Larry was putting on a brave face. Of course Harriet had been frightened and if honest he would have to admit that he had felt a shiver go down his spine when she'd whispered that someone was there. It wasn't an impossibility that someone could be there, in the theatre, who might have harmed Harriet when she was a child and living on the streets. Whether she *had* caught a fleeting glimpse of the midwife and not actually recognised her or had simply felt her presence or even picked up on her scent on the way into the small theatre was neither here nor there. As far as Harriet was concerned, she was there. Her sixth sense had told her so and her sixth sense had always been right in the past as far as Larry was concerned.

Praise for Sally Worboyes

'An excellent book combining humour and passion' *Telegraph and Argus*

'Unbridled passions run riot' *Daily Mail*

About Sally Worboyes

Sally Worboyes was born and grew up in Stepney with four brothers and a sister. She now lives in Norfolk with her husband and three children. She has written several plays broadcast on Radio 4, and has adapted her own play and novel, WILD HOPS, as a musical, THE HOP-PICKERS. Already an established writer, Sally Worboyes continues her brilliant East End sagas to which she brings some of the raw history of her own family background.

SALLY WORBOYES

Banished From Bow

HODDER

First published in Great Britain in 2002 by Hodder & Stoughton
An Hachette UK company

This edition published in 2016

2

Copyright © Sally Worboyes 2002

A CIP catalogue record for this title is available from the British Library

Paperback ISBN 978 1 473 65371 9

Typeset in Plantin Light by Palimpsest Book Production Limited,
Falkirk, Stirlingshire
Printed and bound by CPI Group (UK) Ltd, Croydon, CRO 4YY

Hodder & Stoughton policy is to use papers that are natural, renewable
and recyclable products and made from wood grown in sustainable
forests. The logging and manufacturing processes are expected to
conform to the environmental regulations of the country of origin.

Hodder & Stoughton Ltd
Carmelite House
50 Victoria Embankment
London EC4Y 0DZ

www.hodder.co.uk

For Margaret Kent who gives light to those who live with pain. Many are called but few are chosen.

Thanks as ever to my editor, Sara Hulse.

I

Spring 1905

———◆◆———

Lillian Redmond had woken three or four times during the night and not entirely in a semiconscious state, but quite alert. Now, her dreams disturbed once again, she gave in to her restlessness and roused herself properly. There seemed little point in trying to sleep simply because dawn hadn't broken. Stretching and yawning, she told herself that soon the world would be up and about and she would hear the call of the baker and the tinny noise made by the clattering of milk churns, as the old carthorse clip-clopped into the square.

Lighting the gas mantle above a small ornate mirror, she glanced at her pale face, which had over the years captivated men from all walks of life since she was fifteen years old and had drifted into a life of promiscuity. The face that had been her fortune was now gently lined and her thick dark wavy hair a fine silver grey and more reminiscent of a bright crescent moon rather than a glistening autumn chestnut fresh from its husk. Her deep hazel eyes shone as brightly as they did on the day she was born. Not only had this woman the looks that men of distinction had risked their reputations for, but a sharp intelligence and good common sense. Time had also been kind to Lillian's figure which although somewhat fuller, had retained its gentle sensuous curves.

From a young age, Lillian had felt a strong need to be admired and respected. Coming from a poor background, with no family to speak of, she had soon discovered that to achieve her ambitions she would have to make the most of her attributes. This thought however, had struck her *after* she had made her first big mistake of believing that her first love affair would end in marriage. A painfully hard lesson had been learned when she fell in love with a young sailor who promised her the world and then abandoned her carrying his unborn child – a beautiful baby girl, Lizzie. Summoning every last bit of will power and strength, she had forced herself to rise above her shame by securing work below stairs in a grand house in Kensington where she had toiled from early morning until late at night, always showing a smiling, albeit tired, face. Her reward was promotion from scullery to parlour-maid, which meant that most of her working hours were spent above stairs. She had hidden her secret with a stout corset and had watched, listened and learned how to behave like a lady. She also learned how to be discreet when the gentleman of the house was flirtatious and how to be wicked when visiting gentlemen made amorous advances. The idea of having men pay for their pleasures came to her when, on leaving, one particular guest had mischievously whispered that he would happily give a guinea to feel the inside of her drawers. To mix business in search of pleasure and in such rich company not only flattered her ego but lined her coffers with enough guineas so that once she could no longer hide her condition, she could afford to pay the rent for decent ground-floor rooms in a clean street which had a convenient back door entrance. She gave each of her gentlemen clients a slip of paper before she left her employment with her new address written on it: Flat A, 7, Raven Street, E1.

After she had given birth her client list grew and Lillian was able to not only be a good mother but sport the appearance of a well dressed young woman. The one thing she hadn't bargained on was falling in love again – this time with a married titled gentleman. This second time however, her love had been passionately returned, and before Lizzie had turned five, Lillian's lover had set her up in the very house she lived in now, in Beaumont Square in Stepney, turning a blind eye to the way in which it was discreetly used as a House of Assignation, for gentlemen of the city. For almost two decades Lillian had been gloriously happy and deeply in love. Why her secret lover and benefactor had disappeared from her life was a mystery and a loss she'd had to live with. It would have been a bitter pill for any woman to swallow, especially for Lillian when no reason had been given and no contact had been made since the last wonderful evening they had spent together. For all she knew he may well have passed away.

Sweeping her fine silver hair up into a pile and pinning it into place, Lillian questioned the unsettled and anxious mood that had caused her to sleep badly. She had paid her bills, her client list had not fallen during the past month, Lizzie and her family were living a comfortable life in Wanstead. But something was in the air.

She pulled on her worn cashmere robe, tied the corded belt and relished the softness against her skin. More reliable than a lover, she thought, then went quietly out of her bedroom and down the sweeping staircase to her favourite room, her snug.

She was not entirely alone in the silent house. Her faithful companion, business adviser and book-keeper, Polly, was sound asleep in her own room and a young married couple, who served as maid and handyman-cum-gardener in the basement rooms. Between them they ran Lillian's House of Assignation where the loveliest of girls came in day and night to play hostess to gentlemen of means. The house had seen better days it was true – the curtains had once been changed regularly and decorators were called in to trim, cut and paste hand printed wallpaper, but although the decor and furnishings were now jaded the atmosphere was such that even a prince could feel at ease.

Once in her snug, the nagging worry at the back of Lillian's mind subsided, soothed by the distant sound of the town hall clock striking five. Most people would soon be up and about and in full swing. She put a match to the oil beneath her shining brass kettle, lit the gas fire and settled down to read yesterday's copy of the *Daily Graphic*. Turning to her favourite page – Wonderful London Yesterday – which was crammed with society gossip, she was struck by a headline above a column in which another would-be detective had reported his theory as to the identity of the infamous Jack the Ripper. He hinted that Frederick Charrington, the evangelist who had launched an attack on the East End brothels two decades ago, might have taken it upon himself to cleanse the streets of whores. He had been known to prowl the streets at night on the hunt for men who went in or came out of whorehouses and had written their names in his black book and handed it to the police. Fortunately for Lillian, the self-righteous man had somehow never learned of her house in Beaumont Square.

Lillian read on, amused by the newspaper report. She recalled the time before the killings had begun, when Mr Charrington had invited prostitutes to breakfast with him at the assembly hall to show he bore them no animosity. Word had spread quickly through the back-streets of Whitechapel and at least thirty street girls were there like lightning for the princely feast of bread and butter, ham, cold beef and hot coffee. Characteristically they scampered off before the sermon.

Folding her newspaper she leaned back and rested her head on a feather cushion. In those dark times fear had permeated every alleyway and courtyard, even the most resilient and destitute street girls who had found somewhere to hideaway and sleep after dark were terrified of what might happen to them. The thought flashed through Lillian's mind that her Lizzie might so easily have become a victim had she not had the safety and protection of working at the

House of Assignation rather than trawling the dark streets of Whitechapel looking for business.

Forcing herself out of this dour mood she dismissed the thought and brought the happier times to mind. Apart from those months of terror in 1888 when she, too, feared she might have been on the Ripper's list, her own life had been a whirl of glamour, romance and illicit love.

She reached out and turned down the oil burner beneath the kettle as the desire to close her eyes overcame her. Curling up on the comfortable sofa, she yawned and drew her rug over her. She would wake again when Polly came stomping down the stairs at seven thirty. She smiled at the thought of the thirty year old in her curlers and housecoat who sometimes behaved as if she were still the high spirited girl Lillian had known.

At thirty, Polly was no beauty, but she had a warm personality and a lively sense of humour and Lillian loved her as much as she loved her own daughter, Lizzie. She had grown up in the House of Assignation, and as far as she was concerned, men wanted women for one thing and one thing only. To warm their parts the sun didn't shine on.

With no more thoughts of impending doom Lillian slipped into a light drowsy sleep. A little later, when the clock struck six, she opened her eyes, wondering why she was not in her bed. Recalling her disturbed night of unrest she gazed into the silent tree lined square, where a few dead leaves were fluttering in the breeze and was filled with a comfortable sense of belonging.

Glancing at the railings surrounding the square, she noticed that the gate into the garden was slightly ajar and creaking softly in the breeze. As she looked more closely she could make out the outline of a human figure lying on one of the iron benches. A tramp had obviously found refuge for the night. To Lillian this was a sign of things to come, and this was not the first time a vagrant had slept there. Soon there would be more wretched souls who were homeless and alone finding their way into a respectable place where they could lay down their heads in more pleasant surroundings instead of the dank and filthy back streets of Whitechapel and Shoreditch.

She raised her eyes and looked across the Square into the window of number ten, opposite, where the warm glow from a table lamp radiated across the silhouette of the lady of the house who had also been awake on and off during the night. There was no need for a wave of recognition, the women simply gazed at each other . . . their worlds seemingly miles apart.

Grace Wellington turned first from her window, leaving Lillian with a feeling of uncertainty. Did this proud and courteous young woman know? And if so, how long had she known? Or perhaps she had always been wise to the truth and had had no choice but to accept betrayal passively. Whatever the case, Lillian dared not allow herself to feel guilty. Not now. Not after all this time.

Later that morning, in her long green silk skirt with a matching lace-edged blouse, she listened as Polly told her which clients were booked in for that

day and evening. Matching her girls to the right
gentleman was an art, and Lillian had only once
made a mistake. Several years ago, she had placed
her beautiful protégé, Mary Dean, with a new client,
a rich, handsome gentleman. On her first appointment
with him, he had been swept off his feet and soon
afterwards had carried her off to be his kept woman
in a house in Bow. It had been an excellent match for
Mary Dean but bad for Lillian's business. Innocent
young virgins of twenty were like gold dust in her
profession.

'The only one I'm not sure abaht,' said Polly, breaking into Lillian's thoughts, 'is double chin Donald.'
She narrowed her eyes and grimaced. ''Ave you seen
him lately? Belly like a balloon.'

'Match him with Pearl but let her know beforehand
that we'll add a little extra bonus to her fee. I take it
that Mary Dean hasn't called this week while I've been
out and you've forgotten to tell me?'

'No. How much for the bonus then?'

Lillian shrugged. 'Five shillings?'

'Nah, not enough. Make it seven and six,' said Polly
thoughtfully. ''Er name's not Mary Dean no more so
why d'yer still call 'er that?'

'She'll always be Mary Dean to me.'

'Why'd she change it to Birchfield anyway?'

'I don't think that's any of your business, Polly.'

'Oh, suit yerself. Do we give seven and six or not?
Pearly girlie'll lick Balloon Belly to death if you do up
the fee. Then you can charge 'im an extra guinea.
He won't complain once she's finished wiv 'im. Over

sexed that one – if you asks me. Business on the brain,' she added slyly.

'If you say so . . .' Lillian sighed.

'We've run out of port and three of today's gentlemen drink it. D'yer want me to send Ben out for some or give them a bottle of sherry?' Polly had no time for the finer details. It was Saturday and she wanted to go to the municipal baths to watch a few rounds of prize-fighting in the boxing ring. 'And why're you worryin' over soddin' Mary? She's feathered 'er nest all right. Lucky cow.'

'I'm not worrying over her! I was just thinking of her. She didn't call in last week either. Tell Benjamin to check the drinks cupboard and refill it as required,' said Lillian, and moved to the window. Once again she caught sight of her neighbour at the window of the house across the square. 'It doesn't have to be the best port but neither must it be poor quality,' she advised, her eyes moving from the young woman to her husband, Mr Wellington, who was at his study window. Each of them was watching for someone or something. She was intrigued, especially since Mr Wellington's regular hackney cab had arrived and was about to pull up outside number ten.

The fact that the man disappeared from the window was an indication that Lillian was right. This was indeed his cab and no sooner had he got into it and slammed the door shut than his wife appeared, striding purposefully towards the cab and wrenching open the door to join him.

'Oh dear . . .' Lillian sighed, 'That won't be a

pleasant surprise. I do hope this isn't going to mean that another good client is to be struck off our list. Tobias Wellington is about to be found out or your name is not Polly my dear.' She paused and watched as the driver urged his horse onward bound and out of the square.

Polly joined her at the window. 'You must be kiddin' me. 'Im? Stop comin' over 'ere for a roll between your sheets? Never in a month of Sundays.'

'If I'm not mistaken . . . his determined young wife is about to discover the girl he keeps in Brick Lane. If that's the case . . . I feel for her.'

'Why? He comes 'ere don't he? What's the difference?'

'A whole world. Discovering that your husband has been keeping another woman as if she were his wife is much worse. That is betrayal at its blackest.'

'Well, let's 'ope she's a bloomin' good listener, this girl from Brick Lane, 'cos our girls 'ave to put up wiv all 'is daft talk while he's cocking 'em. How comes you know abaht 'er anyway?'

With her back to Polly, Lillian smiled to herself. 'My clients sometimes tell me their secrets. Your language, Polly, is worse than ever and so is your cockney. Do we have a reason for this?' She managed to keep a straight face.

'Yeah. You stopped me from talkin' nice when I was a kid so I can't start gabbin' like a toff now, can I? It's too late.'

'Do you want me to send you to elocution lessons – is that it?'

'Might be – dunno. I'll 'ave to think about that,' she said, rubbing her chin. 'It won't be as easy as when I was ten and wanted lessons.'

'So what *do* you want?' Lillian was enjoying their banter and always had done. Polly, the illegitimate child of her closest friend had been placed in her care at birth.

'To be made a business partner.' This request was nothing new but Polly liked to throw it in now and again.

'I see.' Lillian hid a smile. 'Well, I shall have to think about that.'

'Thanks,' said Polly, grinning at her. 'I'll talk properly again now then. So, who we gonna put with Sidney the soddin' salesman?'

'You decide,' said Lillian, still at the window and watching as a familiar figure approached her front gate. 'He's not fussy.'

Polly looked up from her writing pad, narrowing her eyes to get a clearer picture of Lillian's expression. 'Who've you spotted?'

'How do you know I've spotted anyone?'

'By your expreshun.'

'Oh? So your eyes have improved enough to see me across a room? The carrots must have worked.'

'I should reckon so. I've eat enough of 'em.'

'It would be easier and more simple if you were to wear—'

'*No*. I ain't wearing no spectacles for no-one. So who is it, then?'

'Harriet, looking very lovely in her emerald green

coat and matching hat. Very feminine.' Turning slowly around to face Polly, Lillian assumed an earnest expression.

'If that's s'posed to be a hint you might as well pee in the wind. Anyway that green coat of hers is old and shabby and the fur collar and cuffs ain't all they're cut out to be.'

'Let's hope she isn't here to bring bad news,' mused Lillian, 'I've had a sense of trouble looming all night long.'

'Should 'ave looked into your crystal ball then, shouldn't yer?' said Polly, but she was pleased that her friend was paying a visit, Harriet could brighten the dullest day.

'I don't need a crystal ball, Polly. Go and let Harriet in before she pulls six times on the door bell. And don't spend too long together. We're running a business here.' With that, Lillian ushered her out of the room and closed the door. She was pleased that Harriet had appeared. She wanted to be alone. The sense of doom was back and she needed to think things through. True, her business was waning but that hadn't worried her in the past. So why now? She picked up the newspaper again and ran through the situations-wanted column. Polly's idea of giving clients the opportunity to be entertained whilst enjoying a candlelit meal in the lavish but largely unused dining room, seemed an excellent way of lifting not only the atmosphere in the house but also her declining income.

She ran her eyes down the column of names of

professional cooks offering their services and stopped at one which looked interesting. The advertisement was short and to the point with no overly worded self praise. It read: 'Newly arrived from America and available. Cook to cater for small intimate dinner parties or formal banquets.' She circled it with her pen. She couldn't imagine herself giving banquets . . . but what about a small, exclusive restaurant for City gentlemen? A place where they could hold informal meetings in an ambience of comfort, taste and style, with special arrangements to take a luxurious room for the night with one of her girls? Losing no time she went to her writing desk and penned a letter in answer to the advertisement.

Meanwhile, downstairs, in the kitchen parlour room, Polly listened as her friend Harriet poured out her heart over the way her neighbours were treating her. She had always shrugged it off in the past but now it was different. Not only had she been to see a doctor who confirmed that she was pregnant but she was certainly beginning to show. It was time for her and her sweetheart, Arthur, to marry – which meant that they would be shunned by everyone who believed them to be brother and sister.

'It's not like you to take notice of what other people fink, Harriet,' said Polly, brewing a fresh pot of tea. 'It's probably 'cos you're in the family way.'

'If you saw the looks they give me, it'd get your goat too. We ain't that much different, you and me.'

Polly grinned and gave her a mischievous wink. 'We are now.' She leaned forward and tapped Harriet's belly. 'You've got a baby growing in there. A little Arfer.'

'Silly mare,' murmured Harriet, pleased at Polly's response. 'Might be a little girl for all you know.'

'Or one of each. You might be 'avin' twins. Two gingernuts to cope wiv. I wonder what your neighbour'd think of that?' she chuckled.

'I won't be around to find out will I?' said Harriet sadly. 'We were all happy in that house.' Her mind filled with the day when she was ten and Arthur nine, and he and his sister, Mary Dean, had left Stepney and poverty and taken her with them. 'I was no more than a filthy ragged street urchin when we first moved into Bow.'

'Mary's only mistake was to let your new neighbours believe that you was 'er younger sister.'

'She didn't want 'em to know I'd bin sleeping rough in coal yards and that. Her and Arfer was orphans, don't forget. Mary knew what it felt like to be destitute. And anyway, she didn't want them to look down on me. That's why she told the lie. She just never bargained on me and Arfer fallin' in love, that's all.

'Sometimes, when me and my Arfer strolled arm in arm and kept to the shadows, we still got spat on and cursed and called heathens. Now that I'm carrying 'is baby, it'll be much worse. I came today to ask if Lillian might let me and Arfer lodge in the attic for a while.'

'I don't fink she can, Harriet. One room we don't use is full of junk.'

'Oh, well that's that then,' she said, leaning back in

her chair and staring pensively at the floor. 'It was kind of Mary to take me in all those years ago, Poll, but she should 'ave said right from the start that I was a vagrant and be done wiv it. We would never 'ave 'ad these worries now, would we, if she 'ad of done?'

'Well, that's spilt milk and no mistake. No point harpin' on about it.' Polly was trying to get her friend back on track. 'This ain't like you, Harriet, gone all soft 'cos you've slipped up. Look at yer – all serious and grown-up. Where's the scatty ten year old that banged on this front door all them years ago wiv a message from Mary Dean? She must be in there somewhere.'

'So must that snooty firteen-year-old who came to the door wiv 'er nose pointed to the sky.' Harriet chuckled, 'You looked a sight in that tweeny outfit.'

'That was Lillian's idea. Cost enough – had to go to a shop in Bond Street for it.' Polly drifted back in time. 'I loved that outfit. Neat little black frock, starched cuffs and collars that clipped on and my little white pinny and hat wiv pretty cotton edging . . .'

'You was the bell gel in a brothel not a bleedin' maid in Buckingham Palace!'

'Impressed you, though, didn't it?'

'Don't look so smug. I only made friends wiv yer so I could come back and 'ave a bath in one of the washrooms.'

'You'd better not mean that, Harriet Smith! If I thought you was only—'

'Oh, shut up and pour out the tea. I s'pose you'll wanna be its godmuvver?'

A huge smile spread across Polly's face and her eyes lit up. 'Can I?'

'Course you can. I'll 'ave two godmuvvers . . . you and my other friend, Flora Brown.'

'Who I've still not met.'

'Well, we drifted apart for a while and when we met up again she was busy gettin' on wiv 'er own life. All right now, though. Now that 'er married man's disappeared into the night and left 'er 'oldin' the baby. She's more like the Flora I knew all them years ago. See, a good friend never changes. You should always try and keep in touch wiv best mates.'

'I'll take that as a compliment and we'll say no more about it,' sniffed Polly, pouring them both a cup of tea. 'An' you should stop worrying.'

'I'm not worrying.'

'No? Well it looks like you are to me . . . by yer expreshun you look dead worried.' In silence, Polly poured them a cup of tea and Harriet wondered for the umpteenth time how she and Arthur would manage to keep their heads above water. She was going to have to give up her job one day and then Arthur would have to feed and clothe her and the baby. She had read in a Sunday paper that the minority report of the Poor Law Commission had pointed out the differences in standards of health-care services and had urged the government to take action. The response was a promise of benefits for the unemployed and pensions for the elderly, but there had been no mention of free medical treatment for workers at the bottom of the wage scale. She was going to have to pay to have her baby delivered safely, and to visit the doctor before and afterwards, should it be necessary.

'Look at yer,' said Polly, piercing her thoughts. 'All doom and gloom when you should be rejoicing. You're gonna have a *baby*!' Harriet lifted her face and looked directly at Polly, who was grinning at her. 'You're gonna 'ave a baby, Harriet,' she repeated. 'One all of yer own to cuddle up close.'

'I know and I'm chuffed over it, course I am.' She didn't want Polly to guess that she was worried about money so she improvised.

'It's the neighbours that're gettin' me down. They sneered at me when I first went to Bow Terrace and then changed once Mary 'ad smartened me up. It wasn't my fault that I'd 'ad to scavenge and live rough all me life. But as soon as Mary got me to 'ave baths and dressed me in nice fings, that was all right. Stuck up sods. I wasn't any different was I? My hair might've bin combed and I changed me drawers more often but I was the same underneaf. One of the posh kids called me a vagabond. Never said it twice, though.'

'Ah, but look at you now, Harry girl. I wish I 'ad lovely red 'air wiv red lights in it. Big blue eyes. You've got freckles, mind, which I wouldn't like. But then, 'ow would you like to 'ave bin born looking like me? And I need spectacles.'

'I'd 'ave jumped out of me muvver's arms and into the Cut. Drowned meself.'

'Thanks very much. Don't say much for personality, do it? You're cruel, you are!'

'Honest, more like. You could do somefing with

yerself if you wanted. You could 'ave your 'air done. You could borry Lillian's hot tongs and make it nice and curly and put a colour on it. A chestnut tint'd look nice. Wear a bit of rouge and powder,' she glanced from Polly's face to her large round breasts squashed under her white blouse, 'and a boned bodice. You're more like a man than a woman 'alf the time.'

'Am I?' smiled Polly. 'That's what you know. Still, at least I'm not up the gum tree.'

'Don't be too certain of yerself,' Harriet mumbled, helping herself to a piece of shortbread. 'An ill wind blows wherever it bleedin' well feels like it. Not for Mary, though. If there's a bit of sun out it'll shine on 'er all right. Lover boy's gonna marry 'er or so he says.' She raised her eyes to meet her friend's. 'What if I die giving birth? Who'll look after my baby?'

Determined not to let her friend bring her down into the dumps, Polly straightened and sniffed. 'Well, it won't 'ave to go into the workhouse or a lousy children's 'ome will it? It might go into a foster 'ome though,' she gently teased. 'That little baby could end up in a mansion 'ouse and be brought up like a princess.'

'Yeah and it could end up being taken in by guardians who'd feed it on bread and water 'til it's old enough to work for its keep. Anyway, who says it's a girl?' said Harriet. 'It might be a little boy and the image of my Arfer.'

'Be a darn sight better off than if it's a girl and the image of you.'

'I s'pose Mary might take it in. Take it to bleedin' Berkshire.'

'Ah so *that's* it? They're gonna move out of Bow and into the countryside and you're goin' to be left behind, Harriet Smith,' smirked Polly, leaning forward, with her hands on her hips.

'You look as if you're gonna bust into song. And you can wipe that stupid grin off yer face. You look like a witch or wizard, I can't tell. Anyway, I'm not put out over it. Couldn't care less where they go. At least them spoilt brats of Mary's will be gone out me life. As soon as they could talk they took the rise out of me and Arthur. Poked fun at our Cockney accents. I used to give 'em a clip round the ear when Mary wasn't looking. That 'ad to stop, though, once the little sods caught me and Arthur 'aving a cuddle on the settee. Blackmailed us, they did. Little bleeders. No more clouts or else they'd tell.'

'Mary should 'ave told 'em you wasn't brother and sister.'

'Course she should! I don't know what she was finkin' about. I liked Mary better when she worked at Bryant and May's match factory and we lived in that lovely little 'ouse in Whitehead Street. She was more down to earth . . . even if she did talk a bit proper. Her mum and dad was churchgoin' people. Lot of good it did them. Both dead before their time.'

'Well, then, Mary Dean deserves a bit of luck, don't she? She'll be a lady now right enough, married to *Sir* Walter—'

'Wrong. *Sir* Robert. That's 'ow much he trusted 'er

not to make trouble for 'im. Now he's gonna marry 'er, he's told 'er 'is proper name. *Sir Robert Montague,*' she said, bowing and curling a hand in the air. 'She never even batted an eyelid, you know. After all this time! And she still calls him Walter—'

'Old 'abits die 'ard, Harriet. He was married when she met 'im . . . and she met 'im here, don't forget, in a brothel. Most of the clients give false names. Stands to reason . . . if you fink about it.'

'Sly sods. I told 'er the rich couldn't be trusted further than you could throw 'em. We 'ad a row over that. Me and Arfer ain't good enough for Mary now. We embarrass 'er in company. She wants to fink about that. Snobs 'ave to come from somewhere, don't they? And she's gonna turn into one if she ain't careful. You mark my words.'

'You've got hard, Harriet Smith. Tough as old boots. If you ask me your 'ead's up your skirt and you can't see for the dark. Mary's all right. She's done a lot for you.'

'I know! Anyway . . . you'd be bleedin' 'ard if you was pregnant wiv nowhere to live! Most landlords are robbers. They charge six shillin's a week for one room wiv 'orrible furniture, a tap in the back yard if you're lucky and a lavatory shared by all and bleedin' sundry.'

Polly realised there was no point in saying any more. When Harriet was in this mood there wasn't much that Polly could do to jolly her out of it. Words of advice or comfort would be as much use as pouring clean water down a drain. 'You'll find a place that's more than a cubby-hole,' she said finally. 'Mary's bound to cough up some money.'

'I wouldn't take it and neiver would Arthur. She can keep 'er money. See what good it'll do 'er in the end.'

The door suddenly opened and Lillian came in. 'Hello, Harriet. How's Mary? I've not seen her for a few weeks.'

'She's fit enough. Gonna get married and move away wiv them brats of theirs. Prince Charming's proposed at last. Me and Arthur are looking for somewhere to stay.'

'Married?' Lillian raised an eyebrow, pleased. 'Good for her! Now then, Polly, this idea of yours to arrange small dinner parties for gentlemen wishing to discuss business. I've decided to go along with it.'

'Ah . . .' A new thought flashed through Polly's mind. 'So you'll be needing a spare pair of 'ands . . . or two?' She was thinking of Harriet and Arthur.

'Not spare,' she replied, glancing at Harriet, 'experienced. If we're to do this at all we must do it properly. A trained cook and trained butler is what I have in mind.' She looked from Polly to Harriet. 'I'm going to have to drag her away now, dear.'

'Oh, don't mind me,' said Harriet, standing up and scraping the legs of her chair on the tiled floor. 'I've got to get back to work – tired and down'earted or not.' She snatched up her handbag from the scrubbed-pine table and raised her chin defiantly. 'I shouldn't be 'ere anyway. This is a whore house and I've got me and my baby to fink of!' With that she turned and walked proudly out of the room, hiding her disappointment and bottling her tears.

'She's in need of help, said Polly softly. 'She and Arfer'll be 'omeless now.'

'Don't be dramatic. Besides . . . there's a recession on, dear, we have to fend for ourselves. If our client list continues to fall and our new enterprise fails to attract City gentlemen, we may find ourselves without a roof over our own heads. Mary Dean won't see them in the street, you can take my word for it. Now then, young woman, we have work to do. Charity is not at home today.'

'No, it never really is nowadays. Everyone's lost interest in the struggle for our rights as well. Even the newspapers don't bovver to report on the suffrage meetings.'

'Precisely,' said Lillian. 'Which is why we must all look out for ourselves.'

Later that day, after a busy afternoon at the local soap factory, Harriet arrived home in Bow Terrace in a far from tranquil mood. She let herself into number thirteen and slammed the door behind her. As she went up the wide staircase to her room, she could smell the familiar fragrance of Mary's lover's cologne. He was in residence again! She went directly into her bedroom, slammed the door and threw herself on the bed and stared defiantly at a spider on the ceiling. 'Blooming rich sod . . . coming 'ere and spoilin' fings. What do she wanna marry you for? Doin' it on purpose to get rid of me an' my Arthur! Well, blow the pair of yer!

You can go to kingdom come for all I care!' A soft tap on her door silenced her.

'Who is it?' she snarled.

'It's me, Harriet. Mary. May I come in?'

'*May* I come in?' she mimicked quietly. 'It's a free bleedin' country ain't it?'

'Are you ready to tell me what's wrong?' said Mary, from the doorway.

'You know wot's wrong. I'm bein' slung back to where you found me as a kid. Back to shackin' down with an old carthorse next to a pile of steamin' dung in a dirty old stable. Still, it's no less than what I expected, sooner or later.'

Mary closed the bedroom door and leaned against it, considering her options. She could do one of three things: give Harriet the sharp end of her tongue, try a little kindness or stay silent. Sitting down on the edge of the bed she looked into that lovely freckled face of the girl she had come to love as a sister. As expected Harriet out-silenced her.

'First of all, Harriet, you're not being slung out. Second, there's no reason why we can't find a little two up two down for let. And third, when was your last period?'

'Ages ago.'

'Ah . . . so I guessed right. Does Arthur know?'

'What do you think?'

'Is he pleased? He should be. I am. I suppose you went to see Polly to give her the good news?'

'Might 'ave done.'

'How is she then? Perky as ever? And Lillian?'

'Go and see for yerself.'

Mary swept her fingers across Harriet's forehead, brushing wispy strands of hair away from her eyes. 'Nothing's as black as it seems, you know.'

'How d'yer make that out? Me and Arthur's not exactly trained in a profession, are we? Him fetchin' and carryin' for the railway and me fillin' boxes at the soap factory. An' I won't even be able to do that once the baby comes. I'll work right up 'til I drop it, though, so that'll be all right. But I don't fink they'll let me work in a factory with it tied to me bleedin' back wantin' a feed every hour.'

'How far gone are you?' said Mary, suppressing a grin.

'Mind yer own business.'

'Does Arthur know?'

'Ask 'im.'

'I will,' said Mary, standing up and brushing a crease out of her silk skirt. 'If I'm to be an aunt, I'll need to know when it's due so I can be there at the birth.'

'Whatever you say, Mary, whatever you say.'

'Are you goin' to stop sulking, then, and talk to me?'

'Nuffing to say.'

'Fair enough. Then I'll leave you on your own 'til you come round. We've brought the wedding forward a week to fit in with Walter's business arrangements. We'll be moving out of this house and into the country in three weeks time. That doesn't give us long to shop for my outfit and yours.'

There was a flicker of response in Harriet's eyes as she looked at Mary. 'A double wedding?' There was also a touch of hope in her voice.

'No, Harriet. You know that wouldn't work.'

'Why not? His lordship'd feel a bit embarrassed, would he?'

'Of course he would, and you know why! Stop being difficult. It's not clever and it's not helping either of us. Our wedding'll be a quiet, private affair. Just the two of us and a witness, Walter's closest friend.'

'I thought 'is real name was Robert,' Harriet sniffed.

'It is and you know that, and you know why I can't just start calling him that.' Mary turned away. 'Let me know if you want me to come shopping with you to buy a nice outfit. My treat.' With that she left the room. Harriet was off the bed in a flash and after her. 'Mary!'

'Yes?'

'Where are me and Arthur gonna live?'

'I told you, there are plenty of places around that you could rent. Something like the one we had in Whitehead Street. You remember that – a nice little two up two down.'

'Course I remember it! I lived there for a while wiv you, didn't I? What about rent money?'

'With both of you at work you'll afford it. We can furnish it with good quality things from the second hand shop in Mile End Road.'

'And once I 'ave to give up me job?'

'That's for you and Arthur to work out Harriet. I

can't ask Walter to support you both, it's not right. You're adults and working. You've got to make your own way one day.'

'Yeah, living in a poor'ouse while you're in the lap of luxury,' she sulked.

Mary shook her head. 'It's the way of the world, Harriet. I've not always had it easy, don't forget. Stop being jealous. With your quick brain and Arthur's dedication to work, you'll better yourselves in time. And you won't have me to thank for it, will you? Your pride won't be bruised and Arthur won't feel indebted to me and Walter.'

'Well, if we do manage to get and keep our own roof over our 'eads, it'll be no fanks to anyone else.'

Halfway down the stairs Mary shuddered as the slamming of Harriet's bedroom door echoed through the house. Yes, she thought, it's time for them to stand on their own feet. Arthur and Harriet were too used to relying on her and her generous lover. They seemed to think that he was a millionaire without any cares in the world. Now, with divorce proceedings finalised, his bank balance would be down by fifty per cent. His wife would receive half of his liquid assets. He had already made it clear that this was his intention. Once they were married, Mary and he were to move into his spacious country house and their children would be going to boarding school. They could no longer be expected to support Arthur and Harriet, who were now in their mid twenties. They could and should have had savings by now, instead of spending every penny in taverns and music halls.

She was being cruel to be kind but she should have known that Harriet, in her present condition, would not see it like that. Surely her brother Arthur would though?

Two weeks after Harriet's visit to Lillian Redmond, she was no closer to finding a solution to her and Arthur's problem. They had looked at a few rooms to let but none was suitable. They were either unfit to live in or the rent too high. Determined to make her way without help, Harriet refused any help Mary offered. Arthur, though, without Harriet's knowledge, had accepted twenty-five guineas from his sister and Walter, and was keeping it for when they found the right place, which would no doubt need refurbishing.

A date had been set for Mary and the children to move out of the lovely house in Bow and into the country house in Berkshire. Soon after this, she and Walter were to be married, with as little fuss as possible. On the surface, Harriet appeared unruffled at the prospect of being homeless again. Her pride would not allow her to show worry or disappointment so she went about the place singing. She could keep this up during the day, but once in her bed she tossed and turned, and cried into her pillow. When eventually she fell asleep she had nightmares of being back in those dark childhood days when she had been treated like vermin by those fortunate enough to have a roof over their heads and food in the larder.

Waking in a sweat in the middle of the night after another of those bad dreams, she all but screamed out in the dark for Arthur – her worst recurring nightmare having disturbed her again. The past, it seemed, was not going to release Harriet. As a child of ten, when she had first been taken in to the house in Whitehead Street, by Mary, she had suffered a bloodcurdling experience. No one, not even Arthur, had managed to get her to talk about it, and although she could push it out of her mind she had not been able to wipe it from her memory.

Out of her bed, she stole out of her room and along the passage with only the glow of a night light in the hall to see by. Creeping into Arthur's bedroom, she closed the door and slipped in beside him, comforted by his low breathing. Then she let her mind wander back to when she had escaped a horrible death by the skin of her teeth. It was early winter 1888, when women checked every shadow in fear of Jack the Ripper, scared to go out after dusk and before dawn. Harriet at the time, was a tough ten-year-old who had spent her life glancing over her shoulder – peril was everywhere. During her battle to survive in the worst of East London, she had grown too bold for her own good and too interested in the affairs of Mary's neighbour, Miss Jacqueline Turner the midwife.

One bright wintry day, Harriet had presented herself to the midwife and offered to do some housework for free so that she could keep warm. The woman had taken pity on the child, and agreed to leave her in the house while she went out on her rounds. Harriet was to dust and polish the downstairs of the small house but not to go upstairs, where there was only her bedroom and a tiny boxroom. That settled, she had gone out; she had too much on her mind to worry about whether Harriet could be trusted. The child had an open, honest face and in any case the midwife knew her quite well. The midwife, whose only desire had been to live passively and deliver life into this world and to one day sail off to America and whose very appearance, as she strode purposefully through the back streets at unsociable hours, had been consoling for those women who also worked during the night. With her dark hat, cloak and black medical bag, she had had a certain air of authority about her even though her heavy footsteps echoing through an empty dark street could be a touch chilling.

Jacqueline Turner lived a solitary life in her small terraced house in the back and beyond of Whitechapel with only her nephew, Thomas Cutbush, for company. Although he did not live with her, she fed him a hot meal most evenings before he returned south of the river to his demented mother, her sister. The midwife had first come across Harriet when the child had pleaded with her to rush to the aid of her mother who had been on the brink of death in a damp room in a slum. Jacqueline had delivered the breech baby in the nick of time. A month or so after the near-tragedy the midwife had discovered Harriet in a doorway at dawn, freezing cold and very hungry. It was then that she had taken her to Mary Dean.

Once Jacqueline had left Harriet to the housework and gone on her rounds on that fateful day, the inquisitive ten-year-old had been unable to resist temptation. That winding staircase had beckoned her more than once during those evenings when she had gone in to play cards with the midwife. She had gone upstairs to the woman's bedroom, walked towards a bureau and sat in a tall-backed chair, slowly opening one drawer after another. The drawers had contained diaries, marked by the year and going back to 1848 when Jacqueline Turner had been young. With mixed feelings, Harriet had slid the journal marked 1888 out of the drawer and opened it.

She had only recognised those words made up of three or four letters – but it was enough to make her blood curdle. Engrossed, she had not heard the street door below open and close again. Neither did she hear the midwife creep up the staircase.

Harriet's punishment for trespassing into that very private place had been restraint: hands and feet tied, mouth gagged, she had been left in the boxroom with no light and little chance of escape. She had read a diary, which would, without doubt, see Jacqueline Turner and her nephew, Thomas Cutbush, sentenced to death.

By the grace of God and her natural instinct for survival Harriet had eventually wriggled free and got away while the midwife was out on her rounds. Her mistake had been to break the lock of the bureau on impulse and take the diary. Soon afterwards she had heard that the midwife had sailed for America.

Now, safe in bed, knowing that Arthur would always be there to protect her should the midwife ever return, she slipped her arms around his warm body and snuggled down to sleep.

Hours later, with the early-morning light shining through the window, she woke to the sound of her sweetheart's voice as he stroked her hair. 'You're a daredevil, Harriet, that's what you are,' whispered Arthur, giving her a peck on the cheek. 'Let Mary find you in 'ere and all hell will be let loose.'

'She won't care,' murmured Harriet, sleepily.

'And I say she would. I say, and I know – she'd go berserk.'

'Well, you don't know much, then, do yer?'

'I know more'n you. Now get up and creep back into yer own room. We'll be married soon and 'ave years of sleepin' in the same bed.'

'I don't wanna get up. I ain't goin' to work today. See what Mary finks of *that*.' She curled into a ball and pulled Arthur's pillow over her face.

'All right, then,' he said, swinging his legs out of bed. 'You 'ave a nice rest. I'll pop in to the factory on my way to work and say you've twisted your ankle bad at work yesterday. How's that?'

'No, you bleedin' won't. Say I've bin sick. They know I'm pregnant.'

'They'll stop you a day's pay as well as sack you.'

'No, they won't. We've got new rules now. I'll go down to the women's-movement office and get advice.

Now, sod off and let me sleep. Or do yer wanna hear about my nightmare?'

Harriet could see that Arthur was taken aback. He had often asked her to tell him about her bad dreams and she had always refused. 'What difference would it make if I did want to know?' he asked. 'You won't tell me.'

'Do you want to know or not?'

'Ummm, no, I don't think I do.' He kissed her cheek, then her nose. 'Don't wanna upset the apple cart, do we? Why bother with all that when everything's tickety-boo and you're all nice and settled in my bed?'

Harriet sat bolt upright and glared at him. 'How d'yer make that out? Nuffing's bleedin' well tickety-boo! We've gotta find somewhere to live!'

'I know, I know,' he said, soothingly. 'Larry Cohen might know someone—'

'Yeah, and so might a lot of people if they'd only come out of the woodwork.' Harriet slid back down into her bedclothes and turned her back on him. 'Where are your mates when you need 'em, eh, Arfer?'

'Well, Larry and Moira intend to be waitin' for us outside the Pavilion at seven o'clock tonight. Tickets are on them.'

She looked up at him slyly. 'Well, that's something I s'pose. Anyway, Larry's old man owns that little music hall. He's entitled to give us complimentary tickets.'

'He don't own it,' said Arthur, pulling his working trousers over his long johns. 'Got shares in it, that's all. He said you could do a little turn before the show starts if you want. Must be worth 'alf a guinea to see you dance, eh?'

'Oh, I see, Arthur Dean. I've gotta *dance* for my ticket and sing for me supper. Might 'ave known.'

'I never said that. I said he'd give you 'alf a guinea. The tickets are a treat. I'll take 'im a little bit of fish anyway. Collecting from Billingsgate today. Four or five runs, I reckons. Should be some tasty 'addock and cod on board.'

'You get caught and you'll go away for a very long time, Arfer. Then what'll 'appen to me?'

'I won't get caught,' he said, knotting his tie. 'Stop worryin'.' He kissed her again, then left for work.

Caught in her own turmoil of guilt, Harriet struggled against the voice inside telling her to get up and go to the factory. Angry with herself for not being strong-willed enough to stay where she was, she ripped back the covers and leapt out of bed. When Mary's illegitimate eleven-year-old peeked round the door, she scowled at him. 'What do you want?' she asked defensively – she was in the wrong bedroom after all.

'I don't want anything from *you*. But I shall tell my mother—'

'Oh, get out, you little smartarse!' she said, showing him the back of her hand.

'You're not supposed to be in Uncle Arthur's bed. It's very rude.' With that he bounded down the stairs in search of Mary. Instead he met Walter in the front hall, on his way to the study.

'Charles, really! How many times have I warned you not to run inside the house?'

'I know, Father, but this is very important. Aunt Harriet is in Uncle Arthur's bed and I believe she's been there all night. That can't be right, can it?'

'Right or wrong, young man, it's none of your business. Now, get yourself into the bathroom and be washed and dressed for schoolwork within . . .' he pulled his gold fob watch from his waistcoat pocket '. . . ten minutes. Your tutor will be here shortly.'

'I can't possibly be that quick, Father. You wouldn't want me to look like a chip off the old block, would you?'

'What on earth are you talking about?' said Walter, amused. 'Old block?'

'Yes. Uncle Arthur. He tells me I'm just like him – a chip off the old block. I don't think I am at all. But he does and so does Aunt Harriet. Who, by the way, is in Uncle Arthur's bed at this very—'

'So you said. Be off with you and no more arguing.'

'But aren't you going to scold her?'

'Your aunt is not a child, my boy. Furthermore, I am not her keeper. She will do as she thinks fit.' He ruffled his son's hair. 'But thank you for telling me. You can stop worrying about it now. We'll soon be out of this house and this district – thank goodness.'

'Exactly, Father, and I wanted to speak to you about that too. Aunt Harriet told Petusha that she is coming with us. Is she lying or were you? You promised Petusha *and* me that *they* would be staying in Bow. Now—'

'Young man,' said Walter, 'my patience may only

be stretched so far. Now, please do as you're told and make haste to the bathroom. To answer your question and to end this conversation, neither Aunt Harriet nor Uncle Arthur will be coming to live with us in the country.' He placed a hand on his son's shoulder and guided him towards the staircase. 'Not another word or I shall be cross.' With that he turned into the study, laughing. Charles was a character and, if he hadn't known better, Walter would have said that he had been blessed with Harriet's spirit. Since she was no relation to him, though, he could only think that the boy had been impressed by the fiery young lady and had mimicked her, whether he knew it or not. That aside, he would have to speak to Mary about the bedroom scenario.

That evening, arm in arm and dressed in their Sunday best, Harriet and Arthur strolled along Bow Terrace, not caring who might spit at their feet. The rumour that she was going to marry Arthur had started with Mary's daughter, Petusha, who had heard it from Charles, who had been listening at the door while it was being whispered. Now it was spreading through the terrace and further afield. The expression on a neighbour's face as she passed them made it clear that she had heard from the gossips that a marriage between brother and sister had been planned. This lady of means was above spitting but she was not above hissing, '*Devils! Burn in hell.*'

They continued on their way, trying not to let it upset them and smiled at an approaching couple.

Both Harriet and Arthur liked this friendly pair, who always looked content. No doubt they had also met with hostility when they first walked out together and especially when they married – and yet the West Indian gentleman and the lovely Irish girl could run circles around the middle class in this part of Bow. Urban Turner was from a wealthy family of glass and marble merchants.

Characteristically, they smiled broadly. 'What's this I hear on the terrace my friends? Brother and sister to be married?' Urban roared with laughter and slapped Arthur's shoulder. 'You know, they actually believe it.'

'So they should,' Harriet blurted, ''cos it's true. Well, part of it. Me and Arfer are getting married but we're *not* bruvver and sister. Mary took me in off the streets when I was ten and 'ad to scrounge for a bit of bread.'

'Really? My goodness. Well, then, you fooled them all and the last laugh shall be with you.' With that he raised a hand in farewell and the couple continued on their way.

'See? It takes a black man to understand,' murmured Arthur, 'a foreigner.'

'Who cares anyway, Arfer? We've got each other – and our baby, when it comes. I'm happy and I don't care who knows it.'

Compared to her wretched childhood, Harriet was much better off now and had enjoyed a good life in Bow with Mary and Arthur. She had watched her mother struggle against hunger and bring up her children in squalid conditions: broken windows repaired with newspapers, rags stuffed into holes in the walls to stop the icy wind coming in. Rats had been a never-ending battle but mice were accepted. When Mary took her in, Harriet's life had changed and she had got used to living in a lovely home, always being clean with nice clothes. She didn't want it to change now.

Harriet's anxieties over what might or might not happen once Mary moved out of Bow soon drifted away, now that she was all spruced up and arm in arm with her sweetheart on their way to the Pavilion to meet up with Larry and Moira. She was happy again. 'What d'yer reckon to that scent, then?' she blurted suddenly, shoving her wrist under Arthur's nose. 'French, that is.'

'Waste of money. You've got your own nice smell. How much did that cost me?'

'Didn't bleedin' well cost you nuffink. I had a squirt from Mary's bottle.'

'Don't look now,' Arthur spoke out of the side of his mouth, 'but guess who's coming.' It was old man Rosenberg with a blonde on his arm. 'Still gettin' a bone in 'is prick at 'is age.'

'Don't be so crude, you dirty bleeder! I bet she 'as to work her rump off to get 'im to rise to the occasion.' Harriet smiled and nodded at the couple as they passed. Uncharacteristically she kept her mouth shut: they were easy meat and wit or sarcasm would have been unkind.

'She won't care about that,' grinned Arthur. 'He's

not short of a few quid, is he? A tie factory of all things. Who'd 'ave thought there was money in men's ties?'

'There's money in horse shit, Arfer, if you put your mind to it. And put our minds to it we will one day. You ain't gonna be fetchin' and carryin' for the railway all your life.'

'Who says so? Good prospects there. And the perks come in handy. Give it five years and I'll be in the governor's chair up in that railway office wearing a nice three-piece suit and a gold fob watch.'

'Your boss ain't got a gold watch.'

'No, but I'll 'ave one. Once I'm up there.'

'Stop talkin' out the back of yer arse and dip yer 'and in yer pocket. I want some coconut ice. A big bag of it. What's on at the Pavilion anyway? Not a Yiddish show I 'ope?' she joked.

'Dunno. Larry did say but I can't remember. It was written by a bloke called Oscar Wilde, I do recall that much.'

'I should fink you would. He was in the paper, what he and his kind got up to. Why d'yer reckon he married in the first place? To keep up appearances? Arfer?'

'I don't know! Stop talkin' for five minutes. It was nice when you was quiet. Might 'ave known it wouldn't last long.' He steered her towards Larry and Moira who were waiting outside the Pavilion, dressed up to the nines in their Sunday best. They had both been to the Russian vapour baths in Brick Lane that afternoon.

'I swear Larry's nose is still growing. What a conk, eh? And look at that frock she's got on! Talk about

Victorian. All their money and walkin' about like that. One I've got on's more in vogue. Good quality an' all. Used to belong to some Lady Somefing-or-other over—'

'Arthur! Harriet!' called Larry, excited. 'Over here!'

Within minutes, the four were relaxed in each other's company and laughing at one of Larry's jokes. There were at least fifty people outside the Pavilion eager to see this amateur production of *The Importance of Being Earnest* and a few people going into the restaurant next door. Nearby pubs and taverns were in full swing with children outside, cavorting around a musician with pleating organ and accompanying female singer. Street vendors were in good voice too, calling out for people to try their pies, hot sausages, barley-sugar sticks and toffee apples.

Going into the theatre, Harriet glanced across at two scruffy ten-year-old girls who were holding hands and dancing around in a circle. She was reminded of herself at that age and felt like joining them. She squeezed Arthur's arm and looked into his eyes remembering when they had been street kids. Destitution was dwindling in this part of London and Dr Barnardo, who had died prematurely from exhaustion, was the man to thank for it. Thousands of starving homeless children had been given a better life under his care, and his good work was continuing. Barnardo had pulled open the curtain on untold misery when children in Spitalfields market had been discovered sleeping under a dirty tarpaulin, hungry, frozen and ragged. He had vowed to let all England know of it.

'We did all right, didn't we, Arfer?' whispered Harriet. 'We came through.'

Arthur nodded. 'Yeah . . . and we mustn't ever forget why. Mary.'

With a touch of remorse, she said, 'Well, she's bound to 'ave wanted the best for yer, Arthur, you being her brother.'

'She's bin a sister to you too, and you should know that.'

'I s'pose. Ne' mind . . . I'll make it up to 'er for gettin' me temper up when I shouldn't 'ave done. I was forgettin' where I came from. The stinking gutter.'

At this, Larry raised an eyebrow, then gave Harriet his practised expression of deep thought. 'You know why a Jewish tailor from Savile Row keeps a needle and thread in his top pocket?'

'Yes, Larry, you told me. More than once. Lest he should ever forget his dirty boots.'

'Roots,' he corrected, 'is what I said.' He leaned back and sported his favourite expression of doubt. 'You know I said that?'

'*You* know you bleedin' well did, so that's all right. Now, move yer arse and let's find some seats before they're filled. Not that we shouldn't 'ave 'ad a special box – compliments of the part-owner . . .' she looked slyly at him and then smiled . . . '. . . and some free chocolate.'

'It doesn't work like that,' said Larry. 'And, in any case, who paid for the tickets?'

'Not the point,' sniffed Harriet. 'We shouldn't be 'ere with all this lot is what I'm saying. I thought we was gonna be treated like royalty. I wouldn't 'ave bovvered to wash and brush my hair if I thought different.'

Larry gazed from her mass of red locks to her bright face and lifted a strand of her hair with two fingers. 'So *this* is the new style, then?'

'Sod off, Larry!' Harriet strode into the foyer, looking forward to a good time in one of the taverns once they came out of the theatre. She was in the mood for dancing . . . and Harriet could dance. Her gift of floating through the air, seeming not to touch the ground in her childhood had often kept her from starvation. Her favourite place to perform had been around the chestnut-seller's glowing coals in Aldgate East.

Coming up from behind, Larry took her arm and guided her away from the milling crowds waiting to go into the auditorium. He drew her to another door, which led to one of the boxes. He whispered, in his mock-posh voice, 'Did you really think I'd have us sit with the plebs?'

'I was testin' you, Larry. Seein' how far you'd go with your tricks. Me and my Arfer *always* sit in the best chairs,' she said, making herself comfortable on a worn red velvet seat.

As she gazed at the rowdy audience below, Harriet was struck by the resemblance this outing bore to another, years ago, when she and Arthur had been no more than nine and ten. Mary and her best friend, Lizzie Redmond, had taken them to see a variety show at a local music hall where the atmosphere had been tremendous with everyone singing along to Miss

May's naughty number. Caught up in her own rec-
ollections another face flashed across Harriet's mind.
Daft Thomas Cutbush, the midwife's nephew. He was
meant to be there that night but hadn't turned up
and then went missing. She shivered at the memory.
Thinking aloud she said, 'I was right, though, wasn't
I? But none of yer would listen.'

'About what?' said Larry.

'He was left to rot in a lunatic asylum . . . poor
devil. No one deserves that.' There was a faraway
expression in Harriet's eyes. The midwife had come
into her thoughts again and the comfort of Arthur's
arm, as he slipped it around her shoulders did little
to help.

'She's here, Arfer,' whispered Harriet, curling her
arms around herself. 'She's down there – among that
lot.' The blood had drained from her face and the
sparkle had left her eyes.

Arthur knew who she meant. 'Don't be daft! Of
course she's not down there. She's miles across the
ocean in America.'

'I want to go home, Arfer. I don't like it here. I
can *feel* her,' she whispered urgently, looking around
wildly as if she expected the devil himself to emerge
from the shadows. 'I want to go home, Arfer. I want
Mary. I never meant to spoil the evening – or waste
good tickets.' She looked into Larry's worried face.
'I'm sorry, Larry, but I don't feel too good.'

'I look upset?' he said, flapping a hand. 'I didn't
pay anyway. Go on. Get yourself off home and leave
us to enjoy the show. Bloody nuisance.' He turned to

Arthur and shook his hand. 'Tuck her up in bed with a glass of sir's best brandy.'

'Thanks, mate. Next time eh.' Arthur leaned forward. 'She's been a bit contrary since this baby thing . . .'

'I know, I know,' Larry said, then, sounding impatient, 'Get her out of here, will you? I don't wanna miss the beginning. Go on, the pair of you.'

Once they had left, Larry turned to Moira and raised his eyebrows. 'That wasn't like Harriet. Nothing like her.'

'But all that stuff about someone being left to rot in an asylum? What kind of talk is that? You've got some strange friends, Larry. I'm not sure I want to see too much of that couple.'

Larry spread his arms. 'Why give me the third degree? Leave it alone, Moira. The lights'll go down any second. Enjoy the show, for God's sake.'

'Did you hear what she said to Arthur? What she whispered?'

'No,' he sighed, 'but I'm sure you did. Go on. What did she say?'

'I couldn't catch it.'

'Well, if it was something worth catching you would have. Now, forget it or we'll leave.'

Larry was putting on a brave face. Of course Harriet had been frightened and if honest he would have to admit that he had felt a shiver go down his spine when she'd whispered that someone was there. It wasn't an impossibility that someone could be there, in the theatre, who might have harmed Harriet when she was a child and living on the streets. Whether she *had* caught a fleeting glimpse of the midwife and not actually recognised her or had simply felt her presence or even picked up on her scent on the way into the small theatre was neither here nor there. As far as Harriet was concerned, she was there. Her sixth sense had told her so and her sixth sense had always been right in the past as far as Larry was concerned.

It had been seventeen years since Harriet and the midwife had set eyes on each other and still the woman's face haunted her. She hadn't considered the possibility that Jacqueline Turner might have changed during that time or that she herself would not be recognised. After all, she was no longer a ten-year-old ragamuffin but a lovely-looking young lady. But the threat that the woman might return to retrieve her damning journal continually plagued Harriet.

America was a good place to live, according to what she'd read in the newspapers, but England was the midwife's birthplace and was most likely where she would want to be spend her last days and where she would want to be buried. For anyone to return to this part of London where they had committed murder would be foolish and Harriet was aware of this, but the midwife was no ordinary woman.

As they walked home to Bow, Harriet was quiet and Arthur decided it best to leave her be. He relished the silence, which was short-lived. Soon she said, 'I never saw 'er, granted, but it felt like she was in that place, Arfer, I swear to God.'

'Mmm . . . maybe she was then.' He didn't believe this for one minute but neither did he like the idea of getting into a debate over it. He was more concerned over Harriet's state of mind – the nightmares kept coming and now with this business of her *feeling* the midwife's presence . . .

'People used to say I'd bin 'ere before, when I was a kid . . .'

'I remember you telling me that.'

'Said I had a sixth sense. Said I'd go far if I didn't fall first.'

'Yep. I remember you sayin' that too.' Best keep it all on a light note, he thought. 'See? I don't forget a word you say, sweetheart. Not a word.'

'Good. So you remember I said the other day that if you didn't get your arse moving and find us a place I'll 'itch a ride to Mary's country mansion.'

'No,' he said, pulling down the peak of his cap. 'I can't say I recall that and I would 'ave done because it's the best promise you've made me so far.'

'I bet that country 'ouse is big enough for all of us. I could be the cleaner and you could do the gardening and odd jobs and—'

'No!' snapped Arthur. 'We'll stand on our own two feet.'

'Well, let's just see if we—' She stopped short by the sound of Larry's voice as he wove his way through the bustling pavement of Whitechapel calling them.

'I meant to tell you,' he puffed, 'there's a couple

of rooms going cheap in a turning off Jubilee Street. They're gonna pull down the row of houses sometime next year. God knows when. But I spoke to the landlord, Harry Cohen, and he said you could 'ave the rooms but you're to go first thing in the morning. No later than nine or he'll be gone.'

'Must be in a right state, Larry, if they're gonna pull 'em down.'

'So? You whitewash the bloody place! Scrub the floors and clean the windows. Block up any holes where mice or rats might set in. How long's that gonna take you? A couple of days? A week?' He hunched his shoulders and threw his arms wide. 'How bad?'

'Arfer works six days a week, Larry, don't forget.'

'It's springtime! The days will get longer and a man can make a lot of a Sunday. It's number four Musbury Street. A turning off Jubilee Street on the right. You can't miss it.' That said, he turned away.

'Larry!' yelled Harriet. 'When am I gonna dance at the Pavilion?'

'In a couple of weeks' time. They're putting on a variety show. I'll come and see you in the week.' With that he wove his way through the Saturday-night revellers, back to the theatre.

'You're gonna dance on stage, then?' Arthur thought she was the best dancer in the world.

'We'll see.'

Laughing quietly, Arthur pulled her close to him. He knew that, given half a chance, she would dance anywhere and love the applause. Her only problem was her pride: she would never be able to ask for an audition. Pride or fear of failure. Still, he looked forward to the day when he would see her in the footlights, her golden red hair flowing as she floated through the air.

'You'd win an audience over in no time, Harriet, love, no question of it.'

'I know that. I'm not daft.' That was her final word on it, Arthur knew. He could read her like a book.

3

First thing the next morning Harriet and Arthur were washed, dressed and out of the door before Mary had left with the children for church. Walking arm in arm, Arthur in his three-piece suit and best cap and Harriet in her Sunday outfit, they looked a treat in the crisp early-morning sunshine. 'If this place is all right, Arfer,' said Harriet, 'you can go straight to Brick Lane and buy a big tin of whitewash for the walls and some white paint for the woodwork. I'll nip into the Yiddish shop on me way back from Flora's and get some washing-soda and a scrubbing brush.'

'Who says we're gonna take it? And why you goin' to Flora's today of all days?'

'We'll take it – unless it's an old ruin. What choice 'ave we got? Whatever it's like it'll 'ave to do till something else comes along. And Flora's my best friend, that's why I'm going round there. I 'aven't seen 'er baby yet. And I've gotta tell 'er we're movin', 'aven't I?'

'S'pose so.' He sniffed. 'If you must. I don't think you should, though.' With his eye on an oncoming hackney cab, he guided her across Bow Road. 'You're only being nosy about Flora's house and you might come away jealous.'

'Don't be daft. Jealous? Poor cow 'asn't got no 'usband, don't forget. How can I be jealous of that? Don't matter how nice her place is – a house isn't a home without a man.'

This was a compliment but if Arthur dared acknowledge it, Harriet would likely snatch it back.

He smiled at her serenely. 'Flora's bloke stood by 'er, anyway. Got 'er a place to live.'

'What d'yer mean, stood by 'er? Her married man's done no more than any of the rich who keep a woman on the side. They're all the same. Shove their mistresses out of the way in a nice little place so they can pop in and knob 'em whenever they want. Dirty sods. Now, flag a cab – I'm not walkin' all the way to bloomin' Jubilee Street!'

During the short journey Harriet hardly said a word. She was enjoying the vision of herself with a baby in her arms in a place of her own. But when the cab pulled up in Musbury Street the silence was shattered. 'Bleedin' 'ell! I ain't livin' down 'ere!'

'Why not? Looks all right to me.'

'Opposite a bloomin' brick wall? I'll wake up and fancy I'm in prison!'

Arthur helped her out of the cab and paid the driver. 'Let's see if it's fit to live in,' he said, thumping the door with his fist. The door knocker had fallen off years ago.

The landlord opened the door with a smile, grabbed Arthur's hand and shook it vigorously. 'Good morning!

Come in!' He put his arm around Arthur's shoulder and urged him along the passage. 'Don't let first impressions put you off. Spit, polish, a bit of carbolic soap and—'

'It stinks,' said Harriet, following the men. 'It's like a bleedin' rat run. I've left the front door open to let some air and light in, else we'd all fall arse over 'ead.'

'A woman after my own heart,' said the man, winking at Arthur. 'I said to myself only yesterday, "That front door's got to go and another with a window put in its place." And what d'yer think? I picked one up from the junk yard – good as new.' He flapped a hand in the air. 'Bit of stained glass too. My lucky day. I was just gonna fix it on but forgot to fetch it with me. Go through, go through.' He stood on the narrow staircase and waved them into the kitchen-cum-scullery.

'I can 'ardly breathe,' gasped Harriet. 'Open that back door, Arfer.' The kitchen reeked of decaying vegetables and stale cooking fat. She heaved, and then, from the corner of her eye, she spotted a decomposed rat in a mucky corner. She pushed past Arthur and rushed out into the back yard.

When she returned Arthur was looking down-hearted. The blacklead cooking range was thick with layers of grease and old food. The butler's sink in the corner was in a worse state but at least there were no cracks. A dull brass plug hung from a metal chain, which had been fixed in two places with rusty wire.

Ash, coal dust and soot from the fireplace under the copper boiler covered every surface, and a pile had been swept into a corner where it had almost solidified. Harriet asked the landlord how long it had been since anyone had lived in the place.

'Not long . . .' was the shifty answer. 'The old boy passed away in the front room, in front of the fire. I don't think he used the kitchen much. His daughter brought hot meals in and did his washing.' He was lying, and it was a mystery to Harriet as to why he would want to. She could see plainly that no one had lived here for some time.

She returned to the back yard, with Arthur following, opened the door into the privy and closed it again. The pan was a brownish black and there was no seat. She shuddered and marched back inside. She thought of leaving never to return, but instead she went into the front room, where she found an old brass bed that had lost its mattress. It was solid and, in its own way, quite pretty. At least she could make use of the soot and coal dust, turn it into a paste that would soon have the brass gleaming, with a little elbow grease.

She turned to the landlord. 'This place ain't fit to live in. The authorities would condemn it out of 'and. We'll 'ave a month's free rent in payment for me cleanin' it up then pay rent of . . . four shillings a week. Take it or leave it.'

The man made feeble sounds of protest but the expression on Harriet's face was enough to wilt a rose. 'You push a hard bargain,' he murmured, 'a very hard bargain indeed. If I was a wealthy man I could understand it. I know landlords who don't even provide sanitation.'

'We all know that – but I wasn't born to pee in a bucket. Anyway, landlords such as that 'ave bin found out. One or two 'ave gone to prison for it.'

'Oh, I wouldn't go as far as to say that.'

'No? Well, I know different. You should pay a visit to St Joseph's Hospice in Hackney. Talk to them poor sods who're incurable from illnesses brought on by disgusting rented rooms. Ask 'em what it's like to 'ave bin struck down with tuberculosis, diphtheria, smallpox, blood poisonin', bronchitis, pneumonia . . .'

'You're talking about unscrupulous landlords working the worst slum areas,' he said, a wounded expression on his face. 'I'm just a working-class man trying to make a living.'

'So this nice coat,' she said, feeling the material between her fingers, 'it's not pure camel?'

'Okay, okay. Four shillings a week and a month free in return for you clearing out the rubbish.'

'I never said we'd get rid of the rubbish. You get the junk out. All of it – except the brass bed, the chest of drawers in the back room and the sideboard in 'ere and them four chairs and the table. Who's living upstairs?'

'No one. You've got the place to yourselves. It's a bloody bargain. I'm letting you have the first look because Larry's a friend. I could let this for—'

'So the upstairs is condemned. The rain comes in the roof as well as the four-legged friends, and if you show it to the wrong person they might report you. The houses either side of this one would be condemned too and you'd lose all the rents. When are these due to be pulled down?'

'In a year or so,' he said, rubbing his chin.

'Show me upstairs,' said Harriet, making her way out of the room. 'I need to know what's above me if I'm to sleep at night.'

The landlord flapped a hand with an exaggerated sigh. 'Up is up and down is down. Nothing that's going on up there will interfere with you. These rooms below are dry and sound.'

'Fair enough, landlord,' she said, keeping her thoughts to herself. 'We'll keep the upstairs locked up and say no more.'

'You drive a hard bargain,' he said again, shaking his head.

'So you keep saying, but you're a businessman so I'm sure you appreciate it, eh?' She winked at him and offered her hand.

The landlord shook it and was out of the house in a flash with sixteen shillings in his pocket – the rent for the second month. It had all happened so quickly, and Harriet was aware that Arthur had had a hard time keeping up with her keen mind. She could find an answer to everything, no matter who she was dealing with, and mostly she was right. Landlords had to be watched.

It wasn't so long ago, back in the 1890s, that families occupying single rooms had had to take in a sleep-only lodger, whose meagre rent paid for the family to use the public baths once a week. Most lodging rooms and houses had been foul from defective sewerage and drainage, faulty taps, scant ventilation and damp. In such neighbourhoods it was expected that at least one member of a family would catch a serious illness. The death rate was high but it was thought by some that to change things radically would be to upset the law of nature. Death was one way of countering over-population in the slums of Whitechapel and Bethnal Green.

'I didn't think you'd wanna take this place Harriet,' murmured Arthur, looking miserably around the room. 'I never in a million years thought you'd wanna live 'ere.'

'I wouldn't 'ave done if the upstairs was occupied – or about to be. We've got ourselves a little bargain, Arfer. A two-up three-down for four bob a week.' She turned and smiled into his puzzled face. 'What a find, eh?'

Arthur looked stunned. And well he might, Harriet thought. But she wasn't having second thoughts. Her eyes sparkled. 'Well, say somefing, then. I did well, didn't I?'

'It's cheap, Harriet, I'll grant you that. But it's a pig-sty.'

'Ah,' she slipped her arms around his neck and kissed the tip of his nose, 'but it won't be, will it? Now, then, we ain't got no pencil and paper so you've gotta remember the list. Paint, rat poison, bleach, carbolic, a bucket, scrubbing-brush, broom and a second-'and wheelbarrow to fetch the lot of it back 'ere. We've only got the one key so leave the door ajar. You'd best get a couple more cut. Oh, and pick up some old sacks to put this rubbish in. That crafty sod won't be back to clear it.'

'Is that all?'

'For now it is, yeah. It's all I can fink of at the moment. I'm brainy, Arfer, I'll grant you that, but I'm not a wizard.'

'Why can't you come with me?'

'Because I'm going to see Flora. I 'aven't seen the baby yet, 'ave I?'

'Oh, right,' he said. 'A bit of homework, is it? Seein' 'ow she feeds it and that?'

She wrapped her arms around him and gave him a big squeeze. 'We're gonna be all right, sweet'eart. I know Mary gave you a lump of money and that'll go a long way. But if we run short, she'll be there for us, I bet yer.'

Pulling back, he peered down at her. 'How did you know about the money?'

''Cos I went in your trouser pockets. That's summink else you're gonna 'ave to get used to an' all. No secrets.'

They parted company in Jubilee Street, where Arthur headed north towards Brick Lane in Bethnal Green and Harriet towards St Mary's Court in Limehouse. With the spring sunshine on her cheeks and her thoughts on the house and how it would look once they had got to work on it, she was grinning and passers-by eyed her with suspicion, perhaps wondering if she might have escaped from the Bethnal Green lunatic asylum.

Happy and carefree, a light spring in her step, anything now seemed possible. They were going to have their own house to live in and she was going to turn it into a proper home. Every wall and ceiling was going to be whitewashed twice until it gleamed like the icing on a Christmas cake. She would scrub the floorboards clean and, out of the money Mary had given them, they would buy linoleum to cover them. She wanted it to smell brand new. She would ask Mary if she could take the tiny oil lamp from her bedroom: she had come to think of it as her own and it had been her comfort in the night when she had woken in a cold sweat and not been able to get back to sleep.

She would run up curtains on Mary's old sewing-machine and make simple covers for the second-hand three-piece suite they would purchase. They would have a little rug in front of the fire in the back room and sparkling white linen and a lace runner on the old pine sideboard – the filthy sideboard that she would clean with liquid soap, then polish until it shone. In the corner of the front room where they would sleep, she visualised a crib with a sleeping baby. Her and Arthur's baby.

She was entering the narrow archway into St Mary's Court before she knew it. The quiet flagstone area was enclosed by an ivy-clad brick wall and terraced two-up two-down cottages. In the centre of the courtyard a flowering fruit tree was in bud. Had she arrived in the depth of winter, however, she would have found the court was a dark, scary place at night, with just one gas light, especially when the fog was low and thick.

As she stood at the door and knocked quietly so as not to wake Flora's baby, she could feel her heart pounding – she was excited at seeing her friend in her new home but mostly at having the chance to hold a baby. When the beautiful dark-haired Flora, wearing an ankle-length grey frock with a blue overall on top, opened the door, the pair gazed at each other then hugged and squealed as if they were children.

'You should have written and said you was coming. What if I'd been out?' said Flora. She covered her mouth with a hand. 'I can't believe you came, Harriet. I'm that pleased to see you.' Then she burst into tears and threw her arms around her friend.

'Come on, Flo, it can't be that bad.' Harriet pulled back and looked into her face, then brushed strands of Flora's thick black wavy hair away from her eyes. 'Been up all night wiv the baby, have yer?'

'No. She's as good as gold,' said Flora, wiping away her tears with the back of her hand. 'Come in and shut the door before anyone sees.'

'Why should you care about other people?' Harriet slammed the door behind her and followed Flora into her warm, friendly sitting room. She had created a homely scene with second-hand armchairs and slightly moth-eaten curtains and rugs. The cushions and covers were a mismatch of colours and patterns – faded reds, pinks, golds and varying shades of green – all lit up by the rays of the spring sun shining in through the window past the old lace curtain.

'See?' said Harriet, dropping into a comfortable old armchair. 'It's right what they say that class and taste don't go 'and in 'and. A chambermaid might well have taste and a princess might not. You weren't a chambermaid, Flora, but you've slaved in kitchens. And look at this room. It's beau'iful.'

'I never slaved in kitchens – well, only at first. I was an apprentice to the cook's help in the director's dining room. There's a difference.'

'Same fing. Well, come on, then, where's the baby?'

'Mum and Dad 'ave taken 'er out in the pram to Meath Gardens to gimme a break.'

'Oh, it's really 'ard work, then, caring for a baby?'

'Oh, it's not that,' said Flora filling a kettle. 'She nearly goes through the night but I'm still always tired.'

'Well, I s'pose you would be. It's not been long since you were in labour.' Harriet glanced at her friend, and saw suddenly that she was letting herself go. Once upon a time Flora had looked beautiful, in a natural kind of way, at any time of day or night. Now her hair was a little greasy and scraped back with hair grips instead of a pretty comb and she wore no makeup, not even a touch of rouge. And she was dark under the eyes.

'Seems like ages ago that the midwife came in the middle of the night.'

The word 'midwife' sent an icy chill through Harriet. 'Well, best forget about all that. It's over and done wiv now and you've got a beau'iful baby girl.'

Flora smiled through a new rush of tears. 'She is beautiful, Harriet, and I love 'er so much. I've called 'er Beanie 'cos—'

'You've *what*? *Beanie?* What kind of a bleedin' name's that?'

'I know it don't sound like a proper name to you but, well, she is a little Beanie. It was Prince Charlie who first—'

'Oh, gawd! I might 'ave known. They can do what they like, the rich, can't they? Some of the names you read in the society pages make me scream.'

'He never *said* to call 'er that! It's just that when I first told him, you know, that I was . . . having his baby, he smiled and whispered in my ear, "I've planted a little bean inside my lovely Flora."' She looked at her friend for a response.

'Stone the flippin' crows,' chuckled Harriet. 'Just as well the dozy sod 'as scooted off and left you 'oldin' the baby. Some father he'd make. Planted a bean!' She burst into laughter. '"Planted a bean in my lovely Flora,"' she mimicked. 'You should 'ave called 'im Prince Jack. Jack and 'is great big beanstalk.'

Flora tonged a couple of lumps of coal on to the fire, smiling now. 'I've not seen 'im since we moved out of Brick Lane and into this place – and that was over a month ago. That's the worst of it, really. I believed 'im, Harriet. I believed he would get a divorce. I expect it's because he's such a gentleman that he doesn't want to break 'er 'eart.'

'Never mind he's broke yours, though,' said Harriet, without thinking. Then, on seeing the hurt expression on her friend's face, she changed her tune. 'Blimey, Flo . . . is that 'ow long it's been since I've seen yer? Nearly two months?'

'Yeah. I was disappointed, to tell the truth. Baby's nearly seven weeks old. I thought maybe Arthur told you to keep away from me. You know what men are like.'

'No, he's 'ad other things to worry over. Gonna be a dad.'

'Never? Not you as well?' Flora looked startled.

'You can smile, I'm 'appy about it, but it's not all roses and sunshine. The gossips 'ave bin givin' vent to their filthy minds – they all seem to know I'm pregnant and they still fink me and Arfer are brother and sister. So you can imagine.' Harriet could tell from her friend's expression that she had rocked her – and Flora was always calm and collected. 'A cup of tea would be nice.'

Flora's smile faded and a look of worry swept across her features. 'Oh, Harriet, you can't live there now. Not if they *really* believe you're brother and sister. You can't. You mustn't.'

'I'm not going to, don't worry. I've not said too much to Arfer about it, but the way people look at me now, it's 'orrible. One minute they've got me feelin' ashamed when I shouldn't be and the next my temper's up higher than I want it to be – and all over nuffing.'

'But why can't you just tell them? Or tell one at least. Word'll soon get round that you were adopted into the family and brought up as one of them.'

'Because the stone's bin cast, Flora, that's why. Most of them women are wives of successful men in the City. They ain't got much else to do but gossip. If I take this away from 'em, the focus'll go straight to Mary who, don't forget, is livin' in sin with two illegitimate children.'

'Oh,' said Flora, a hint of despair in her voice. 'So they found out about that too?'

'No, they never. That *is* a tight secret, and so it should be. I'm not that keen on her little ones but it wouldn't be fair if it all came into the open. So far as they're concerned, they're an ordinary family. Mary's bin good to me and I wouldn't do anyfing to spoil fings for 'er. I love 'er like a sister.'

'I can see what you're getting at,' said Flora, taking her friend's hand. 'You're a good person, Harriet. Not everyone'd be prepared to keep their mouths shut to spare another.'

'They fink they'll be banishing us from Bow – and they will be, but I'll never let on 'ow much it 'urts. I like livin' there – even though I'm comf'table down this end where I'm more used to the people and their ways.'

'I s'pose I've been lucky, movin' into this court-yard. They know this isn't a gold ring on my finger,' murmured Flora, thumbing the gold-coloured band, 'but I've not once had a black look. I can't imagine having to put up with neighbours saying such horrid things.'

'I've known worse, Flora. Stop pulling me down. You might be in the dumps today but I'm not and I don't wanna be.'

'I'm sorry. Of course you've known worse. Anything must be better than your childhood.'

'Yes and no. It wasn't all bad. Lighten up a bit. You'll 'ave me slittin' me wrists if you're not careful. We 'aven't done bad, 'ave we? Think of them poor cows livin' on the streets in the back of beyond in Shoreditch. We're pigs in shit compared to them.'

An hour later, the girls were sitting before the glowing fire having caught up with all the latest gossip and sharing one of Flora's cigarettes. Once Harriet had mentioned the house that she and Arthur were to rent, the conversation turned to decorating, furnishing and babies. Flora was going to show Harriet the best second-hand shops, which were out of the area in Kensington, Hampstead and Mayfair.

Then Flora told her that she had joined the women's-rights movement and the Women's Social and Political Union, founded by Emmeline Pankhurst, which aimed to recruit working-class women to struggle for the vote. Flora had gone to the East London People's Palace for company when she was lonely, living in Brick Lane and pregnant. She had found the women there lively and inspirational: she had got into conversation with them and became interested, especially after a talk on equal pay for women, maternity and infant care. Also she had found that at every meeting she attended on women's suffrage, the class barrier was almost non-existent. Suddenly, ladies of distinction and factory girls had something in common.

But Harriet was not interested in political meetings and pulled the conversation back to a more personal topic. 'So, is Prince Charlie gonna come back, d'yer think?' she asked.

'I don't know, Harriet. I wish I did. One way or another it would make it easier.' Flora evidently didn't want to discuss the lover who had deserted her, and returned to what she had been saying earlier. 'The Pankhursts are not just suffragettes, you know. One of Emmeline's daughters is an artist as well as being political. I saw an exhibition of her watercolours and drawings.'

'Don't tell me she paints pretty flowers?' said Harriet, curling her lip.

'No. She draws women in their grim working conditions.'

'Good for 'er. So, what about Prince Charlie, then?'

'I don't know. I wish I could say something for certain but I can't.' She turned away her face. 'I mustn't 'old you up.'

'You're not 'oldin' me up, Flora.'

'Well, maybe not, but . . . well, it was a lovely surprise you turning up out of the blue like that.' Flora became pensive, gazing into space. 'I don't have any other friends – not proper friends. I lost touch when I was with Prince Charlie and then, once I was pregnant, I had to keep myself hidden away for most of the time, till I couldn't bear it and went out, to public talks on women's rights. There was some nice girls and women there, but they thought I was married so I couldn't get too close.'

'Well, neiver 'ave I got any friends, so that's all right. Well, except for Polly. Once I'm settled you can both come to tea and meet each other. You'll get on, I know you will.'

'That'd be lovely.' Flora smiled. 'Something to look forward to.'

★   ★   ★

As she walked slowly home, through the back-streets and out on to the Mile End Road, Harriet said a little prayer to the Lord Jesus. She asked him to let things turn out well for Flora, herself and Arthur. She also suggested that he might like to arrange for the house where Flora's Prince Charlie was hiding away with his family to be struck by lightning.

She sang as she strolled through the streets, a song from her ragged childhood days. She had learned it from watching the Salvation Army when they played it: 'Jesus Loves Me'. Then, as ever when drawn back to those times, a feeling of dread returned to her. Harriet shuddered as she remembered the unyielding expression on the midwife's face when she caught her peeping at the diary. She forced it from her mind and pictured the blackened face of the warm, friendly coalman instead. The man who had let her sleep in his yard. She also thought about her mother and her little sister, whom she had missed so badly when the family had been split up all those years ago when they had gone to live with an aunt and uncle who had had no room for Harriet. Soon she would take Arthur to visit them. He had only been to her aunt's house once and that was several years ago when she was ten and he was nine.

They had made the journey from East London to Camberwell on the omnibus, clutching small paper parcels of hot faggots and pease pudding that they had purchased with ill-gotten gains: Harriet had shown Arthur how to pick a purse. The wealthy gentry were always in and around Whitechapel at that time, their morbid curiosity overcoming their disgust for deprived areas and their filthy inhabitants. The ride had been a highlight of Harriet's life, sitting in the bus with smart, affluent folk who had been visiting the scenes of the Whitechapel murders. She had been amused by the buzz of conversation. The adults had given their opinions as to the identity of the murderer. They had spoken of East London as if it were a different place from the one Harriet and Arthur knew. They had said that women were asking for trouble if they went out after dusk, whether or not horrific murders were being committed. They pitied the children and said they should all be put into an institution. They had thought that most of the men, if not all, should be in prison.

Harriet had felt insulted by this, and had told Arthur, voice raised, a fabricated story as to how she and her baby brother had been kept in a cellar without food or drink until they finally clawed their way out, and how her father had tried to slit her mother's throat because he'd caught her with the rent man. Then she had spotted the midwife going into the Lambeth asylum to visit her nephew, Thomas Cutbush. When she could read properly, she had gleaned from the midwife's diary that the twenty-two-year-old was insane and for some reason, she had felt a wave of sympathy for the pathetic creature who had had no friends whatsoever.

Harriet turned into her street and nodded at a neighbour as she passed – the woman was whitening her front doorstep with a block of chalk. She nudged open her own front door and went inside the dark, narrow corridor. With no window and no gas lighting, she had to feel her way into the scullery where the sun just managed to shine through the small filthy window. Harriet slid the bolt on the back door, kicked it open and all but fell out into the yard, desperate for fresh air. Nauseated, she went to the outside lavatory, but as she pulled open the door, it came off in her hand and a worse smell filled her nostrils.

As the lavatory door crashed to the ground and shattered all she wanted was to run from this place, but there was no gate leading out of the yard and her only escape was back through that dark passage.

'I thought you were out your skull taking that place on.' A voice drifted over her head. 'Wants fumigating.' A woman pulled a couple of loose planks out of the fence. 'Squeeze yourself through and come inside before you pass out. The kettle's just boiled.'

Harriet raised her head and gazed into a square face. Her neighbour looked as if she could cope with anything life threw at her. 'Do yer know what you are?' she said, wiping her eyes with her sleeve. 'An angel of mercy.'

'If that's meant to be a compliment, it's wasted on me. I'm offering a cup of tea and not much more than that.'

Grateful to escape, Harriet followed the unsmiling woman into her house and could hardly believe the difference between this one and next door. The scent of Sunlight soap and bleach was in the air. 'It smells nice and clean in here,' she said, at the same time noticing the bleak atmosphere. 'Was yours as filthy as next door when you moved in?'

The woman, who looked to be in her forties, raised an eyebrow as she spooned tealeaves into a china teapot. 'I was born in this house. My mother wasn't overly fussy but neither did she let it go. She passed away years ago and Father went just before her. The name's Greta.'

'Mine's Harriet. I'm getting married soon . . . to Arthur. He's gone down Brick Lane to get some cleaning things and paint.' She glanced out of the open doorway into the narrow passage, and shuddered. Something felt wrong in this house. And this woman reminded her of the midwife.

'And you're both working, are you?' asked Greta, breaking into her thoughts.

'Arfer works for the railway – deliveries – and I've got a little job at Yardley's soap factory. Me and him have been livin' wiv his sister over in Bow. But she's movin' out to the country with her little family so we're on the trot.'

'Very nice for her, too. This part of London's not everyone's cup of tea but you can stick the open countryside. All very well for a day out now and then,' said Greta, as she poured boiling water into the pot, 'but the thought of drifting into boredom like that turns my stomach. You should have next door shipshape in a day if you both work at it.'

'The state of that place is beyond me,' said Harriet. 'How can anyone live like that?'

'The old boy who was there before you never knew

whether he was coming or going. Kept himself to himself, though, and that's no bad thing. Bit of a dark horse but that suited me. At least he never drank himself silly like some.' She looked directly into Harriet's face, giving her a clear message.

Harriet shivered inwardly. 'Be all right, next door, once we've scrubbed it top to bottom,' she said, and thought, Be a darn sight better than this one. 'I take it there ain't no evil spirits lurking about?'

'I should hope not. No evil and no spirit. I can't abide people who use gin to get them through the day or go out in the evening just so they can come back full of drink and behave like degenerates.'

'Just as well you don't live in the Jago or down Whitechapel,' said Harriet trying to lighten the conversation. 'They're all bleedin' drunks, if you ask me. But then wot else 'ave they got?'

Pouring the tea, Greta acted as if Harriet hadn't spoken. 'Be sure to complain every time the rent collector comes. It all gets reported back to the landlord. Or most of it anyway. If you behave too proud of what you've done he'll put up the rent and we'll all suffer. And don't ever let him know if you decide to use the upstairs. Always complain about the damp, vermin and bugs. And that's another thing. Get rid of them straight away. I don't want the devils finding their way through cracks and crevices. I've made up a solution that works. I'll give you the recipe.'

'My muvver used to click the bedbugs between her thumbnails,' said Harriet, determined that this woman wasn't going to bring her down. There was only one way to deal with women like Greta and that was to goad them with a friendly, casual manner. 'Muvver used to say that lipstick factories used the blood from the bugs to make lipstick. I never knew if she was kiddin' or not.'

'Well, you can click them if you like but it'll take an age. They love dark damp places to hibernate then multiply when it's warm.'

Harriet sipped her tea. 'So, you live on your own, then, do you?'

Her familiarity seemed to irritate Greta, who wasn't too clever about hiding it. 'As a matter of fact I don't. I've taken a girl out of the depravity of the workhouse and given her a room upstairs. In payment she cleans and shops for us. For Edith and me, that is. Edith works for the Whitechapel art gallery. In the office above it. Practically runs the place. She's an artist in her spare time. Painted that picture up there.' She nodded at a brightly coloured abstract oil painting. 'Not to everyone's taste, but what does that matter?'

'And what d'you work at?' asked Harriet, pushing her luck.

'I'm bookkeeper for a Jewish tailor four days a week, and I do the accounts for the Anarchist Club.' Greta looked slyly at Harriet's face for her reaction. The anarchists weren't too popular among the ordinary folk in Stepney. 'But, then, I don't expect you want to know about that.'

'Each to their own,' Harriet didn't know who Greta was talking about or what they stood for. Politics, so far as she was concerned, was for others. 'I can't be doing with all that – too busy getting from one pay day to another.'

'As so many people are. Maybe you should pop into Alexander Hall for half an hour and listen to one of the speakers. You might learn something.'

'Where's that?' sniffed Harriet. 'Up West?' Her indifference was meant to end the conversation.

'It's in Jubilee Street. Right on your doorstep.' Greta stared into Harriet's eyes. 'We get some good speakers coming into Whitechapel, you know. Lenin's been once or twice.'

'Is that right?' Frankly, Harriet couldn't care less who came and went so long as they didn't preach on a soapbox in her street.

'William Morris used to visit and give a talk in the old days, and Bernard Shaw. Then there was Eleanor Marx . . .' Greta waited but Harriet didn't respond so she went on, 'It takes a strong woman to defy such a father as she had. Karl Marx wouldn't soil the soles of his shoes by coming into the slums. *She* did, though. Learned Yiddish so she could help to unionise the immigrant tailors.'

'Well she'd 'ave to, wouldn't she? The foreigners stick together. It's a pity none of your famous people couldn't speak up for us English – the poor who were born and bred in East London.'

'Then there was Annie Besant,' Greta had ignored her remark, 'leading the women while the men fol- lowed—'

'She did well. I'll give you that. Got more pay for girls at the matchbox factory. She's not one of your anarchists though, is she, Annie Besant? I only saw 'er once and she seemed nice. Very feminine for a union woman.'

Greta narrowed her eyes and looked thoughtful. 'I think we could get along as neighbours, living shoulder to shoulder, so long as we don't meddle in each other's affairs. I would rather you didn't get into conversation with the girl from the workhouse. She's a compulsive liar and can't help making mischief. I shouldn't like it if she was to be upset – with you being a stranger. We've managed to get her nicely settled into a homely atmosphere.'

This little speech immediately put Harriet on her guard. Why was she telling her to keep out? 'Well, maybe I could be 'er friend. Sounds like she could do with one.'

'No. She'll engage you in gossip, which will be all lies. She can't help being crafty. So, if you should see her in the back yard or in the street, best to leave her in her own world where she feels secure.'

'Well, we'll see,' said Harriet. 'You never know, I might be the makin' of 'er. I 'ad it very hard as a child and only just escaped the work'ouse so I do know a little bit about what I'm thinkin'. And I'm thinkin' she might want a friend. If not, I'll leave 'er to 'erself.'

'Well, I'll thank you not to encourage her. She lives in a world where it's always bedtime. A lazy and ungrateful girl. Edith and I feed and clothe her after rescuing her from the workhouse and I don't think she even knows where she's been or where she is now. She'd sleep all day long and go out at night if she had a chance.'

'Sounds to me like she never appreciated you,' said Harriet. 'I bet she's never satisfied either. Give her three pennies and she'll want four.'

'Good. You've got the picture. I thought it best to start as we mean to go on. That's why I called you in for a cup of tea. I shan't make a habit of that. Don't believe in it. Ladies taking tea together makes for gossip.'

Harriet stood up. 'And a lovely cup of tea it was. Once I've got my place all tickety-boo and shinin' like a new pin I'll return your hospitality. Right now I'm gonna chuck all the junk out into the back yard and burn it. Don't put yer washin' out today, will yer?'

Harriet left through the gap in the fence and went into her house with two thoughts in mind. One was to keep out of her neighbour's way and the other to open wide every window to let in some fresh air. Then she would work systematically from the front room to the back and then the kitchen, carrying out rubbish and broken furniture. As far as the girl from the workhouse was concerned, if Harriet felt like talking to her she would. Sod the lesbian.

Next door, Greta was none too pleased to hear banging and crashing and wondered if this peculiar ginger-haired young female was going to be a nuisance. A nosy-parker. 'Best keep on her good side,' she told herself. 'Persuade her along to one of the radical meetings and get her so involved she'll have no time to poke her nose where it doesn't belong.'

Hearing a creaking sound from above she guessed that the workhouse girl had finished polishing the floor and was about to steal a ten-minute rest. Well, that suited Greta. The ginger-headed bitch from next door had got her worked up and now she had excess energy to burn. Opening the small cupboard beneath the stairs, she unhooked her father's old leather strap and ran it slowly across the palm of her hand.

An hour or so later Arthur, his wheelbarrow piled high, was puffing like an engine and red-faced. He had purchased all that Harriet had ordered and more – six rolls of damaged wallpaper. Stopping short at number four he was careful not to unbalance his barrow as he set it down and took a breather. He dabbed his sweaty brow with the sleeve of his jacket and noticed that there were signs of brass beneath the filth on the old brownish-black letter-box. He walked up to it, and rubbed his thumb over it. He'd have it gleaming before he painted the door black. He knew not to expect the landlord to deliver another.

His mind charged with the vision of red roses climbing over it, he banged on the door, exhausted from his trip but excited to have his own place at last.

Harriet opened it and he laughed to see her dirty face. When she spied the rolls of pretty wallpaper on the wheelbarrow she was thrilled. 'Arfer, you crafty bleeder,' she grinned, 'you went out and got that specially for me.' She threw her arms around him.

'I love you, Arfer, do you know that? I really, really love yer.'

'Well, that's just as well, then, seeing as you're 'avin' my baby.'

'You bought that wallpaper for me so I'm gonna make you a steak and oyster pudding as soon as we move in. I am. With tatters and greens and gravy. A proper dinner – jest for the two of us. Wiv a spotty dick and custard for afters.'

But Arthur wasn't thinking of his stomach. He couldn't wait to be back at Mary's house with Harriet in his bed.

4

Leaving Bow Terrace had been emotional and traumatic for both Harriet and Arthur. With Mary, Walter, the children and all of their belongings gone, the last few days in the silent and echoing house were sad. They hadn't expected to feel lonely – in fact they had looked forward to having the house to themselves. However, not only did they miss the family, they were bombarded with notes through the door, some disgusting, some religious and so damning that Harriet and Arthur felt guilty, as if they *were* brother and sister.

There had also been a few pulls on the doorbell and nobody there when they had answered the call. Instead there was always something on the step, linked to the devil or God. On one occasion a raw egg had been smashed against one of the downstairs windows. It was more than a blessing that they had their little house to go to and they couldn't wait to get out of Bow.

When the horse and cart arrived to take them and their belongings to their new home in Stepney, the neighbours had gathered in small groups. The smug expressions of the women, as the cart was loaded with items they considered good enough only for the rubbish dump, had upset and embarrassed Harriet. She was crying inside when she climbed up next to the driver but mostly because she was leaving what had been her home. However, she had given a fine performance as a proud young woman moving on to pastures new, her head high and chin up. She glanced back once at the lovely house and suppressed a deep sense of loss. Then she thought of her and Arthur's two-up two-down and the way it would look once they had settled in. She compared it with the stable where she had had to doss down as a child. This tiny house in Stepney, their new home, was a palace in comparison and in her imagination the old horse-drawn cart was her carriage, taking her to a grand ball she would not have to leave at midnight.

Harriet's Prince Charming, Arthur, had been on the back of the cart making sure that none of their possessions fell out during the journey along the cobbled streets from Bow to Stepney.

A month after they had moved in and enjoyed a whirlwind romance with their new home, cleaning, painting and furnishing it, Harriet and Arthur were tired, but proud of their achievements. Before setting out to the soap factory each morning, Harriet had had a bout of morning sickness, but now, on this bright Sunday morning, lying in bed with the sun streaming through the window, she was in seventh heaven. Arthur was fetching her tea, toast and honey. She plumped the pillows, positioned them against the brass bedhead and sank back content. She wanted to share her happiness with her younger sister. Alice was almost twenty but young for her years. As a child she had always been quiet but it had been said that she would grow more out-going, like Harriet. However, as the years had passed she had withdrawn further into her own world . . .

Arthur arrived with the breakfast tray. 'The toast's a bit overdone, love,' he said. 'That old range is too flippin' good at times. Roaring, it is. I've scraped off the worst of the burnt bits, though.'

'That's all right, Arfer, I like charcoal.' She grinned at him then spread on some honey given to them by an old boy along the street who kept bees. The generosity was not so much a neighbourly gesture as a bribe. At times his bees could be a touch on the angry side. When he had been introduced to Harriet he had known straight away that she would be on his list of those to mollify.

Arthur sat on the edge of the bed and sipped his tea. 'I've just seen that poor cow on 'er hands and knees in the back yard, scrubbin' the steps. I wouldn't mind bettin' she ain't seen a square meal once in 'er life. All skin and bone.'

'I know,' said Harriet, licking her fingers, 'and I'm gonna say somefing soon.'

'Rather you than me. That pair of lesbians frightens me to death. They're both a penny shy of a shilling.'

'More like a penny over the bob. Sharper than a fox. Who told you they're lesbians?'

He gave her a sideways glance and pulled a face. 'You did. You said they was a pair of dockers in frocks.'

'Well, we don't know for sure, do we? They might
be wicked torturers. They might not be givin' 'er any
food. She was sobbin' again last night. I've a good
mind to poke around that hole in the plaster and go
right through to—'

'You've not bin upstairs again?' He shook his head.
'Wastin' your time even thinkin' about it. Too much
work. Be satisfied with what you've got.'

'I wasn't finkin' of it for us, Arfer. I was finkin' that
I might let our Alice come and live wiv us.'

'Whatever for? She's all right where she is. Got 'er
own little bedroom an' all. What 'ave we got to offer
other than a couple of derelict rooms that even mice
won't move into on account of the rats?'

'There's no rats up there! Stop tormentin' me.'

'Oh, so you *do* agree wiv me, then? It *was* a waste
of a tanner gettin' the rat man in?'

'Arse'oles. Now go and pour me another cup of tea.'

'It is Sunday, you know.'

'Yeah, well, wot wiv us forgettin' to go to church
today . . . it slipped my mind. May God forgive me.'

'Shouldn't swear, no matter what day it is. I dunno
what Mary'd say if she 'eard you use that word.' Arthur
took her empty cup and left the room.

'Well, Mary won't ever 'ave to listen to me swearin'
now, will she? Madam's swannin' around 'er country
mansion! She's forgot all about us!'

'You're talkin' a load of rot!' His reply floated in to
her from the kitchen. 'She's written twice and said we
can go and visit as soon as she's settled in prop'ly.'

★   ★   ★

Arthur poured the second cup of tea then gazed out of the window into the back yard at the girl, who was now sweeping leaves away from the back door. Suddenly he opened the tiny window, called to her that he'd made a fresh pot of tea and asked if she'd like a cup. The expression on her face was a mixture of shock and terror, and in answer she lowered her eyes and turned her back on him. But Arthur was not prepared to give up easily. He carried his own cup out into the yard and stood smiling at her, waiting for a reply.

'Come on,' he coaxed her, 'everyone takes a little tea break. It's not poisoned!' She raised her eyes furtively then wrapped her thin arms around herself. Frightened eyes fixed on his face, she stepped cautiously towards him, a lamb to the slaughter. She reached out with a trembling hand and took the cup from him. In her face he saw something he had never seen before: unequivocal despair. This girl had all but given up. Her eyes were dead.

'They're at church,' she whispered, looking about her, agitated.

'Good for them. Now, you get that tea down yer before it turns cold.'

'You won't tell them?'

'Course not. It's none of their business. My name's Arfer and my wife-to-be is called Harriet. She's 'aving breakfast in bed. Toast and honey. We're gettin' married in a fortnight.' In his wisdom, Arthur knew that that short-and-to-the-point introduction was enough. He waited while the girl drank her tea.

'Thank you,' she murmured, handing him the empty

cup. Then, before he could say another word, she turned and scurried back inside the house, closing the back door without making a sound. Well practised, thought Arthur. The poor girl had been taught to go about as if she were invisible, as if she didn't exist. He went back inside, leaned against the passage wall and pressed his hands to his face to stop himself shedding tears. He had no idea why he should feel sorry for the wretched girl. Then Harriet called him, and he pulled himself together. He went into the bedroom and sat on the edge of the bed again.

'I 'eard you go out into the yard, Arfer. What did you see through the winda? More than one rat?'

'There's no rats out there, Harriet. They won't bother us now that all the rubbish 'as bin cleared away. If you're still worried I'll go down the lane and buy a cat.'

'Well, if it wasn't a rat that's brought you down, what was it?'

'The girl from next door. She can't be a day over fourteen. It's not right. She's all skin and bone and . . .' He buried his head in his hands and, for the first time since he had mourned his mother and baby sister, Arthur shed a tear. 'I swear to God she's covered with bruises. Don't ask me 'ow I know, I just do. That grey frock she wears 'as got long sleeves but you can see bruise marks beneath the cuffs.' He cleared his throat, wiped his eyes with the back of his hand and took a long, deep breath.

'I told you I was gonna look into it,' murmured Harriet, looking ashamed.

On the same wavelength, Arthur knew that the girl next door was a haunting reminder of Harriet's own life before Mary took her in. 'That could be you,' he said. 'Or me, come to that.' He half turned and caught her eye. 'What do we do about it? If we say anything them two cows'll send 'er back to where she came from and she might not want that.'

'We'll 'ide 'er upstairs and tell 'em she must 'ave run away.'

'Don't be daft. They'd call in the police. Have to. No, we'll leave things be and wait. It's not as if what's goin' on in there has just started. She's not at death's door. Besides, I wouldn't choose either of them two next door for an enemy.'

'Oh, right, so we'll wait till she *is* at death's door, then, shall we?' Harriet swung her legs off the bed and sat next to him. 'Are you sure you saw bruises?'

'I think so. But it's not that so much as the lost look in 'er eyes. At least she took a cup of tea off me. That's a start. I think we've gotta go slowly, love.'

'All right,' said Harriet, calming down, 'we'll leave it for now – but I don't wanna leave my sister in South London. I want Alice where I can see 'er.'

Arthur was beginning to feel the burden of having a place of their own. 'I don't know if we can afford it,' he said. 'You'll 'ave to give up work in a few months' time and my wages won't keep the three of us.'

'Alice can go out to work. I'll get 'er a job at Yardley's wiv me. Poor cow's never 'ad the chance to earn a wage. She stops at 'ome doin' the washin' and . . .' Harriet was looking troubled '. . . I don't trust my uncle. He makes my flesh creep.'

Taken aback by this disclosure, Arthur felt a chill rush through his veins. She had never so much as hinted that there might be something afoot in her uncle's house, that her sister was not only keeping the house and laundry spotless but perhaps having to satisfy her uncle's sexual demands. It was not unheard-of but never in his wildest dreams had he imagined it could go on inside Harriet's family. Of course, she might be wrong but she wasn't the type to imagine sin where there was none. The opposite, in fact. Conjecture did not bode well with Harriet. To her the truth was what you saw and not what you thought.

'We could go over there this afternoon, love, if you want – put the idea to your mum. Would that make you feel better?'

'Yes, it would. But you must promise me that if Alice wants to come and they try to stop her, you'll stand by me when I put me foot down.'

'All right. If it means that much to you. But then again, wouldn't it be more sensible if we made the upstairs liveable first? I've got some paint left over and the timber yards are open of a Sunday. We could do it today and go to your aunt's place next Saturday afternoon.'

Harriet pinched her lips tight. 'I love you so much, Arfer Dean, d'yer know that? I love you more than anyone could love anyone.'

He slipped a hand around her neck and gently

pulled her face close to his. 'An' I love you, sweet-heart.'

Later that day, while Arthur got to work on the upstairs rooms, Harriet took a break from washing down the paintwork and went to see Lillian Redmond. She had two reasons for her visit: first, she wanted to invite Polly to her and Arthur's register office wedding, and second, she was hoping that there might be some bedlinen or curtains going spare. She had seen the spacious storage cupboards packed with folded white sheets and towels. Since the once highly successful and busy House of Assignation had seen a decline in business, she felt there must be a surplus now.

When she arrived in Beaumont Square that sunny afternoon the trees surrounding the green were in full leaf with pink and white blossom, and the grass was a tapestry of colour, with bluebells, hyacinths and daffodils spreading at random, filling the air with scent. It was a treat simply to stand and gaze at the marvel of nature. She was a touch startled when the soft voice of Grace Wellington, a young lady the same age as Harriet, broke the quiet: 'It's quite breathtaking,' she murmured.

Harriet turned to her and smiled. 'So are you in that lovely outfit.'

Grace was wearing a cream and light blue ankle-length coat and matching hat. 'Why, thank you,' she said. She was blushing. 'Do you live in the square?'

'Chance'd be a fine thing. Mind you, I expect one or two of these grand places 'ave bin turned into lodging rooms. All the same, me and my fiancé could never afford to live 'ere.'

Harriet looked from Grace to her daughter, a two-year-old with lively eyes. 'What's your name, then?'

'Sarah,' the child murmured.

'Very good, darling. Well done,' said Grace, radiant and proud. 'She's been practising for weeks now. Her brother had been teasing her.'

'Well, I think she said it perfectly!' Harriet placed a finger under the child's chin and lifted her face. 'I think you're gonna grow up to be famous, never mind what your brother says.'

'Oh dear, I hope not.' Grace chuckled. 'From what I hear of celebrities they're all high on something else other than success.'

'I wouldn't know,' said Harriet, impressed with this stranger. 'Do you live on the square, then?'

'Yes.' Grace nodded at one of the impressive houses opposite.

'Very nice too.' A warm glow filled Harriet. She was talking on intimate terms to a graceful lady of means with no obvious barrier between them. 'This time next year I'll be pushing a pram.' She patted her stomach and tested her: 'I'm to marry my sweetheart in a fortnight.' A look of reprobation was not forthcoming. The remark seemed to float across Grace's head. 'That's why I've come today to see my friend Polly. To give 'er an invite. She's a maid-of-all-work.' Harriet jerked her head towards the House of Assignation. 'Per'aps you know 'er employer? Lillian Redmond.'

'No,' said Grace. 'I love the house, though. We tend

to keep ourselves to ourselves on this square – except for the staff, of course. The nannies know each other. It's a sight to behold on sunny days when they go *en masse* to the Bethnal Green gardens or Victoria Park, pushing their charges in their prams.'

I bet it is a sight to behold, thought Harriet, a touch enviously.

'Well, I must get on,' said Grace. 'Little Sarah is ready for her nap and there's a women's suffrage meeting at the town hall that I should hate to miss. Emmeline Pankhurst is giving a talk on women's rights.'

'If I don't bump into you again like this I'll fetch my baby over to show you, once it's here.'

'I'd like that very much,' said Grace.

As she opened Lillian's ornate gate, Harriet couldn't help looking back at the woman and watching as, with the child's hand in hers, she climbed the wide steps leading to her front door. For all her wealth and beauty, she seemed a lonely, sad soul. Then, before she went into her house, Grace turned and gave a delicate, almost secret curl of her fingers. Harriet returned the gesture with a flick of her thumb. Both knew that they would not socialise and that if their paths crossed again they would say no more than hello, but it didn't matter. They had discovered that the class barrier was not impenetrable.

'Oh, Gawd, look what an ill wind's blown in,' said Polly, opening the door to her friend. 'I s'pose you were a bit lost for somewhere to go of a Sunday, eh?'

'Oh, shut up.' Harriet laughed and pushed past her. 'Is Lillian at home?'

'Yes. Why? What you after?' Polly closed the door and looked slyly at her friend. 'She won't give you a job, you know. Not with you in the family way.'

'I don't wanna job, Polly. I want to unburden 'er. Take some excess weight off her shoulders – or out of her cupboard to be precise. I'm after some linen, and anyfing else goin' begging. Oh, and I've come to invite you to the wedding. Just you, mind. No one else. There'll be you, me, Arfer, my sister Alice and my mum, if she wants to come. Oh, and Mary, of course.'

'Well, you'd best come down into the kitchen 'cos Lillian's not in the best of moods. She'll say no to anyfing at the moment.'

As she followed Polly down the winding staircase to the basement, Harriet asked if she'd ever spoken to the woman across the square with the two-year-old daughter. The response was robust laughter. 'I swear to God you're a witch, Harriet Smith.'

'I've got a sixth sense, if that's what you mean. Dunno about witch, though. I'll play around wiv the idea and make an effigy of you and put a pair of spectacles on it. What's give Lillian the rats, then?'

'I'll tell you over a cup of tea.'

Once they were settled at the scrubbed pine table, Polly leaned forward, eager to tell her friend the latest gossip. One of Lillian's most popular courtesans, Rebecca, a dark Austrian-Jewish beauty, had been seeing one of the clients away from the House and that was against the rules, especially when the client lived so close by – across the square. He was the husband of the young lady Harriet had just asked about.

'What d'yer reckon to that, then?' Polly was full of it.

But Harriet wasn't amused. Not that it bothered her that Rebecca had broken the rules. After all, Mary had met Walter in this house, had seen him *and* had become his kept woman. What bothered her was Polly's teasing. She was keeping something back and Harriet had a good idea what it was.

'So the woman across the square is the client's wife. I think that's terrible. He needs to be hanged, drawn and quartered, if you ask me. She's got two children, you know.'

'So?'

'Polly, stop it. You've got some scruples, surely?' Harriet sipped her tea and eyed her friend. 'If you fink it's all right for someone's 'usband to be keepin' company with another woman, a whore, and just yards away from where you live, you're just as bad as the whore.'

'Oh, Miss High and Mighty now that you're gonna get married! And as it just so 'appens, Harriet Smith, I never said I fink it's all right! None of this is all right but none of it's all wrong eiver. So there!'

Dipping a biscuit into her tea, Harriet shrugged. 'Each to their own. Does she know? His wife, I mean.'

'Course she don't! Wot's wrong wiv you? I wish I'd never told you now. Making me feel guilty for nuffing. What 'ave *I* done?'

The sound of footsteps caused Polly to sit up straight. 'Oh, Gawd, if this is Madam I'll be in for it. Last thing she'll want to see is me entertaining my friends, the mood she's in.'

The door flew open and crashed against a cupboard. It wasn't Lillian, it was Rebecca, and she was crying. 'Who does she think she is? She doesn't own me!'

'Where is Lillian?' snapped Polly, agitated.

'In her snug. Don't worry, she won't come down here but as soon as you hear the door bell you'd better move like lightning. She's expecting the woman who's going to be the chef.'

'Don't you mean the cook?' Harriet was pleased she'd come on this day to visit. It was all happening – dramas all over the place.

'Of course she's a cook but we must call her *chef*! Can you believe that?'

'Sit yerself dahn, Becky, and stop wailing. D'yer want me to put summing in yer tea? A drop of whisky that Lillian don't know about?'

'Yes, please. It might help. She was very hard on me. Said I must choose between working here or taking my chances with my beloved. She said he's hardly likely to want to know me if I'm not associated with this house. I don't believe her.'

'Well, you should give it more thought,' said Harriet. 'My best friend was left 'igh and dry by a married man she thought loved 'er. And she's got his baby. What makes you fink your chap's gonna be any different?'

'Because I know him! And this isn't something to make fun of.'

'Course it ain't. It's the end of the road for you and that's no laughin' matter. I can see that. Your bloke's got a beau'iful wife. I met 'er in the square. She's lovely. So's 'er little daughter. You'd best stick wiv Lillian, Becky.'

'Rebecca actually, Harriet.' She dabbed her cheeks dry. 'Most of the men who come here are married with families. Didn't Mary Dean tell you? She should know!'

'*No?* Mary's knight in shining armour was never *married*, was he?'

'Yes, and he didn't desert *her*, did he?' She began to weep again. 'You see, Polly? *Everyone* is going to make fun of me! *Everyone!* When I leave here today I will never return!'

'But if you do that, you'll never see lover-boy again, will yer?' Harriet did her best to sound sympathetic.

'Actually, you're wrong. I'm already living in a charming room for which he has paid a year's rent in advance. I am to be his second wife. But I shall miss coming here.' The tears began to flow again. 'I feel like throwing myself into the river! How could Lillian be so angry with me? I am her best and most favoured courtesan.'

'Well, maybe that's why.' Harriet leaned across the table and peered into the silly woman's face. 'She can't afford to lose you at the moment, can she? And she definitely can't risk exposure because, like I said, his wife lives across the square. Use your noddle!'

'You see!' Rebecca spread her hands dramatically. 'I can't win. I lose my Toby whichever way I turn!'

Harriet rolled her eyes in exasperation. 'And Lillian's gonna lose out if you go. As you say, Becky, you're the most favoured girl. Clients stop coming if their favourite disappears.'

'Well, what am I supposed to do?'

'Give up seeing the *married man* away from 'ere! Find another lover to sing your bleedin' 'eartbreaking love songs to. You've got more'n a lot of people, Becky! You've got the looks and the voice and we all know you can act – Gawd 'elp us, we know that! Drama's in your bleedin' veins, my old cock!'

Rebecca stretched herself to her full height and, in her best theatrical manner, threw back her head, looking down on Harriet. 'You are so coarse. I should never have come here in the first place. And you're right. I can always get work in the theatre – and my Toby loves to see me on stage. You may tell Lillian that you are to blame for my decision to leave.' With that, Rebecca flounced out of the kitchen and out of Lillian's life.

Harriet shrugged. Her thoughts were on the lady opposite, who surely would not continue to live in the house if she found out about her husband's affair with Rebecca – never mind him using this whorehouse, although, apart from the clients, everyone thought it was a finishing school for young ladies.

'Well,' said Polly, 'you've put your bleedin' foot in it, all right. I could 'ave talked 'er into stayin' with Lillian and only seein' lover-boy during business hours. But there we are, you 'ad to put your pennyworth in.'

'Oh, shut up, Polly. He's paid a year's rent on a flat for 'er. Course he'll be seein' her away from this place. I feel sorry for 'is wife. Bleedin' upper-class men. Think there's one rule for them and another for the rest of the world.'

'There is,' said Polly, straight-faced. 'Becky don't know it but Mr Steamin' Long-johns 'as got another mistress who he's paid out on a place for. Some silly moo over Befnal Green's bin left 'oldin' 'is baby.'

'It's his poor wife I feel sorry for,' Harriet said. 'What if she finds out?'

'She 'as, if Lillian's right. His wife followed 'im there one day – well, she jumped in the 'ansom cab just before it pulled away and went wiv 'im to the rendezvous.'

'See?' Harriet grinned. 'I knew there was somefing about that young lady across the square. She's got more guts than you and me put together, Polly. Bloomin' good luck to 'er. I 'ope she kicked 'is arse – *and* 'is bit on the side!'

If Harriet was as perspicacious as she liked to believe, it might have dawned on her who the girl in Bethnal Green was, but her good friend Flora was the last person on her mind.

'Each to their own, Harriet. Them that judge others might not liked to be judged themselves.' This statement was a touch too philosophical for Harriet, but she had learned that there was more to her friend than Polly let on and sometimes a leading remark from her was best left unanswered.

'Well, that's as may be but all I know is that there's a

strange mood about this place today. As if somefing's about to 'appen. I'll see you at Stepney Register. Don't lose that invitation or make the excuse you lost it and not turn up.'

'Invitation? It's written on the back of a sugar bag!'

'It's still an invitation. I jotted the details down quick before I came out. And don't forget to—'

Before she could finish her sentence, Polly grabbed her friend's arm. 'Shush!' she whispered. 'Lillian's coming. Gawd – listen to them footsteps. She's out for blood.' Polly closed her eyes and crossed herself.

'Stop bein' so dramatic. Anyone'd think—'

The door crashed open and Lillian strode towards the larder. She took a half-full bottle of brandy from the shelf and collected three small glasses. She poured all three of them a drink. 'Three for sorrow and three for joy,' she said, handing each girl a glass. 'We'll drink to the departure of Madam Rebecca!' With the glass to her lips, she threw back her head and downed the burning liquid, then waited for them to do the same. At the look on her face. they did so, coughing, spluttering and laughing.

'Another!' she said, refilling their glasses. 'This time we'll drink to our new venture. Intimate dinner parties for City gentlemen!'

This time the girls were a little more cautious and sipped, slowly.

'She gone then?' said Harriet, matter-of-factly.

'Yes, and good riddance. Tobias Wellington will no longer be welcome in my house! I should have known he'd sneak one of my best girls away.'

'Don't be so daft,' said Polly. 'Business is business. You've gotta pretend that nothing untoward has 'appened and offer 'im the best of the bunch. Give 'im Rosa Lee. He likes 'em dark and fleshy.'

'And when he asks after Becky? What then?'

'She's gone to make 'er fame and fortune on the stage. Make it sound as if you're proud of 'er and pleased. Like it was your idea.'

'See?' said Harriet, grinning. 'She might be as blind as a bat but there's not much sawdust between our Polly's ears.'

'There isn't *any* sawdust, my dear. All of my girls, whether they entertain my gentlemen in the boudoir or the drawing room, are carefully picked for their intelligence.' Relaxed, now, Lillian floated around the table, her rich green and pink ankle-length crêpe frock flowing behind her, a matching fringed silk shawl cascading from her shoulders. On her hips she wore her favourite belt of tiny pink flowers, clasped at the front with a small sapphire-blue glass buckle – a present from her former lover. 'Society gentlemen, my dears, require so much. Wit and charm are at the top of the list, and an interest in literature, of course – a passing comment on a character from our author Charles Dickens is a better tease than a flash of silk knickers.'

'I'm surprised you never made 'em 'ave elocution lessons.' Harriet winked at Polly, who was too cautious to laugh.

'Ah, but *my* girls are taught never to lose their Cockney inflection, Harriet. The upper classes love to bed someone out of their realm. My gentlemen expect more from the girls than they do from their wives. It gives them a reason and an excuse . . . should they ever be found out.' Floating down on to a padded, high-backed chair, Lillian waved a delicate hand. 'It's all a matter of etiquette – once learned never forgotten.'

'But you never 'ad to learn it, did yer?' said Harriet, encouragingly. 'It must 'ave bin in your blood.'

'There is nothing in my blood, my dear, but working-class cells. But never, never let on that I said such a thing. Let those who need to believe otherwise do so.' Lillian held up a hand and, spoke with pride: 'Girls . . . I worked my fingers raw in the beginning, scrubbing floors and polishing copper from dawn, until I dropped into my bed at night. But I watched, I listened, and I learned.

'I learned that, there but for fortune, we should *all* be mixing in circles of a higher station, should we so wish it. We are all the same beneath the skirts, rich or poor.' She crossed her legs gracefully. 'The face and the figure are our fortune, and we must always treat both with the greatest respect.'

Harriet and Polly had heard all of this before but they loved to watch her acting out the scene.

'I always tell my ladies never, under any circumstances, to ask questions and never to *offer* sexual favours but linger as if reluctant to leave a man's side. Occasionally one of our gentlemen may not make an advance and is happy enough to keep company, in these lavish surroundings, with a beautiful woman.'

'Good job Polly never went in for it, then. She wouldn't be able to keep 'er gob shut for five minutes.'

'I wouldn't sell my body for nuffing,' sniffed Polly.

'Just as well, cos nobody'd be buying.'

'I bet you'd lay down for a guinea, though.' Polly smirked. 'If you wasn't so coarse and vulgar you'd be workin' 'ere, I bet yer.'

'Course I would. If you're gonna 'ave a bloke knob you, you might as well 'ave 'im bleedin' well pay for it.'

'Oh, and your Arfer coughs up, I s'pose?' Polly was enjoying this break. She had checked Lillian's expression and believed that her employer was miles away, in her own fantasy world, but she was wrong.

As if she were looking into another world, Lillian murmured, 'Lust and love, my dears, do not wear the same glove. This House is a place where lovers meet in secret. Always keep that in mind and the magic and stardust may brush off on to others who are of a different mind.'

'We're gonna 'ave to replace Becky a bit sharpish. Rosa's got a good client list already.' Polly's sense for business was back.

'No,' said Lillian, gazing at the ceiling. 'That won't be necessary. I shall come out of retirement. Had I left it much longer my carnal prowess might have been lost altogether. Lillian Redmond, my dears, is coming out of mourning. It's been fifteen long years since my beloved Robert found it necessary to forsake me. I am ready to love again.'

Neither Polly nor Harriet could think of anything to say in response. But Lillian was not searching for encouragement. As far as she was concerned, her gentlemen would welcome her back with open arms and rock-hard passion.

She turned her head to her *protégées* and smiled warmly, a new sparkle in her eyes. 'Polly,' she said, 'put on the kettle. We are going to tint my hair chestnut.'

'I'm just finking . . .' Harriet paused '. . . finking aloud that is . . .' She cocked her head to one side and peered at Lillian. 'These business meetings over dinner, you'll be needin' an attractive waitress, I should reckon.'

'I shall indeed, but if you're about to ask whether that someone might be you, Harriet, the answer is no. You're far too impertinent and perky. You have the looks I grant you but—'

'Bloomin' cheek!' roared Harriet. 'I'm not impertinent! I speak me mind but that's another fing altogether!'

'Anyway,' said Polly, a little high and mighty, 'I shall be applying for the post. You can take my job, if you like. Be a skivvy.'

'No, Polly,' Lillian sighed, 'I already have someone in mind. One of my girls is ideal for the position.'

'Position? We're talkin' abaht a soddin' waitress, Lillian.'

'Indeed we are, Harriet, which is why I must be very particular. She must be someone whom one or more of our guests around the table would find desirable.'

'Kill two birds with one stone, you mean,' said Polly, sullenly. 'Some gentlemen like plain girls, you know.'

'I'm sure they do, but we are talking about desire not love, which is an entirely different kettle of fish. Wouldn't you agree, Harriet?'

'No, I wouldn't!' snapped Harriet, rising from her chair. 'You talk a load of tripe at times, Lillian Redmond, and if you can't help out someone who's bin a friend for years you're not much of a person to my way of thinkin'! I wouldn't work in a whore'ouse in any case.' Angry and insulted at the rejection, she grabbed her hat from the back of the chair and stood defiantly in front of Lillian, prepared for ructions. She was interrupted by the door bell.

'Ah, that will be the new cook.'

'Don't you mean *chef*?' taunted Polly. 'I s'pose I'd better let 'er in. Peculiar sort, if you asks me. I only saw 'er the once when she came for the first interview and that was enough to make my flesh creep.'

'Don't be too hasty with your opinions or the way you greet her. She does appear to be a lone creature but I imagine she could be quite contrary, if you rattle her bones.'

Once Polly had left the kitchen, Lillian turned on Harriet. 'And as for you, madam, I suggest you try to remember that familiarity leading to contempt cuts a friendship!'

'I never came here to be contemptuous, Lillian. As a matter of fact I never came looking for work either. Although if you really considered me a friend you might 'ave considered me for the new work that's coming. The reason I came, apart from a friendly visit, was to ask if you could spare some bed linen and towels and, well, any linen you're not using. I know you've got too much now that you're not as busy as you used to be.'

'Really? Polly's been discussing business out of hours, has she?'

'No, of course not. I picked it up for myself. And them cupboards up there, Lillian, they're jam-packed with stuff. You've not even used some of it.'

'My, my, you *have* been poking around, haven't you?' Lillian smiled.

'I had a look ages ago when I realised Mary was really gonna go to the house in the country. I knew we'd be homeless and I was worried. I didn't fink you'd mind me looking.'

'Of course not. I've long since realised that there are really only two rooms in this house that I may think of as my home.' There was a touch of regret in Lillian's voice.

'So, will it be all right if Polly sorts out stuff you don't need?'

Preoccupied with her own thoughts, Lillian gazed into Harriet's face as if she hadn't heard what she'd said. 'The thing is, my dear, we may – indeed, I hope we shall – be needing the bed linen. Would that I could be charitable, but I fear that is not the case.'

'But you'll never get round to using all of it.'

'Oh dear.' Lillian checked her dainty fob watch. 'Time is running on, as it will.' She raised her eyes to meet Harriet's. 'Was that all, then, dear?'

'Well, I s'pose it must be! You wanna try being a little bit more benevolent, Lillian. Don't forget where you've come from. If it wasn't for your benefactor settin' you up 'ere, you might well be leanin' on a lamp-post 'opin' for a shillin' trick to buy you a bed for the night!'

'Charity, my dear, begins at home, and justice next door. Remember that and you will never be embarrassed. I'm sorry if I hurt your feelings.'

'Well, don't be 'cos I won't be crossing your threshold again! Ever!' With that Harriet stormed out of the kitchen, up the stairs and into the lavish hall, where Polly was receiving the woman who was here to finalise her new post as cook. Seeing the expression of fury on Harriet's face as she stormed up the stairs towards them, the woman discreetly withdrew into the shadows and watched. She recognised the face and the hair and if she was not mistaken, she knew this young lady very well.

'You'll 'ave to come and visit me in future, Polly,' Harriet snarled, as she strode past her, ''cos I ain't comin' back to this house!'

The slamming of the front door caused Polly to shudder and the woman to smile. She had recognised the face, the hair, the voice too.

'Sorry about that but our Harriet's a little 'ot-blooded on account of 'er ginger 'air.'

'Don't apologise,' said the midwife. 'It's not settled that I shall be taking up employment here. I haven't seen my room yet.'

'All the rooms 'ere are lovely, except mine. I'm in the smallest one.' Polly showed her into the study and went back downstairs to tell Lillian to get a move on.

Angry with herself for having gone begging to Lillian Redmond's house, Harriet vowed that from now on she would never again ask for charity. She would make her own way in the world or go without. There were numerous stalls down Petticoat Lane where she could purchase second-hand sheets, curtains and all sorts of linen for no more than a shilling a bundle. There were also stalls where she could buy remnants of fabric for cushion-making. White sheets and towels, boiled in the copper in soda water, could be brought back almost to their former glory.

On arriving home she turned the key in the lock and glanced instinctively up at the window of the house next door where she saw the girl from the workhouse staring down at her. Stepping back, she motioned for her to come down and go out into the back garden. The response was instant withdrawal and the closing of the curtain. Not satisfied, Harriet knocked boldly on the front door, hoping that the crones were out and, if not, she would ask to borrow some milk. There was no reply, so she knocked again. She had to get the message across to the girl that she was not going to give up.

When the door creaked open and she stood face to face with the timid creature, she knew that she had to throw caution to the winds if she was to help her.

'My name's Harriet and I'm new to this area,' she said. 'I 'aven't got no friends and I wondered if you'd

like to come in for a cup of tea. I'm a bit lonely in
there when Arfer's not at 'ome. He's gone down the
Lane and won't be back for a couple of hours yet.
So will you come in for just five minutes to keep me
company?'

The girl glanced over her shoulder, then murmured,
'I'm not allowed.'

Harriet smiled. 'What the eye don't see the 'eart
can't grieve over. When are the two old bats due
'ome?'

'They might come back early,' said the girl.

'We'll know soon enough 'cos if I stand at a certain
angle by my front window, I can see along the turning.
You can soon slip back through the loose fence in the
garden.'

'They might not be back for hours,' the girl murmured, wringing her hands.

'Well, there we are, then. Nuffing to worry over.
Close the door and come through the back. I've got a
bit of fruit bread left over from yesterday. You could
'ave a slice of that an' all.'

'But they might find out.' The girl looked near to
tears and was trembling.

'Look, if you don't come through the loose bit of
fence to me then I'm gonna come through it to you
– and if you lock the back door I'll stop there till the
witches come 'ome.'

A faint smile spread across the girl's face. 'I'll come
through – but only if you keeps lookout.'

'I said I would, didn't I? You can make a pot of tea
while I stand on guard by the winda.'

'I'm from the work'ouse,' she said, warningly, as if it was a prison where she'd been placed for serious wrongdoing.

'Yeah, and so am I. I was only there a couple of days, granted. I legged it quick as you like. Go and unlock the back door.'

While the pair enjoyed a cup of tea and a slice of fruit bread Harriet did as promised and kept post by the window. To her surprise the girl relaxed in her company, although the look of mistrust remained in her eyes.

Knowing that this might be the one and only time that she could have the girl to herself, Harriet's perception was to the fore. She watched for any show of flesh beneath the long-sleeved grubby blouse. The girl's long skirt covered her ankles, leaving only her ill-fitting old boots on show. Her collar covered her neck right up to her ears. But to Harriet, there was no need for evidence: the girl's white face and dark puffy eyes were enough. She was being mistreated by the two women next door, that was clear, but to what extent, she would not find out today. She would have to be patient. She held back from quizzing the girl, just asked what her name was.

'Wot sort of a name?' She gazed at Harriet with a sad, blank expression.

'The first one. The one you was christened wiv. Or if you wasn't christened, whatever your mum and dad called you. Mine's Harriet, for instance.'

'But I said I was from the *work'ouse*. I was born there. I never 'ad a proper name like folks wiv families 'ave. They calls me Bony cos of me bein' born all skin and bone. I s'pose that must be it. Next door don't call me anyfing. Well, sometimes they does but not a name like you got.'

Harriet refrained from asking what they called her. Her blood was beginning to boil and she didn't want to frighten the girl off. 'It don't matter anyway. But as it 'appens, I think Bony's all right. I like it. I'll call you Bonny, though, shall I?'

'I don't mind.'

'I'm sure you don't but would you like me to?'

'I don't mind.'

'But what would you prefer, Bonny?'

'Don't bovver me.'

'All right, Bonny, that's sorted out, then.' Harriet made a show of checking no one was coming along the street then smiled down at the girl. 'All clear.'

'I'd rather Pony,' murmured the girl, her eyes lowered. 'Pony. I'd rather you called me that. I used to 'ave to look after the milkman's pony when he came to the work'ouse. Give it a drink an' that.'

'I can't call you Pony – you'd get the piss taken out of you somefing rotten. Did you feed the carthorse as well?'

'It weren't no carthorse, it were a pony. Milkman said so. I fed it wiv stale oats off the back of the cart.' The girl was opening up, talking, albeit quietly, but still she avoided Harriet's eye. Either that or her shoulders had bent so much that it was easier for her to look down rather than up or straight out.

'So you was its feeder. We'll call you Freda. How about that? Freda the feeder.'

'I don't mind.'

'But you'd prefer it to Bonny?'

'I would, but I don't mind.'

'All right,' said Harriet, sighing. 'Bonny it is. It's a free country and you've got the right to choose yer own name.' At last she had managed to slip in something to give the girl food for thought. 'Bleedin' good job an' all that we live in a free country, don't you reckon?'

'I don't know wot you mean. I shall 'ave to go now. I've to blacken and polish the lead range before I spits and irons.'

'What about yer dinner? It's Sunday and they're out so I s'pect you'll cook for yerself?'

'I cooks everything but not if they're eatin' out.'

'So you won't be 'avin' no dinner, then?' Harriet meant to draw as much information from the girl while she had the chance. 'No 'ot meal for you today, eh?'

'I don't 'ave no 'ot meals!' Panic had crept into her voice. 'They only burns your tongue. I 'ave chunks of bread. Wiv drippin' sometimes. An' soup. I makes it from carrot and tatter peelin's and that. I dips me bread in it. I 'ave cheese rinds as well. Puts it in the soup. Goes all soft. I cuts it up first, mind.'

'How d'yer know that hot meals burns your tongue if you don't 'ave 'em?'

'They gives me some on a fork. A sizzlin' tatter out of the roastin' pan. It blistered my tongue.'

Harriet controlled her temper. Her own childhood had not been a bowl of cherries but compared to this poor cow's it was easy. She only just managed a smile as she stood up. 'Well, Bonny, I reckon you'd best get back to your duties, then, eh? Don't want to give them two anything to complain over, do we? But we've got neighbourly now, you and me, so you pop in whenever you want. If me or Arfer's not at home, you can make yerself a cup of tea and help yerself to biscuits from the flowery tin. Or cut a slice of bread and jam.'

'I wouldn't come in,' said the girl, standing by the door. 'I wouldn't come in if you wasn't 'ere. They'd lock me in the cupboard for that.'

Her guts screaming at her to keep cool, Harriet walked the pathetic fourteen-year-old through to the back door. 'Well, they wouldn't know, would they? But, then, you know 'em best. Don't wanna take risks.'

Back inside her own little kitchen, thankful to be alone again, Harriet slumped down on to a chair. The vision of her hard-working mother scrimping and scraping to make ends meet and scrubbing until her knuckles were red raw came flooding back. Her mother had worked every hour God sent so that she and her sister didn't starve and it had all been done with love and kindness.

She had seen the bruises under the cuff of the girl's frock and she had seen weals on her neck. Harriet's father might have shouted and sometimes clumped Harriet and her sister, their mother too, but at least they had never felt the sting of a whip or been locked in a cupboard where, no doubt, rat and mousetraps were set.

By the time Arthur returned she had come out of her low mood and had had an idea. The girl next door should be rescued to coincide with Alice's arrival. She would be given a very short haircut – a ha'penny all-off – and wear boys' breeches and shirts purchased off a second-hand stall. Once dressed for the part they could let her go out and pass her off as Harriet's brother.

'Do I smell rabbit in the range?' said Arthur, coming into the house and pecking Harriet's cheek.

'You do, sweetheart. And roast potatoes and carrots. I'm just about to put the greens on. Did you get all you wanted?'

'I certainly did. Got a deal on the paint too. Gonna drop a bit of fish off now and then, which meant I 'ad a little bit left over for a present. Go and 'ave a look on the wheelbarra. See what you think.'

'You better not 'ave wasted good bleedin' money, Arfer Dean, is all I can say,' said Harriet, making her way outside. When she saw the array of bright flowering plants for the back yard, she all but wept. So much so that she turned a blind eye to the second-hand birdcage and the two boxes pierced with air-holes. Inside one was a pair of goldfinches and in the other a pair of songbirds.

Happy to see the new feathered friends, she hardly had to force herself into looking at the bright side after her upsetting day so far. The birds would not only make Arthur happy and cheer her on a dull day but would please her sister and the girl from next door. 'They're lovely, Arfer,' she said, picking up a tray of flowering primulas. 'Beau'iful.'

'I thought you'd be pleased.' He followed her through the passage, carrying a tin of paint in each hand.

'Course I am, but that don't mean to say I don't worry over you barterin' with strangers. You get caught pinchin' fish and I'll be left 'igh and dry.'

'Perks, love. Everyone does it. Part of the job.'

'Don't make it right, though, does it.'

'Course not. If the employers paid us a fair wage we wouldn't be forced to do it. Some would – but, then, some are born thieves and it don't matter where they work. Rich or poor, a born thief is a born thief.'

There was no arguing with this. Even among the middle-class clerks, managers or directors the stealing of funds was commonplace. The fast-expanding business and commercial world was providing opportunities for fraud and embezzlement, which were seen in the same light as the low-wage labourers' so-called 'perks'.

Dockyard workers were probably the pioneers of what was considered fair robbery since their pay was no more than a pittance. Drivers of the omnibus pocketed a percentage of fares and this was also common knowledge. Fraud was a more complicated offence, not always seen as criminal: successful cheating was the result of a good education, which was only available to the middle classes. However, such offences were not unique to the business world: certain gentlemen helped themselves to the poor rates and collections for the poor.

Clerks of unions were known to fiddle thousands of

pounds, and treasurers of town-relief funds pocketed similar amounts. If a crate of fish, meat or fruit 'fell off' an open carriage during a train journey to London from the countryside or fishing port, it was a small loss by comparison and no loss at all if the appalling low wages were taken into account.

'You not getting paid enough for the hours you work, Arfer, won't persuade a judge in court,' said Harriet.

'Court? Talk sense. That'd cost more money than all the fish I could snuck in a lifetime.' Arthur lifted a bird out of the box and cupped it in his hand, stroking its silky feathers. 'You're gonna brighten up our little back yard, my friend. See? Lovely little things, ain't they? And when you're out there relaxing on a sunny Sunday, you can watch my lovebirds. Did you go and see Lillian, then, about the sheets and that?'

'Yeah, and what a waste of a Sunday *that* was. She was in a peculiar mood. One of 'er best girls 'as left and she took it out on me. I offered to wait at the table for 'er, once she's got these business dinners off the ground, and she said I was too impert'nent! Soddin' cheek. I ain't never goin' back there!'

'You've said that before and back you go. Can't keep away from the place. Let Polly come and visit you 'ere. We can 'ave visitors now we've got a nice 'ome.' Arthur, a touch on the lordly side, sat down in his favourite chair by the range. 'Yes,' he smiled, 'we've got a home to be proud of!'

'Well, it ain't Buckingham Palace, sweet'eart, but you've got a point. I don't need to go visitin' now, do

I? They can walk round to us and wear their own shoe leather out.'

'So, do you wanna hear the latest gossip from the Lane or tell me your news first?'

'What news?' She couldn't imagine how he would know she'd had the girl from next door in and learned a thing or two from her. 'What are you talking about?'

'Lillian's place. I know there's more to it than what you've said. So rather than bleat on and off about it all day, get it off your chest now and be done with it.'

'All right.' Harriet pulled up a chair. 'You're gonna love this. The goings-on in that place! Well, Arfer, I can 'ardly believe it. Bleedin' affairs all over the shop. One of the whores, a dark-looking Jew – and beautiful, mind – 'as bin entertainin' a married chap from across the square to Lillian's and 'is wife ain't got a clue! He's a regular visitor. In and out all the time, by all accounts. And he's set Rebecca up in a nice little lodging room so he can see her away from Lillian's place. And she's not the only one and his wife is a lovely woman. So what d'yer make of that, then?'

Arthur pulled a face. 'I fink someone's been telling you porky pies, sweetheart. No one'd take silly risks like that – goin' in and out of a whorehouse and right opposite where you live? Pork pies,' he chuckled, then burst into laughter. 'That Polly should be a story-teller, if you ask me. Write books and that. Things she comes out with!'

'I saw it with me own two eyes, Arfer Dean! Lillian's kicked the Jew out over it. I'm tellin' yer, a right old 'ow's-yer-father it is. Our life's a bit on the boring side next to that, don't you fink?'

'Well, you could always be one of Lillian's girls,' said Arthur, earnestly. 'Line your pockets that would. You could earn ten times as much as you do slavin' in that factory. Why don't you walk back there and 'ave a word with Madam Lillian?'

'What? And you'd go along wiv that, would yer?'

'Course I would.'

'Me crawlin' naked over another man? You'd be all right about it?'

'I'm thinkin' of a nice post-office savings account, love. It'd be nice to 'ave a few pounds put by for a rainy day.' Nodding slowly, eyes narrowed and thoughtful, Arthur rubbed his chin. 'To be honest, that's why I thought I'd marry you. How much does she pay? You're not worth as much as them tropical women with great big bosoms and arses but—'

'Do you know what I reckon? I reckon you mean all of that. That's come from somewhere deep down, that has. Well, that's just as well 'cos it's exactly what I was gettin' round to. Lillian made me an offer too good to turn dahn. I'm glad you agree with it all.' Harriet stalked out of the room and unhooked her coat from the hat stand in the passage. 'I'll go back an' book m'self in for as many men as I can – and arrange to go there every night except Sundays. That suit yer, sweet'eart?'

'You'd best be pulling my leg,' barked Arthur. 'That kind of talk, jokin' or not, is for low street girls.'

'Oh, is that right?' Harriet simpered. 'Well, I s'pose

I'd best put me 'at and coat back on the hook and be'ave like a decent girl. And to my mind,' she said, stepping slowly towards him, 'decent girls do decent fings for them that are less fortunate.'

'What's that s'posed to mean?'

'My sister Alice, and the girl next door. I wanna rescue both of 'em as soon as possible.' She straddled Arthur on his high-back chair and ran her fingers through his hair. 'D'yer fink you could put up wiv three females in the 'ouse?'

He gazed into her lovely freckled face. 'I don't know. It's not what I want but, then, I mustn't be greedy, must I? Life's all-out splendid and I don't want anyone or anyfing to spoil it. I agreed to yer sister comin' and I'll stick by it, but this business of the girl next door, we could get into a lot of trouble.'

'I know, sweet'eart, but I've got that 'orrible worry in the pit of me stomach again – my sixth sense is working overtime.'

'Yeah, but it's not always bin right, 'as it? Sometimes you worry over something that you can't put yer finger on and nothing 'appens.'

'But we don't know, do we? And I wouldn't want to take a chance. She might not agree to anyfing, anyway.'

'Well, just don't rush it, that's all. Rome wasn't built in a day.'

'Just as well.' She unknotted his tie. 'Would 'ave fell down be now if that was the case. Anyway, who cares about all that? We've got a lovely Sunday afternoon all to ourselves. D'yer wanna little cuddle before dinner or after?'

'Afterwards. I've got some floorboards to fix and some walls to paint and a winda frame to seal. Keep it warm on the back burner.' He smiled, kissed her lightly on the cheek and lifted her off his lap. 'Now, get them greens on or the meat'll burn to a cinder.'

'And you really don't mind about my sister comin'?'

'I'll answer that once she's bin 'ere a week. Two bloomin' Smiths in the place might be too much to bear. We'll just 'ave to wait and see.'

'You'll love it, sweet'eart,' said Harriet, winking at him. 'Three women all fussin' over yer.' Left to herself, Harriet mused over the idea of Arthur coping with not only three females but three very different personalities. Her mind went immediately to Lillian's house and Beaumont Square where she, Harriet Smith, a girl from the gutter, had so easily conversed with Grace Wellington, a lovely young lady from the upper classes. This had thrown a new light on the snobbish middle-class neighbours in Bow. It dawned on her that the problem did not lie with her and Arthur, but with them. Maybe they had been a little too close to their true roots for comfort? Lower class folk who had climbed the ladder perhaps?

Little did Harriet know that Grace Wellington had taken comfort from the same thought. She had no idea of what went on behind the closed door of the house opposite to hers or that her husband frequented it, but all things considered, it was as well that she did not.

Truth may be the cause of heartache, but ignorance, in certain circumstances, was bliss. Her brush with the honest, open Harriet, from a different walk of life, had lifted her spirits and she was happy not to wonder why. There was no need.

5

Jacqueline Turner, the midwife, had experienced a momentary shock when Harriet had stormed past her in the entrance hall of the house in Beaumont Square – there could be no mistaking that unruly ginger hair and obstinate expression. Fate had certainly dealt Jacqueline a fair hand, for had she arrived ten minutes earlier or later she might have missed seeing the girl and would by now have signed an agreement to work where the troublemaker might be employed as scullery-maid if not prostitute, and she did not want to be recognised at this stage.

Not wishing to waste any more of her time, she had left Lillian's house with no intention of returning. Fate had led her to Harriet Smith and, after this stroke of luck, she decided to use her energy in working out the best way to get back her diary. The spiteful child of ten whom she had trusted, had tricked her then stolen her most precious possession.

Striding through the back-streets, mind racing, the midwife realised that she was walking too quickly – an old habit she had not shaken off. Pausing at a jeweller's she glanced in the window and caught sight of her reflection. Although over sixty and raw-boned, she looked, and was, more stalwart than most of her age. Her sunken cheeks and protruding jowl emphasised her wide steely grey eyes with their defiant, determined expression. Now the rage was returning – the rage that had haunted her since the day she left for America, in the winter of 1888.

At a more sedate pace, she passed a butcher's shop, which had not changed since she was a child running errands for her mother. Her thoughts drifted back and she recollected the time when her father had carried her in one arm and her sister, Celeste, in the other to the meat market to see the cattle herded in after being walked all the way from Wanstead. She would always remember the odour of the animals. It was a smell she had warmed to from the first time she had swept her tiny hand against the sweaty hide of a cow. Her sister, however, had been repelled by the beasts and had said so. Jacqueline had adored her father and been saddened by the way her mother and sister treated him. Taking advantage of his good nature, they had often ridiculed and teased him, as if he were too weak in spirit to keep up with them. They had been wrong: he was a wise man who saw and heard everything and kept his thoughts to himself.

'Your sister has a dark future. The poor child takes after your mother and no mistake,' were the words he had mumbled one evening, when Jacqueline had found him sitting by the fire in an unlit room. At the time she had not understood what he meant, but as the years passed his prophecy had been fulfilled. Both her mother and sister proved to be of unstable mind, their personalities changing from one minute to the next, from dour and moody to towering rage or manic laughter. At least Celeste had been blessed with beauty – with her raven tresses and dark brown eyes she attracted most men. Beside her, Jacqueline had always been made to feel plain and lumbering. Eventually Celeste had married John Cutbush, a true gentleman who earned a decent living as a clerk in one of the London banks. Sadly he died young, leaving his son Thomas to survive the best way he could, but Jacqueline had come to love the lad as if he were her own son.

Back in her two furnished rooms above a tobacconist's on the corner of Sidney Street, the midwife took a sixpence from her worn leather purse and pushed it into the gas meter. She didn't want to run out of fuel and be cast into darkness later in the day. She settled at the small table by the window and enjoyed her meal of saveloys and pease pudding, bought from a street vendor, then sipped her gin and smiled as the picture of Harriet striding out of the house in Beaumont Square came into her mind. She wondered if the high-spirited young woman had been interviewed for the position of cook and turned down.

After placing an advertisement in the local paper Jacqueline had gone to the house in Beaumont Square with the intention of taking up employment. She had hoodwinked Lillian Redmond into believing she was qualified and experienced as a cook. Now, with her savings from the years spent working in prosperous America as a midwife and having found Harriet Smith sooner than she had expected, she could afford to relax and not look for immediate employment, providing she continued to be frugal.

Jacqueline recalled the September night in 1888 when she had seen what she had assumed to be the work of a raving lunatic or the devil himself, then pushed the macabre scene from her mind. Instead she reflected on how she had saved Harriet's baby brother's life just minutes before. Harriet had led the midwife to her pregnant mother through dark cobbled streets where there were no gas lights, only the moon and the glow from the paraffin lamps hanging inside the decrepit houses to illuminate their way.

The Smiths' dimly lit lodging room had been their only living space with an old kitchen table covered with matchboxes spread out to dry. There was a fireplace with a small oven and a hob on which a black kettle was simmering. In two opposite corners of the room there had been two straw mattresses with blankets, an old chest of drawers made of tobacco barrels, and a coal cupboard with shelves above it for storing food. The father had been sitting in the one and only chair. His request had been that Jacqueline save his wife at the expense of the child.

The midwife having lifted the thin grey blanket that covered the woman had witnessed a sight she had not come across before in all her twenty-four years as a midwife. Between the white legs of the pregnant woman had dangled the tiny blue-mauve leg of the unborn child. Little Harriet had been on the verge of tears and terrified for her mother. But God had been willing and Jacqueline had managed to deliver the baby boy.

When she was making her way home afterwards, in the early hours of the morning, she had not fully taken in the petrified call of a man, whose high-pitched voice had echoed through the desolate street. When he appeared in front of her, wide-eyed and trembling, and begged her to go with him, she realised that another vile Whitechapel murder had taken place. When she saw the spreadeagled body of a woman lying in a dark pool of blood with her throat slit and her body mutilated, Jacqueline had had to grip a railing to overcome the nausea that assailed her. The prostitute's eyes had been open, showing the terror of her final seconds.

The sound of the man's voice, echoing through the back-streets as he ran off, came flooding back. He had reported the nightmare scene in graphic detail for all to hear. The piercing shrill of a policeman's whistle and fast echoing footsteps had caused the midwife to cower back in the shadows. An urgent voice inside her head warned her to get away. To go home.

Back in the present, covering her face, the midwife wished, as she had wished so many times before, that she had left for America soon after that incident, thus avoiding worse events that had followed: more macabre murders, two of which had been by her own hand in order to cover for her beloved nephew, Thomas, the insane whore-killer. Her maudlin thoughts too much to bear, Jacqueline picked up her glass of gin and swallowed the contents.

The newspaper headlines and explicit reports that had followed her to America had not surprised her. By then, she had accepted that the lad, her nephew, was out of his mind. His next victim, while she sailed away from England, had been the most horrific of all. Thomas had made the murder look like the work of a crazed Freemason who had adhered strictly to the words of the Bible in offering the prostitute Mary Jane Kelly as his sacrificial lamb, according to Exodus 29:22–23.

Shuddering, the midwife lifted the lid of a trunk in the corner of the room and pulled from beneath a pile of papers a package tied with string. It contained numerous articles cut from various newspapers printed in the American press, which had reported the murders. She untied the string and carefully removed the cuttings from the brown wrapping paper where they had lain for almost two decades. On the top of the pile was an article dated April 1891, which reported that Thomas Cutbush, who had been arrested for stabbing young ladies in the rear, must surely be Jack the Ripper. Thomas's rooms had been searched and rough drawings of the bodies of women and their mutilations found. Another which told of the discovery of his overcoat in his lodging rooms and that a young man in a similarly described garment had been seen talking in Backchurch Lane to a woman whose dismembered body had been found later in sacking under a local railway arch, in nearby Pinchin Street. The same year the remains of two more bodies had been discovered in the Thames, in Battersea Park and on the Chelsea Embankment; Alice McKenzie was found in Castle Alley with her throat cut, and Frances Coles in Swallow Gardens with a similar grotesque injury.

Thomas Sadler, a fireman, had been arrested on suspicion of having committed the crimes, and eventually discharged. His offences were to have been in Whitechapel around the time of the later murders, to have a bad temper, drink too much, and like the company of prostitutes.

Certain officers in charge of the Jack the Ripper murders had known that the midwife's nephew was the culprit. It came as no surprise to some of them when Thomas's uncle, Charles Cutbush of Scotland Yard, shot himself through the head in his own kitchen around that time. He knew the truth and had decided to take it with him to his grave. Other than two of his colleagues he had told no one who was responsible for the Jack the Ripper murders. Thomas was finally certified insane and detained at Her Majesty's pleasure but had not been tried for murder. The mystery of Jack the Ripper's identity continued to intrigue the press and the public – but the midwife's diary, which Harriet had taken, would soon change that, if it fell into the wrong hands.

Jacqueline leaned back in her chair and shut her eyes tight. She had read enough to remind herself why she had not opened this package for so long. Filled with grief and remorse for the part she had played, and which, in a sense, had led to her nephew having to spend the rest of his life in a lunatic asylum, she found herself shedding a tear. Had she adopted her nephew and brought him to live with her, she might have helped him to live a sane and orderly life, she thought.

She wiped her face with the palms of her hands, hardly able to believe that tears were streaming down her cheeks. She could not remember having cried before, except once when she had been punished as a child for soiling her bed, and a second time when she had been flogged for questioning something in the Bible.

She hauled herself out of her chair, went to the mirror over the tiny fireplace and stared at her reflection. She embraced the tears and welcomed the release and the warm glow that spread through her chest. It seemed all right, after all, to cry. Especially in the privacy of this lodging room, which was now her home.

Back in her chair, she turned up the oil lamp and began to read again, with no thought of skipping over those too-painful or bloodcurdling reports. Now she would lay a ghost.

The following two weeks for Harriet were among the best days of her life. The small, modest wedding tea went off without a hitch: her sister had been there, her mother too. Polly had been the maid of honour, looking quite feminine and attractive in her own way. Her mousy hair had been given a henna rinse and then, after a session with the curling tongs, pulled up into a chignon with a silk and pearl band. Having been ordered to wear a corset, she was as surprised as anyone by her new figure and how nice she looked in her hired silk skirt and jacket with the row of tiny glass buttons. However, after the wedding tea and back in the House of Assignation, she could not wait to pull everything off and slip back to her old comfortable self.

Harriet's mother had cried when the thin gold band was placed on her daughter's finger. She had been through so much anguish and suffering that to see one of her children radiantly happy was the best compensation she could have asked. It had also been a joyous relief to her when her second daughter, Alice, moved in with Harriet. No questions had been asked when Harriet had made the suggestion and no resistance was forthcoming from Alice's aunt or uncle. But the expression of joy on her sister's face had told her that her instincts had been right and she thanked God for the insight.

The upper floor of the house off Jubilee Street was now looking quite different. On closer inspection Arthur had realised that the walls of the small bedroom where Alice was to sleep had at some time been covered with embossed paper and when he had whitewashed them the pattern could be seen more clearly. He repaired the wooden floorboards and painted them black; now a second-hand rag mat almost covered them. Alice's single bed and a chest of drawers, which had been sent by horse and cart along with a tea-chest filled with her clothes and her white twill bed cover, were in place and Harriet had placed a vase of fresh flowers on the window ledge.

Shy at first and missing her mother, Alice spent much of her time in her room, and Harriet decided to let her come out of her shell when she was ready. She had continued with her work at the factory and was grateful that at the end of a tiring day she now came home to a house where the beds had been made, a fire lit and a meal was either simmering on the stove or baking in the range. This evening, though, there was a little sparkle in Alice's eyes: she had made friends with the girl next door. Whether it had been engineered by Bonny, was neither here nor there: she had come out into the back yard and begun to sweep away some leaves while Alice was hanging washing on the line, but. Bonny had made the approach. She had caught Alice's eye and smiled timidly. The conversation was limited but enough was said to enable two withdrawn girls to bond and Alice had already planned to invite the other in for a cup of tea.

Now Harriet slumped down in Arthur's chair by the range and untied her boots. 'Gawd, Alice, my feet are tired. That cottage pie smells lovely.'

'Does it? That's good. Did they make you stand up all day, then?'

'Not likely, but they still ache. Wouldn't mind a cup of cocoa.'

'That's a bedtime drink.'

'Not in my book it ain't. I drink what I like when I like, if it's in the larder. Our aunt 'ad certain rules, I s'pose?'

'She did, yeah. But I never minded. Shall I make it with milk or water?'

'Boiled milk, if there's enough. I'm feeding two, don't forget.'

'Course you are,' said Alice. 'I was forgetting. You'll need plenty of calcium, won't you?' She opened the mesh door of the cool cupboard and took out a jug of milk. 'I wonder if it's a boy or a girl.'

'Don't bleedin' well care what it is so long as it don't keep me up all night. Remember our baby brother? He was always cryin', poor little mite.'

'That's because he was hungry. Mum told me that. I can't remember, really, but she said her milk dried up and she never knew. Shame, wasn't it? I would 'ave liked a little brother to look after.'

'If you ask me it was a blessin' in disguise. At least he passed over peacefully in his sleep. No more hunger pains for him. He's better off with Jesus.'

'That's what Mum said, so it must be right. We'll all be with the Lord Jesus one day – she said that too.'

'Not all of us, please, God. The rotters go else-where, is all I 'ope. You wouldn't want Uncle George followin' you up there, I bet.' This was the first time Harriet had broached the subject and she wasn't sure if she'd spoken too soon, but she went on anyway. 'I always thought he was a dirty old man. Dunno why.'

'Because he *was* a dirty old man.'

Harriet was ready to ask the question but dreaded what the answer might be. 'I thought he might have . . .' was all she could say.

Pouring milk into a small enamel saucepan, Alice shrugged. 'It don't matter any more. I'm away from him now.'

'Put 'is hand up your skirt, did he?' A horrible feeling was creeping over Harriet, but even though she felt she was going down a road filled with shadows, she had to go on for her sister's sake. 'You don't 'ave to answer that if you don't want to,' she murmured. It would be painful for both of them if her instinct had been right. The look in her sister's sad brown eyes confirmed that she was about to hear something she dreaded.

Alice leaned against the wall next to the range, arms folded, and slipped into her own world. Harriet waited, not sorry that she had mentioned it now. She had turned the key of a locked door. Now Alice looked directly into Harriet's worried face. 'You can do anything, you know, to get through things you hate. I invented a tiny switch that no one could see or feel, only me. It's just here,' she tapped the side of her head with a finger, 'hidden by my hair. When he had that look on his face and no one else was in I just flicked my switch down and then I couldn't feel anything. You could 'ave stuck a knife in me and I wouldn't have felt it. That's how good it was.'

'Alice,' whispered Harriet, choked, 'tell me about it later on, eh?'

'No, it's all right. It's not really bad. I pinched two of his big white handkerchiefs and always had one tucked up my sleeve, just in case. By the time he'd got me where he wanted and was ready to put my hand on his thingy, I covered it up with the nice clean handkerchief and did what he wanted. He tried to talk me out of it but I wouldn't give in on that. So, what with me being switched off and a clean white handkerchief between my hand and his thingy, it wasn't as horrible as it would have been. There wasn't anything I could do about his hand, though. He put that where he wanted. But my switch was turned off so I never felt that either. I'll never get married, though, Harriet. Never.' She raised her eyes from the floor and looked into Harriet's stricken face. 'Do you think it might have been my fault?'

Shocked and upset by her sister's speech, Harriet was unable to answer. This was her younger sister, whom she should have been able to protect, her little sister who had been through the worst of all childhood horrors and hadn't been able to tell a soul. Now that she had been asked, the poor girl was only too ready to unburden herself of the guilt she had carried for something that was no fault of her own.

'You should 'ave told Mum,' she whispered shakily.

'And have her turned out into the streets again? I couldn't do that. I was payment, I suppose. I don't know if Aunt knew about it, but she was frightened of him, I think. She couldn't 'ave children. Or, at least, that's what she said. I don't really know.'

'I'm sorry, Alice, I never knew, I swear it. But the way he leered at me, and that smile that made your flesh creep, I should 'ave asked you about 'im ages ago.'

'How could you? You never hardly came to—' At

this point, Alice wept. 'I missed you so much but you never came. Sometimes I didn't know if you was dead or not.'

Harriet got up, went to her sister and held out her arms, hating herself for having thought only of her own welfare since the day she had been separated from her family. 'I couldn't help you or Mum, Alice,' she said, clasping her sister to her and stroking her dark hair. 'I ran away from the work'ouse after just a few days then slept rough in the coalman's yard. He looked after me, though. Gave me dried oats in hot tea and another mug of tea to wash it down wiv. Then I got into real bad trouble wiv a midwife who tied me up and locked me in a room not much bigger than a cupboard wiv no light or nuffing.'

Alice smiled at her. 'It's all right. I'm so safe and happy now that I'm with you. It's over now. We can be together always. I wasn't criticising you for not coming, I just missed you, that's all. And I didn't like thinking you might be dead. Mum used to cry in bed at night and I had to pretend I never knew. She was so sad you couldn't live wiv us as well but there wasn't any room.'

'I know – and out of the three of us I was toughest. If I never wanted to do somefing I wouldn't bleedin' well do it. Bit like Dad, really.'

'That's what Mum used to say. She used to cuddle me when I couldn't get to sleep and say that you'd be all right because you had Dad's will.'

'Yeah, well, I was all right, then, wasn't I? But you do need friends, Alice, I found that out. I've got some now. I've give Polly me address, and Flora. Once summer's broke and the days are longer, they'll be round.' She glanced at Alice to see her smiling. 'I'm dying for a cup of somefing – I don't care if it's tea or cocoa so long as it's hot and wet. You get on with that while I go out to the lav, eh?' She looked around for an old newspaper, but Alice had tidied up again.

'It's all right. I've cut up two lots of squares and hung both bundles on a nail. The smaller ones are for wipin' your fanny dry and the bigger ones for when you do numbers.'

Rolling her eyes, Harriet left her sister in the kitchen. Alice certainly was an asset with her houseproud ways – her aunt in South London had trained her well. So long as Arthur and Harriet were working, there was no need for her to have to face a world unknown to her. Once the baby was born and Harriet at home, it would be Alice's turn to earn a wage and by then she would have learned more about the ways of the world. As for what she had been through with her uncle, Harriet could see no point in harping on about it or talking it through any more than they had this first time. Alice had said all she had to in one clean swoop. There would be a problem once she met her own sweetheart. She might have it in mind that anything physical between man and woman was rude. All of this was running through Harriet's mind while she sat on the lavatory pan reading bits of the cut-up newspaper. At least her sister was safe now with her and Arthur.

She pulled another piece of paper from the string and noticed an advertisement headed 'People's Palace,

Mile End Road, E'. The illustration showed groups being taught technical drawing, painting, needlework, carpentry and various other skills. A new thought struck her. Why not go with Alice to one of the evening classes and learn a skill that they might not only enjoy but could use, perhaps, later on to earn a living? Excited now, she couldn't wait to talk to Alice about it. She was surprised to hear a quiet tap on the lavatory door and her sister whispering her name urgently.

Sensing that something was wrong, Harriet was out of the brick hut in a flash. Alice was trembling as she mouthed, 'Come inside.'

Harriet followed her into the kitchen, closed the back door and leaned on it. 'What's the matter?'

Her sister looked scared. 'Come into the passage . . .' Alice murmured, and crept out of the kitchen, signalling for Harriet to be as silent a mouse. Once in the passage, she stopped and put a finger to her lips, then pressed an ear to the wall, encouraging Harriet to do the same. Together, they listened and could hear the distant sound of muffled screams and the crack of a whip. Harriet turned quickly and took the stairs as fast as she could, making as little sound as possible. In the tiny back room her fears were confirmed. The girl from the workhouse was being savagely beaten.

'We've got to do something,' whispered Alice, wringing her hands.

Harriet signalled for them to go back downstairs and into the kitchen. There, she poured them both a glass of water. 'We've got to play this very carefully, Alice.'

'But she'll die if they don't stop!'

'No, she won't. This must 'ave been goin' on for months and she's survived it so far. Another hour won't make no difference.'

Beside herself, Alice stood in front of Harriet and stamped her foot. 'We've got to stop them! They're whipping her, Harriet!'

'*Stop it!*' hissed Harriet, then raised an arm, showing the flat of her hand. '*Stop it, Alice!*'

Her eyes wide and disbelieving, Alice went to a corner and slid to the floor where she sat clutching her knees, her eyes focused on Harriet and what she might do next. But Harriet's attention was no longer on her sister: she was pacing the floor. She stopped suddenly. 'It is Tuesday today?'

'I don't know. Why? Why you looking so serious now?'

'Is it Tuesday? Is it?'

'Yes! It is Tuesday, because I've made a cottage pie! We always have cottage pie on Tuesday! Aunt and Uncle have cold meat on Monday and stew on Wednesday so—'

'All right!' snapped Harriet. 'Today's Tuesday. That's good. They go to their club, whatever that is, and they don't get back till gone nine.' She looked at the clock on the window-sill. It was a quarter to seven. 'They'll leave soon. We'll wait till they've gone out.'

'I can still hear her crying out. They're torturing her!'

'Stop it, Alice! I've got ears!'

'Well, why can't we bang on the front door and

tell them to stop? Why do we have to stay here and let them carry on doing it? I don't understand you, Harriet. I don't know what's going on.' Tears were rolling down Alice's face. 'Are things so different in East London? Does everyone whip the girls who work for them?'

'No, of course they don't,' said Harriet. 'She's from the work'ouse, and if we go bargin' in or call the police, the best that can 'appen to her is that she'll be sent back there. They'll lie through their teeth and say she's done all manner of fings, and who d'yer think the authorities will believe? A work'ouse girl or two upstandin' citizens? And women at that.'

'So as it's Tuesday we *can* call the police – because they won't be in. Is that what you mean to do?'

'No. I mean to prise open the back window and go in there. I'll collect 'er things – not that there'll be much to collect – and you'll be at our front door keepin' watch. Then you give me the all-clear that no one's in the street – not a soul, mind! No one must see us when we fetch the girl in here. No one!'

'Then what will we do with her? She can't stay shut up all day, and we won't be able to leave her by herself in case they break into our back window and—'

'Alice,' Harriet interrupted, 'we'll change the way she looks. Arthur'll give 'er a 'aircut and we'll get boys' clothes off the ragman down the Highway till we can afford something better. We'll pass her off as our brother. If a sister can come and live wiv me, so can a brother, right?'

'Yeah,' said Alice. 'I just heard that whip again.'

'I know – but we're gonna 'ave to bear it. It'll stop soon – unless they've changed their mind this week and don't go to their club.'

'Shush!' Alice held her breath. 'It's gone quiet.'

Tense, Harriet and Alice sat waiting for the next crack and cry, but there was nothing. No sound, other than the closing of a door. It was all a little too silent.

'You don't think they've killed her, do you?' Alice's eyes were wide and her mouth curled down. She was petrified.

'No. She must know the routine by now: stay tight-lipped in case they come back in for a second innings.'

By now both girls were ready for something a little stronger than tea or cocoa. In the kitchen, Harriet went to the old pine cupboard above the sink and took out a small bottle of much-needed medicinal brandy. To have to listen while a slip of a girl was whipped mercilessly was more than anyone could bear. But they did not know that this whipping session was only the half of it . . .

Greta and Edith, of similar disposition, had both practised nursing and had met during their time caring for the women in a workhouse. The girl now living with them had been one of the children in their care, and when they left to follow different careers and live together, she had been placed with them as an apprentice, in the hope that she would return to care for others. This was no humane act on the part of Greta and Edith, since anyone who was willing to take on a so-called apprentice was given ten pounds towards expenses. The workhouse girls were meant to be used with a degree of humanity but, as with the poor waif in the house next door, this rule was rarely observed.

Bonny's first taste of things to come had been a while ago. Just a few days after she had moved in, she had blackened the iron fireplace but had not polished it highly enough for their liking and had smudged some of the blacking on to the surrounding red tiles. Her punishment for this was to be laid across two chairs in the kitchen and whipped with ferocious, unrestrained cruelty.

The old man who had once lived next door had been stone deaf and posed no threat to Greta and Edith, but once Harriet and Arthur had moved in, a change had had to be made: beatings were administered in the boxroom upstairs, where the women believed the girl's cries would not be heard. Punishment was meted out frequently, mostly while Harriet and Arthur were at work. The two women sometimes concluded the beatings by dipping Bonny's head in a pail of freezing water.

On one occasion Bonny had managed to escape but had met Greta in the street and been forced to return. From then on her punishment was more severe. Stripped naked she was beaten with a hearthbroom, a horsewhip or a cane until she lost the power of speech and could only manage a sound to compare with a dying kitten. Then, and only then, would Greta instruct her partner to stop.

As well as beating her, the women kept Bonny on the brink of starvation. Occasionally she cut herself a slice of bread from their loaf or stole a biscuit from their tin. Naturally she was punished for this and kept without food, which meant she had to steal again – and so the vicious circle had gone on.

Until they moved her upstairs, her sleeping quarters had been a cupboard next to the coal-hole and her bedding no more than straw and a thin, moth-eaten cover. In the depth of winter she almost perished with cold and this seemed to be her destiny, always close to the brink of death but not close enough for her misery to end.

On one occasion, she had had to spend a night with a collar and chain fixed round her neck, the end of which was fastened to the coal-cellar door. The swollen weals remained for a week before the blistered skin dried and peeled. The wounds, there for all to see, mercifully stopped this practice: anyone visiting would see the evidence of cruelty, a risk neither woman could take. The collar and chain, however, hung inside the coal-hole as a threat.

Bonny had become overly subservient, timid and silent. Kindness, in the form of Harriet speaking to her and Arthur giving her a cup of tea, had been previously unknown to her. But when she saw Alice in the back yard hanging out the washing, she had taken her for another apprentice from the workhouse and hoped that at last she last found an ally.

'Shall we wait for Arthur to come home, Harriet,

before we break into next door?' whispered Alice, hoping her sister would want to act straight away. 'Or shall we go in when they've gone out?'

'Be quiet, Alice,' murmured Harriet. 'I'm tryin' to fink.'

'Only they might come back before him and—'

'Alice! Shush for five minutes. You're worse than me. I told yer, I'm finkin' it through!'

Shrugging apologetically, Alice held her tongue and the house seemed eerily silent until the sound of their neighbours' door slamming broke the stillness. Knowing that her sister's eyes were fixed on her face, waiting for a sign of what their next move might be, Harriet walked quietly out of the kitchen and listened at the front door. The low conversation between the women as they turned away from the house was followed by echoing footsteps.

Harriet waited until it was quiet again, then opened the front door and looked cautiously along the gas-lit street. She could hear nothing but the clip-clopping of horses' hoofs on the cobbled road at the end of the turning. She shut the door, then went back into the kitchen and nodded at her sister, a determined look on her face. 'I'm going in through the back door. You set the table with three cups and saucers, some biscuits and a pot of tea. When we come in, try to look normal as if you don't know anyfing of what's bin goin' on next door.'

'All right,' said Alice. 'I won't say a word.'

'Good.' Harriet delved into Arthur's orange crate where he kept his tools, next to the copper boiler. She had seen him use a small crowbar when he had eased up the rotten floorboards in Alice's room. Holding it up as if it were a flag she grinned. 'This should do the trick.'

'But they'll see if you damage the door or break the lock, Harriet. Why don't you just knock on the front door?'

'Because the poor kid won't be in any fit state to open it. They always use a key so she'll wonder who the hell it is.'

'But she might guess it's one of us,' said Alice.

'She won't be finking straight after the whipping she's just 'ad.' Harriet picked up a candle, stole into the back yard and went through the loose part of the fence. She examined the lock of the back door, then the small kitchen window to see which might be the better of the two to ease open. To her relief, the back door was not locked so she turned the handle and went inside.

She climbed the stairs and opened the door into the back room. The wretched girl was curled up in a corner with sacking to cover her naked bleeding body. As she stared down at the whimpering child, tears welled in Harriet's eyes. This was the most pitiful sight she had ever seen – and she had seen worse than most people. 'It's all right, Bonny,' she whispered. 'It's me, Harriet, from next door.'

The girl was semiconscious and in shock, but these whipping sessions happened at least once a week, whether a reason had been found or not. She had learned to live with them.

'I've come to take you away from here,' Harriet continued, picking up the girl's small bundle of clothes. 'It's all over now, sweetheart,' she said, stepping towards her. 'You're gonna live wiv me and my sister next door and no one'll know. I swear to God those two witches won't ever know. We'll let 'em fink you've run away.'

Lifting her face, the girl peered at her through swollen eyes. She opened her mouth to speak but closed it again. Then, using every bit of strength she could muster, she eased herself up on to her elbows. Licking her dry lips she mouthed, 'Water.'

'Yeah, you can 'ave a lovely glass of water, Bonny, but we've got to get you out of 'ere.' She stepped closer and held out a hand. 'Come on, it's over. No more sufferin'. You don't 'ave to put up wiv it any more.'

As Harriet had thought, there was no response other than a look of suspicion that swept across the girl's face. Her eyes darted from Harriet to the door, as if she expected her tormentors to charge in at any second. Harriet laid a hand on Bonny's red, swollen cheek, stroked it with a finger then lifted her chin. 'It's over now. You're gonna live like a normal person from now on. We don't live in a palace but it is a proper home.'

Still no response. She tried another tack. 'My sister Alice wants you to come and live wiv us. She's 'ad a bad time too.' Forcing a smile, she added, 'We're gonna make you look like a boy and say you're my bruvver. No one'll recognise you, honest to God.' This time there was a reaction, the girl's brow furrowed, but the expression in her eyes changed from a look of defeat to a new dawning.

Harriet knelt in front of her, and looked into her face, 'We don't 'ave to rush but we should get a move on. My sister, Alice, is keeping lookout. Can you manage to stand up, Bonny?'

'I finks so,' came the trembling reply.

'Good. Pull that sacking round yer.' With an arm around the pathetically thin waist, Harriet eased them both up to full height. 'Come on. Once we're next door I'll wrap a nice thick blanket round yer.'

Flinching with every painful step, Bonny allowed Harriet to guide her out of the room and down the stairs, the candle lighting their way. 'They might come back. What if they comes back?' she whimpered.

'The state you're in, they're not gonna argue. They could go to prison for what they've bin doing. Trouble is,' said Harriet, while negotiating the back door with the girl, and the candle, 'bruises and blisters do disappear. Time we got to court you'd be as pink as a peach. So we ain't gonna take no chances.'

Before she had time to wonder how she was going to get them both through the loose fencing, Alice was there to help and they made their way to safety inside Harriet's house, with the back door bolted and the curtains closed. True to form, Alice had set the table as Harriet had asked. She had also opened the tiny iron door beneath the range so the glow from the fire would add to the homely feeling.

'Now,' said Harriet, a touch breathless but not yet

finished, 'I'm gonna go back in there, open the front door and leave it ajar so they'll fink that that's the way you left.' She leaned over the girl and spoke softly so as not to alarm her. 'Is there anyfing you want me to collect for you?'

'My coat. It's on a hook by the coal-hole door.'

'And that's all?'

'I s'pose so.' She hung her head and shrugged. 'I can't take everyfing.'

'You can 'ave wot's bleedin' well yours. Now, what else? We can't really afford to 'ang about, Bonny.'

'It's just a bit of ribbon with somefing on it. A medal. It's 'idden in that up-the-stairs room.'

'Where?'

'Behind the skirting board under the winda behind the pile of old newspapers.'

'And that's all. A coat and a medal?'

'But they might come back!'

'Well, it'll be too bleedin' bad if they do. I've gotta see to the door and we need to get yer coat out of there so I might as well get your medal while I'm at it. Alice, keep watch at the front and whistle out the back if they come along the turning.'

Once Harriet had slipped out of the back door, the girls looked at each other, frightened. Neither said a word and the silence grew until Alice broke it with a whisper: 'I must go to the front to keep watch. Don't move or anything.'

'Shouldn't I hide upstairs?' The terror was back in the girl's eyes. 'In case they comes back?'

'I don't think so. Harriet never said that. No. I'll just go and make sure they're not coming.' Backing out of the kitchen, Alice offered a brave smile but she herself was trembling.

Standing in the dark, desolate street, she listened intently and, to her horror, she heard distant footsteps approaching. She peered along the turning but couldn't make out who was coming, or even if it was one person walking alone with another following, or a couple. Her heart beating rapidly, she took no chances. She ran through to the back and whistled, while Bonny sat shaking with terror. Alice whistled again, with more urgency, and sighed with relief when Harriet finally appeared with the girl's long black threadbare coat over her arm.

'Get inside, Alice, quick, and turn down the lamp.'

'It might not be them,' she said. 'I don't know who it was but two people are coming along the turning.'

'Just do as I say.' Harriet went inside and urged Bonny to follow her into the front room, which was her and Arthur's bedroom. 'You must get into our bed and lie very flat,' she hissed, 'just in case one of 'em barges in lookin' for you.'

'I wants to go back before they sees I'm missin'! Please let me go back! You don't know what they're like – please!'

'No! You're never goin' back in there! You're safe now. Do you understand? Safe! Now 'ide under them covers and try not to bleedin' well tremble!'

The sudden rat-a-tat on the door sent a wave of terror through them but Bonny's glimpse of better things to come strengthened her will to survive. Instead of cowering in a corner she was on Harriet and Arthur's bed faster than a rabbit could scurry into its warren. A smile spread across Harriet's face. Bonny was spreadeagled so flat under the eiderdown that only the smell of her unwashed body could give her away.

She went to the street door, shoulders back and determined. She would pretend to be shocked that the workhouse girl had run away. The knocking changed from a rat-a-tat-tat to three loud, purposeful bangs, which did not intimidate but served only to provoke her.

She wrenched open the door and was a touch disappointed to see Arthur standing there. He had forgotten his key. 'Oh, it's you,' she said. Of course she was relieved to see him but she had been ready for a verbal battle of wits.

'Who did you think it was, then? Rent man?'

'No. Come in and shut the door. We've got a guest. You didn't see next door in the street, did yer?'

'No. Only the bee-keeper. Why?' Arthur pulled off his cap and went through to the kitchen. 'Oooh, something smells nice, Alice. Meat and crust pie, is it?'

'No,' said Alice, looking nervous. 'It's shepherd's pie.'

'Better still. So, what's goin' on, then?' He sat in his chair by the kitchen range and waited. 'And don't tell me there's nothing in the air 'cos I know different. Harriet said we've got a guest. I can't see anyone other than you, Alice, and you're not a guest, you're family.'

'She'll come in from your bedroom in a minute. She can tell you, eh? I'll just strain the greens. Did you want the greens water?'

'Yes, please. Salt and plenty of pepper.' Lighting a roll up, Arthur wondered if Harriet's mother had decided to unload herself too. If that was the case, he would have none of it. She could stop over the night and squeeze in the bed with Alice but be gone by the time he returned from work the next day. Enough was enough.

'Did you want a little drop of vinegar in it?' Alice asked.

'No, ta. Just pepper and salt. So who is it, then, Alice? Yer mother?'

'No, not Mum. Best wait for Harriet. She explains things better than I do.'

Harriet came into the room, with her new ward in front of her. She placed a hand on each of the girl's shoulders and patted her gently. 'We've kidnapped Bonny, Arfer. She's gonna sleep in Alice's room. We—'

'Stone me blind . . .' murmured Arthur, gaping, his cigarette stuck in the corner of his mouth. 'Who's done that to yer, gal? Them two next door?'

The girl pushed herself against Harriet and her eyes widened as she stared at him, frightened he would send her back and that they would know she had been out of her room. 'No one,' she whispered. 'No one did nuffing.'

'It was them two lesbos, that's who it was. She ain't goin' back there no more, Arfer. Me and Alice heard the crack of the whip, over and over. They've bin torturin' 'er, Arfer, and starvin' 'er 'alf to death.'

'Too bleedin' right she's not goin' back in there. Dish up dinner for four, Alice, and you fetch my clippers, Harriet. We'll 'ave you lookin' like a boy, Bonny, don't you fret.' Arthur looked from the skinny waif to Harriet. 'Did you break the lock to go in and get 'er?'

'No. I never 'ad to. I took your small crowbar but I never 'ad to use it. The back door wasn't locked. They're not as smart as they bleedin' well fink they are.'

Arthur looked around the kitchen, then glanced at his makeshift toolbox in the corner. 'Where is it, then? The crowbar.'

'Oh, sweet Mary Mother of Jesus . . .'

'Not the time for prayin', Harriet! Where *is* it?' The look of sheer terror on her face was the answer to his question. She had left it behind and they would find it and know exactly where the girl was.

'You're not goin' back out there, Arfer. They might come in and catch you and—'

'We'll see about that,' he snarled, taking a lighted candle off the window-sill and going out into the back yard. 'I might not be a wrestler but I'm not frightened of two silly cows like them!'

On his heels, Harriet racked her brain as to whether she had taken it inside the house or left it in the yard but she couldn't think straight. Arthur was in a temper, and if the women did return there would be an almighty row and they might send for the police. 'Don't go upstairs, Arfer, *please*!'

He spun on his heels and glared at her. 'Is that where it is? Upstairs?'

'I don't know! I can't remember what I did with it. I wasn't finkin' straight!'

'Tellin' me you wasn't,' he mumbled guiding his candle around the step outside the door before opening it. Once inside the house next door, he walked slowly, peering at the floor, not missing an inch. When he arrived at the stairs, he stared at the treads, concentrating, and almost missed what was under his nose. Harriet had placed the crowbar there before going up the stairs. Had Arthur not trodden on the end he wouldn't have seen it.

'Don't go upstairs!' hissed Harriet, from the yard door. 'Arfer!'

'Shut up for five minutes! I've found it! I'm just gonna 'ave a little look round.'

'You bleedin' well ain't! Get yer arse back inside next door or—' The sound of footsteps echoing in the street stopped them both in their tracks. Arthur didn't need Harriet to tell him to move. He was out of the back door in a flash and closing it silently behind him.

Settled in the kitchen and listening intently, their hearts lurched when they heard their neighbours' door slam shut. 'They're back early,' whispered Harriet, glancing at the clock. 'I bet they practise black magic and the devil warned them to come back!'

'Don't talk rot,' barked Arthur. 'And stop whisperin'! This is our place and no one's gonna make us to do anyfing we don't want! Now, then, Alice, go in the front room wiv Bonny and shut the door behind yer. You'll 'ave to sit in the dark but at least you can watch to see that the girl don't do anyfing daft.'

'But what if they come in there?' cried Alice, terrified.

'They'll do no such thing. This is my 'ouse.' Three loud bangs on the door stopped him short. He looked from one to the other, and gently guided the girls out of the room into the next, quietly closing the door behind him. Then he opened the street door in none too good a frame of mind. Both women were standing there, and he put on a fine display of nonchalance. 'Hello, ladies. What can I do for you?'

'The workhouse girl has run away and we—'

'Run away? Good Lord. But the wife's brother saw 'er this afternoon, out in your back yard. Never looked at him, mind, but she never does look anyone in the face, do she? He never said she was upset or that, although . . .' he rubbed his chin thoughtfully '. . . the wife did say she heard screams coming from somewhere. Could 'ave bin your 'ouse. I'll get my jacket and fetch the police.'

'You'll do no such thing,' snapped Edith, red-faced and furious. 'We only knocked to ask if you'd seen or heard anything.'

'Well, I never,' he said, 'but my wife and her brother did, didn't they? Earlier on, when you must 'ave already gone out. Sounds a bit worrying to me, 'er screamin' like that. Someone must 'ave broke into your place and she tried to stop 'em thievin'. So you'll need the police.' Suddenly he looked aghast, as if a new and dreadful thought had struck him. 'Good grief – she might 'ave bin murdered and dragged off.'

'Mr Dean,' said Edith, tight-lipped, 'there's no sign of struggle and I'm surprised that today was the only time that screaming was heard. The workhouse girl is not sound in the head. She takes it upon herself to throw her body against the wall whenever she sees fit. She also inflicts pain by striking herself with anything to hand. Sometimes she will use my belt and sometimes a length of garden cane. She has run away and taken a silver candlestick.'

'Which, no doubt, she will sell,' added Greta.

'Oh, I see what you mean.' Arthur sucked in air. 'So, really, it's none of our business and you'll be bringin' the police in yerself, 'cos of the candlestick. Well, I'm sorry you've 'ad such a bad time with the selfish girl and I 'ope you find 'er.'

'Oh, we will, Mr Smith, we will.'

'Well, when you do find 'er, and she's back in the fold, so to speak, I'll get an aunt of mine to check 'er over and try and see if she can stop the girl 'urtin' 'erself. My aunt's a mind doctor as well, you see, so she'll soon draw out the poison from 'er mind.'

Greta and Edith looked at each other. 'I shouldn't bother, Mr Smith. Don't worry your aunt over that girl. I doubt we'll see anything of her now. We always suspected she'd take advantage and run away. At least it was only one candlestick and not two. We'll say no more about this, if you don't mind,' Greta stated.

Arthur put on an anxious expression. 'I don't know so much . . . My wife's gonna worry over the poor kid.

All skin and bone, wasn't she? Can't see 'er survivin' out there.'

'Thousands like her do,' said Edith. 'You either turn a blind eye or dedicate your life to those who will stab you in the back at the least chance. My advice is to leave it to men like William Booth and Dr Barnardo. Unlike many do-gooders, such men dedicate a lifetime to the cause, not a ten-minute flash in the pan.' She turned away and Greta followed her back into their house.

Arthur opened the door of the dark front room and struck a match. 'Come on, you two, it's time for a bit of grub. They won't be back.' He looked from the petrified face of Alice to the bed, which seemed to be unoccupied. The girl was as still as a corpse and as flat as a pancake beneath the bulky eiderdown, which Mary had given to Harriet and Arthur.

'If you're still breathin' under there,' he joked, 'there's an 'ot meal waitin'. If you don't move yerself there'll be two 'elpings for Alice, who eats like an 'orse.'

The first thing to appear over the bedcovers was Bonny's pale, thin hand as she gripped the edge and slowly pulled it down to show a hot, sweaty face. A hot, sweaty, smiling face. The first smile she had offered in a very long time. 'They finks I've run away.' She chuckled.

Alice helped the girl out of bed, looking, as far as Arthur could tell, happier than she had since her arrival in Stepney. This abduction of the workhouse girl meant yet another mouth to feed but, that these events it seemed as if another hand was at work, an invisible hand. Had his parents not been churchgoing Christians he would not have given the Almighty a thought, but these two girls had been through worse things than he liked to think about over and had been delivered into his and Harriet's arms.

'You know where we're goin' this Sunday?' he said suddenly. 'We're goin' to church.'

Both girls were agog.

'Too right an' all,' said Harriet, from the doorway. 'From now onwards, we're gonna be church-abidin' citizens.'

'Why?' said Alice, who had never been to church in her life.

'You don't 'ave to, but me and Arfer are gonna go and when my baby's born, it's gonna 'ave a proper christenin'. Church ain't no bad place. I've bin a few times to keep Mary 'appy and, to tell the truth, I rather liked it, not that I was bleedin' well gonna let on. She'd 'ave 'ad us there not only on 'igh days and 'olidays but every bloomin' Sunday.'

'But you just said we'll go every week.'

'No, I never, Alice. I said we was gonna become church-abidin'. I might go every Sunday, I might not. But when I do go, we'll all go together. All five of us.'

'I says me prayers every night,' murmured Bonny. 'But it never made no difference if I asked the Lord Jesus for deliverance – not when I was in the work'ouse or next door.'

'Well, He's got a lot of people to look after, ain't He?' said Arthur, in a new, fatherly fashion. 'Bit like Santa Claus. He got to you eventually, though. Delivered you to next door and then to us.'

'Yeah,' said Alice, 'and he did the same for me. It must be something about this house. It's got a lovely feeling to it. I think angels must have lived here once.' She looked about herself and smiled faintly. 'I think they're still here.'

'Better not be,' sniffed Harriet. 'Me and Arfer ain't always law-abidin' and I don't 'spect you will be either, Bonny, once you feel yer feet.'

Before the girl could answer, Arthur let out a groan. 'I'm sorry, we can't call 'er Bonny. Bloody daft name.'

'We can't do now, no. Not if we're to pass 'er off as a boy. Don't fink I 'aven't thought of that, Arfer Dean. We'll call 'er Bo.'

'Oh – I likes that!' exclaimed the girl, her face lighting up.

'Well, that's settled, then. Bo it is. Now come in and eat the shepherd's pie before it's burnt to a crisp.' Harriet went into the kitchen, forcing herself not to shed a tear. If the girl only knew that when she smiled like that it was she who was the angel in this house! She couldn't wait to see what colour her hair would come up once it was given a good wash and the years of grease and grime had gone. There was no doubt in Harriet's mind as to who Bo reminded her of: herself, long ago, before she had overcome the belief that she was nothing more than an extra being the world could do without. The coalman she ran errands for once she was out on the streets had soon put her wise to that. He was a quiet man and spare with his words, but when he had spoken, wisdom was there for the hearing.

———◆—◆———

6

A few weeks passed before Jacqueline Turner could bring herself to walk along the Whitechapel Road, which held memories of bad times past that still haunted her. Having read the newspaper articles on the Whitechapel murders twice, she had finally burnt them in her tiny fireplace in her rooms above the shop in Sidney Street. Now she felt ready to inch her way forward into settling back into this country, her birthplace. She had been to visit her sister in Peabody Buildings in Albert Street, Kennington, only to find that she had been evicted for disturbing the peace. A neighbour, who had been pleased to see the back of her, was only too ready to fill her in with all the details. By all accounts, Celeste Cutbush's manic behaviour had gone from bad to worse when her friend and companion of years had passed away with tuberculosis.

Another neighbour, eager to join in with the gossips, had told the midwife where her sister now lived. Back in her midwifery outfit, Jacqueline was receiving spontaneous respect and, within the walls of the Peabody Buildings, had been treated as if she were an officer of the law, which had gone some way to help boost her morale.

She walked back slowly from Kennington on this sunny Saturday, stopping once in tea rooms for light refreshment; she had got as far as Aldgate before she began to feel her age. In the old days she would have charged along at twice the speed and hardly noticed other people, but now the pavements seemed packed with street vendors and people going in and out of shops and taverns. And there was certainly more traffic coming in and out of side roads, not only hansom cabs and bicycles but the occasional motor car too. Things had changed quite a bit during the seventeen years she had been away and it seemed obvious to her that, in this new twentieth century, life would move at a faster pace.

Now, resting on a bench by a water fountain, resentment engulfed her. This area where she had been born and bred now seemed like a strange place. Even the street beggars looked different from those she remembered, not quite so wretched, starved, or at death's doorstep. Seeing a young man wearing a mackintosh and trilby, striding along purposefully, she thought of Thomas, her nephew, and how he might have turned out if things had been different. She still hadn't been brave enough to find out how he was from the authorities. He had been detained for life in an asylum, that she knew, but was he still alive? Would he know her if she were to visit him? Would it break both their hearts to meet again only to have to part?

'No wonder your uncle Charles shot himself, lad,' she murmured. 'Would that I had had the courage to do the same.' As the superintendent in charge of the Ripper case, the wretched man had had no choice but to commit suicide when it looked as if the cover-up over his mad nephew was about to discovered. It would have caused a scandal and the public disgrace would have been too much for any man to bear, never mind one in his position. The saving grace in the whole affair was that no one had realised Jacqueline Turner, respectable citizen and midwife, had been involved in the gruesome murders.

'Wouldn't we all, gal?' The thin voice of a leathery-faced woman drifted across to Jacqueline. A vagrant had parked herself on the bench. 'Ain't got no gun, that's the trouble. And you try finkin' of a way of finishin' it. I 'ave – Gawd, luv, I 'ave. Too risky, that's the trouble. Wot if you was to survive and end up in prison for it? In prison and only 'alf dead. Don't bear finkin' abaht. So jest push on, I says. Jest push on.' The woman ended with a long drawn-out sigh, enjoying the chance to revel in self-pity.

'Isn't Raven Street along Whitechapel and on the left?' murmured Jacqueline, taking no notice of the tramp's ramblings. 'Next to the London?'

'Yus, it is,' she said, all knowing. 'Not me, though, oh, no. Wouldn't catch me livin' on the doorstep of an 'ospital.' She blew through the gaps in her teeth and pushed her face close to the midwife's. 'Bit of an inconvenience, wouldn't you say? Eh? Stone me blind if I 'ad to. They'd be draggin' you off when you was asleep to run tests on yer. They thieve the bits you can't see and use 'em on royalty an' that.

No, you wouldn't get me in no 'ospital. I'll be all right on the platform. Whitechapel railway. Got a very nice bench there. That's where I shall meet my maker. Have you marked your place yet, lady? 'Cos you should, you know. A friend of mine's going dahn one of them underground lavatories.' She shook her head. 'Wouldn't suit me. No. Tch, tch, tch. Die in a public convenience? I shouldn't fink—'

The midwife heaved herself off the bench and left the woman to her rambling. The vagrant had injected her with the determination never to be thought of as one of them. Passing the Whitechapel railway station she thought of catching a train to some other part of London but something was driving her on and before she knew it she had arrived at Brady Street where she had to cross the main road into Raven Street.

She stood in front of the towering block of flats and was thankful that Celeste lived at number thirty, on the third storey. She gripped the iron rail and began to climb the filthy stone steps, wondering what she would find. She could hear shouts echoing and stray dogs barking but in this block it was relatively quiet. She arrived at her sister's door, knocked and waited for abuse to be screamed at her from within. But, to her relief, she could only hear the shuffling of feet, then the creaking as the door opened half-way and her sister stared at her, with a puzzled expression in her eyes. She was a shadow of the woman Jacqueline remembered, and all skin and bone.

'Hello, Celeste. It's Jacqueline, back from America.'

'I don't know no such person. Who sent you?' The

woman was already closing the door. 'Go away and leave me alone.'

'I'm your sister, Jacqueline. Don't close the door. I've come to see how you are.'

'I don't know no sister. She died. So did my brother Thomas. I don't know you.'

'You mean your son, Thomas. Let me come in, Celeste. I'm tired and my feet ache.'

'You mean Jacqueline Turner? You've come about Jacqueline Turner?'

'No. I *am* Jacqueline. Your sister.' The midwife lost patience and, with a sweep of her arm, brushed the frail woman aside and went into her flat. There was a tiny sitting room with a tin bath in front of the fireplace, a shabby armchair and a table with two chairs pushed in close. Sacking hung at the grimy windows, tacked into the timber frame.

Jacqueline pulled a high-backed chair to the fireside, sat down and watched as Celeste put her hands to the fire, which was unlit. She felt an overwhelming sense of pity. 'How long have you been living like this?' she asked.

'Like what? Don't talk in riddles. You're just like the others. They kept on asking questions. Said my brother Thomas was Jack the Ripper. He never wore a black cloak and top hat. Never.'

'Thomas was your son,' said Jacqueline again, 'not your brother. We never had a brother. There was just you and me, Mother and Father.'

'Riddles. Just like the rest of 'em. What do you want from me?'

Sighing, Jacqueline looked around the depressing room for a gas meter. Seeing none she got up and went into the tiny kitchen, which contained a filthy sink and a gas oven, in which were stacked dirty dishes and bags of rubbish. Above the cooker was the gas meter. She took a threepenny bit from her purse, pushed it into the slot, turned the handle and went back into the sitting room. There she turned on the gas tap, and put a match to the fire, where a few lumps of coal were waiting to be burned. Coal which was covered with a thick layer of dust and grime.

Celeste turned slowly to face the midwife, who was back in her chair. 'Why did you do that?'

'Nothing like a fire in the hearth. That's what our father used to say. A house isn't a home without a fire burning.'

Celeste turned back to the flickering flames. Then, without any prompting, she said, 'He never did kill them women. Poor boy. They put the blame on him. Did they hang him for it? I don't know. They all talk in riddles.'

'They never put the blame on him. So far no one's been found guilty. They arrested more than one man over it. Thomas was put into a hospital, not a prison. He wasn't right in the head, Celeste – we must at least accept that or else we shall both die in torment.'

'He was a doctor,' said the woman, who looked older than her years. 'And a detective. He saw things, that boy, saw things that no one else saw. Should have been a priest. That's what God wanted but no one listened. I burned the Bible. Burned it and made a roaring fire.'

'When was the last time you ate a square meal?'

'I don't need food. He never did kill them women. He never boasted over it and he would have done. They deserved to die. He would have boasted over it if he'd been the instrument of God. Did they hang him? No one told me. They took him away. Dragged him from me. God was a witness. He saw it all. Let them all burn in hell. His uncle did. Charles Cutbush. He burned in hell.'

As she gazed at her demented sister, the midwife felt more than pity. The face of their father came to mind, sad and disappointed. 'If Thomas is dead, he'll be in the arms of our father.'

'God doesn't cradle man.'

'Not God, Celeste, our own father. You remember him, surely? And Mother.'

'Riddles. You all talk in riddles. You'd best be going now.'

'Yes,' murmured the midwife, 'but I shall come back, Celeste. With cleaning materials. You don't have to live like this. You shan't live like this.'

'I live the way I want and none of you will interfere. I'll thank you to leave now. I've a lot to do, people to see. I'm not short of company.'

Jacqueline stood up and looked down sadly at the pathetic figure. She was filled with grief. How could Celeste have sunk so far? Their father had been an upright citizen and Celeste's husband had been from a good middle-class family. What had gone wrong?

Where had the insanity come from? Their grand-parents were of sound mind, clean and decent folk from south of the river.

'You'll want to go now. Soon be dark.' Celeste was staring into the fire as if it was there by magic. It had been a long time since she had seen flames in that fireplace.

'I've taken rooms not far from here.'

'Whitehead Street.'

Jacqueline was taken aback that her sister had remembered the name of the turning where they had lived as a family. 'No, I let that house go when I went to America. Thomas stayed there for a while, I believe. Before they took him into hospital.'

'Prison. That's where they put him. If they never hanged him he'll be there now, rotting away.'

'My rooms are within walking distance. I'll come back tomorrow and we'll make this a nice place for you to live in.'

'You leave it be. It's my home. I don't want no interference. Go back to America where you came from.'

'Remember to turn the tap off once the gas runs out,' said Jacqueline. 'I'll call in a day or two.'

'I shan't open the door. You're just like the rest of them. You think my Thomas ripped them women apart. What if he did? They deserved to die. God saw to it. He used my son as His disciple. He should have been given a gold cross to wear round his neck. A medal.'

'No one deserves to die, Celeste,' murmured

Jacqueline, her own guilt weighing heavily on her. In America her days had been filled with people, mothers who wanted not only to have their babies delivered safely but to be pampered and fussed over, and she had fulfilled their wishes. And lined her purse. But now that she was home, in these familiar, haunting surroundings, she could hardly believe that she had ended the lives of two prostitutes.

So who was to blame for things going so badly wrong? The government? Society? God? Or Mother Nature weeding her garden? All of these thoughts were going round and round in Jacqueline Turner's mind as she walked through the back-streets making her way to Beaumont Square, where she had seen her foe, Harriet Smith. When she arrived Jacqueline was pleased to see that no one else was sitting within the enclosed green with its cherry trees in full blossom. She opened the iron gate, went inside and sat down on a bench, with a view of the House of Assignation, the same bench on which her nephew, Thomas Cutbush, had placed himself all those years ago just before she had left for America when he had taken it upon himself to act the sleuth. He had told her all that had happened, but at the time she could not accept what she considered wild ramblings. Had she not been so worried about his state of mind and paid more attention to all he had said, things might have been different now.

After a meeting at Scotland Yard in 1888 when the Commissioner, Sir Charles Warren, had given his top men a dressing down for their failure to find the so-called Jack the Ripper, Sir Robert Anderson, one of the officers on the case, had come into this square to see his mistress, Lillian Redmond, and tell her that she must close down her House of Assignation until the Whitechapel murders had stopped. All brothels in the area, high class or low, were being watched to see who came and went, and gentlemen of standing frequented Lillian's house.

Outside the House of Assignation, Sir Robert had looked discreetly about him and seen his colleague's nephew, the twenty-two-year-old Thomas Cutbush, sitting on a bench reading a book while smoking his pipe. The position the young man had chosen afforded him an excellent view of the entrance to Lillian's imposing white house. Losing no time, Sir Robert Anderson had approached Thomas with the intention of seeing him off. He had warned his colleague's nephew that the team working on the investigation of the house he was watching would not be best pleased if he continued to interfere. His threat to report back to Scotland Yard that Thomas, the amateur, was hindering police investigations had fed Thomas's ego. It had confirmed that Thomas had been right and that the residence was being improperly used. The twenty-two-year-old had then disclosed his anxiety that Sir Robert had been frequenting the whorehouse and that he was glad to know it had been for law-abiding reasons. He had all but patted the officer on the shoulder.

Believing that he had satisfied the young man, Sir Robert had asked him to leave the square but he was not dealing with an ordinary or sane person. Thomas had gone on to explain that he had new information about the murder of the prostitute Annie Chapman: that she had been pregnant. This had been his trump card but the officer had simply waved it away as another of the silly amateur theories bandied about at the time. But Charles Cutbush's nephew had not been easily put off and his patronising smile had irritated the officer. He had insisted that Thomas leave the square and did not return causing Thomas to rise slowly from the bench, and murmur, '"*Qui tacet consentire videtur.*" He who is silent seems to consent.' His next sentence had been his downfall: 'I shall hope to be joining the Grand Lodge very soon, Sir Robert.'

As he watched Thomas walk away, his books under his arm, his head held high, the officer had questioned not only himself but his colleagues. How could they have let things get so shockingly out of hand? That young man had murdered three women in the most horrific manner and had the entire country in a state of panic and fear – yet they had left him to roam the streets. Had they not have covered up the first time when he had killed a prostitute out of passion, further gruesome killings might have been avoided. Shame lay on their shoulders. In their position they should have realised the potential consequences.

The idea of secreting his colleague's nephew in an asylum had come to Sir Robert in this square. Thomas had been rendered senseless with a drug, and then, with the help of a member of the Freemason Society, a Dr Browning, taken by hansom cab to a lunatic asylum. They had decided to tell Charles Cutbush of Scotland Yard that his nephew had lost all sense of right and wrong in a heated argument during a meeting when a member of the Lodge had disapproved of him joining.

On the way to the asylum with Thomas, Sir Robert had been mostly silent, cursing himself for having agreed to cover up the first murder, when Thomas had slashed a prostitute with a penknife. A week later she had died from infection of the blood. Thomas had confessed to his uncle, Sir Charles Cutbush. It had seemed right at that time to cover the unfortunate incident since the chief inspector of the Yard would most certainly have had to resign.

Set in their belief that Thomas had to be locked away for good, Scotland Yard had not taken into account on the love and determination of the lad's aunt, Jacqueline Turner. Once the midwife had learned of her nephew's confinement she had had two reasons to rid the world of a prostitute Catherine Eddowes. First, the woman knew too much to report her as, and second, if another killing took place while Thomas was interned he would be exonerated and the authorities would forced to discharge him. Little did she know that, set free, Thomas would continue in what he now believed to be his calling: to cleanse the streets of all prostitutes.

Now, five years into the twentieth century, the midwife was haunted and plagued by the past. In the quiet of that tree-lined square, where birds sang and the sweet scent of flowers drifted through the air, her determination to retrieve her diary grew stronger. Every detail of Thomas's confessions and her own hand in the murders had been written into it.

Leaving the square, the midwife resolved to continue with her work, and find out where Harriet Smith lived. Also, she had her sister Celeste to consider, and the least she could do for Thomas was look after his mother. If Harriet Smith was intent on selling her journal to a newspaper or turning it over to the police, she would have done so by now. The possibility of her having tossed it into the river years ago seemed more likely than her having hidden it away – but until she knew for certain, the midwife would not, could not, leave anything to chance. This square was a perfect place for her to enjoy a respite from her work while keeping an eye on the house she had seen her enemy leave.

Pleased with the way things were turning out, the midwife left the square, with no idea that she herself had been observed from the window of Lillian's snug. Although she was wearing her long black cloak and hat, she had been recognised as the woman who had come to the house for employment as cook and had left without a by-your-leave.

Watching from her window, Lillian was puzzled and the nagging anxiety in the pit of her stomach had returned. She had a strange feeling that it had something to do with this woman, who had introduced herself as a cook yet was now wearing the uniform of a midwife.

The door of the snug opened suddenly. 'Who you spying on, then? The house over the square?'

'I wasn't spying, Polly, merely glancing at the house in case Mr Wellington was on his way over.'

'Well, then, it ain't me who needs spectacles but you. He's just arrived. Shall I show 'im into 'ere or the dining room?'

'I'm not sure,' said Lillian, pensive. 'What do you think? Which will impress him the most?'

'Neiver – but you know my opinion on that. I told you to take down the flowery curtains and leave the windows bare. It's too old-fashioned and more like a flippin' boudoir. It's gotta be more like a men's smoking room if this is to work.'

'Well, then, show him in here. I'll tell him we're expecting decorators with regard to the dining room.'

'Not decorators, a designer. Let 'im imagine panelled walls and dark red and green wiv a hint of gold.'

'Yes, Polly. Show him up, please.'

'Yes, madam,' she said, dropping a fancy curtsy and grinning.

Presently, there was a soft tap at the door.

Lillian opened the door to Tobias Wellington, smiled and waved him in. 'It's very good of you to spare the time, Tobias. I shan't keep you long, I promise, but I need the advice of someone like yourself.' She patted the back of a comfortable chair.

'Happy to oblige, my dear Lillian.' He sat down. 'I do hope you're not going to tell me you're bankrupt,' he said, jesting.

'Of course not, my dear.' She sat opposite him, her desk between them. 'I'll come straight to the point. I know how busy you gentlemen of the City are, but I've a new project and I want your opinion.'

'Is that all?' He smiled, with evident relief. 'I thought you might perhaps have had it in mind to scold me over the voluptuous Rebecca.'

'Of course not. I'm much older than you, my dear, and have seen love lost and won many times over. I can only hope that you find the happiness you seek with your mistress without encumbering your marriage. You will not be the first gentleman to have fallen in love with one of my girls.'

'How I love coming into this house, my dear! You are doing a great service to the upper level of society who must be discreet in affairs of the heart. Please, if I can advise you in any way, it will be my pleasure.'

Catching a certain look in his seductive dark eyes, Lillian felt a tingling inside her crêpe-de-Chine underwear that she had not experienced in a long time. She hoped he would not notice her blush. 'Now, then, to business.' She leaned forward. 'Wining and dining are on my mind. Intimate dinner parties for gentlemen of the City who would rather not leave this house until dawn has broken.'

He tilted his head. 'Gentlemen's relish,' he murmured, not taking his eyes off hers. 'How clever.' He leaned a little closer too. 'Of course, I may only take up such an enchanting offer should my family be in the country for a weekend.'

'Understandably. But what of your colleagues?'

'They will be bursting at the seams, my dear.'

'Thank you, Tobias. Your passion does you credit. I had it in mind that you would either reject the idea out of hand or—'

'In your company I could not reject any idea so easily.' Still he held her gaze. 'I give you my wholehearted support and shall indeed pass on this good news to my trusted friends and colleagues.' He raised an eyebrow. 'I trust that my old acquaintance, Rebecca, will not be returning?'

'You trust right, sir.' Lillian was enjoying the flirtation. 'Am I to presume that she and your good self are no longer a story?'

'You are, madam. I have seen to it that she shall have a roof over her head for twelve months. She is very gifted and will, I am sure, make her own way in the world.'

'And the girl from Brick Lane?'

'In my diary and no more. I have said goodbye long since.'

'Very wise,' said Lillian, impressed. She stood up, a clear signal that this business meeting was over. 'The gentlemen's dining room will be ready in a few weeks. Should you find, say, half a dozen trusted associates – or a few more – drop a note through the letter-box naming a day that suits you.'

'And if, at the dinner table, the numbers exceed the girls available?'

'Tobias, I have twenty girls on my list.'

'And should there be one-and-twenty gentlemen,

must I be the one to spend a cold night in my own bed?'

'I'm not sure I understand, my dear,' said Lillian, all innocence. 'Whatever are you suggesting?'

'I think you know, and your answer is appreciated.' He reached out his hand to take hers, then gently kissed her fingertips.

'My dear Tobias,' purred Lillian, 'I think I am a little *too* mature for a handsome young devil. I could not possibly add my name to the list.'

He pulled her close to him, laid a light hand on her buttock. He trailed a finger across to her thigh, then kissed her lips. 'You are a very beautiful woman, Lillian.' Kissing her again, this time with a touch more passion, he squeezed the top of her leg and very slowly pushed his warm hand into her groin, massaging gently. She instinctively opened her legs a fraction. Stroking her lips with the tip of his tongue he gazed into her soft hazel eyes. He pressed his lips to hers once more, moved his hand between the soft fleshy part of her legs and slid a finger up and down until the silky material of her gown grew warm. Slowly inching her skirt up he slipped a hand inside the leg of her silk drawers and squeezed until she begged with her eyes for more. 'Women are like wine,' he whispered. 'The longer they are left lying in the dark the more they improve.'

He pushed a finger inside her and slid it to and fro while smothering her neck with kisses. Then he eased them both towards the closed door of the snug, pressed her against it and lifted her skirts. He pulled aside her silk undergarments and, using his leg to ease hers further apart, drove himself slowly inside her. She could feel him burning hot and throbbing as she stretched her legs wider, moaning with rapture. Still he teased her, moving rhythmically, in and out, evidently resisting the urge to quicken and have it over too soon. But even he, the man of many women, could not control himself once Lillian turned the tables and seized his erection with hot spasmodic gripping. Her eyes pierced his soul and her smile screamed seduction.

'Temptress . . .' He groaned, thrusting himself hard inside her and, with the lack of control of an adolescent, he flowed as he had not flowed before.

The climax over, the throbbing easing, he withdrew slowly and held her tight until their breathing slowed. 'My God,' he murmured, 'that was unbelievable. Your timing, my dear, is exquisite.'

'I'm so pleased you think so,' gasped Lillian. She eased herself out of his arms and let her gown fall back into place. 'They say the unexpected is the most rewarding.'

'Indeed,' gasped the young man, twenty-five years her junior. 'Indeed, indeed.'

She looked into his face. 'And there must be no talk of love or passion or loyalty between us.' She could hardly believe what she had let happen. She could hardly believe that this tall, handsome young man had fucked her.

'Absolutely,' he said. 'Absolutely never to happen again.' Dressed properly, he gave her a hint of a bow.

'I don't know what came over us but, my dear Lillian, it was quite, quite wonderful.'

'You flatter me, Tobias.' She looked at him with a certain glint in her eye and he looked back with the same in his. Before they could say another word they were in each other's arms again. This time, they used the thick beautiful floor rug.

Sitting in the kitchen, waiting for Lillian to come down and tell her how the meeting had gone, Polly was snoring. The house was extraordinarily quiet, but then, the walls of these old houses on the square had been built to be soundproof. The sound of the knife-grinder's machine outside, however, brought her sharply to her senses. She checked the clock and realised that she had been asleep for nearly an hour. She brushed the creases from her skirt and splashed cold water on to her face.

The sound of the front door opening and closing mystified her. If this was Mr Wellington leaving so late after their meeting, she could only imagine that it had gone well. She wondered if Lillian had made it all sound so profitable that he had seen an opportunity to be a business partner. With Mr Wellington one could never tell. To her mind he was a peculiar sort: he had a penchant for working-class girls when he could easily afford to go to a West End establishment and bed a high-class prostitute. If he hadn't realised that such places existed, he wasn't as worldly as she imagined.

What Polly and most other people didn't know was

that Tobias Wellington had working-class blood in his veins. His family roots were in the East End. His parents had worked their fingers to the bone to build up a trade in men's tailoring. Although the house in which he lived at the time he had met his wife Grace had been fairly grand, his parents had been born and bred in East London. Before their success in business, his mother had worked from dawn to dusk, cleaning dusty old offices while his father had filled every waking hour with labour in a small tailor's shop, first as a machinist and then as a pattern-cutter. Their ambition was to give their one and only son a decent education.

Encouraged by his wife, Tobias's father had rented a small room above a solicitor's office, where there was just enough space for a cutting table and sewing-machine. Gradually his small, select clientele had grown until he had gained a reputation as *the* bespoke tailor for gentlemen. Ten years later he was running a prosperous factory in Aldgate.

Now Polly went into Lillian's snug to find her resting in her favourite armchair, eyes closed and smiling faintly. She went to the window, peered out and caught sight of Mr Wellington in the square. Polly turned from the window to her surrogate mother and let out sigh. 'You've let 'im cock yer, 'aven't you? Him of all people to set you off again. You need your brains tested as well as your fanny.'

Eyes still closed, Lillian flicked her fingers towards the door, indicating to Polly that she should leave the room. 'Go and have a lie-down, dear, you work so hard.' She spoke as if she had had ten glasses of sherry.

'He's bin in this room for over an hour! Is he gonna pull in some clients for us? What did he fink of the dinner parties? Was he any good? Is his winkle the size of a pea-pod? Did he say he'd come to one of the dinner parties?'

'Yes,' drawled Lillian, half asleep, 'and he thought it an excellent idea, and yes, and no, and yes. Now go away and let me sleep.'

'Did you ask about Rebecca? Is she coming back?'

'No. He's not seeing her any more. He's given up all women – except for coming here, of course.'

'How much did you charge 'im?'

Lillian wiggled her fingers again and brushed the air with her hand. 'Off you go, dear.'

'You never bleedin' well did charge 'im, did yer? We're not runnin' a charity, you know. Look at you. It's nearly killed yer! You should 'ave said no!' There was a quiet pause as Polly stood, hands on hips, staring into Lillian's serene and smiling face. 'Are you gonna open yer eyes or not?'

'No. Go away.'

'I'll go away and make out a bill. He was wiv you for over an hour. I'll knock on the door and ask him for the money.'

'Polly . . .' There was a hint of warning in Lillian's voice. 'Don't overstep the mark, dear. Close the door quietly behind you.'

Polly marched across the room, grabbed the door handle and murmured, loudly enough for Lillian to hear, 'Disgustin' behaviour for a woman of your age. Should be ashamed of yerself.' A loud slam followed. Even this did not ruffle Lillian's feathers. She was not going to let go of this moment for any one or any thing. It had been an experience quite out of this world. Tobias in his passion, had whispered that she was the queen of all queens. Chuckling quietly she recalled his fare-ye-well compliment – *From now on I shall call you Queenie. My Queen from across the Green . . .*

Back in the kitchen, Polly was not only angry with Lillian but worried for her. If Tobias Wellington had broken two hearts, and there might have been more, he could easily hurt the woman Polly had come to love as a mother, the woman who had taken her in and saved her from going down the road so many had travelled: the road to impoverishment and vulnerability. She poured herself a glass of water and wondered how she could stop the affair before Lillian was hurt. It had taken her years to get over the rejection of Sir Robert, the man she had loved deeply and believed she would eventually marry.

She opened the door of the range, pulled up a chair and sat watching the glowing coals, thankful that the maid was not there, chopping vegetables or dicing meat for their evening meal. She glanced out of the window in the direction of the house across the green, and felt a surge of anger. She was in two minds about whether to march over and give Mr Wellington a piece of her mind. Then she caught sight of the newspaper boy and went to the door before he could ring the bell. His fresh, freckled face grinning at her softened her mood.

'I've got a nice present for yer, mush,' he said. 'The paper bill.'

'Very generous, I'm sure.' She took the newspaper from him, spurned his cheeky wink and closed the door. Then she turned to the front page and saw a small headline: 'Woman's Body Pulled Out of the Thames'. She went back to her chair by the glowing coals to read the reports.

Half-way through, Lillian came into the room. 'You shouldn't jump to conclusions, Polly. Mr Wellington and I were discussing business arrangements and no more.' Polly kept her eyes down.

'He is such a gentleman,' said Lillian, taking the coffee pot off the range. 'He thinks our idea – *your* idea – is a stroke of genius, and he is going to pass the word among his colleagues. Things are looking up, my dear.' She glanced at her ward while she poured her coffee. 'Something in the headlines to strike you dumb, dear?'

Polly slowly raised her eyes to Lillian's. 'It's Rebecca. They've pulled her out of the river.'

That afternoon, shocked by the news of Rebecca's suicide, Polly felt the need to get away from the square and see her friend Harriet. As she walked along Jubilee Street towards Harriet's turning, she was crying – crying for Rebecca and questioning her own life as she never had before. Why had her own mother given her away at birth? Where was she now? Was she alive? And, most important of all, why hadn't she kept in touch with Lillian so that she could know how her own flesh and blood was faring? If her mother was alive, had she married later in life and had children? Did Polly have brothers and sisters? A family she could call her own?

Questions she had never needed to ask were filling her mind and she was seeing things differently. There was another side to the East End where she had grown up. Music-hall productions always showed noisy, jolly Cockneys with their hands on their hips hollering and shouting, never the abortionists, thieves, body-snatchers and hordes of prostitutes. Rebecca's suicide would either hit the headlines or be ignored, but since the Whitechapel murders, a spotlight had illuminated this tiny area of London, casting an exaggerated light on everything bad and leaving the ordinary good working-class folk in shadow.

In no time at all, Polly was on Harriet's doorstep thumping on the door. A stranger opened it, and Polly assumed she had come to the wrong house and was so disoriented that she was rendered incapable of speech.

'Did somebody attack you?' the woman asked. Her voice was soft and her expression sympathetic. 'Did you want to come in?'

Polly allowed the woman to guide her to the kitchen. Then Harriet's voice calling from the back yard brought a smile to her face. She was in the right house after all. 'Harriet?' she whimpered.

'Who is it, Alice?'

'It's me, Harriet, Polly!'

Coming into the kitchen drying her hands on a tea towel, Harriet was shocked to see her friend in this state. Never before had she shed a tear or showed sorrow. She held out her arms and Polly fell into them. 'Oh, Harriet,' she muttered, 'I feel that bad over this.'

'Over what? What's 'appened now?' Harriet guided her to Arthur's chair by the range.

'It's really awful. More awful than anyfing.'

A horrid sensation sped through Harriet. Was her friend here to break bad news? If so, only a tragedy involving Lillian would leave her in this state. She lowered her eyes, dreading what she was about to hear. ''As something 'appened to Lillian?'

'No. It's Rebecca. She chucked 'erself in the river! She's dead!'

Gripping the back of Arthur's chair, Harriet steadied herself. She looked at her sister and nodded towards the pot of tea just made.

'Everyfing tickety-boo?' Arthur had come in from the yard and was washing his hands in the sink. 'What d'yer think of our place, then, Poll? More cosy than Mary's 'ouse in Bow?'

'Polly's upset, Arfer. She won't be able to talk till she's 'ad a nice hot strong cup of tea.'

'Well, that's good 'cos it's why I've come in. Lovely bit of earth out there, Harriet. We'll 'ave the best runner beans growin' up them poles in the summer.'

'And tomatoes, eh?' said Alice. 'You *are* going to let me grow some up the back wall, eh?'

'Course I am. Bo not back yet?'

'No. She's gone to the grocer's as well as the 'ardware. I forgot to buy a chunk of suet for the spotty dog,' said Harriet, stroking Polly's hair. 'We're gonna 'ave to give you another tint, Poll. It's nearly all washed out.'

The room fell silent, a clear indication that they were going to have to address the bad news. Harriet was aware of this but, uncharacteristically, she couldn't find the right words. 'Polly brought some sad news, Arfer.'

'Oh, yeah?' he said. 'What's that, then, love?'

'One of – one of our girls, Rebecca. They pulled 'er out of the river.' Polly was trying not to cry. 'She said she was gonna throw 'erself in the river but we never thought she would. Not Becky. She ain't the type, is she, Harriet? No matter 'ow bad things are she wouldn't do that, but she did, and we could 'ave stopped it.'

'Oh, no,' said Arthur, resolutely. 'You won't ever stop someone from jackin' it in if that's what they want. Not once they've got it into their 'ead. No.' He glanced at Harriet and raised his eyebrows. 'At least she's out of her misery, eh?'

'But she wasn't miserable. She 'ad a little room he was payin' for and he was gonna keep 'er an' all. She never found out about the girl from Brick Lane. Only me and Lillian knew about that and we never said a word.'

'You're talkin' too fast for us, Polly,' said Arthur. 'What girl from Brick Lane?'

'The one he got in the family way. He paid for 'er to go into a little 'ouse as well but he never went to see 'er no more. She lives over Lime'ouse so Becky couldn't 'ave found out. Becky stays round Aldgate way wiv the theatrical lot. We never ever let on – I swear on my life.' Polly crossed herself.

'What was the girl from Brick Lane's name?' Harriet asked.

'I don't know! How am I s'posed to know that? Becky never knew nuffing about it. Only Lillian. Some of the men tell 'er everything. She's more like a bleedin' mind doctor at times, listenin' to all their carryings-on.'

'So why did your friend throw herself in the river?' said Alice.

''Cos he gave 'er up,' muttered Polly. 'I got that much out of Lillian. She and Becky 'ad a row 'cos of 'er seein' a client away from our place.' She looked at Arthur, as if he was the one she had to answer to. 'It wasn't Lillian's fault. How was she to know that Mr Wellington would drop Becky so he could still come over to us?'

'Someone should tell that nice wife of his about 'im,' said Harriet, angrily. She had heard enough to realise that Flora's so-called Prince Charlie and Mr Tobias Wellington were the same man. 'She's a lovely lady, young enough to get divorced and remarry. I've a mind to go and see 'er.'

'You'll do no such thing! In fact, from now on,

Harriet, you'll keep away from Lillian Redmond's place. It's a brothel when all's said and done. Never mind the goings-on. Suicide's against the law, apart from anything else.'

'Yeah – and so is nickin' a bit of fish 'ere and there.'

Arthur's stern face ended that line of thought. 'You've got enough to keep you busy!'

'Oh, stop it, you two,' whispered Alice. 'You shouldn't row now, not with your friend here and so upset.'

'It's all right,' said Polly. 'Arfer's right.' Then, looking around, she managed a smile. 'It is a nice place, Arfer. You've got it nice and homely. I wish Lillian would settle down and just live in that place or sell up and—' The sudden rat-a-tat on the street door stopped her short.

'That'll be Bo back from her errand,' said Alice, and went to let her in. Bo hadn't wanted to go out by herself but Harriet had insisted, saying it was an important step forward. The wretched girl had been too terrified to go out into the yard for fear of her oppressors.

When Alice opened the door the fourteen-year-old was trembling and smiling – she had made the purchases and had the change gripped in the palm of her hand. She was quite pale, but with an expression in her eyes that none of them had yet seen. It was a look of triumph.

She charged past Alice and through to the kitchen. 'You's won't never guess!' she blurted, standing before the man of the house. 'Yous won't.'

'How many goes do we get, Bo?' Arthur laughed. 'And take your bleedin' cap off when you come inside.'

Bo snatched it off her head, threw it up in the air and caught it. 'I saw 'em. I walks right past and they looks at me but they never knew it was me!'

Polly wondered where this person had come from. The voice didn't match the short back and sides or the clothes. It looked like a boy but talked and acted like a girl. 'Funny sort of name,' she said, looking from Bo to Harriet, puzzled. 'Someone's bruvver, are yer?'

Arthur chuckled, pulled his cap back on and left them to it. 'Fetch my cup of tea out into the yard, will you, Alice? It's all right for you women but I've got work to do.'

Settled round the small kitchen table with their tea, Harriet and Alice took it in turns to tell Polly all that had happened next door and how they had kidnapped Bo. Through it all the girl never said a word but kept her eyes on Polly's face, waiting to see if she was going to suggest they send her back. The one thing that Bo had learned in life was to watch silently. Watch and listen.

'You're lucky they never sent for the police,' said Polly, when she had heard the full story. 'Don't want them poking their noses in.' She sniffed and turned to Bo. 'Have you got anyfing on 'em?'

Frowning, Bo looked from Polly to Alice. 'I don't know what she means.'

'Take no notice,' said Harriet. 'She's just makin' certain we've covered our tracks.'

'No such thing,' snapped Polly. 'I asked because you need to 'ave a bargainin' point in case they do clock what you've done. A scar or summink from where they've cut you. That sort of fing.'

'They're too clever for that, Polly. Mind you, there are marks that might never go away, across 'er back where they whipped 'er. You could call them scars, I s'pose.'

'Well, there you are, then. Nuffing to worry about. Mind you, I wouldn't want 'em livin' next door to me. Ravin' lunatics! Never know what they might do next. Good job you ain't got a cat or they might tie it to a tree when you're out and—'

'Polly! Either brighten up or sod off!' Harriet had heard enough doom and gloom for one day. 'Now, then, I'm gonna knock up the spotty dog and put it in to boil then go out. Who's for coming up the People's Palace to find out about instructions?'

The three other women gazed at her, mystified. 'Instructions on *what*?'

'On whatever takes your fancy, Polly. Carpentry, joinery, dressmakin', tailorin', modellin' in clay, art. Oh, and wood carvin'.'

'Wood carvin'?' exclaimed Bo.

'What about typewritin'?' Polly was half interested.

'Yep. That an' all. So, what d'yer fink? Shall we go? Who's for it?'

Bo shot a hand in the air, her face radiant. 'Wood carvin', please!'

Harriet peered at her. 'That's not the sort of fing girls go in for, Bo. I know we cut yer 'air but don't go and forget what you are, will yer?'

'I can do it. I carves wood all the time. When I can. I uses me medal.'

'That thing on a bit of old ribbon? That ain't a bleeding medal!'

'No. It's a lock-picker. A boy give it to me. At the work'ouse. Showed me 'ow to pick a lock wiv it but I never uses it for that. I uses the point to scrape away at wood.'

Polly sighed. 'Well, if there's typewritin' classes, count me in. I'll need lessons on that if I'm to be Lillian's secretary. My 'andwriting's cop.'

'I'll show yous if you like,' murmured Bo. 'I'll show you what I can do.' She pushed her hand deep into the pocket of her breeches and pulled out a piece of wood she had been working on. 'The man from the timber yard down the turnin' give it to me.'

'Did he now? And when, may I ask, did he come sniffin' round 'ere?' Harriet didn't like the sound of this.

'He never. He never came. I wents down there 'cos I likes the smell of sawdust and that. There's a box of bits of wood . . .' she paused, remembering '. . . off-cuts. That's wot he calls them.' She relaxed and smiled. 'And I can 'ave a bit of wood when-ever I want 'cos they only goes on 'is fire.' Her fingers clenched around the wood as if it were a piece of treasure, and she looked coyly at Harriet. 'It's not finished. I've only carved the face. But it's gonna be a baby doll so I won't 'ave to cut curls or that.'

'Well, show us, then,' said Harriet, intrigued.

'It was meant to surprise you. The wood man said I could go back and he'd put by the right bits for a body and arms and legs. It will 'ave fingers and toes. And I can do it so the arms and legs move. It takes a long time but it'll be ready when you 'as your baby.' Bo uncurled her fingers to reveal the small, beautiful face of a doll. 'If you 'as a boy we can save it for when you 'as a girl.'

Harriet took it from Bo's pale thin hand and a lump came into her throat. 'It's – it's beau'iful.' She looked from the doll's head to Bo's face. 'I never knew . . .' she murmured, and cleared her throat. 'I never knew you was makin' this for me.' She placed an arm around the girl and hugged her. 'You're such a lovely person, Bo.'

'Am I?' came the whispered reply. 'But I'm from the work'ouse.'

'That's right, and you've proved it don't make no difference where any of us come from. 'Cos you're not only nice but you've got a special talent. I don't know anyone who can carve wood like this.' Harriet turned to Polly. 'What do you say, Poll?'

'I agree wiv yer. It's not where you come from but where you're goin'. Talking of which, are we gonna go to the People's Palace or not? This is my afternoon and evenin' off, so far as I'm concerned.'

'No clients today, then, Poll,' said Arthur, all knowing. 'Lillian's business a bit low, is it?'

'We never 'ave clients of a Saturday, Arthur, and if you fink about it, you'll know why.'

'Gotta be at home with the family?'

'In a way. Men don't like to feel repentant on a Sunday for what they did of a Saturday and are gonna do on a Monday.' Polly looked around at the others. 'Well, then? Are we goin' out or not?'

'We are. All four of us. But first fings first. I want a private word wiv you, Poll, in the front room. Won't take a minute.' With that, Harriet left the room and Polly followed her.

'Shut the door,' whispered Harriet, in the privacy of the bedroom. 'Now, listen, I'm sorry about Rebecca and I know it's a shock for yer but, well, there's something I'm gonna tell you, Poll, and you've got to promise me on my baby's life that you won't ever mention it again, not to me or anyone else.'

'I promise,' she said. 'But you don't 'ave to 'ave me swearin' on the baby's life. Leave the poor little soul out of it – it's not even in this lousy world yet.'

'No, all right, but that was just to let you know 'ow important it is that you keep this secret.' After a short pause, Harriet told her friend that Tobias Wellington was not only responsible for Rebecca's suicide but for making her good friend Flora pregnant, then leaving her to get on with it.

Of course, Polly was shocked and wanted confirmation. She asked question after question until she could really believe it. 'I know what I'd like to do to 'im,' was her final word.

'Well, you can't do anyfing and nor can I. We just

'ave to let 'im get away wiv it. If you tell Lillian I'll never forgive you, and nor will God.'

Polly turned away. 'Come on. Let's go and find out about typin' lessons. I fink I'm getting past working in a whore'ouse. If I could only persuade Lillian to turn it into something else – run some kind of business from there and get rid of all those lecherous men.'

'Never in a month of Sundays,' said Harriet, following her friend out of the room. 'Lillian's too set in 'er ways to change now. But you're not. You can do what you like. We all can, if we put our minds to it. A bit of education won't come amiss.'

'I s'pose not, but to tell the truth,' Polly grabbed Harriet's arm to stop her going into the kitchen, 'I'm not really in the mood for socialising. You go wivout me. I'll come another time.'

Harriet shrugged. 'If you're sure. But it might cheer you up a bit. Nuffing's gonna bring back Rebecca, Polly, no amount of grievin'.'

'I know, but it's not just that. I was thinkin' about things on the way over, about me and where I come from. I've never asked and Lillian's never told me so—'

'So what?'

'So I s'pose people fink I don't give a toss, but I do. It would be nice to know who my muvver was. Is. She could be alive and all right, for all I know.'

'I expect she is. Not in this country, though. You're gonna 'ave to save up if you want to go in search of 'er. She went to Germany with 'er mum and dad after she 'ad you. I thought Lillian would 'ave told you that. Mary told me ages ago. It's not the sort of fing you bring up, really, is it?'

'No, Lillian never said. So she was German, then? Is that wot you're saying?'

'By all accounts. 'Er grandparents emigrated over 'ere with 'undreds of others to work in the sugar refineries in Whitechapel. Lived around Aldgate in Little Germany. The Germans that came over weren't all poor. Your ancestors was middle-class merchants, be all accounts. You would 'ave been a bit of an embarrassment for 'em, Poll. Snobs, see – can't take a little bit of scandal in the family. You're better off wivout 'em.' She winked at her friend and smiled. 'Lillian's bin like a mother to yer so don't go upsettin' 'er now, eh? She thinks as much of you as she does of 'er own daughter, Lizzie.'

'But you can't blame me for bein' a bit inquisitive about where I'm from – can yer? You'd want to know, wouldn't yer?'

'Course I don't blame you. Get yerself an education and then go in search of 'em. Let 'em see what they've missed out on by not takin' you wiv 'em.'

'I could do that, you know. I've got a brain for figures and a lot more common sense than Lillian.'

'I know that and so does she. The world's your oyster, Poll. You've got no 'usband to answer to and no kids to fend for.'

'You don't 'ave to remind me. I'm well aware of that. Nearly thirty years old and still thought of as a girl.'

Harriet missed the touch of regret in her friend's voice. 'Well, there you are, then. You can do what you want. This is the twentieth century – we're out of the dark ages. It's a new world that's coming. We'll all 'ave this new electricity they're ravin' about in our places one day, you'll see. And my Arfer will 'ave 'is own little motor car. It's the age of change and not soon enough. And do you know what? I'm gonna get myself a profession. Somefing I can do from 'ome to make a few shillin's while I'm taking care of the baby. Dressmakin'.'

'Not a bad idea,' Polly said, thoughtfully. 'Come on, then. Maybe I'll come wiv you after all. But I doubt this People's Palace is for the likes of us. Too bloomin' posh. Anyway, I can't be long – Lillian'll be worried. Wonderin' where I've got to.'

'Well, that shows she loves yer, then, don't it? So stop bein' so downhearted and put a smile on yer face. Now, give us a hug.'

'Why?' Polly pulled back and peered at her.

''Cos I love you. We all do. Just don't get more cantankerous than me or I'll start actin' like a staid old married woman and give you another lecture.'

'Some chance,' chuckled Polly, opening her arms to her friend. 'It's a funny old world, innit?'

'No. It's you that's peculiar not the world.'

Arm in arm they went into the kitchen to find Arthur giving the girls a lecture on the workings of the great railway. They *appeared* to be all ears and mesmerised.

★　　★　　★

Harriet was surprised by all the buzz inside the grand building of the People's Palace in the Mile End Road and immediately drawn in. People from all classes were there and a fair share of Europeans too; men and women with a common goal, to advance their education or take up a new hobby. Bo lost no time in slipping into the woodcarving class. Harriet disappeared into the dressmaking room and Polly into the local-history lesson, since there was no class this evening for typing and book-keeping. Alice, having taken more time to consider all that was on offer, finally drifted into the wig-making and hairdressing group. Local history interested her but she didn't want to appear to be copying Polly. At first, she regretted her choice; this evening the talk and demonstration was on wig-making and the tutors in attendance were two older ladies. As it turned out, they caught and held the attention of the entire class.

Amid scholars and illiterates, Polly was enthralled. The old Yiddish gentleman with wispy silver hair, in a tired grey suit and a skull cap, had a voice to listen to for ever and all he said was spell-binding.

He began his lecture in the middle of the previous century when thousands of Europeans had emigrated to London. By 1891 twenty-five thousand Germans had settled in England, predominantly in the East End. Such was the concentration at one time around Aldgate that it had become known as Little Germany. In 1870 Leman Street had been commonly known as the high street of German London. The tenement houses had been inhabited by several thousand of these hard-working foreigners.

The first wave of immigrants had tended to be from the middle classes, merchants and artists who had been lured to England with the Coronation of George I, the first Hanoverian monarch who had come to the throne in 1714. Then, between 1840 and 1900, due to a series of failed harvests, millions more had packed their bags in search of a new life. Most had been bound for the USA and had travelled the northern steamer route from Hamburg to Hull then overland to Liverpool and across the Atlantic to America. Others had travelled to the Channel ports, then on to Liverpool via London where many stayed as they were too poor to afford the onward passage. But thousands, including the Communists Karl Marx and Friedrich Engels, had deliberately sought a fresh start in London, attracted by the capital's religious and political tolerance.

In and around Whitechapel and Aldgate the low value of German labour had forced new arrivals into the sugar refineries where conditions were dire. They worked in a vast cellar lit by small windows at pavement level. The heat was oppressive, and an oily steam, thick and vaporous, permeated the atmosphere.

But not all was sweat, toil and labour. Numerous German bands had livened up the streets during the day and evenings, and there was an underclass of thieves, swindlers, pimps and prostitutes. According to the speaker, the majority of his countrymen were honest and hard-working – tailors, bakers, hairdressers, waiters, bankers and musicians. The flourishing community had its own church, St Georgeskirche, in Little Aalie Street, and a German hospital in Dalston. The immigrants formed social and football clubs, and opened a seaman's mission in East India Dock Road that played host to thousands of German sailors. One of whom had fathered Polly.

By the 1890s the Little Germany of the East End had dispersed as the sugar-refining industry collapsed. Many had made their way back to their homeland or set off for the USA. Some stayed in Bethnal Green, Stepney and Hackney, while others chose nearby West Ham and Canning Town.

The speaker talked for two hours, and the sense of wonder in the room had a notable effect on Polly – especially since she had learned only that day that her mother was German and might easily have been among those who had had to make their way home after the closure of the sugar refinery. If Polly's mother had been single when she became pregnant, she would have had no choice but to give up her baby. And who better to trust the child to than Lillian Redmond, a lovely, kind woman who had also at a tender age been smitten then deserted by a German lover. A sailor, no less.

Filing out of the Palace with hordes of others who had enjoyed their evening, Polly linked arms with Alice, who was looking flushed. 'How'd you get on, then, Alice? Good, was it?'

'I liked it. I didn't think I was going to when I first went in but I did. I'm going back on Tuesday evening, and next Saturday, and the Tuesday after that.' She glanced at Polly. 'Did you enjoy your talk on local history?'

'I'll say I did. Had to sit next to a woman whose armpits reeked but I kept me face turned the other way. It was still in the air but I got used to it. I can't tell you how good this fresh air smells.'

'Oh dear, that wasn't very nice for you. I had a lovely time. We can all tell each other about our talks when we get back, can't we? That way we'd be learning a lot more.'

'Depends.' Polly grinned. 'Your sister don't look none too pleased.' Harriet had obviously been one of the first out for she was waiting by a lamp-post. 'Look at that face. Could wilt a bleedin' rose.'

'You don't think she came out early because she was bored, do you?'

'Probably. But the strings of my 'eart ain't gonna vibrate over it. I've enjoyed meself and she's not gonna spoil fings.'

Hanging on to Alice's arm, Polly stepped up the pace a little. 'Dropped a shillin' and only found a farthin', 'ave you, Harriet?'

'What a bleedin' waste of time that was. I'd 'ave bin better off stoppin' at 'ome and sittin' round the fire with my Arfer. Silly drawers in there ain't got a soddin' clue. Said nuffing about pattern-cuttin' or how to machine bones into a bodice or anyfing that's bleedin' useful.'

'Oh, that wasn't right,' said Alice. 'Didn't you say something?'

'Course I never. Not my place. The other soppy cows liked it enough. Bleedin' embroidery and fancy stitchin'. As if that wasn't enough she showed us how to hand stitch. Smockin'! With silk and gold thread! This is Stepney, not Hammersmith Terrace!'

'What's Hammersmith got to do with it?'

'It's where she and all the other spoilt rich live! Mrs la-de-da Halliday-Sparling!'

'I've 'eard that name before.'

'Course you 'ave. She was May Morris before she got married. Go and take a look at the family shop in Oxford Street. Just because she's William Morris's daugh'er don't mean to say she can come down 'ere and tease us wiv her silks and gold threads.'

Roaring with laughter, Polly took her friend's arm. 'You're jealous, Harriet Smith.'

'Harriet *Dean*!'

'Sorry, Mrs *Dean*, I meant no 'arm. But you are jealous all the same. You'd love to work with fine materials and you know it.'

'Who wouldn't?' she snapped. 'And where's Bo got to?'

'She won't be long, eh?' Alice, always the peace-maker, offered both women a gentle smile. 'She never goes out. I expect she's making the most of it.'

'Take no notice of yer sister, Alice. She loves to be in a snit. Ain't that right, Harry old girl?' grinned Polly, using her mock-posh voice. 'And because of that she don't always fink straight. Best class for 'er, that was, if she only thought about it.'

'About *what*, Polly?'

'About starting up a little homebound business. Doll-makin'? Bo's the genius at carvin', Alice ain't complained about the talk on wig-makin', and you've just been listenin' to a member of a famous arts and craft family on fine stitchin'. Dolls' dresses?'

'Talk of the devil,' smiled Alice, 'here she comes.'

Running towards them, her face flushed and green eyes shining, Bo was clutching a piece of wood carving. 'He said I was talented!'

'We already knew that. What 'ave you got there?' Harriet held out her hand. Then, on seeing the intricate piece of carving, she gasped. 'Bleedin' hell! You never did that in a couple of hours, did yer?'

'I did. Teacher give me a proper tool to borrow and I can use it again when I goes back. He said I was a star pupil. He said I can go back three times every week. He said—' She stopped short, her eyes wide. Lowering her voice to a whisper, she said, 'This is 'im.'

Harriet turned her head and let out a low whistle. She was impressed, and so were Polly and Alice. John Seymour was tall, blond and blue-eyed, with a lovely smile. 'Evening, ladies, I was hoping I might catch you. Which of you is Harriet?'

'I am,' croaked Harriet, her eyes fixed on his smiling face. 'Why?'

'Your brother has the makings of a genius. Did you know that?'

'Course I did. Why d'yer fink I fetched 'im?'

'We're gonna form a little business venture,' said Polly, getting in quick. 'Doll-makin'. I'm to be the business adviser and book-keeper, Harriet's to make the clothes with fine materials and guidance from May Morris and—'

'And you're going to make the wigs,' the young man cut in, his eyes on Alice's face.

'How did you know that?' she asked, her eyes lighting up. 'He must be a mind-reader,' she said to Harriet.

'No. I saw you earlier, going into the class.' He offered Alice his hand, 'I'm John Seymour. Pleased to make your acquaintance. Your choice of course was excellent. Wigs will never go out of fashion. Sadly, not many women are blessed with lovely hair.' He was admiring hers openly. 'I shall look forward to seeing you again. All of you.' He turned to Bo and gave her a gentle slap on the shoulder. 'Keep up the good work – and the wood-carving too.' He gave her a wink and walked away.

Never before had any of these women been speechless, yet here they were unable to utter a word. It was the smiling Bo who broke the spell. 'I finks he took a shine to you, Alice.'

'Don't be daft.' She giggled and blushed.

Having crossed the Mile End Road at the Whitehorse Lane junction, Polly said her goodbyes and, in a much lighter mood than she had set out earlier that day, made her way home. In no time at all she had arrived in the square and was pulling on the bell of Lillian's house. Expecting the house maid to open the door, since she was not there to do it, she was a touch surprised to see Lillian.

'Lazybones lyin' down again, is she?' Polly went inside, unpinning her bonnet.

'It's Saturday, Polly. They're entitled to free time. And you know they prefer to be invisible.'

'True,' she said, and unbuttoned her ankle-length coat. 'They're a married couple, after all. I s'pose the less they see and mix wiv us the better, really. Can't be all that much fun livin' in.'

'They don't complain,' said Lillian, leaning against the closed door, arms folded. 'They keep themselves to themselves and that suits us both.'

'I never said otherwise.'

'Where have you been, Polly? I've been worried.'

Polly held out her arms. 'I'm sorry. I never meant to worry yer.'

Lillian hugged her. 'You must be hungry,' she murmured.

'I'm not but I will be. Wouldn't mind a drop of sherry.'

Lillian pulled back and studied Polly's face. 'Well, then, let's go into the kitchen and you can tell me where you've been and who's put the light into your eyes.'

'Not the kitchen, your snug. You get the drinks and I'll go up and light the fire. I've got fings to say and I want us to be nice and cosy.'

'That sounds mysterious, but since you're smiling I'll assume it's not something that will upset me. I'll bring up a snack for both of us. Cold mutton and crusty bread?'

'Perfect. Don't forget the mint sauce.'

Once the fire and the oil lamps were lit, Polly made herself comfortable in an armchair, her legs curled under her. She was looking forward to their time together. She and Lillian had always been close but their relationship had tended to err on the side of detachment when it came to the personal side of their lives. Quips and witticisms had been a shield, and she was only just realising it. Lillian had said, more than once during the past weeks, that something was in the air, about to happen, and that it had caused her to have disturbed nights. Maybe this was it. After a lifetime of living together in this house, they were going to have to confront the truth. Events had brought them to this moment and Polly wasn't sorry. The talk on the German immigrants had touched a chord in her. She wanted to know if her mother had had to travel back to Germany alone or with her family – her parents . . . Polly's grandparents.

'Did you go to see Harriet?' asked Lillian, arriving with the tray of refreshments and pushing the door shut with her heel.

'Where else would I go? She's the only friend I've got – well, was the only friend. Now that I've met her sister, Alice, I've got two. Then there's fourteen-year-old Bo who seems to 'ave taken to me.'

'Bo?' said Lillian, easing herself down on to the sofa. 'What kind of a name's that?'

'Well, it started out as Bony, 'cos she was born all

skin and bone in the workhouse. Then it changed to Bonny when Harriet and Alice rescued 'er from two lesbos who was torturin' 'er. Then Arfer said change it to Bo 'cos Bonny's a girl's name and they've cut 'er hair off and dressed 'er like a boy so's not to be recognised by the witches next door.'

'Goodness,' murmured Lillian, handing Polly her plate. 'Rescuing is one thing but living next door to female torturers is rather dark. Are you sure Harriet wasn't pulling your leg?'

'No. I saw Bo wiv my own two eyes. She shares a room wiv Alice, Harriet's sister.'

'I didn't realise she had a sister. She's never mentioned it, and neither has Mary Dean.'

'Well, then, that begs a question, don't it? How comes you never asked 'er if she 'ad a family? Poor cow 'ad to come from somewhere. We all come from somewhere, after all. Take me, for instance . . .'

'Pour yourself some sherry and fill my glass to the top. I've a feeling I'm going to need it.'

'We both are,' said Polly.

Lillian emptied her glass in one swallow. 'Well, then, Polly, here we are. I suppose we'd best get this over with.'

'Get what over with?'

'Well, I imagine after my little session with Mr Wellington and then your reading that dreadful piece of news, you have little desire to stay on in this house. Am I right?'

'No, you ain't. But Mr Wellington is part of why I want to have a little chat.'

'There's no need, I assure you,' said Lillian. 'It was a flash of passion and no more than that. It will not be repeated. I'm too wise to lose control twice.'

'I should reckon so. Anyway, it wasn't that either. Well, not exactly. But I do want you to know what kind of a rotter he is. And to do that I've gotta break a confidence. But I think it's right that I do – but you 'ave to promise me on the Bible that you'll never, ever, repeat it.'

'Polly! Are you telling me that you don't trust my word?'

'Of course I trust yer, but this is very important. Someone would be devastated if they ever found out what I'm to tell you.' She lowered her eyes. 'We don't want another suicide on our conscience, do we?'

Lillian refilled her glass. 'These things happen, Polly. A day doesn't pass without a death or two being reported. Suicide, murder, accident, illness – it's all very sad, whatever the cause. But, yes, Rebecca's end is particularly upsetting for more reasons than one.'

Polly popped a piece of bread into her mouth. 'Mr Wellington is the man who made Harriet's friend Flora pregnant then walked out on her.'

Silence filled the room until Lillian managed to say, 'The girl from Brick Lane is Flora? Harriet's friend? No, Polly, you must be mistaken.'

'It is. By all accounts, Flora doesn't know that 'e lives in these parts or that 'is name is Wellington. She only knew 'im as Prince Charlie and he told 'er he lived in a posh part of town – Westminster, I fink she said.'

'Well, then, what on earth makes you think that it's our Tobias?'

'*Your* Tobias, not mine, thank you very much.'

'You know what I mean.'

'Harriet put two and two together. I can't remember the details but it's true.' She stared into Lillian's face. 'It's real.'

'I see.' Lillian sighed. 'Well, let's hope Harriet doesn't deem fit to bring the girl here, visiting. That's all we need, to have her storming over the square and telling all to his wife.'

'There's no reason for her to come 'ere. Why would she? I just wanted you to know what kind of a man he is, that's all. And there's another fing, was my mum a German?'

Caught off-guard, Lillian could do no more than gaze at her ward.

'That's somefing else I learned today. Harriet told me. But only because I mentioned it. She never saw it as a secret or anyfing. Just somefing that wasn't talked about. As if I wouldn't want to know. As if it would upset me.'

'And does it?'

'No, Lillian, it don't. But I just need to know a bit more about 'er. What was she like? Was she pretty, or plain like me? And what about my dad? I must 'ave one somewhere. Who was he? What was he like? Did they love each other? Was he a German as well and did they both go back to their own country?'

'I suppose Harriet was bound to break it to you

one day. You found her in one of her high-handed moods no doubt.'

'No, I never. She was normal. More normal than normal, in fact. Sad about Rebecca but too worried over other people who've had a worse time of it to break 'er heart. It was me who raised it. Rebecca going like that did somefing to me – 'ere all lively and 'igh and mighty one day and wiped out the next. Like we took the rubber ourselves and polished 'er out of our picture.'

'She wiped herself out, and I can't say I'm surprised. She was a born actress – her parents worked in music halls and were both gifted, the mother a singer and her father a musician. If Rebecca threatened to end her life once she threatened it a dozen times. In the end she probably thought she was giving the best dramatic performance of her life in throwing herself into the river over a lost love.'

'Sayin' it is one thing, doin' it is somefing else. She must 'ave felt terrible knowin' she'd never see summer again.'

'She wouldn't have thought that far ahead. She probably had an audience and acted out a part in a drama that had not been fully written. Rebecca did not think of consequences, ever. You may trust me on that, Polly. I do get to know my girls quite well.'

'You mean she expected someone to jump in and pull 'er out?'

'No. Like I said—'

'She wouldn't 'ave thought that far,' said Polly, finishing the line for her. 'You could be right.'

'I am. Trust me. It was almost ordained that she'd
do something like this. Ordained by herself. Throw
mud at the wall enough times and eventually it will
stick.'

Then Polly asked quietly if Mr Wellington had
mentioned it, if he'd seen it in the papers. And if
he had, what kind of a person was he to come over
and carry on as if nothing had happened. Lillian put
her straight on that and in no uncertain terms. He
was, after all, a client, and the girls working at the
House had been briefed enough times about staying
within the boundaries and not getting involved with
any of the men outside business. Tobias Wellington
hadn't seen it in the papers – even he was not so
callous as to be uncaring about something so tragic.
Polly accepted this and half apologised for thinking
the worst.

'All of that aside,' said Lillian, 'let's talk about you.
Or, rather, your real mother and father. I shall be
breaking my promise to your mother, but I feel it is
right that you know the truth.'

'Go on, then.' Polly was all ears.

'They were both German. Ziglinda, your mother,
worked in the same house as myself, some thirty-
odd years ago. We were in the kitchens, she along-
side Cook and me. I scrubbed floors, your mother
scrubbed vegetables. We became close friends. She
knew I had got myself in the family way and slipped
extra little food parcels into her pocket for when I
woke hungry in the night.'

'You shared the same room, then?'

'We did. A tiny room with hardly any space between our narrow beds. And before you ask if our employers were short of space, the answer is no. It was a huge house in Fitzroy Square but they were an uncaring family. Bankers and politicians.'

'Were they 'orrible to you?'

'They might have liked to think so. But we showed one mask to them and another when we were by ourselves. We learned much in that house and we ate well. Moneyed people are not necessarily clever, my dear. They just like to think they are.'

'And my dad?'

'A German sailor who gave up the life to work in the sugar refineries once he'd met Ziglinda in a tavern. We'd gone out for the evening and had a lovely time. By then I had had Lizzie, who was being looked after by your grandmother. They fell in love but the family had to go back to Germany when the refineries closed down. Your parents weren't married when you were born and it was thought best for you if I brought you up as my own child. By then I had met my sweetheart, Sir Robert. Not long afterwards he set me up in this house. The rest is history.'

'But you must 'ave kept in touch?'

'No. That was the bargain struck between us. We thought it best at the time if all ties were severed. Your mother entrusted you to my care. We were very good friends – close.' Lillian swallowed. 'I suppose you'll want to find them?' she said, hoping Polly would say no.

'One day, but not just yet. When I'm in the mood for it and when I've saved enough for the boat trip.'

'Well, I'm relieved you're not going to run away to find them, Polly. And when you're ready, I hope you'll allow me to come with you. I'd love to see my German friends again.'

'Course you'll come wiv me. You owe me that much.' She grinned. 'You're me muvver, ain't yer?'

'Broad Cockney again, my dear? Harriet's family must have made an impression.'

'Aha,' laughed Polly, 'that's where you're wrong. Her sister, Alice, was brought up in South London with an aunt and uncle who like to think of 'emselves as middle class. Lower middle class, granted, but middle class all the same. Alice talks nice. You'd be proud of 'er.'

'Oh dear,' said Lillian, mischievously, 'I suppose that means Harriet will be bringing her over to show her off.'

'That'd be all right, wouldn't it?'

'Providing she knows what sort of a business we run and providing Harriet does not bring her other friend here – the girl from Brick Lane. On that I stand firm.'

'Fair enough. Soon said as mended. I won't mention Flora again.'

'Good. Now, tell me about this girl who is being passed off as a boy and who's been tortured by two lesbian neighbours. It sounds better than a novel.'

'Oh, and that's not all. Us girls – me, Harriet, Bo and Alice – went along to the People's Palace. We loved it and we're goin' back. I'm gonna take up the study of local history, as well as typewritin' and book-keepin'. What d'yer say to that, then?'

'And Harriet?'

'Sewin' in gold thread and silks. Which is somefing else we need to talk about. I've changed my mind about this place bein' used as a restaurant with sleepin' accommodation. I fink it'd be too much work and you might get the authorities pokin' their noses in.'

Lillian's face brightened. 'My thoughts entirely. It all sounds like too much work, in the end. I would rather carry on and let things take their own course. If we stop making money we can sell this house and move into a smaller one. If we continue as we are, we'll not starve.'

'Good, because the rooms we don't use could be put to use, a sewin' room or a wig-makin' room, or a room where people who like to write or paint could come along . . .'

Lillian stretched out her legs. 'I thought there would be a sting in the tail. Go on, break it to me gently.'

'I'm thinkin' of an arts and crafts school.'

Lillian pressed her lips together and Polly could see she was trying not to laugh. Then Lillian said, 'It sounds a lovely idea but a little too ambitious. We're in the heart of the East End of London, not the West End or Bloomsbury where artists and writers prefer to gather.'

'That's where you're wrong. Them sort of people love to come into this area. You should get out more. Go to a few lectures. Come with me to one of the classes. You're never too old to take up a hobby, you know.'

'I'm sure you're right, but I've realised that I'm too tired to start using my brain for anything other than trying to keep this little business of mine afloat. It's enough, Polly.'

'So you won't consider turning it into a crafts school?'

'No, dear. But who knows? Once I am with the angels, *you* might. Nothing would surprise me, these days. Nothing. We may well see intellectuals and artists moving in to soak up the salt-of-the-earth atmosphere in the East End. Only time will tell.' She glanced at Polly and raised an eyebrow. 'And God help *us*, who are the salt-of-the-earth, the inhabitants, should that ever come about.'

'Stop bein' a snob. You're surrounded by rich people in this square and you don't seem to mind that. Especially not since one or two are good customers.'

'Yes, but sadly the day will soon be upon us when they make an exodus into better parts of town. Another grand house is to be converted into flats for academic students. The owner has caught on to the trend and will add his name to the list of greedy landlords who know when the time is right to line their pockets.'

'Oh, and you wouldn't, I s'pose? You wouldn't do the same fing to get rich? You'd make four flats out of this place and not only coin it but own a property that'd go up and up in price. Greedy landlords are always on the lookout.'

'I would never have this house altered. Never. It is

the House of Assignation for gentlemen of the City and that is what it shall remain as long as I live. And I intend to live for a very long time.' The smile was back on her face.

'Dirty cow. I know what you're thinkin' about. Good, was he?'

'Yes . . . but not as good as me.'

7

Four months later

━━━━◆◆━━━━

Now seven months pregnant, Harriet had every reason to feel exhausted after a day on her feet, packing soap into boxes at the factory. But she and Arthur could not afford for her to give up work yet. She had been collecting things for when the baby arrived and had taken up Flora's offer to borrow her baby's crib and clothes. Bo had offered to work in the markets as a porter, but it had already been decided that she had to have a qualification to be independent in the world when the time came.

Once again, their faithful friend Larry had come to their aid. Having heard the story from Arthur, he had made it his business to put in a word for Bo at a local cabinet-making factory where his cousin worked. Two weeks later, she was taken on as general dogsbody with a small weekly payment on condition she was given instruction and training. Larry had not divulged that she was a genius with a wood-carving tool. Had he done so they would have had her carving timber for a pittance and give her no time off to learn other skills.

Alice, following in her mother's footsteps, was now working in the local library, menial work with low wages but fulfilling. Her position included shaking and dusting the thousands of books and keeping them in strict order. She also had to dust and polish the furniture, in which she took great pride, including the long oak counter with a sliding glass top that held yards and yards of borrowers' tickets, the dark bookcases, which fanned out from all angles, the long tables in the reference library with seats at either side and, finally, the grand staircase with its metal balustrade and highly polished mahogany handrail curving upwards. She also regularly removed and washed the glass shades on the gas-lights.

During the telephonists' lunch break, Alice worked on the new wooden switchboard. Here she was happiest of all, talking to people from all walks of life and from all over London. The magic of the telephone for ordinary people was still a novelty. Not that ordinary people had much to do with it but here in the library they could watch as the plug on a lead was pushed in and out of the sockets and listen to a telephonist speaking to people they could not see.

Now that most homes had gas to light their rooms as well as oil lamps, there was more and more talk of electricity being commonplace within the next twenty or thirty years. However, unlike gas, electricity was feared and only wealthy Londoners were having their homes wired in readiness for the new commodity. Ordinary people would live in fear of being electrocuted, and the proof of their trepidation could clearly be seen by the way in which they watched Alice working the switchboard at a good distance from her.

Knowing that she sometimes had an audience boosted

Alice's confidence, as did the people who spoke to her on the other end of the line. She was treated like a proper clerical member of staff. Her ordinary accent was ideal for the work, as was her polite, easy manner. She loved coming into the building each morning and enjoyed the reverential hush throughout the day. The atmosphere of knowledge and learning, with the smells of books, leather and wax polish, was simply wonderful. She could not in her wildest dreams have wished for better employment. The chief librarian, a gentleman in his early thirties, was her favourite person there, and she looked forward to chatting to him over a cup of a cup of coffee during their break. His comment on her first day had struck a chord: 'Anyone can come in here and read themselves out of the gutter.'

His name, similar-sounding to her own, caused them both to laugh quietly at their first introduction. Alice and Alfred were also of a similar disposition and had led comparable early lives: they had been lonely children wandering through a bustling world. The only difference was that Alice had grown up in a relative's house where books were read as a family pastime, and Alfred in an orphanage where they had been non-existent. Each of them had strayed into a library for refuge, and each had discovered a thirst for books.

Outside the library, in the busy Whitechapel market, a stall sold food for horses and hay would drift into the library. Sweeping this away was Alice's favourite occupation. She likened it to having a foot in two different worlds and being at the centre of everything.

Added to her joy at working here, she could borrow books to take home, which encouraged not only her sister to join the library but Arthur and Bo too. Arthur could not get enough of Sherlock Holmes, and Bo was learning to read with Harriet's help. Her favourite story was Robinson Crusoe.

Alice had three books piled on the counter ready to take out when she caught the eye of the librarian, who was smiling at her. 'Who is it this time? One of the Brontës or Jane Austen?'

'Oh, these are not for amusement,' she smiled, 'more for learning, really.'

Alfred picked up the top book and read the title. '*Wax Dolls.*' He looked impressed. 'A hobby, is it?'

'Well, in a way, I suppose so.'

Alfred glanced at the other two books: *Wigs Through the Centuries* and *Dressmaking for Beginners*.

'Well, it's a variety,' he said, baiting her.

'There's a reason for it,' Alice told him. 'We're going to make dolls – with wax faces, not porcelain. We couldn't do that.'

'Wax, eh?' He scratched his head. 'Wouldn't last long, would they? Bit of sun and they'd melt.'

'Oh, not ordinary wax like they use in candle-making. And only the face would be wax. The body will be soft material and stuffed, but I think the arms and legs might be wood. My sister's found out where they make all kinds of wax. Our neighbour, a bee-keeper, told her where to go.'

'And the idea's to sell them, is it?'

'If it works out. Little Bo, my brother, carves wood.

He's very clever. And I think the carved face of a doll gets pressed into a plaster cast, then taken out, and when the plaster's set the melted wax is poured into it. And then when that's set, the face and the back of the head, which is in a different plaster cast, are tapped out, and then put together with a little bit more melted wax. As if it was glue. That's how it works, I think. I'm not sure which of us will paint the faces.'

'And who'll make the wigs?'

'Oh, well, that's me,' she said, smiling shyly. 'You know it would be me. I told you I'm learning at the People's Palace.'

'So you did. I was thinking of going along there m'self, as a matter of fact.'

'Oh, you should. They have all kinds of classes there, you know, and they give interesting talks.' Alice tidied her pile of books. 'My sister, Harriet, is studying how to make really small clothes for the dolls.'

'Do you know what I'm thinking, Alice?' said Alfred. 'I'm thinking that you should come along on one of the evenings when the Whitechapel Arts Group are in the reference library. They're mostly members of the art school but they don't just talk about art. They discuss the great poets and philosophers. I think you'd enjoy it.'

'Oh, but I don't belong there, and I'm not an artist or a poet.'

'Course you're an artist! Making dolls' wigs by hand? That's art.'

'But I'm only learning.'

'So are the members of the art group. They're

students mostly. Anyway,' he shrugged, 'it's something for you to mull over. They meet on the fourth Thursday of every month upstairs in that small room off the reference library.'

'Do you go in to listen to the discussions?' She was too modest to ask outright if he was a member of the group. 'With you being the chief librarian, I just thought you might go in . . . now and then?'

'No,' he said, shaking his head. 'I'd like to, of course I would, but no. I'd be an impostor, wouldn't I? Whereas you, well, you're a young lady of learning to do with the arts. And, well, you're not exactly like everyone else, are you? Coming from South London and not having a Cockney twang. I think they'd take to you, Alice.'

Alice blushed, and rubbed at a tiny bit of dirt on the polished counter. 'I'm not educated enough. Well, I've not had a proper education other than school. I've always read books, though. Even when I was a little girl. I loved reading.'

'Well, there you are, then. You'll be able to put your ha'pennyworth in. Self-educated?' He let out a low whistle. 'Not many can boast that.'

'Well, I wouldn't say educated . . .'

'I would.' Alfred lifted his eyes from her face and glanced at a young sailor who had come into the library and was looking at him. 'Well,' he said, 'off you go, then. It's five past four and you know you like to be out sharpish.'

'I do, but only because I like to have the tea ready when they all come in from work.'

Arriving at Alice's side, the sailor looked at Alfred with a pleading half-smile. His earnest expression was heartwarming. 'See you in the morning, then, Alice,' said Alfred, 'Don't be early or you'll put me in a bad light.' Had he not said this more than once before, Alice would have taken it seriously, but she was getting to know him now. She turned away and left.

'Hope I never interrupted anyfing, Mr Wood.'

'Course you never. Go on up to the Reading Room and I'll be with you in a tick.' This polite, illiterate lad was here for a favour. Alfred penned the love letters the sailor dictated to his girlfriend in Portsmouth. This was something he did for several young men who could not read or write, and to know that true love and romance did exist seemed to have helped him get over his own broken heart. Now it was a hobby.

Alone at the counter, Alfred gazed at the door after Alice had gone and enjoyed a few minutes imagining himself walking out with her. She had won a place in his heart, but he believed that the nine-year difference in their ages meant that he was too old to win her affection. He had not felt this way about a woman since the day his fiancée had jilted him after their three-year engagement.

The warm, calming atmosphere of the library, or the silent creativity of the minds of poets and authors past, had helped forge many romances within these oak-panelled walls. Almost adjoining the library was a curious little museum with a natural-history section that housed stuffed rabbits, weasels and birds. A number of glass jars stood on a long shelf with water and flowers in them, or a sprig of soft fruit. Alfred often wondered if the matchmaking that went on in the library had something to do with the natural-history museum – the birds and bees.

On arriving home, having called at the butcher's and greengrocer's, Alice was ready to put her feet up with a cup of tea and a biscuit, and was surprised to see Harriet already settled in the armchair with her feet on a footstool.

'Lucky cow,' grinned Harriet. 'I've just made a pot of tea.'

'You're back early,' said Alice, worried. 'Is everything all right?'

'Apart from a few twinges. The foreman told me to knock off early. He's gonna shorten my hours and keep quiet about it. See, Alice, that's what comes of workin' 'ard and bein' reliable.'

'You sound just like Mum.' Alice bent over and kissed her sister. 'I'm glad you're all right. I've bought some pigs' liver for tea. I got the butcher to cut it really thin and he gave me some breadcrumbs out of his machine. I'm gonna coat the liver in them and fry it with onions. Butcher said that's the best way.'

Harriet put down her teacup and covered her face. 'Just do it eh? Don't give me a bleedin' runnin' commentary.'

'I was only saying—'

'I know what you was sayin' – but don't! Baby's on

the bleedin' move again. Little cow won't settle down. And I've got wind. Pass me the bottle of gripe water.' Harriet winced.

'Did you want me to run round to the doctor for you?' said Alice, pouring the medicine on to a spoon. 'You do look a bit pale.'

'No. I ain't payin' another shillin' out for nuffing. This is normal. I remember Mum 'avin' wind when she was carrying our little bruvver.' She opened her mouth and allowed her sister to pour in two spoonfuls. 'That should do the trick. Don't start moanin' if I break wind. Gripe water's good for the heart but the more you take the more you fart.'

Alice pushed the tiny cork back into the bottle. 'You're funny you are. And it might not be a girl. You keep saying it is, but how do you know?'

''Cos of me dreams, that's why. I know the name as well now. Last night I dreamt Arfer came in after I'd given birth with a flower for me out of the garden. An iris.'

'Oh, Harriet, that's a lovely name.'

'It'll do.' Harriet pushed on her belly and let out a long, loud belch. 'Better out than in. Fink yerself lucky it never came out the other end.' She glanced at the clock on the mantelshelf. 'Bo's late.'

'No, she's not. Well, a quarter of an hour, maybe, but that's not late, Harriet. Don't go on at her, will you? She's nearly fifteen.'

'Who said I was gonna go on at 'er? I worry, that's all. Case them witches next door try to snatch 'er back.'

'They wouldn't do that. They don't even know it's her.'

'I wouldn't bet your dinner on it. Witches, that's what they are.'

'Ne'mind. Perhaps they'll move away.'

Harriet went quiet. 'That's a point,' she murmured, more to herself than to her sister. 'That'd be just the job if they did that. We could rent that 'ouse as well. Bo should start earnin' soon, and what with the piecework . . .'

'What piecework?'

'Oh, didn't I tell yer? I was chattin' to one of the women at the sewin' classes and she's puttin' some work my way for when I turn it in at the factory. Reckons you can earn up to six shillin's a day once you get the 'ang of it. Runnin' up skirt seams which 'ave already bin tacked. Once I get goin' on Mary's machine I'm quick as lightnin'.'

'I know. I watched you, didn't I, when you made me a skirt?'

'So you did,' whispered Harriet, pensively. 'You know, we *could* drive them two out. What silly sods we've bin. Tiptoein' about when we should 'ave bin stampin'. Talkin' quiet when we should 'ave bawled.' A huge smile lit up her face. 'Didn't our uncle say he wanted to get rid of that old piano his mother 'ad left 'im?'

'He did say that, yeah. All the time. But he never did anything about it.'

'Well, we will. Might as well get somefing out of the old sod. Did any of you ever play it?'

'Mum could play. They said she was a natural. No one ever showed her, Harriet, but she could listen to a tune and pick it up. She told me how to do it. You just listen with one ear then pass it through your brain to the other. From left to right. She insisted you had to listen with your left ear, then let it pass slowly through to your right.'

'And did it work?'

'Oh, yeah. Always. It's easy, really. Much easier than trying to read sheet music.'

'So you can play as well, then?'

'Oh, yeah, but I don't need to now, do I? Uncle never came into that room where the piano was – probably cos Mum sat in there mostly. I loved that piano. I don't think he'd want to get rid of it now. I think he only wanted to so I wouldn't spend so much time in there. He liked to sit and look at me.'

'Leer at you, don't you mean? Filthy sod! I know what I'd like to do to 'im.'

'Oh, but you mustn't, Harriet. You promised. Mum would be so upset it would kill her, I'm certain of it.'

'I know. I ain't gonna say anyfing, don't worry. You're all right now, anyway,' Harriet said, checking her sister's expression, 'now you're wiv us. Well? Say so, then! You *are* all right?'

'Course I am. I was just thinking, that's all. Thinking how lovely it would be to play tunes again.' Her face was glowing. 'Oh, Harriet, I did love to play – especially when me and Mum played together. There's nothing like music to cheer you up. You kind of lose yourself in it.'

'Yeah, all right, don't get carried away. I'll see if Arfer can borry an 'orse and cart and go and fetch it with one of 'is mates. Bleedin' 'eavy, them pianos.'

'But where will we put it? There's no room anywhere.'

'In the passage.'

'You can't do that,' said Alice. 'We'd 'ave to squeeze past it every time we came in or went out.'

'Not for long, though.' Harriet grinned. 'I'll drive them two old cows out if it kills me. All night long we'll take turns plonkin' on it – good and loud.'

'You mustn't play during the night, Harriet, that's disturbing the peace.'

'Up to midnight, that's all.' She threw back her head and laughed. 'Right up to bleedin' midnight! See 'ow the wicked cows like that!'

'Well, they do deserve it, don't they?' said Alice. 'They were horrible to Bo.'

'No, they treated her like angels would! *God!* Open the back door for me. I'm having a flush.'

'Don't be silly, course you're not. Only mums and aunts have those when they're in their change of life. You're too young for hot flushes, Harriet. It's this weather. It read seventy-five degrees on the thermometer at work. And in the newspaper it said it's going to be the hottest August in ten years.'

Alice pushed open the stiff back door and looked out in wonder. Between them, Arthur and Harriet had turned the back yard into a haven. Along one side old rosebushes had been brought back to life after a severe pruning, a hydrangea was bursting with beautiful pink flowers and the ground-covering blue and white flowers that Harriet had planted earlier that year were like a spreading carpet. On the opposite side, Arthur's vegetables were strong and healthy, and Alice's tomato plants were bearing fruit. The scent coming off the roses was heavenly.

It was a delight, especially compared to the back yards at either side. The two women next door had no interest whatsoever in gardening and the old couple on the other side kept rabbits and chickens for the table. Alice sighed with delight. Life could not have been more pleasant. She hadn't missed her mother as much as she thought she might, because she knew she could jump on the omnibus or train to visit her. Since she had come to live with Harriet she and her mother had exchanged letters regularly and her sister was now in the habit of scribbling a little note at the bottom.

She turned to Harriet, and whispered, 'I never thought in a million years that I could be this happy.'

'Is that right?' said Harriet, her voice strained. 'Well, there we are, then. What goes round comes round. You deserve a bit of happiness, Alice.' She closed her eyes and rested her head against the back of the chair. 'Fetch me a glass of water, will you?'

'Harriet, why are your freckles showing up so much? You're as white as a sheet. Harriet?' She leaned closer until their faces were almost touching. 'Harriet?'

'It's all right. I've not passed out. Just need to keep my eyes shut, that's all. It'll go off in a minute.'

'What will?'

'Pain.'

Alice stared at Harriet's pale, drawn face. 'I'm gonna run for the doctor. This isn't right. You shouldn't be in pain yet. You're only seven months.'

'Stop it, Alice. Gimme a drink of water.'

Alice fetched a glass and held it to her sister's lips. She couldn't stop her fingers trembling. 'I'll make you a cup of tea,' she said.

Harriet pushed away the glass, took a few long deep breaths, then eased herself up. 'Give me your arm. I'm going abed. I need a doze, that's what it'll be. I'm dog tired.'

'All right,' said Alice, helping her up and into the bedroom. 'You're sure you don't want me to run for the doctor?'

'No need. I was on me feet too long today, that's all. Don't bovver wiv the tea for now. Fetch me a cup in about half an hour and wake me up if I'm asleep. I don't want Arfer to see me like this. You know what he's like – he'll panic and make fings worse.'

Alice helped her on to the bed and made her comfortable. 'I'll draw the curtains too and that'll help cool the room. Shall I open the window a little bit?'

'No,' whispered Harriet. 'Leave me in the dark and shut the door. Let me sleep.' She was already drifting off.

Alice stood by her bedside, staring down at her beloved sister. Harriet's face was still white against her thick ginger eyebrows and freckles.

An hour later she was still sleeping soundly, and Bo had not returned from the cabinet factory. Arthur was due home at any time. In the kitchen, Alice went about her duties, hoping that when her sister woke she would be ready for a nice hot meal. As she stirred the gravy in a small saucepan, deep in thought, she all but jumped out of her skin when she heard the sound of three loud bangs on the door. Arthur had returned from work and forgotten his key again.

She rushed to the street door and tried to look serene and composed when she opened it so as not to alarm him, but as soon as she saw his smiling face she burst into tears. He took her into the kitchen and sat her down, then rushed into the bedroom. Harriet was lying there, smiling faintly at him.

'Sorry, sweet'eart,' she said. 'I 'ad a little lie-down and must 'ave fell asleep.' She sat up and plumped her pillows behind her. 'Is Bo 'ome yet? Alice 'as bin worried. You know what she's like.'

Arthur eyed her. She wasn't as rosy as she had been of late. 'Is that why she's cryin'?' he said.

'I expect so. Silly cow – cries at the least bleedin' fing.' Harriet eased her legs off the bed and held out her hand for him to help her up. 'This is a big baby, Arfer. Or it's twins.'

'Better not be a pair of 'em,' he joked, 'or one'll 'ave to go in the work'ouse.'

'Over my dead body,' she said, and made her way into the kitchen. Arthur, satisfied that all was under control, told Alice to keep the dinner warm while he went out to look for Bo.

'You don't 'ave to do that, Arfer,' said Harriet, easing herself on to the kitchen chair. 'She's not a baby. Probably doin' a bit of overtime.'

'I'm sure you're right, love, but I'll take a walk over to the factory anyway. 'Don't overcook the cabbage.'

Once the girls heard the front door slam they relaxed.

'At least the colour's come back to your face,' murmured Alice, 'but you still look drawn.'

'Fanks very much. You're all I need. I'm seven months' pregnant, Alice, and still doing a full day's work. I'm bound to feel it now and then.'

'I suppose so,' she said. But Alice was not persuaded: her sister didn't look tired but ill.

When Greta opened the door she was far from pleased that Arthur walked straight in and declared that he had heard rats in the loft. He wanted, he said, to take a look upstairs to make sure that they hadn't chewed their way through to the bedrooms. He marched from the main bedroom to the boxroom, came back downstairs, walked around, then went out into the yard and checked the lavatory.

Satisfied that they had not waylaid Bo, he smiled at the confounded women, tipped his cap and left them to stare after him.

As he went into his own house, he chuckled to himself. He couldn't imagine anyone taking those two old women for anything other than a couple of spinsters who liked nothing more than knitting and gardening.

'What's tickled your fancy?' said Harriet, trying her best to sound normal. 'Caught 'em in their underwear, did yer?' She had guessed what he was up to and the look in his eye told her so.

'Oooh, perish the thought.'

'I expect Bo's stayed on a bit longer at the factory because they're busy,' said Alice, placing the steaming gravy boat on the table.

'It don't matter so much now.' Arthur pulled off his cap and tossed it on to a hook on the back door. 'She can stay out for as long as she likes, so long as we know she's not next door.' He pulled some fish wrapped in newspaper out of his pocket. 'Put this in the cool cupboard, Harriet. Nice bit of smoked haddock for tea tomorrow. Enough for us lot and more for the cats if we 'ad any.'

'I love smoked haddock.' Alice spooned a piece of liver on to each of their plates. 'I've got a special recipe. It'll be a nice surprise.'

'Don't you ever talk about anyfing except food?' Harriet was still feeling a touch nauseated and the smell of liver wasn't helping.

'I do, actually. I was telling my friend Alfred about our project. He thinks it's a good idea and that wax faces will look lovely once they're painted, but not very practical if our dolls are to be played with. Wax dolls are really more like an ornament – wax fashion dolls. They're made so that fashion experts can display new styles on them.'

'So it'd be a waste of time us making dolls with wax faces for children, then?'

'Well . . .'

Sighing, Harriet flapped a hand. 'Blooming daft

idea of Polly's in any case. I'll make more money by running up sensible fings, like workin' skirts for workin' women.'

'Oh, but he thinks it's a good idea! We just 'ave to find a way of making porcelain heads, that's all. A small factory with kilns where they fire teapots and cups.'

'Or pipes.' Harriet smiled. 'Flora's dad works in the clay-pipe factory. Bin there for donkey's years.'

'There we are, then,' said Arthur. 'Another good reason for you to visit and hold her baby. Now you're so close to your time you'd best get some practice in.'

'Too right an' all,' said Harriet, hiding her inner worry that something wasn't quite right with her. 'I might take the day off tomorrow and visit 'er. You can go in and say I've twisted my ankle and I'll only be out forty-eight hours.' Harriet gazed at her dinner plate, at the liver and the greens in particular. She didn't feel like eating but if she was to stop them fussing over her she had to, hungry or not. 'I think I'll wait for Bo to come in. You two 'ave yours an' I'll put mine on steam. That little nap seems to 'ave—' Four rhythmic taps on the door stopped her short. That was Bo's knock. Off his chair in a flash, Arthur went to let her in. Evidently he had been more worried than he'd let on.

She came into the room, her face shining. 'I've got a present for yer.' She brought her hands from behind her back and showed them a small wooden rolling-pin made by her own fair hands and with a tiny carving on each end. 'The foreman showed me 'ow to use the lathe. And he said I can make some more in my own time and sell 'em in the market. They're for rollin' pastry.'

'Well, they wouldn't be for rollin' leather, would they?' grinned Arthur. 'Nice bit of timber that,' he said, taking it from her. 'Looks like a bit of elm.'

'Why's he bein' so nice to yer?' asked Harriet. 'Not after any favours, I 'ope.'

'No. All I did was a little bit of carving for 'im on a . . .' she closed her eyes, '. . . a bureau!'

Silence fell in the kitchen. She had been allowed to carve into a hand-made bureau? A fourteen-year-old apprentice? 'What sort of a carving?' Arthur asked suspiciously.

'A rose. He showed me the drawing – the design – and gave me a little bit of instruction and then I did it. The customer wanted a rose carved into the top of it. Tomorrow I'm to carve two grooves eiver side to hold 'er pen and pencil.'

'Well, I'll be blowed . . .' murmured Arthur, sounding as proud as punch. 'You really must be a little genius, Bo. A cabinet-maker letting an apprentice get a tool anywhere near a piece . . .' He let out a low whistle. 'Was it a hard wood?'

'Oak.'

He burst out laughing, and looked from Harriet to Alice, who were smiling and watery-eyed. 'Looks like the doll-makin' could be a success with our little genius carvin' different faces and different expressions. Reckon you could do a baby cryin', Bo?'

'I fink so. Anyfing's possible, Arfer – ain't that right, Alice?'

'Yeah,' she said, smiling. 'So long as we're healthy.'
She glanced at Harriet, who turned away.

'Hurry up and eat yer dinner, Arfer. You've got a
little trip to make. Down to the stable to borry the
milkman's horse and cart then over the river to visit
my aunt and uncle. You're fetchin' us a piano home,
sweetheart.'

'Whatever for?'

'So we can 'ave parties and liven the place up on a
dull day, why else?'

'Lyin' cow,' Arthur said, with a broad grin. 'You
wanna drive away them old cows next door. You're
after more space for your little business. I wasn't born
yesterday. You wanna turn next door into a family
factory!'

'All right, clever clogs, so what if I do or I don't? No
'arm in gettin' rid of them two old bats, is there?'

'No, sweet'eart, course not. I'll get your piano for
yer.' He started to laugh again. 'Things you come up
with. Blowed if I would 'ave thought of it.'

'The thing is,' said Alice, 'it's not a very big rolling-
pin, is it?'

'That's right,' returned Bo. 'Foreman says that in
this twentieth century people won't be 'avin' such big
families so pastry for pies won't be such a big lump.
Little pies for little families.'

Holding up the rolling-pin, Harriet shook her head.
'He's not wrong. This is a more sensible size, and I
reckon that now Queen Victoria's gone, women won't
'ave so many babies. Especially now that a rubber
johnny's gettin' to be more usual.'

'Rubber johnny?' said Bo, mystified. No one could find the right words to explain. 'And what's a rubber johnny got to do with a rolling-pin?'

'Ask your foreman,' smiled Arthur. 'He'll tell you.'

'Don't you dare, Bo,' said Harriet, throwing him a black look. 'It's something that you don't 'ave to worry over yet. It's to do with 'avin' babies. Or, rather, not 'avin' them.'

'Oh, well, I'll learn all about that when the doctor comes and delivers yourn, won't I? I'm gonna watch, if that's all right? Or will the doctor tell me off?'

'Doctors don't deliver babies, Bo,' said Alice. 'Midwives do that.'

'What's a midwife?'

'Someone to keep away from unless you've got no choice,' said Harriet, the old wave of dread rushing through her. Immediately she was picturing Jacqueline Turner and wondering where she might be now and what she was doing.

'But they're good people, Harriet, surely?'

'Course they are, Alice,' Arthur put in. 'But enough of that kind of talk. Dinner'll be freezin' cold by the time we get it down us.'

Passing number thirteen where Mary Dean's family had lived, the midwife continued on her way, entering a past life she would love either to be back in or put behind her once and for all. In this quiet turning she had spent a happy childhood, at first, living in the larger house at the end of the street. Later on, once her sister had married and her parents had passed away, she had moved into her own two-up two-down, a spinster content with her own company and engrossed in her calling as a midwife. Then, to deliver life safely into this world had been enough for her.

She stopped outside the house that in 1888 she had been in a hurry to leave, once she had made up her mind to go to America. The small family living there now were European immigrants who kept it in good order. The windows were clean, the doorstep was whitened, and the brass letter-box on the front door, had been polished. She continued to the end of the turning, wondering if anyone she had known still lived here. When she arrived at the old brick wall that separated this turning from the pretty Trinity almshouses beyond, she turned the handle of the small door in the wall and found that, with just a gentle shove, it opened. While she had lived in Whitehead Street she had never known it to be unlocked. So many times, as a child, she had yearned to slip through it into what she believed must be another world.

Now she entered this enchanted place, with alms-houses surrounding a green, and felt an overwhelming desire to live there. Beneath most of the windows were boxes of colourful trailing plants and in the centre of the green was a statue on a marble plinth: 'To the memory of Captain Richard Maples who dying a Commander of a shipp in the East Indies in the year 1680 left to the Trinity House ye value of £1300 with which part of these almes houses were built. The said Corp. caused this statue to be erected Anno 1681.'

She strolled through the enclosure, feeling as if

she belonged there. She had entered this little oasis only twice before, through the main gates leading in from the Cambridgeheath Road, both times at night and in the dark to give her services as midwife.

Now, with the sun streaming down and the smell of freshly cut grass, it seemed a different place. Beyond another high brick wall, which had no gate, was a small church and the larger, grander Trinity almshouses, which had been built in 1695 on land given by Captain Henry Mudd for retired merchant seamen and which led out to the Whitechapel Road. These cottages had been restored to their former glory in 1896, while Jacqueline had been in America. When she had seen them on her return, behind the ornate black gates, she had felt that better things were to come in her neighbourhood.

As she came out through the gates of the almshouses into Cambridgeheath Road Jacqueline Turner vowed to spend the remaining years of her life living in a Trinity almshouse. She would go to the authorities soon to put in a request for tenancy. With her good reputation and long career, she had no doubt that her name would go to the top of a waiting list, should there be one. Crossing Cambridgeheath Road, dodging between horse-drawn carts and trams she stopped on the pavement to gaze into the face of a horse harnessed to a dray and stroked its sweaty hide. She was outside the entrance to Mann, Crossman and Paulin, the Albion Brewery, which had been established in 1760 and provided work for several hundred men. The smell of brewers' yeast, malt and hops was familiar to the locals.

More at peace with herself, Jacqueline decided to visit Celeste, and persuade her to come outside into the warm fresh air for a stroll. It had been good for her to return to her family roots. Soon she would be ready to find out what had happened to her nephew, and perhaps visit him, if he was still alive. She wandered along, remembering her childhood, her loving parents. Even though her mother had developed a split personality later in life, there had been times when she had cuddled Jacqueline by the small fire in their front room and sung to her.

Finding herself in Buck's Row where the prostitute Polly Nichols had been found with her throat cut, Jacqueline's thoughts flew back to when she had seen Martha Tabram, one of her nephew's victims, lying in a pool of blood near George Yard Buildings. She continued to walk towards the place where she had murdered Annie Chapman, in Hanbury Street.

As she went through the narrow passage of number twenty-nine and into the back yard, an icy sensation rushed through her. Here, in this filthy place, at dawn, she had strangled and mutilated a woman who had threatened to blackmail her and had let slip that she knew Thomas was guilty of the murder of two of her friends.

Jacqueline stood at the top of the three stone steps that led down into the yard, and stared at the fence to which she had pinned Annie before squeezing her throat until the last putrid breath had left her mouth.

She remembered the chimes of the brewery clock striking six after she had left the place and was making her way though Bethnal Green. She also remembered stripping the rings from the dead woman's fingers and laying them at her feet, with other items taken from her pocket. She could not remember why she had done this. She had also removed the wretched woman's womb and buried it in her back garden in Whitehead Street, to hide the evidence that she had been pregnant.

Jacqueline left the place in turmoil. Her blood was beginning to boil. She was angry because she had allowed other people to drive her to such diabolical lengths. Mary Dean came to mind: she had introduced Jacqueline to the whore Annie Chapman. In turn, Annie Chapman had signposted her to Catherine Eddowes, the prostitute who had had Thomas's initials inked into her arm as evidence, should he ever attack her.

Striding through the back-streets of Whitechapel and was soon in the street where her sister lived. She had been so caught up in her thoughts and tormented by what she had been forced to do in the past that by the time she had climbed the steps to the third floor of the dark, dingy building her legs were heavy and aching. She had not visited her sister for three weeks and could only hope that she was in a better, more sane frame of mind now that summer had set in.

She tapped on the front door and heard a young woman yell shrilly for her noisy children to be quiet. She stared at the door, wondering if she had walked into the wrong block of flats or come to the wrong floor. When the door opened and a young Polish woman looked into her face Jacqueline felt sick. This was the right flat but the wrong person. 'I'm looking for my sister, Celeste,' she said.

'The old woman? She was your sister?' The woman shrugged sadly. 'She did not put a match to the fire. The fumes from the gas killed her. They say that she committed suicide. I did not think she had family. Nobody said she had family alive. I am sorry for you. Very sorry.'

Jacqueline gripped the iron banister to steady herself. She felt weak, her legs buckling under her. Using every bit of the strength she had, she edged her way down the stairs, shuddering when she heard the door of her dead sister's flat shut.

Once in the Whitechapel Road, she flagged down a hansom cab. Today she would not be frugal. Today she would pay to be delivered to her rooms above the tobacconist's. Today, Jacqueline Turner felt alone and vulnerable. Thomas had been incarcerated for life, her parents were long since dead, and her sister had committed suicide. On her own now, in this strange, fast-changing world, she had only the past to cling to. Harriet Smith had much to answer for. If she had not stolen the diary, Jacqueline was sure that her life now would have been very different. She would not have gone to America and Thomas would have been living with her in the little house in Whitehead Street.

Back in her lodging rooms, the midwife brewed a pot of tea and sat at her table by the window with the family photograph album. Now it was all she had to remind herself of her family. There was a picture of her father, as an upstanding young man in his early twenties, but her favourite was a pen-and-ink drawing of her great-grandparents: in it, they were standing outside a thatched cottage and pretty garden in Stepney at a time when it was a village, ruled by the Lord of the Manor. Another drawing, by the same hand, showed a small wooden church among the cottages, fields and marshland of Bethnal Green.

Jacqueline's father had begun his working life as an officer in the Wapping fire brigade and gradually worked his way to a senior position elsewhere. On turning to a photograph of him, herself and Celeste at Southend-on-Sea where the family had gone for their annual summer holiday, she closed the album, unable to go on. She had hoped the pictures would comfort her in the solitude of this quiet, lonely room but they had not. They were a sad memento of better times past and a glaring reminder of the way things had turned out. Her entire family had been wiped out. She had lost the small hope that Thomas might still be alive, and if he were, he would most likely be in a catatonic state worse than death. She could no longer feel him in her soul. She gazed at a photograph of him as a small boy and felt, deep down, that he had died in the asylum. She lifted the album from the table and hid it away in a small cupboard. She no longer wished to be reminded of happier times.

Sipping her tea, the midwife stared out of the window to the deserted street below, where the only movement was paper and leaves blowing in the breeze, and was reminded of herself and her life now. 'No more than a piece of paper blowing where the wind takes me,' she murmured. Once again, her mood switched from melancholy to hostility with a vision of the yard in Hanbury Street where she had had little choice other than to end the miserable life of Annie Chapman. She had only previously seen the woman in the back-streets of Whitechapel when the prostitute was touting for work.

But Annie Chapman had not only sold her body to earn a living: according to one newspaper report, she had tried to earn some money selling flowers or doing crochet work. At one time she had been married to a coachman at Windsor but they had separated. Then, she had received an allowance of ten shillings a week from her husband but that had suddenly stopped and she had learned that he had died. They had had children, who had been living with her husband. After his death her young son, a cripple, had been sent away to school, and her daughter to an institution in France. With no money coming in and unable to visit her children, the woman had turned to drink. Cheap gin with a touch of arsenic was her favourite cocktail.

She had been drunk on the evening when she had almost tricked the midwife into giving her an abortion, which had overshadowed all the midwife's feelings of humanity towards a lost soul. Now, though, Jacqueline was carrying a worse burden: guilt. And her resentment of Harriet was worsening. Harriet had the upper hand, which made the midwife uncomfortable.

If Harriet still had the diary, she had total control over Jacqueline's destiny. And the worst of it was not knowing.

Now she opened her diary and wrote:

It has been another hot, wretched day. Celeste is dead and buried. Soon it will be dusk and I shall light the oil lamp. I shall request a change of area. I no longer wish to work in Whitechapel. I must attend mothers in Stepney in, around and close to Beaumont Square. I shall enjoy my wrapped sandwiches and gin in fine surroundings. From the green and through the trees there is a clear view of the house. Once seen, the street urchin with the unruly red hair will be marked. I am impatient to see where she lives. May God allow me to live until the day the troublemaker is ready to give birth. I shall be her midwife. Ha, ha.

With the old piano installed in the passage of number four Musbury Street, the mood inside the house had changed from calm and content to cheerful. Not only could Harriet, Arthur and Bo sit back and enjoy Alice's lovely music, they had fun playing the tune Alice had taught them, 'God Save The Queen'. All three could pick it out now. In the evenings they sang along with whoever had chosen to play, not once, but four or five times as if they were rehearsing for a show.

The thumping on the wall from the women next door roused peals of raucous laughter, which served only to fuel the anger of their neighbours. One week of this treatment, with their complaints ignored, was enough for the two women.

Now, humming a tune as she hung out the washing, Harriet had no idea that Greta was staring at her. Her mind was on her baby and whether she might be carrying a boy or a girl. Secretly she was longing for a daughter the double of herself, but whenever Arthur asked, and he often did, she said she didn't mind what she had so long as it was healthy. She planned to have three children, one daughter and two sons.

She lifted the empty washing-basket from the ground, and paused to admire the rosebushes. With the house looking comfortable and homely and the back yard so lovely, she thought it was time she invited Mary and her family for Sunday tea. The trouble was, of course, that since they lived so far away, arrangements had to be made in advance: her sister-in-law had to book a room in a hotel for an overnight stay. 'You never know,' Harriet thought, a dead-heading a rose, 'one day we might live in an 'ouse good enough to 'ave Mary and Walter stoppin' overnight. So long as they leave their snooty brats at home with the nanny.' She didn't hear her neighbour come out of her back door so the sound of the woman's voice, never mind what she was saying, startled her. The words that struck her cold were 'filthy incestuous pair'.

She turned slowly to face her tormentor, and her stomach lurched: the expression on Greta's face was no less evil than that of the midwife when she had caught Harriet looking at her diary. 'Piss off,' was all she could say and she hated herself for it. This was exactly what the woman had wanted to hear.

'Your name is linked with black worship in Bow – did you know that, whore?'

'Is that right?' said Harriet, walking forward slowly, her basket lodged between her hip and her hand. 'Well, if all you've got to do wiv your spare time is go wanderin' around looking for sick lies and gossip, maybe it's time you stopped livin' wiv a woman and found yerself a man.'

'I spit on that baby,' said the hag, safe behind the fence and keeping her distance. 'Satan's child! I spit on both of you.'

Using all her will-power not to reveal that she knew the woman and her friend were sick-minded torturers, Harriet drew a deep breath. Bo was in the forefront of her mind now and she had to protect her. If she let the cat out of the bag, she might have the authorities dragging Bo away. This woman would stop at nothing to take her revenge for the rescue of her victim, never mind the piano-playing.

'I'll say this and I'll say no more, witch. Arthur is *not* my brother. You need to get your facts right before you point your crooked finger. His sister adopted me.'

'A likely story – and even if it were true, you were pregnant well before you were married! Sleeping with a man out of wedlock! Filthy whore! We were sickened and ashamed to be living next door to heathens!'

'Well, thank the Lord for that! 'Cos you're going and that's exactly what we want! You warped, twisted cow!'

The veins on the woman's neck bulged. 'Damn you and damn that devil child spawned by evil! We were ready to move out as soon as we saw you and that man of yours. The smell of the gutter is all over you. You've come from dirt and you'll never wash it away!'

Harriet threw down the washing-basket and strode forward, ready to rip away the loose fencing and strangle the woman. But Madam Greta knew when to retreat, and she went back into her house then bolted the door behind her.

Harriet picked up her washing-basket and hurled it with all her strength against her neighbour's back window, breaking a pane. Then, arms folded and defiant, she waited for her neighbour to come out. She was ready for her – ready to give her some of the treatment she had given Bo. But the house was silent. This at least was an accomplishment. She had frightened the woman who had terrorised Bo.

Harriet went back inside and sank on to the kitchen chair. She wasn't sure whether she was going to laugh or cry. She did neither. The anger had gone as quickly as it came. She felt nothing except a tiny glow inside at the thought of the women leaving the house next door. It hadn't been certain that they would leave, but now there was no question of it. 'I dunno, God, you do work in mysterious bleedin' ways, don't yer?' she murmured. 'Why put me all through that to see the end of them cracked nuts? You don't make life easy, do yer?'

On a sunny Saturday, when the horse-drawn removal wagon turned up at the house next door a loud cheer filled number four. At last Bo could act like a girl and wear a long skirt and a bonnet on Sunday instead of breeches and a cap.

Harriet sent Arthur to see the landlord with regard to renting the house next door and even though he was unable to strike a deal as good as Harriet had managed with their house, he had had the weekly rent knocked down from eight shillings to seven, and still Mr Cohen had no idea that each house had been made good upstairs and was in use. Luckily, Larry's friend had too many properties to look after to think too hard about Musbury Street. His only real worry was that the local criminal fraternity, the Aldgate mob, who extorted protection money from shabby restaurants, pubs, gambling dens, street bookies and honest shop-keepers, might turn on him.

Property owners were not yet on the list of the East End's flourishing and violent gangs but others, like Mr Cohen, knew that it was only time before they would be approached by men who carried cudgels and knives inside their jackets. With the new century, ill winds were blowing across the ocean from New York. Here and now in this part of London, the protection racket was worked by a powerful mob of up to forty Russians, the self-styled Bessarabian Tigers; they preyed mainly on fellow Jews who were too intimidated to inform the police. For this reason landlords kept in the shadows. They could no longer afford to threaten eviction over short rent, which in itself was a blessing for the poor and certainly a bonus where Harriet and Arthur were concerned.

But for all the crime and fear there was a brighter side to life. Even though dogs still cocked their legs against lamp-posts and litter was dropped everywhere, the newly appointed street cleaners were doing a grand job and East London looked much better. A birth-control shop had opened, more public lavatories were being built and a new Sunlight laundry was doing a roaring trade in Limehouse. In Bethnal Green the new eel-and-pie shop was a tremendous success, offering a cheap, hot, nourishing meal at a marble-topped table, and the East London Art Gallery in Whitechapel was attracting revolutionary artists into the area to show their work.

But the poor still had to beg their living and sleep rough under bundles of rags, while thin, hungry children ran wild in the back-streets stealing food from market stalls and picking pockets.

The local doctor had advised Harriet to stop working at the factory, so she had been secretly to see the manager of a clothing sweatshop just east of Spitalfields where mostly Jewish immigrants worked. The innovation of piecework was a stroke of luck for Harriet. She was fast and efficient on the treadle sewing-machine and because of this she negotiated for the work to be delivered to her door. It arrived on the back of a cart in great bundles tied with string.

The room Harriet had chosen for her workshop was the one in which she had found Bo after the last flogging from her tormentors. The small window gave enough light to work by and there was space for Mary's hand sewing-machine, a chair and the two heaps of piecework from the factory – one pile to be machined and the other of finished work.

Today she had to add three rows of pale blue satin ribbon to the bottom of light grey ankle-length skirts and corresponding silk braid to the long pointed collar of short, matching fitted jackets. After three hours' working non-stop she was feeling tired and, as luck would have it, the sound of the door knocker gave her a welcome excuse to take a break. She imagined the caller was the door-to-door hair-cutter. So far the woman hadn't persuaded Harriet to have her hair cropped, and neither would she, but they were about the same age and had taken to each other on their first meeting.

On opening the street door, she was surprised to see Flora standing there holding her baby girl, Beanie, who was now seven months old. She was very pretty, with reddish black hair and one tooth showing. 'Well, I wasn't expecting you, Flora, but I'm pleased you came. I was gasping for a cup of tea but wouldn't stop. Once I get on that machine I lose all sense of time.' She kissed the baby. 'Look at yer! Beautiful dark blue eyes, just like your mum. So, what you brings you 'ere today, then, Flora? Bored or missin' me?' Harriet filled the kettle and a thought struck her. 'How did you know not to knock at our 'ouse? I 'aven't seen you since we took over this one.'

'A neighbour told me. I knocked next door first off. I want to know what's goin' on. Takin' two houses and leaving the factory?' She rested back in a chair and patted Beanie, who was sleepy. 'What's it all about, Harriet? I 'ope you're not overdoin' it.'

As Harriet filled her in on all that had happened next door and how she, Alice, Polly and Bo had followed in Flora's footsteps and were now regularly attending classes at the People's Palace, Harriet's cheeks flushed with excitement and the sparkle was back in her light blue eyes. She told Flora that they were planning to form a little cottage industry, making dolls, and that she had been advised by the doctor to give up work at the factory.

'But with two lots of rent, Harriet, you'll miss the money, surely?'

'No, I won't. I'm doin' piecework upstairs. I'm usin' the little bedroom, Alice is in the other and Bo's in our boxroom next door.'

'And does it pay as well?'

'Better than the soap factory when you work it out. Mind you, I'm bleedin' well brilliant at it. Quick as lightnin' on that machine and learnin' more and more little tricks of the trade up the Palace.'

'Where will you make the dolls?'

'In this place. The downstairs front room, and this kitchen too, if need be.' Harriet handed Flora a cup of tea carefully so as not to disturb the baby. 'I'm gonna make the dolls' clothes, Alice the wigs and Bo the dolls' faces. Polly, who you've still not met, is gonna do the books and sales. She's got the mind of a businessman, that one.'

'Oh,' murmured Flora, looking a touch jealous at

being left out of it. 'At least I had *something* to do with it. I told you about the classes.'

'Course you did – and you can do more. What are you good at?'

'Cookin'. You know that's my first love. One day I'll run my own little café.'

'I'm sure you will, but what about in the meantime? Don't you need to earn a bit?'

'Course I do, but how can I go out to work with a baby?'

Harriet grinned at her as she took the lid off the biscuit tin. 'Work at 'ome, you daft mare. Do what I'm doin'. You can hire a sewin'-machine, you know. Piecework's easy. You can pick and choose yer own hours.'

Flora liked the sound of it, and before they knew it an hour had passed and arrangements had been made for her to go to see the foreman at the sweatshop. This way she could still attend her three afternoons a week at the domestic-science classes and earn a wage. 'You know,' said Flora, pensive, 'Dad worked in the clay-pipe factory keeping the kilns going. You might be able to get your dolls' heads fired there.'

'But I thought you said he'd left and gone back to the brewery?'

'No. Mum's still there on bottle-washing but only part-time. She looks after Beanie for me when I go to my classes.'

'But didn't they 'ave one of the lovely little brewery houses in Bellevue Place off Cleveland Way?'

'They still do. Mum's still at Charrington's, don't

forget, and when the old boy who sweeps the floors in the brewery retires, Dad's got the job if the pipe factory gets too much for 'im.'

'Well, that's somefing. I love Bellevue, Flora. The first time you took me 'ome for tea when we were kids I believed it was a long-lost country village that 'ad been magicked there overnight. All them lovely rosebushes and flowers . . .'

'I know, and all tucked away behind an old brick wall with a green door. And you're right, the cottage gardens fenced with wooden rails make it look magical. My favourites are the lupins and delphiniums. You should grow them in your back yard. Dad's put some in mine. Lovely, they are.'

'Yeah, well, when I've got the time I will. Once the baby's 'ere I'll make somefing of this back yard. Them two women wasn't interested. Not the sort who liked flowers.'

'Makes all the difference. A pretty back yard to sit in.'

'Yours ain't a back yard, Flora, it's a proper garden. Anyway,' said Harriet, as tiredness swept through her, 'you'll find out about the kilns at the pipe factory then, will yer?'

'I said I would, didn't I? Mind you, what about that small doll factory in Cambridgeheath Road? That might be a better bet.'

'I never knew there was one.'

'It's tucked round the back. Fronts on to the main road but it all goes on out the back. I used to nip over there when I was old enough to cross the road by

myself and stand in the doorway out the back.' Flora
smiled. 'My uncle worked there. One time he slipped
me a pair of doll's legs, another the body, then the
arms, and then the head. Then he fetched the wires
round that went through the inside of the body and
put it all together with them.'

'I never knew that. I could 'ave done wiv a bleedin'
free doll. You should 'ave told me about it.'

'If I 'ad you'd 'ave been there every day pesterin'
knowing you. Anyway, my uncle said I wasn't to tell
a soul or he'd go to jail. So I never.'

'Does he still work there?'

'No, but Dad knows the chap who owns it. Old man
Steinberg. I'll get 'im to 'ave a word.'

'Mmmm . . . I'm in 'alf a mind to go for a stroll
over there today.'

'Can if you like.'

'It's a bit of a trek, though. P'raps I'll stroll along
to put the idea to Polly.'

'Well, I've got to get back soon anyhow. You should
fetch Polly to visit me. I'm always 'avin' to work
between the baby's feeds so I don't get out much.
The company would be nice, Harriet.'

'All right,' said Harriet, who had remembered that
Beaumont Square was the last place she wanted Flora
to visit. She might get a glimpse of the man known to
her as Prince Charlie and she was too lovely a person
to have her heart broken. 'We'll come and see you
next Saturday afternoon. How's that?'

'Sounds all right.' Flora glanced at the clock and
raised an eyebrow. 'I'd best be going.'

Harriet saw her friend out, closed the door of number three and went into her home next door. Her mind on the doll factory, she was all for taking a break and paying Polly a visit. Anyway, she enjoyed visiting Lillian's lovely house. The naughty house that Arthur preferred her not to mention.

In Beaumont Square Jacqueline Turner settled herself on her chosen park bench and was a little sorry to see two or three courting couples there, making the most of their thirty-minute lunch break. She took her library book from her pocket instead of her wrapped sandwiches and began to read, glancing occasionally at the House of Assignation. She was hungry but did not relish the idea of eating in a public place when other people were close by. Soon they would be gone and she could enjoy her sandwich of strong Cheddar cheese, raw onion and sliced apple. When she looked up from her book again, she was at last rewarded for her patience: walking slowly towards the House of Assignation was the person she had been hoping to see.

Arriving at Lillian's gate, Harriet felt as if all of her strength had been drained by the walk and she was relieved to have made it this far without collapsing. She was angry with herself for coming out when she should have been resting at home. She ignored the griping pains in her stomach, and put them down to not having eaten enough fresh fruit. By the time she pulled on the doorbell of Lillian's house, she was feeling quite faint.

When Polly answered, the expression on her face told Harriet that she must look as bad as she felt.

'Bleedin' 'ell, Harriet! Wot're you up to? You shouldn't be walkin' about as if you wasn't pregnant.'

'Help me to a chair, Polly,' was all she could say.

Polly gripped her arm, kicked the door shut and sat her on Lillian's prized possession, a beautiful ladies' recliner in the hall. So far no one had dared sit on the ivory silk couch for fear of leaving the tiniest mark.

'Stay there and I'll fetch the smelling salts,' said Polly, frightened, Harriet could see that Polly's hands were trembling. Before she went down to the kitchen she shouted up the stairs for Lillian.

When Lillian appeared from her snug she gazed down at Polly then at Harriet. 'Has she gone into labour?' she asked.

'I don't know! Come and sit wiv 'er while I fetch the salts.' With that Polly was running down the stairs. 'Don't let 'er stand up!' she yelled back over her shoulder.

Lillian sat down calmly next to Harriet and stroked her hair. 'When is the baby due, Harriet?'

'Six or seven weeks' time, I think.'

'Did something happen on the way here? Did you slip or—'

'No,' said Harriet. She didn't want to be questioned at a time like this. She felt ill. Beads of perspiration were trickling down the side of her cold face. 'Can you flag me a hackney cab, Lillian? I want to go home.'

'I don't think you should, dear, not just yet.' Lillian knelt before her, unlaced Harriet's boots and pulled them off. Then she lifted her legs and made her as comfortable as she could on the recliner. 'Polly will be here soon with her smelling salts. Say no to her if you feel you don't need them.'

'I don't. Just a glass of cold water.'

'And a tiny drop of brandy?'

'No. Just water.' Trying to hide another pain, Harriet closed her eyes tight. 'I'll be all right. Overdone it a bit, that's all. Tried to get five hours' work done in three.' Then she opened her eyes and peered into Lillian's hazel ones. 'Will it be all right if I doze off for ten minutes?'

'Of course it will. Once you feel a little better, we'll get you upstairs and into bed.'

'No. No, I don't want to settle down. If I could just lie here for a while, Lillian, I'll be fine.' She licked her dry lips.

Lillian placed a feather cushion beneath her head. 'Try not to worry. I'll have Polly fetch you a cool drink and then we'll see you're not disturbed.'

'What if a client comes in and sees me like this?' Harriet could no longer keep her eyes open. 'Won't be good for business, will it?'

'Hardly,' said Lillian, patting Harriet's swollen belly. 'But who cares about clients at a time like this? I certainly don't.'

Arriving with salts in one hand and a glass of water in the other, Polly looked at Lillian, apparently waiting for words of wisdom but all she received was a smile.

'I always said you were a mind-reader. Or are your ears sharper than your eyes?' Lillian asked.

'What're you talking about?' snapped Polly.

'The water. It's all that Harriet wants. No smelling salts, just water. You read her mind.' She was giving her a message.

'Course I bleedin' never. Anyone who's close to passin' out wants water.' She put the glass to Harriet's lips and told her to take small sips. 'We'll forget the salts.'

'And leave Harriet to have a doze,' Lillian murmured. 'She's exhausted. Been working for hours and no doubt walked too quickly on her way here. She's exhausted, that's all.'

'Well, if you say so, Lillian. You're the wise old woman, not me.'

'Shut up, Polly, and go away,' murmured Harriet, amused but too weak to laugh. 'Let me sleep.'

Before Lillian and Polly were down the stairs and in the kitchen, Harriet was drifting off to sleep. 'She's too strong willed for her own good,' said Lillian, giving Polly a certain look. 'It does nobody good in the end. A stubborn streak is worse than a yellow one.'

'Well I know what I'd prefer to 'ave,' sniffed Polly. 'And so would you.'

Outside, with the sun on her face, Jacqueline Turner was smiling. Not only had she seen Harriet but she had seen her pregnant – and quite close to her time, if she was not mistaken. All she had to do now was keep a low profile and wait until she came out of the house then follow her. At least God had deemed fit to throw her this second crust – he had led her to Harriet in the first place.

Fifteen minutes later, Polly came out of the house, ran off towards the main road and returned in a cab. Once Harriet was settled inside and on her way home, the midwife strolled over to where the woman was now standing outside the gates. She had recognized her as Lillian's cheeky servant. She aimed to engage her in conversation to see if she could find out where the cab was heading.

'Hello again,' she said, looking into Polly's face. 'I don't suppose you remember me but I'm the woman who came for the interview as cook and left suddenly.'

'I do remember you,' returned Polly, giving her the once-over.

'I had meant to come sooner than this to apologise for leaving in such a haste on my last visit.'

'Oh. Well, then, you'll want to speak to Lillian Redmond. I'm not sure if she's still looking for a chef, mind, but you can—'

Jacqueline raised a hand to stop her and managed a friendly smile. 'No. I shan't be seeking work in that field again. As you can see from my clothes, I've gone back to my previous profession as midwife and nurse.'

'So you're not a cook any more?' said Polly. 'Is that why you left without saying goodbye? You changed yer mind?'

'In a way. I lost my nerve. I have worked as a professional cook but never in such a homely place as this. I questioned myself, once I was in the study waiting for the lady of the house, as to whether I was the right person for the position. Intimate dinner parties for gentlemen of the City is something I've not come across before.'

'Well, I wish you'd 'ave come and knocked on the door twenty minutes sooner. My best friend could have done with seeing you.'

'That'll be the young lady who just left in the cab, would it? She didn't look too healthy for someone so close to her time. I should think she must be seven or eight months' gone?'

'More or less.' Polly peered at the woman's face and then said, 'I don't s'pose you've got time to pop round and take a look at her? We've very concerned and she wouldn't hear of us calling in a doctor. A bit stubborn is our Harriet.'

'Of course I wouldn't mind. Looking after pregnant mothers is my calling. Delivering their babies is only part of the work. We must care for the plant if we are to have strong seedlings.' She smiled.

'I suppose that's a way of seein' it. Harriet lives at number four Musbury Street. It's just off—'

'I know where it is. Off Jubilee Street. It's in my territory, luckily. Most likely I would have been called to see to her once her time had come.' Jacqueline pulled a small ladies' fob watch from her top pocket and checked the time. 'If I walk through the back doubles now I'll be able to spare her ten minutes, which is all I need to check her over. I have three other mothers to see this afternoon. Please apologise to your employer for my leaving without a word. I was in the square plucking up the courage to come to the door and explain myself.'

'That's all right,' said Polly, narrowing her eyes and peering at the woman's face. 'You tell Harriet to put her feet up, won't you? She's a proper work'orse that one.'

'I shall indeed,' said Jacqueline, and walked away.

Watching her striding off, in her light grey cape, hat and long skirt, she looked like someone out of an old picture journal. The midwife, to Polly's mind, was trapped in a time warp. Living in the past and unable to let go of the last century. She was an old Victorian in so far as she could make out and that was no bad thing when it came to experience. She was just the ticket for Harriet, she mused.

By the time Jacqueline Turner arrived in Jubilee Street, Harriet was inside her little house and resting on her bed, sipping a hot cup of tea but feeling no better for it. She glanced up at the clock on the mantelshelf and was relieved to see that Alice would soon be home. She was experiencing worse pains now but the feeling wasn't right. She remembered when her mother had been expecting her baby brother and had explained in detail what would happen when the baby was ready to come so that Harriet would recognise the signs and be quick to fetch the midwife for her.

There was no such movement inside as her mother had described but the pain in her lower back and stomach was growing stronger and she was frightened that she might suddenly go into labour and have to do it all by herself. The worry she had been going through, on and off, during the past week or so had now turned to hard facts. She knew she needed the doctor, and wished Alice was home so that she could send her for one.

Standing at the end of Musbury Street, Jacqueline was weighing her options. This was a fine opportunity to call at the house and as likely as not Harriet Smith would be by herself. If there was a husband, he would be at work. But the midwife could not afford to draw attention to herself and the shock to Harriet of seeing her after all this time might set off her contractions and cause a premature birth. If anything untoward happened to her, the finger would be pointed at the midwife – of this she had no doubt. During her years in the profession she had learned one thing: her patients and their spouses treated her as if she was an angel of God when the birth went smoothly and damned her as the devil in disguise when it did not.

She went into a tiny café and ordered a glass of lemonade to give herself time to think things through. It would be wise to walk away now and wait until she was called officially to attend Harriet, but a voice inside her urged otherwise.

Lying on her side with the pains setting in again, Harriet blamed herself for not leaving the soap factory sooner and asked God to forgive her and promised she would be good from then on and never swear again or blaspheme on a Sunday. She believed that her baby was suffering because she had stood day after day packing soap into boxes. Older and wiser women who had experienced childbirth had warned her to take things easier but she had ignored them. Now she knew she should have taken their advice, and was very frightened – for herself and what lay ahead, and for the baby who was going to be born earlier than nature planned.

Questions flew through her mind. What if she wasn't strong enough to help the baby into the world? Had she been foolish to come home in the cab when she should have asked to be dropped off at the local hospital? What if she died giving birth and the baby was born with no one to take care of it?

She held her breath as another severe pain gripped her stomach and back, then grabbed Arthur's pillow and clutched it as she felt a strong urge to bear down. Once the pain had passed she imagined she needed to go to the lavatory. The pain was almost identical to when she had been constipated and had taken a spoonful of thick black bitters to open her. She gazed at the bedroom door, wondering if she could make it by herself to the back yard, and decided against it.

Deep in her own thoughts, Alice was in no hurry to get home. She was thinking about Alfred and his offer to take her out one evening to see a show at the Foresters Music Hall in Cambridgeheath Road. She liked him, but not in the same way as she liked Bo's woodwork teacher at the People's Palace. The tutor hadn't invited her out but was always quick to say hello and begin a conversation. He had beautiful eyes, and the way he looked into her face made her heart beat differently. He was very good-looking while Alfred was quite ordinary – ordinary, but kind and nice. And she felt far more comfortable with Alfred. He and she were alike and had things in common. Sometimes they talked non-stop right through their break and she was never bored.

She decided that she would talk to her sister and ask her advice. She didn't want to lead Alfred on, but neither did she want to put him off. As she approached the house, preoccupied with her dilemma, she did not notice the midwife further along the turning. As she scrabbled in her handbag for her door key she was startled when Jacqueline Turner asked if she lived there.

'Oh!' gasped Alice, a hand on her chest. 'You frightened me.'

'Well, I never meant to, I can assure you.'

'No, of course not. I was miles away.' Alice looked the woman up and down. 'Are you a midwife?' she asked cautiously.

'Yes, I am. A friend of Harriet's asked me to call to see if she was any better. She had a bad turn in a house in Beaumont Square, apparently. I didn't want to knock on the door for fear of waking her if she was resting. You came along at just the right time. I've only just arrived.'

'Oh dear,' murmured Alice. 'Poor Harriet. And I've dawdled all the way home. I'm her sister.'

She pushed the key into the lock, but before she

turned it the midwife grasped her arm. 'A quiet word before we go in.' She smiled. 'I would like you to see how she is first, and if she does need me, come and let me know. Don't tell her I've arrived. Sometimes that panics my mothers. If she's resting on the bed, close the curtains to keep the room shady. Then, and only then, tell her that Polly from the house in Beaumont Square asked me to call round to check up on her. Tell her I'm the local midwife and it's best if she lies nice and quiet while I feel her stomach. And, most importantly, you must stay by her side while I check her pulse. Your presence will help keep her on an even keel.'

'I understand,' said Alice, wide-eyed and innocent. 'Shall I go in now, then?'

'Yes. I'll wait here. Leave the door ajar.'

'I will,' promised Alice.

Jacqueline Turner's mind was working fast. If the girl managed to persuade Harriet to agree to be seen by the midwife, she would have to play it carefully. She would keep her face turned away or her head down so she was not recognised immediately and, she wanted Alice in there as a witness in case Harriet was in serious trouble and things went wrong when the finger of blame would be pointed at herself. If the ginger-headed troublemaker recognised her as the midwife from hell, she would scream blue murder.

Alice appeared, startling her. 'You can come in, midwife. She's lying nice and quiet with her eyes closed although she's not asleep. And I've closed the curtains. She likes it better now that it's darker in there. Did you want to come in, then?'

'Yes. Lead the way, if you please.'

Leaning over her sister, Alice whispered, 'The midwife's here, Harriet. She's going to feel your stomach to make sure everything's all right.'

'Gimme yer hand,' whispered Harriet. 'Don't let go of it.'

'Course I won't.'

Her eyes shut tight, Harriet lay still while Jacqueline felt her stomach and took her pulse.

Her fear of all midwives had finally confronted her. She wanted to scream at the woman to get out. Scream for Arthur. Scream for her mother. Scream for any reason so that she could release the terror of midwives she had been harbouring all through her pregnancy.

Her brief examination over, Jacqueline replaced the quilt over Harriet, picked up her black medical bag and left the room, with Alice following. Once outside in the street, her face set, she showed no emotion as she said, 'I shall inform the doctor, who will come to the house, that your sister's baby is dead. It will be stillborn. Another midwife will accompany the doctor. This is an urgent case so they'll be here immediately. Stay by her side until they arrive.'

'I will, midwife,' said Alice shocked. 'I won't leave her.'

Alice closed the door as quietly as she could, crept into Harriet's bedroom and sat in the chair by her side. Harriet's eyes were still closed and she looked almost as white as the sheet. 'It's not good news, Harriet,' she managed to say. 'It's really not.'

'I know,' said Harriet, in a defeated tone. 'It's all right. I know my baby's stopped moving.'

'Try not to think about it, eh? The doctor's coming soon with another midwife.'

'Another?' Harriet slowly opened her eyes. 'A different one?'

'That's right, but the important thing is that a doctor's coming too.'

Harriet drew her hand to her stomach and stroked it. 'My little baby's dead, Alice. Did she tell you that?'

'Well, she said she thought it might be. It couldn't have been very well in there. It must have got ill, just like babies out here. They get ill and don't always recover. You remember our little brother . . .'

'Course I do. He was beau'iful. I loved 'im so much. But he was only weak through being hungry. My baby wasn't hungry. I ate for two. You said that.'

'Well, then, maybe something else wasn't right. Well, it couldn't 'ave been, could it? Otherwise it would still be kicking.' Tears were slowly rolling down Alice's face. 'Our little brother never stood a chance, really. But yours would 'ave done if it was strong enough to be born, Harriet. You would have made sure of that. It would have been loved. Well, it was loved already. We all loved it. Still do.'

'Did she say how long the doctor would take coming?'

'Not long. She said it was urgent. I think she was

more worried about you. He'll be here soon. Can I get you anything?'

'No. Just leave me be, Alice. I want to be alone wiv my baby. I'm gonna say a prayer now because once they take it away it won't be mine any more. I know they won't let me keep it, and I don't want it to be taken away by strangers. I want to keep it here with me, then bury it in a nice little grave next to the church. But they won't let me do that, will they?'

'I'm not sure. We'll ask, shall we?'

'They won't let me keep it. It's not fair. This is my baby and nuffing to do wiv anyone else. But they won't see it like that.'

'But they're not bad people, Harriet. They'll just examine it, make it nice in a white gown and put it in a nice little bed—'

'A coffin, Alice. They'll put it in a coffin.'

'Yeah, but I've seen a coffin, when my friend's granny died. It was lovely, Harriet, all lined with white satin. They'll put your baby in a silk gown. I'll make certain of that. I'll tell the doctor when he comes. I will. I promise.'

'Did she say it was definitely dead, then? Or that it might be?'

'Well, she thought it had stopped moving.'

'Did she, Alice? Did she say it was dead?'

'Well . . . she said it was going to be stillborn.'

'So it is dead, then.' Harriet turned her face to Alice and burst into tears. 'Why? Why, Alice? I never did anyfing to 'urt my baby. Why 'as it died?'

'I don't know.' Alice held her sister's hand. 'I don't

know why our brother died either. I don't know why anyone dies unless they're old and ready for it. But it just keeps on happening. Over and over. And I don't know why.'

'Look at us.' Harriet smiled through her tears, genuine tears and a genuine smile. 'Soakin' the bleedin' sheet with tears and snot.'

'Shall I make us a nice pot of tea?'

'Why not? Tea makes the world go round.'

Harriet watched her sister leave the room, and laid her head down on the pillow feeling calmer for Alice having been there. She was like an angel. Then she looked around the room that Arthur had whitewashed and painted. It looked lovely with the flowery curtains and simple polished furniture. Homely. Her eyes focused on a tallboy where Arthur had placed a small teddy bear, which he had brought with him from Whitehead Street. He had had it since he was a baby and he had wanted his baby to see it.

Crying again, Harriet was gripped by pain and the urge to bear down. She clutched the iron bedstead with both hands and fought against it. She didn't want to deliver her baby without the doctor or a midwife to help her. The sudden knock at the door brought relief. Help was here. Someone would see her through this nightmare.

Shocked to see Harriet looking so poorly and to find that her baby was dead inside her, Jacqueline walked through the back-streets of Stepney Green, her emotions in turmoil. While she had been in Harriet's room with her, the past had come flooding back to the midwife and now she was trapped in it, assailed by visions of when she had lived in Whitehead Street and had delivered a neighbour's baby or laid out a dead body.

Walking home slowly, she could see her beloved Thomas, happy as a sandboy one minute and a lost, lonely child the next. Pictures of seasonal holidays drifted through her mind, Easter Sundays, when those who could afford to dressed in white for church, Christmas Days when snow lay thick and frost sparkled on the trees and people wore something red. And finally the old Jago, where the poorest of the poor scraped by, half wishing they would not see another winter out. It was a cruel world, a world in which the midwife felt she no longer belonged. She had no one to talk to and no one to love or be loved by.

For most of her life, Jacqueline had taken pride in delivering babies into the world but somehow she had also seen fit to take the lives of two women, who had done her no harm other than to fall below the line of respectability through no choice of their own. Haunting doubts were creeping into her mind as question upon question challenged at her conscience. What had possessed her to murder two innocent women, whose only crime had been to gossip too freely under the influence of drink? Why had she not sought some other way of dealing with them? What had possessed her to mimic the murderous actions of her poor demented nephew? Why hadn't God stopped her? Why hadn't He been there to protect those women and guide her away from sin? Where was He when Thomas had cried out to Him?

And now little Harriet, a child turned out into the street to fend for herself, to sleep in shop doorways in freezing cold winter, to scavenge for food without the art of a London rat. Little Harriet, who had somehow crawled through it all to find herself a husband and a home, a home in which a newborn would be warm and safe. All of this Harriet had achieved and her baby had been taken from her before she had had the chance to put it to her breast.

'The devil's work,' murmured Jacqueline. Pity for Harriet overcame her. As a child she had been on the brink of starvation with no-one to look out for her and now that she had found a loving home she was grieving and suffering over the worse possible thing – the death of her baby.

'At least you have a loving family to look after you, Harriet,' she whispered, seeing things in a different light. The need to be by herself in her small lodging rooms overwhelmed her. Her diary didn't matter any more. Let the world know what really happened. Let them read and realise that with every murder the souls of many more wither and die. Her diary would tell them. Her diary, which was her confession.

In this mood of acceptance and awareness that, at the end of her life, she would be lowered into a pauper's unmarked grave, with no one to be saddened by her departure, calm spread through her. It didn't seem to matter that life would continue as if she had never been, once she had faced her maker. The thousands of mothers she had cared for had most likely wiped her from their memory in the same way that the pain of childbirth faded quickly. She imagined her mothers' answers should they be questioned after her departure from this world and what they might say – '*The midwife? No . . . Can't place her. A strange sort of woman? I wouldn't know. What did you say she looked like?*'

What if her sacred diary did come out into the public domain, what harm could it do now? No harm to her and none to Thomas who she felt sure could not have survived Broadmoor prison. Of all his faults he had always been like a bird, free to flit from tree to tree, watching the world with all of its rights and wrongs. Caging him was the worst of all things she could imagine. No. He could not be alive. He could not have survived the treatment in a prison hospital for the insane. There was no point in her paying a visit. If not dead and buried he would have by now sank deep into his own safe insane world and her presence would disturb him.

She walked on towards the doctor's tiny surgery where she would leave a message that he was needed urgently in Musbury Street and that as she was feeling unwell she would not be making her calls today; another midwife must cover for her.

Continuing with her quiet rambling she gradually raised her voice. She glared at a group of men loitering outside a small tavern and said, 'Whitechapel will be in the history books!'

Satisfied that she at least had turned their dour moods to laughter, she ignored other passersby who cast her curious or critical looks. The difference between Jacqueline Turner and other down and outs who talked to themselves, was that she was wearing the uniform of a midwife – a citizen to respect and have faith in.

At last she reached the tobacconist's and went up to her rooms, removed her outer clothing and boots and piled them neatly in a corner. The fire was out and the room begged for the sound of crackling wood or the hissing of red coals, but if she lit it, memories of her home in Whitehead Street with Thomas visiting every day might flood back and she did not want that. Not now.

In her fireside chair, staring into cold ashes, she wallowed in self-pity and allowed herself to cry. She cried for her sister, Celeste, for her nephew, Thomas, for her beloved father and her wretched insane mother. She wept for the days when she had sat on her mother's lap, listening to the comforting sound of her heartbeat. But most of of all Jacqueline cried for herself, for the years of being lonely with no one to share her grief or her joy.

Eventually she glanced at the small north-facing window and wondered whether to light the oil lamp but decided against it.

She mused over what her father would make of things now – the talk of electricity was on everyone's lips: all homes would be converted and it would be commonplace one day to have light at the flick of a switch. What would he think of the electrically driven trams, which were already appearing on the roads? To Jacqueline they were cumbersome, noisy and dangerous.

Changes were taking place in every direction: ladies of the leisured class were coming more and more into her birthplace – taking part in 'East Ending' was the new fad. It was fashionable now among socialites and the well-to-do to be seen in pubs, taverns and music halls.

'But will the poverty ever be wiped out?' she asked herself. 'Indeed not. The rich need the soup kitchens, sailor's homes, shelters for old Jews, orphanages and lunatic asylums. They need them to feel safe and smug and in control.'

She dried her eyes. At least she had been born and would die before East London became too much of a freak show. She had fulfilled the promise she had made to herself to go back to Whitehead Street, and she had found her sister before it had been too late. She had forgiven Harriet, after all these years, and perhaps saved her life with her impromptu visit. She could think of nothing else that she had to achieve outside this room. She opened her black bag and withdrew a writing pad. She tore off a clean white page and, with her modern ink-filled pen, she wrote, 'The last Will and Testament of Jacqueline Turner. I entrust all of my belongings and savings in Westminster Bank to the National Children's Home in Bethnal Green.'

She signed it, put it into an envelope and addressed it to the local police station. Then she placed it carefully on the table by the window where it would be seen.

Calm and collected, with a warm glow in her chest, the midwife pushed several sixpences, one by one, into the gas meter. Then she turned her attention to the family album which was back on the table and an envelope that contained some loose photographs she had always meant to add to the picture portfolio of her life. She withdrew one of Thomas as a small boy and another, taken when he was eighteen and a diligent office worker, then kissed them before placing them on the mantelshelf. She added one of her mother and father on their wedding day, one of her sister Celeste, when she was a beautiful sixteen-year-old, and one of herself and Celeste together, as children. Last, she placed beside them a faded picture of her grandparents, standing proud and stern in a photographic studio, taken when they were in their seventieth year.

She placed the rest of the photographs on the small table, picked up an old soft cushion, and dropped it to the floor in front of the gas oven. Wistfully brushing her fingers across the worn black cover of the album and the faded gold embossed words, she sadly murmured, 'It's the way of the world, Father. We come into it with nothing and we leave with nothing. And so be it.' She then drank from her bottle of gin before opening the tiny oven door and turning the gas high.

Settled on the floor, her head sinking into the feather cushion, she was ready for a long awaited, and by now, much yearned for sleep. In a strangely reflective mood, with tears silently cascading down her pale and determined face, she felt at peace, as if all her last sorrows were being released and she could leave the world purged and spent. Comforting herself, she sipped her gin, which had been her crutch and seen her through the worst of times and the best of times.

Allowing herself moments of self indulgence, she began to reminisce and let her mind drift wherever it wanted . . . and it wandered back through time to when she was a child, hazy, but with a strange photographic clarity. Celeste, her sister, was young and lovely, laughing, her mother was proud and happy, and she herself was snuggled on her father's lap. The child Jacqueline, full of life, energy and hungry for adventure.

Drowsy, now, she lifted a hand to her face and suddenly began to sob. Thomas's name was on her lips. 'Thomas . . . Thomas, I couldn't help you! They wouldn't let me help you! I pray you are in heaven. Please be there, Thomas! Be there waiting for your devoted aunt who should never have left you. Thomas, if you can hear me . . . please answer! Thomas!'

It's all right, Jacqueline. Thomas is here. It was her father's voice and she was filled with light and joy.

'Daddy?' she whispered. 'Is it really you?'

We are all here, sweetheart, waiting. Open your eyes, Jacqueline. Look into the glow.

Slowly lifting her heavy eyelids, the midwife just managed to focus. It *was* her father. He was holding out his arms to her. He was saying something but she couldn't quite make out the words. She knew his voice and she was beginning to understand what he was saying. Gradually it became clearer. He was looking down at her and smiling, his outstretched arm coming closer and closer. He touched the tips of her fingers and spoke again, his voice gentle and loving . . .

Come on Jacqueline. It's over. You've walked your last mile.

In her silent bedroom, the sun streaming through a gap in the curtains, Harriet was at last feeling less guilty over the stillbirth of her lovely baby boy, but she had cried on and off for days. At least the young midwife had let her cuddle him once and kiss his little face before she had had to say goodbye.

Neither Harriet nor Arthur had wanted a post-mortem carried out on him but it was common practice after a stillbirth. On her follow-up visit the young midwife had sat at Harriet's bedside and listened sympathetically while she poured out the story of her fear of midwives without giving reason for it. At least she had got part of it off her chest and had been almost persuaded by the young midwife that those in her profession were just normal folk like herself, who had had a calling into caring for others, in a similar way that nuns felt it their natural duty to go into a convent. During their brief chat, the young lady happened to mention that an older woman who had served in the profession for decades and had become too tired to continue had chosen to end her life instead of living without a cause. Harriet felt as if a bolt of lightning had shot through her when the midwife told her the woman's name: Jacqueline Turner.

She felt a peculiar sense of loss since she had feared

the midwife's reappearance for so long that it seemed almost impossible to shake off the fear and let it go. Then she found herself feeling sorry for Jacqueline. She wondered now if the woman had been afraid of her too.

Bo came into Harriet's bedroom with a tray containing onion soup and bread. She looked lovely in her long skirt and blouse. Her brown hair was still cropped like a boy's and her bright green eyes still had the look of apprehension from a childhood spent back and forth between the workhouse and the Children's Home in Bethnal Green. When Harriet had asked about her life in the home, Bo had offered no more than a shrug and Harriet knew it was best to leave it at that. She had seen for herself in a newspaper picture the misery of the orphans in the Bethnal Green children's home. It had been the main reason for her escape from the home after one night. Even dossing in shop doorways and queuing at the Salvation Army with other waifs and strays for a farthing breakfast had seemed preferable to living there.

When Dr Barnardo took possession of a house in Flower and Dean Street, then a second in Dock Street, and licensed them as common lodging houses for children, a glimpse of better things to come emerged. At his lodging houses, the doors were open at seven each evening to admit destitute children. A simple nourishing meal was provided, followed by prayers, and the lights were dimmed at bedtime when the doors were locked and bolted. But those trusted with running these places were strict disciplinarians, often with a hidden cruel and twisted streak. However, under the eye of Dr Barnardo the children were safer than they might have been in the National Children's Home in Bethnal Green, where those with perverted leanings were attracted to work.

No doubt, in the photograph Harriet had seen the orphans had been ordered to smile, but it was evident that they had nothing to smile about. Bruised boys and girls, aged from two to eleven, wore shoes that were far too tight with their toes poking out, dirty old clothes, too large or too small, and all had similar expressions, defiant or defeated, the older ones comforting the young. Their faces and hair had been scrubbed for the occasion but the bruises, from a fist, foot or burning cigar, could not be washed away. Neither could the camera hide the pleas for help in their desperate eyes.

Bo, who had been through the mill in every way, had suffered beyond description but now, after a few months in this modest home with people who had grown to love her, she had blossomed. It hadn't cost money, just care.

'I might 'ave put a bit too much salt in the soup,' said Bo, placing the tray on Harriet's lap. 'Shall I plump yer pillows so you'll be more comf'table?'

'No, I'm all right. This smells lovely. Where's yours?'

'I've put it in the tin wiv a lid that Arfer give me. I dipped me bread in it first while it was in the saucepan and ate that. I'll take the soup wiv me to the cabinet-makers and 'ave it when I'm 'ungry.'

'Fair enough. You've got it all worked out. I'll be up and about in a day or so. The nurse said I should get back on my feet now, soon as I feel ready.'

'But not unless one of us is in. Arfer said so.'

'I know what he said. He's always saying it. I already get out of bed when you're all out to work.' She looked into Bo's worried face and smiled. 'When I pee in the commode.'

'Oh, yeah, course you does.'

'Go on, then or you'll get the sack.'

'I won't. I'm doin' another carvin' on the back of a chair. And foreman's gonna pay me a florin for doin' it.'

'Well, that's somefing I s'pose.' Harriet spooned the delicious soup into her mouth. 'I hope he's still givin' you trainin' in other fings.'

'Course he is. Dovetail joints at the present,' Bo said, standing upright and proud. 'See you later on.' Before she went out, though, she turned slowly and became her old timid self, which did not get past Harriet.

'What's that daft look for?'

'I was just wondering . . . if you's all right now? Not as sad as you was? Cos if you was I'm sure we could get you a little baby. They gets lots of 'em at the work'ouse. There's a delivery all the time.'

'What d'yer mean, Bo?' Harriet had visions of a horse and cart turning up with a full load. 'The work'ouse don't want babies. They want you once you can walk and work.'

'No, they don't want the babies – but they just

come. Sometimes in the day but mostly at night. You hears that bleedin' scream and you knows, just knows, another poor little bastard's bin born.'

'Is that right? Well, now, first off, enough of the swearing.'

'But you says "bleedin'" all the time!'

'I was talkin' about "poor bastard". That's swearin', and if Arfer 'ears you say that he'll go berserk. We don't swear in this 'ouse.'

'But you says arse'oles sometimes.'

'That's different. One rule for me and another for you. That's my swear word and I'm not sharin' it. Not even wiv you.'

'Right,' said Bo. 'I s'pose you are better, then? You sound like you used to and you've got fire in yer eyes again. I just didn't want you to go cuttin' yer wrists, that's all.'

'Bleedin' 'ell! Where'd you get that from?'

'A lot of women did it after their baby was took.'

'After it died, you mean?'

'Sometimes they died but mostly they got took. So you won't cut yer wrists, no matter what?'

'No, I won't. Now, go to work.'

Harriet waited until she heard Bo leave the house and the door slam behind her. Then she found herself smiling through tears. She was glad that Bo was out of the workhouse and in her and Arthur's care, but she was a constant reminder of grief and suffering. With a certain look, she could bring Harriet close to tears, yet she had just heard Bo tell of babies dying and being given away. So why was she feeling a little relieved?

Could it be because Bo had deliberately painted a picture of an even worse situation than Harriet had endured? Had this been her way of bringing Harriet back to her old self?

She dried her eyes on the sheet and glanced at Arthur's pillow, which still bore the impression of his head. She pulled it close to her side and stroked it. Poor Arthur. He had been so close to tears while he watched her holding their baby, but had used every bit of will-power to be brave and act like a man. 'Silly old fool,' she murmured. 'Never mind, though . . . There's a reason for everyfing.'

Crying into her soup she nibbled on a piece of bread although she was not hungry. 'Come on, Harriet, got to keep the wolf away from the door. Keep yer strength up.' But no matter how hard she tried, she couldn't eat. She wanted her baby and that was all there was to it. She wanted her baby at her breast drinking the milk that was still trickling out, a constant reminder that she had the food and no one to give it to.

She put the tray on the floor beside the bed, slid down under the covers and cried as she cuddled Arthur's pillow close to her breast. Before she had realised what she was doing, she began to pat it and sing quietly through her tears: 'Hush, little baby, don't you cry, Mummy's gonna sing you a lullaby . . .'

Later, having read Flora's letter once more, she smiled at her friend's touching words. She had been clever enough to find just the right ones. Instead of trying to cheer her up, Flora had confessed that if the same thing had happened to her she would have gone

to pieces. She had gone on to give a brief account
of what Beanie was up to and had ended with a
down-to-earth piece of advice: don't go jumping in
straight away. Wait until you're strong again. You've
got all the time in the world.

It had just turned one o'clock and Flora was due
at three. This would be the first time Harriet had had
a visitor since she'd lost her baby. Now she was just
about ready to face people, even Polly and Lillian who
she knew would find it hard to hide their upset. She
had been disappointed when her mother had written
to say how sorry she was to hear of the baby's death
and that she would get over to see her as soon as she
could. It went against the grain feel sorry for herself
that her mother had not been there when she most
needed her, and Harriet had missed her – had missed
her during her childhood and afterwards. She had had
to be tough for everyone's sake when the family
had been parted, but over the past few days, she had
had time to think and be honest with herself. She
had had a horrible childhood, but she had survived.
Now she was nicely off and happy with Arthur.

Her dad's face was in her mind when she recalled the
birth of her baby brother. Jacqueline Turner had been
a good, hard-working woman, an excellent midwife
who had fought to save his life against all the odds. She
had been kind to Harriet's mother and had handled her
father exactly right, giving him orders he had dared not
disobey. It was rare for her strong-willed father to be
quietened by a woman, midwife or not.

In her present mood, Harriet couldn't help thinking

back to her childhood and happier times spent as a family. At Christmas time they had pulled together to make the most of a special time of year. They had lit a proper fire on Christmas morning, and the only oil lamp had been turned up high. Paper chains and lanterns that she, Alice and their mother had made were strung across the room. A beautiful hand-made family Christmas card, kept from when their mother had been a child, was always placed on the mantelshelf. A small chicken, snatched by Mr Smith from the poultry market, sizzled in the tiny range with roast potatoes and parsnips, greens and gravy.

The present boxes for herself and Alice contained an orange, a few nuts to crack open, a stick of toffee and, best of all, a toy: a home-made skipping rope with wooden handles, a wooden hoop or a whipping top. On Boxing Day, the local priest and his helpers would deliver the charity box to all the families along their turning, with sausages, cold meat, some fruit cake, bread, a packet of tea and a small Christmas card with a picture of Jesus on the front.

For the first time in her life, Harriet was allowing herself to wander down into Memory Lane, to when life was hard and rough but they had been together as a family. The face of her father, smiling at the Christmas dinner table, came to mind. No one could have blamed him for walking out. He had said so many times, when they been hungry and cold with no money to spend on food or fuel, that they would be better off without him, that charity was hard to come by when there was a man in the house. She recalled the funny expressions he made behind her mother's back when she had been nagging. She remembered when he had suggested that she and her sister go carol-singing to those houses where the wealthy folk lived and, in particular, Jewish families. She understood why they should sing humbly to the rich, but to the Jews who didn't celebrate Christmas? His grin and twinkle was his answer. They would be the only carol-singers to dare – and although some might be affronted others would be touched by the innocence. It had worked. One evening when the snow was fluttering down they had done as he suggested and returned home with elevenpence each.

Harriet wanted Alice to be at home with her, to talk about those times when there had been sunny moments as well as dark ones. She wanted to relive them with her sister and, more importantly, she wanted her baby brother back. Oh, yes, they had said he was better off dead, that he hadn't suffered but had slipped quietly away.

'But that wasn't *true!*' Harriet shrieked suddenly. 'He *starved* to death! His mother's milk dried up from *hunger*! *My baby brother died of starvation!*' She burst into tears, threw Arthur's pillow across the room and cried, '*I want my baby!*'

She ripped away the bedclothes, leapt out of bed, wrenched open the top drawer of a chest and grabbed pile after pile of the pressed baby clothes Flora had given her and flung them about the room. Then she lifted the high chair, which Arthur had painted pale primrose, and smashed it against the floor until it was in pieces. Her blood hot and pumping through her veins, she was almost out of breath but not out of steam. As she looked around for something else on which to vent her anger she heard the door knocker. She ignored it, ripped the covers off the bed, then grabbed her pillow. She yanked off the case and then, using her new-found strength, tore at the seam until it came apart and feathers flew out.

Again she heard the door knocker. 'Go away!' she screamed. 'Piss off!'

Flora was tapping on the window and peering in. 'Harriet, stop it! Open the door! Now!'

'Go away! I don't want you near me! Sod off! My baby's dead! Dead! And he's not coming back! I delivered a dead baby! Dead baby, dead baby, dead baby!'

The sound of glass breaking stopped her in her tracks and she stared at the window as Flora's hand came through a jagged hole, grabbed the iron handle and eased it down. When the window flew open and Flora came through, Harriet backed against the wall.

'Don't you ever tell me to piss off again, Harriet Smith!'

'Dean! Harriet Dean!'

Hands on hips, eyes blazing, Flora shook her head. 'I've just risked my life for you!'

'I never asked you to, did I?' screeched Harriet. 'And you've broke my fuckin' winda!'

Flora glanced about the room and started to laugh. 'Well, you've made a fine mess of this, Harriet.'

'So what if I have?' Harriet turned and went out

of the bedroom. 'I can do what I like in my own house.'

Flora followed her friend into the kitchen. 'It'll take you ages to clear that room.'

'Good. I'd rather be in there than in the kitchen.' Harriet was filling the kettle. 'You're five minutes late, by the way. And thanks for yer letter.'

'That's all right,' said Flora, sitting down in Arthur's chair. 'I was gonna fetch Beanie but Mum didn't think I should. She's baby-sittin'.'

'Well, you should tell 'er it's not catchin' – but I s'pose you can't blame 'er for bein' worried.'

'Stop bein' silly.' For all she had written in her letter, Flora weakened and suddenly broke into tears. She mopped herself up quickly, then said, 'You're taking it so well, Harriet, I wish I could be more like you.'

'What – and smash a room up? Pull yourself together. You're s'posed to be lookin' after *me*. I should be in that bed waited on 'and and foot.'

'Shouldn't have messed it up, then, should you?' said Flora, dabbing her eyes. 'But I understand – I know 'ow much you were looking forward to being a mum.'

Harriet gazed at her friend, a touch bewildered. 'Flora, I'm not s'posed to be comfortin' *you*.'

'I know. I'm sorry. It's just that when I think—'

'Well, don't bleedin' think! I've done my cryin', fank you. Cried m'self bleedin' dry. You're all I need! It wasn't meant to be,' said Harriet, spooning tea into the pot. 'That's all there is to it. That's the way I see it now.' She was about to go on but Flora, looking up at her, nodding and smiling through a stream of tears, was too much. She burst out laughing. 'I knew you'd be a tonic – I just knew it!' And the more she laughed the more Flora cried.

Half an hour and two pots of tea later, they were on a more even keel and Harriet was opening up. 'I knew somefing 'ad 'appened deep down. I just didn't want to accept it. I knew it 'ad stopped moving. Never mind the pains – which were labour pains if I'd but known it. My womb was trying to push out the baby before things turned nasty. The doctor said the baby 'ad faded away before I 'ad the pains even. He said it was a blessing that I never died too. Good job that midwife came when she did and called the doctor. She saved my life, according to the doctor. Much longer and I'd 'ave bin a goner too and that wouldn't 'ave been very nice for Arfer, would it? Flora? *Would it?*'

'No! Sorry, Harriet. It's just that—'

'Don't you dare start crying again.' Harriet pointed a teaspoon at her friend.

'I won't. I promise. It's just that—'

'Flora . . .'

'All right, all right. But it's just that I'm so pleased to see you with a bit of colour in your face and back to your old self. There! I've said it.'

'Oh, right, well, that should go down in the 'istory books, shouldn't it? Really important bit of information that was.' Harriet paused. Then she said, 'I'm gonna tell you somefing, Flora, and you must promise not to say anyfing. Ever. To anyone.'

'I shouldn't 'ave to promise, Harriet. You know that.'

'True, but, well, you might think I'm going peculiar above the eyebrows and want to tell Arfer to watch out for my mind in case I lose it. And I won't lose it. Not now. I needed to let it out and I've done it. Alice'll love to tidy the bedroom so that's two birds wiv one stone.'

'Well, go on, then,' said Flora, intrigued. 'What 'ave you got to tell me?'

'The midwife who came first and then went for the doctor, I knew who she was. I kept my eyes shut tight so she wouldn't know I knew but I recognised 'er smell. A soap-and-gin sort of smell. It was the midwife from Whitehead Street.'

Flora looked puzzled. 'So?'

'She came after me. I reckon she's bin followin' me for ages. I swear to God I caught a glimpse of 'er out of the corner of my eye – and more than once.'

'Harriet, what are you talking about?'

Harriet weighed it all up, and decided not to bother. She would have to start at the beginning, and what was the point? Jacqueline Turner was dead. It was over. She could forget her and her nephew, Thomas, and get on with her life.

'I said, what are you talking about Harriet? Why would a midwife come after you?'

'I never said that.'

'Yes, you did.'

'I never – and what's more, I'm supposed to be in my sick bed with you sittin' on a chair next to me, visitin'. How come I made the tea and waited on you?'

'Because I was upset. Now, then, the midwife. You're not gettin' off that lightly.'

Relieved that Flora had insisted, Harriet told her story, from the beginning right up to the time she thought she'd sensed Jacqueline Turner in the Pavilion. 'But what I don't understand,' said Harriet, feeling better for having unleashed her story, 'is why she gassed herself. Because that's what she did. It was in the paper. They reckon it was because 'er sister 'ad done the same thing and she was the midwife's only family.'

'I can understand that,' said Flora. 'Maybe seein' you again and in a sorry old state, she'd 'ad enough of this bleedin' world.'

'Flora!' Harriet grinned. 'You swore!'

'Well, there we are, then. My dad was right. He said too much time in your company and I'd pick up bad 'abits.'

'Bleedin' cheek! You wait till I see 'im. I don't swear.'

'Listen, Harriet, I need to earn some money. When are you going to be well enough to take me to the factory and get me in on the piecework?'

'Oh, I'll put my coat on and we'll go now, shall we?'

'No. Too soon. The day after tomorrow'll do. I'll come round at three and we'll go by 'ackney cab – unless you're up to walking. You decide.' With that Flora stood up, brushed herself down and kissed

Harriet goodbye. 'I'm going to say this, Harriet, and I'll say no more. I know you must be sick of people giving you advice—'

'Go on, then, spit it out.'

'You'll have moods. You might feel sorry for yourself already and been depressed, but the next stage is anger. You might find you'll want to burst at the seams and smash everyfing in sight.'

Harriet felt like hugging her friend. 'Well, I should fink it's started, then. You've seen the bedroom.'

'Well, as long as you know it's normal.'

'All I know is that I feel better for usin' a bit of energy. But I'll be aware of it and try to be patient with Arfer, if that's what you're sayin'.'

'And yourself. And anyone around you. I'll let myself out.' With that, Flora made a hasty departure, closing the door behind her.

'Clever bleedin' cow,' murmured Harriet. 'Thank God for real friends.' Worn out, now, she carried a glass of water back into her bedroom, took one look at the mess and the broken window and made her way upstairs to doze on Alice's bed.

Alice was the first home from work and was as quiet as a mouse so as not to disturb her sister. On one hand she was blissfully happy and on the other she was devastated by the news she had received at the library: Alfred, the librarian, had plucked up the courage to ask if she would like to go with him to a literary evening at the Queen's Palace in Poplar and she had said yes; and Arthur had been arrested by the railway police.

She was so preoccupied with trying to decide the best way to break the news to Harriet that she didn't notice the broken window, and since Harriet had closed the bedroom door she had no idea of the mess inside or the state of her sister's mind. She glanced at the clock and knew it wouldn't be long before their mother arrived. She had telephoned mid-afternoon from the library in Whitechapel to the library in Camberwell and asked her to come straight away.

Believing Harriet to be in her own bed, resting, she filled the kettle and put it on the range. She looked out of the small window into the yard and admired the lovely view of roses in full bloom, old climbing ivy and clematis against the back wall. She imagined herself and Alfred sitting out there on a sunny afternoon, chatting idly. But the vision of Arthur behind bars clouded the lovely picture.

A knock at the front door snapped her out of her reverie. Her mother was early and when Alice saw her standing on the doorstep in her smart blue ankle-length coat and matching hat she burst into tears.

'That broken window-pane wants replacing,' her mother said.

'We have to keep our voices down, eh? Harriet needs her rest.'

'*Who you bleedin' whisperin' to, Alice?*' came the shrill, half-awake voice of her sister from above.

Mrs Smith unbuttoned her coat. 'You don't think it might be better coming from you, Alice? I mean to say, I hardly know Arthur.'

'No. I wouldn't be any good. She's going to need you now, Mum, more than ever.'

'We'll see. She never was one for taking advice so I doubt she'll listen to anything I've got to say.'

'*Alice! Who is it?*'

'It's your mother, Harriet. I'll be up as soon as I've settled.' The ensuing silence brought a smile to Mrs Smith's face. 'That's shocked her.' She handed her hat and coat to Alice, then found her way into the kitchen where she poured herself a glass of water. 'Fetch a pot of tea up, Alice. I'd best get this over and done with. Knowing your sister she'll be all at sixes and sevens when she hears.' She climbed the stairs and went into Alice's bedroom whence Harriet's voice had come.

'Those stairs are a bit creaky,' she said, sitting on the edge of the bed and peering into Harriet's stunned face. 'How're you feeling? Not much colour in your cheeks but you was always a bit too pale for my liking.'

Harriet focused on her mother and at first smiled broadly, then burst into tears. 'Where've you been?' she wailed. 'I thought you never cared about me losing my baby!'

Mrs Smith ran her fingers through her hair. 'You never thought that and you know it. Still on the low side, I expect.'

'Course I'm bleedin' well on the low side. Wouldn't you be?'

Mrs Smith gave her daughter a knowing look. 'I was, Harriet, once upon a time. You don't get over the loss of a baby just like that. It takes a while before you can accept it.'

Harriet lowered her eyes, then pulled herself up. 'Well, it's just as well you came today 'cos I was gonna write you a letter askin' where you was. Why did you take so long comin'?' she murmured. 'I needed you.'

'Life's not as simple as that. If only we could all drop everything and run when the need arises, but we can't.'

'You sound like your bleedin' sister. Bin living too long over south of the river, if you asks me.'

'What about Arthur, Harriet? How's he taking it?'

'Sad inside – that sort of thing. Keepin' quiet over it so as not to upset me. But I'd rather talk about it. Maybe men don't feel the same as women about these things.'

'I expect that'll be it. He's been through it all before, don't forget. You, too, if you think about it. How old was he when he was at home alone with his mum when the same thing happened to her? And she died as well as his baby sister.'

Harriet covered her face. 'That's true. I expect that's what it'll be. I felt terrible for ages after our little James died. Wasn't very old, was he? A month if that. I loved 'im, though.' She searched her mother's face.

'Well, the poor soul never knew much about it. I've had my troubles, none can deny that, but I came through. Nothing but worry on the way, but there we are. I've suffered,' Mrs Smith responded.

'In what way?' Harriet was beginning to get impatient. Every time she had been to visit her mother she had heard the same thing.

'Where shall I start? Your father was a waster in the

old days. I had three little ones to look after till your brother died and broke my heart. Then I had to put you into a children's home and fend for myself with a child in tow – your sister Alice. No one knows the trouble I've had.' She sighed. 'But what's the use of complaining? No one listens . . . There we are.'

The creaking of the door and the sight of Alice with just a hint of a smile on her face was a comfort to her sister. 'Did you want me to fetch your tea in or will you be getting up, Harriet?'

'I'll get up. Did you see the state of my room?'

'Yeah. I went in to have a look at the broken window. It won't take me long to clear it up. Did you feel better for it?'

'Much,' said Harriet, firmly. 'Flora came and she was a tonic.'

'That's good. So you'll come down, then? For tea?'

'Oh, Alice, stop fussing,' their mother said. 'Fetch the tea up, I've got comfortable now. Up and down those stairs, and for why? I'm not getting any younger.' Mrs Smith looked from Alice's face to Harriet's. 'You don't mind, do you, if I stop where I am? I've been at the library all afternoon. I've brought an overnight bag. I'll take your bed, Alice, once Harriet's got herself out of it. Who broke the window?'

'I did.' Harriet offered no reason or excuse and she didn't want to explain why or how Flora caused the breakage.

'Should be more careful. But, then, you always rushed about not doing things properly and breaking anything in your way. Just like your father.'

'Course you can sleep in my bed,' said Alice. 'We've got next door, don't forget. I can go in there. I expect you feel a bit weary, Mum, after travelling over from South London, and especially having lost a grandchild.'

'Tch. Don't be melodramatic, Alice. You can't lose something you never had. Harriet's baby was stillborn at six months or so. In my books that's a miscarriage not a birth.' The room fell silent as Harriet controlled her temper.

'Ne'mind, eh? Everything'll be all right from now on. Ten years' time and you'll have half a dozen children pulling at your skirt, Harriet. Won't she, Mum?' said Alice.

'I should hope not. I dare say she's learned a hard lesson from this. You must wait until you can afford children before you go throwing caution to the wind. Two children are quite enough.'

'If you marry your librarian,' said Harriet, determined not to let her mother bring them down, 'you can 'ave a dozen.'

'Four.' Alice smiled. 'That would be nice. Not a dozen, though. Couldn't afford it.'

'Oh, shut up and go and make me a cheese sandwich. I'm starving.'

'But dinner'll be ready in an hour or so.'

'I couldn't give a tosspot. You've all bin naggin' 'cos I couldn't touch food – well, now you can feed me up, can't yer? I've got some makin' up to do.'

Alice turned to her mother. 'Did you want a sandwich as well, Mum? We could have dinner much later now that—' She caught the warning look in her mother's eyes and stopped dead.

'Now that what? Now that's Mum's 'ere? She's probably more starvin' than I am. Could always eat like an 'orse, couldn't you, Mum?'

'Fetch me a sandwich as well, Alice, but don't rush. I want to have a quiet word with your sister.'

Once Alice had left the room and closed the door behind her, Mrs Smith unlaced her boots and pulled them off. Then, surprising Harriet, she edged herself on to the bed next to her. 'Move over, then, Harriet,' she said. 'Give me more space – I'm not all skin and bone any more.'

'If you're tired, Mum, why don't you get into bed properly and 'ave a sleep?'

'I'm not tired.' Mrs Smith placed an arm around her daughter's shoulders. 'I just wanted to cuddle up to my little girl,' she said, unconvincingly.

Cuddle up to her little girl? This was new, out of character and a touch on the eerie side. 'I'm hardly little – although I will say that when I was little, I could 'ave done with a few cuddles.'

'Well, I never was the cuddling type. But since I've got some dreadful news to give you I thought it best if I was here for you, in case you burst into tears.'

Harriet could hardly believe this. Her mother wanted to be there for her. Had she suddenly changed? 'Well, that's nice, Mum. You don't look too worried so I s'pose it's not that bad. Is it?' There was a long pause. 'Oh . . . Dad 'asn't . . .'

'Died? Is that what you were going to say? Well,

the answer's no, thank goodness. No, it's nothing so serious, but coming just after your miscarriage . . . that's a bit much for anyone. Even you. You might pretend to be tough but no one's made of stone.'

'Oh, I don't know,' said Harriet. 'So if Dad's all right and so is Alice. What is it?'

Smiling and wrapped in her private thoughts, Mrs Smith brushed her hair off her face. 'No, your father's more alive than he's ever been – oh, and he sends his love.' Stunned by this revelation, Harriet could only stare at her mother open-mouthed. She could see it was no jest by the expression in her eyes.

'Dad? You know where he is?'

'Course I do. He got in touch soon after we split up and I met him at London Bridge. He'd got himself a job working for a clearance company and promised that as soon as he was on his feet we'd all be back together again. He goes to some posh private houses after the dead have been carried out and strips them. Not antiques – the grieving family usually takes the good things – but he does all right. Clears factories when they close down too. I dare say he was lean when you last set eyes on him but he's filled out a bit and it's not all fat. Anyhow, the point is that we'll be getting back together, me and your dad.'

Harriet could not believe her ears. She peered into her mother's face. 'You've bin seein' 'im all these years and never told us?'

'Well, I would have told Alice, her being closer to me than you were, but your father didn't want your aunt and uncle to know his business so I kept quiet over it. He's given me little treats now and then. It's not been a bed of roses at your aunt's place but it's more comfortable than what he had to offer at the time. But that's changed now. Anyway, Harriet, that's not why I came.'

'I thought that Dad would have taken me in if he had a room,' murmured Harriet, feeling let down. Had they cast her completely out of their lives when the family had been split up?

'Well, he did suggest it once, but no . . . it wouldn't have been right. Not once I could see he was going to make something of himself. Best we were the carrots dangling. He always had a good brain, just never the opportunities. He learned a lot from the clearance work – what fetches money and what goes on the rubbish tip. After about five years he and his pal started up their own little business, with a broken-down old cart that the borough had discarded. He bought it off them for a few shillings. Said he wanted to use bits of it. But between them they fixed it up good and proper.'

'And?'

'Well, he kept on and on and on, beavering away, until he and his pal took over a yard from a wine merchant who was moving out of North London and who'd gone out of business. That bit wasn't public knowledge, bear in mind. His pal was good at rejuvenating pieces and brought them back to their former glory. Your dad's the salesman, so to speak. I'm sure he'll get in touch soon and give you a helping hand once he's doing well.'

'We don't need handouts, Mum. Arfer would go berserk. Besides, we're all right, what wiv my sewin', Alice at the library, Bo comin' along nicely at the cabinet-maker's and my Arfer doin' well at the railway.'

'Oh, I shouldn't be too proud. Especially not now he's in trouble with the police.' Mrs Smith raised an eyebrow disdainfully. 'Arthur was arrested this morning by the railway police. He's in a cell at the police station in Shoreditch, by all accounts.'

'He's what?' Harriet stiffened and drew away from her mother.

'It's not easy for a mother to deliver bad news, but someone had to do it and best it came from me. Well, Alice thought so, anyway. Really and truly I don't know the chap. How many times have I seen him? Twice? Three times?'

'My Arfer's been *arrested*? Is that what you're saying? My Arfer?'

'I suppose it's better than having to tell you he's had a tragic accident. It'd be much worse if he was dead. I think I would have made Alice break the news if it had been that bad. I remember when my father died, it was such a shock. I loved him so much. I cried and cried and cried. No one knows what it's like when you lose someone you love. My mother never—'

'*Mum!* Stop talking about yourself and tell me what's *happened*!'

'There's no need to shout, Harriet.'

'Where's my Arfer? What's going on?' She was

trembling and a ghastly sick sensation rushed though her. 'Just tell me what's happened. *Please.*'

'He's been arrested, pure and simple, by the railway police. But it's only a minor offence so—'

'Oh, Jesus! I knew this would happen!' Harriet leaped off the bed and paced the floor, wringing her hands. 'He'll lose his job over it. I kept tellin' 'im he'd get caught. What 'ave we done to deserve this? First the baby and now this.'

'Stop laying the blame elsewhere, Harriet. That's the trouble with people. When things go wrong they blame God.'

'I'm not blamin' anyone!'

'No one's perfect. You've done all right for yourself. Look how you managed to drag yourself from the gutter. I don't hear you thanking anyone for that, so don't cast a stone as soon as things go wrong. They were probably doing a spot-check and he was one of the unlucky ones. All they found on him was some fish, according to Alice.'

She looked into her mother's expressionless face. 'Alice telephoned to you at work. And that's why you came, to break it to me gently? Why couldn't she 'ave told me?'

'Well, I am your mother, after all.'

'Yeah, I was forgettin'. So what am I supposed to do now?' She clasped her head with both hands, unable to think straight. 'Alice should 'ave told me instead of draggin' you all this way.'

'She thought it best, under the circumstances. She's not as bright as you, Harriet, but that's no bad thing.

She's sensitive. Always was. I don't expect he'll get more than six months.'

'Six months? He bleedin' well won't get six months! Who told you that?'

'I was only surmising! Dear, dear, you don't change, do you? You always jump before you think. I shouldn't be too hard on your husband when you visit. I expect he was only doing it for you. Not that I know much about him, of course. This is going to set you back but you'll come through. I should know. Look at me and the life I've had. I talk from experience not presumption. I've had to put up with your aunt all these years. Fussy? She'd polish your shoes if you stood still long enough. Or get more Alice do it, more like. I don't know how I've managed to bear it all the while. The nights I've spent—'

Pacing the floor, Harriet was so angry she felt as if she would burst a blood vessel. 'I've a mind not to rush over to Shoreditch till tomorrow. Teach 'im a lesson! He'll get the sack, you can bet your last shillin'. He'll be out of work. Maybe it's as well I did lose the baby. This wicked world's not good enough for my child.'

'Don't say things like that!' Mrs Smith eased her legs off the bed and sat on the edge. 'You'll be all right. You'll pull through. You're hard, and that should help. I wish I had your resilience. I've always been soft, that's my trouble. We'll have our tea downstairs.'

Harriet studied her mother, and her heart sank. The woman was admiring her reflection in the small oval mirror. Yes, thought Harriet, I'm looking at a complete stranger. The strangest thing of all was that she felt nothing for her. No love, no hate, no resentment. Nothing. She no longer felt the need to win her love or impress her. A stranger had come to tell her the worst news possible – that her beloved Arthur was locked in a cell for stealing.

'Does Alice know about Dad?' was all she could say.

'No. He didn't want me to say anything to either of you until he had a place. A proper home you could visit. Tell your sister if you feel you must. Knowing you, you'll do what you want anyway. This kind of a thing upsets me. I'm too soft that's my trouble.'

'Really?' murmured Harriet. 'Well, I wouldn't have said you were too soft, Mum. I would have said you saw what you wanted and worked your way to gettin' it. No shame in that, I s'pose. You always look smart.'

'I should say so. Determination and hard work go hand in hand.' With a faint smile she left the room.

Harriet felt a sense of loss – not just because of the news Mrs Smith had delivered, but because mother and daughter had been on the same bed and all hopes of closeness had been crushed for ever. This woman meant nothing to her and no doubt Mrs Smith felt the same about Harriet. They had been too long apart.

Pictures of her life floated through her mind, and Harriet felt giddy. She had been warned about mood changes by Flora and now she seemed to be swinging from one emotion to another like a pendulum. She was furious with Arthur at one minute and thinking of her lost childhood the next. She couldn't take it in. Arthur in prison? Her father reuniting with her mother? Her mother here to comfort her? The world was closing in on her.

Resentment and rage rose inside her. Continuing to pace the floor, she argued that her mother had had little choice other than to lodge with her relatives all those years ago – but she could have found a tenement flat later where they could all have been together as a family. Her mother had secured a decent position in the library in Camberwell, and her father had been working all these years! And what of Alice? She hadn't had the chance to make her own way in the world. She had been given the job as housekeeper in her aunt's house, whether she wanted it or not. 'All them bleedin' years of pinin' for my parents when all the time they could 'ave come and got me. All those years of missin' them and longin' to be together again! What kind of parents are they? Or does this 'appen to every family?'

Alice came sheepishly into Harriet's bedroom, holding a cup of tea. 'I never meant to deceive you, Harriet,' she said. 'I just didn't know what to do for the best so I phoned Mum at the library. A book borrower I know told me about Arthur. Her husband got caught too. My friend at work, Alfred, told me to leave early. He guessed you'd be upset if you heard it from a stranger.'

'It's all right. You did the right thing, as it turned out,' said Harriet. 'My little chat up here with Mum has made me see the light.'

'Oh, you're all right about it, then?' Alice said, surprised.

'Yeah, I'm all right about everyfing, Alice.' She took the cup of tea. 'You can fetch your tea if you like but I don't really want Mum to come back up.'

'No, that's all right. I expect you want to be by yourself, to think what to do.'

'Not really. I'm upset over Arfer, I will admit that, but I couldn't count the times I told him not to steal from the 'and that feeds 'im.'

'You'll be all right once you've paid him a visit. Will you go this evening?'

'I don't know, Alice. I might say too much. Perhaps I should wait till tomorrow when I've calmed down a bit.'

'Oh, so you really *are* annoyed with him?'

'Not just Arfer. Mum too. I don't want 'er comin' over just 'cos there's a bit of scandal. And don't tell me that's not why she came. She said herself she wanted to 'ave a couple of days away from that 'ouse. You gave 'er the perfect excuse.'

'I just thought you might have drawn a little comfort from her being here, that's all. She can be galling at times though, can't she?'

'It would 'ave been all right if she'd come when she 'eard about me losin' my baby, but, oh, no, that never crossed 'er mind. She don't love me, Alice, and maybe she never did. Worse still, I don't care any more. My friends mean more to me than my own mother. And that's the blunt truth.'

'I've heard some other people saying that. One or two. Oh! That reminds me. You know your friend Larry?'

'Course I know 'im Alice, what of it?'

'Well, you know he comes into the library quite regular—'

'You told 'im,' said Harriet, all-knowing. 'What did he say?'

'Same as you, really. But he said you're not to worry, he could fix Arthur up with work. Funny, really, the way this new century's affecting everyone. They're pulling down lots of old houses and factories and building smart new ones.'

'What's that got to do with Larry – or Arfer?'

'Oh, well, Larry said that's why there's plenty of work. Bit better pay as well, he said, if you're prepared to work the hours. And Arthur would be, wouldn't he?'

'I suppose so. He can think about it while he's in prison.'

'But he's not in prison! He's at the station in a cell.'

'They've locked 'im away, Alice. To me that means prison.' Harriet sipped her tea. 'I daren't even start to fink of missin' 'im. Or what he must be feelin' like. I've got to keep my temper up or I'll go right down. Mum's got under my skin and I could do without that. I don't want 'er stoppin' too long. Did she tell you about Dad?'

'No? Why? Has she heard something?'

Harriet sighed. Why had her mother kept to herself something so important? Did she imagine that Alice didn't miss her dad? Or was she secretly hoping that by the time their dad had found a place to live, Alice, like herself, might be married with a home of her own? One thing had become apparent: her mother was not maternal. She hadn't been too upset when their baby brother died. Their dad had been, though. As tough as he liked to make himself out to be, he had broken down.

Wiping tears off her face, Harriet murmured, 'Ask Mum about 'im. She'll tell you.'

'All right, I will.'

'Before you go, Alice, I'm a bit confused over somefing you said earlier on. You said that Mum missed me so much she used to cry. That you used to get in bed wiv 'er when you missed me and she'd cuddle you to sleep. Somefing like that.'

'That's right. I did say that.' Alice blushed.

After a short pause, Harriet folded her arms and looked directly into her sister's face. 'It was a whacking big fib, wasn't it?'

'Well, I suppose it was stretching the truth—'

'No, it was a fib. Why did you say it? To make me feel better?'

'Not really. It's what I used to make up when I was in my bed crying for you and it sort of became real.'

'She didn't comfort when you was cryin'?'

'Well, she would say, "It's not as if she's dead, you'll see 'er again," that sort of a thing.'

'Not quite the same, is it? Ne'mind, though. I feel better for knowing. Listenin' to 'er, I thought I was losin' my marbles. She 'asn't got an ounce of sympathy in 'er body.'

'I know. But she never ever got cross with me.

Never smacked me or told me off. Never got angry once.'

'And never talked to you either.'

'Not really.'

'Well, do you know what, Alice?' said Harriet, her face screwing up and her eyes filling with tears again. 'Do you know what we both need? We need a great big 'ug, a hug and a cuddle, and not just now 'cos fings are sad but for all the bad times when we 'ad to be brave.'

'Do we?'

'Yes, we do.' Harriet wiped her runny nose on her sleeve. 'So come 'ere and give me a big 'ug.'

'Oh, do you think we should?'

'Of course we bleedin' well should! We're sisters.' She held out her arms, tears cascading freely, as Alice walked slowly towards her, dry-eyed and sombre. Harriet slipped her arms around her sister and laid her head on her shoulder. 'Now, put your arms around me. Come on, I won't bite you.'

'I've not done this before, Harriet,' said Alice, 'not since you and me said goodbye when you went off to the children's home,' Alice said. 'No one's hugged me since then.'

Harriet held her sister tighter. 'You're my sister and we should have cuddled before now.'

'I wanted to, Harriet, but I didn't know how. I so wanted a cuddle up like this but Mum never—'

'I know. Never mind.' As she patted Alice's back and kissed her forehead, Harriet felt a glow inside. 'When we was tiny and shared that excuse for a bed we always cuddled up to keep warm, didn't we? And then we took turns in snugglin' Baby close. Do you remember that?'

'Not really – tiny bits come back now and then like a dream, but that's all.'

'Never mind. From now on we'll hug whenever we bleedin' well feel like it.' Harriet pulled a little away from her sister and smiled when she saw tears trickling down Alice's face. 'Oh, Alice, you look lovely, smilin' and cryin' at the same time.'

'Do I?' she said, wiping her face with the back of her hand. 'Bit salty.'

'Tears are.'

'I wonder why?'

'It don't matter, does it? They're there for a reason. It's all the sorrow comin' out. But you can cry when you're 'appy as well.'

'I am happy,' chuckled Alice. 'I'm crying because I'm happy – and sad. Do you think we should cuddle Mum?'

Harriet laughed. 'Don't let's go too far. She'd stand there like a bleedin' pole from a washin'-line.'

'She must have cuddled Dad.'

'Oh, Alice! I don't wanna fink about fings like that. Go on. Leave me alone to drink my tea.'

Once Alice had left the bedroom Harriet allowed herself to enjoy a little self-satisfaction. During the past hour she had realised so much about the past and was comforted. The truth spoken aloud didn't hurt as much as she had thought it would. And the truth was staring her in the face: if Arthur hadn't been arrested her mother wouldn't be here; her mother celebrating that she and the girls' father were going to reunite at a time like this was thoughtless; revealing the fact that their father had been working for the past seventeen years and that they had been seeing each other but not the girls was vicious; her mother's indifference to Harriet's childhood was painful; her lack of gratitude towards Mary Dean for having taken care of her homeless child was inexcusable; her disinterest at her and Arthur's wedding was a mystery; Harriet being treated as if she were a stranger when she had made brief visits to her aunt's house was unforgivable. Finally, Arthur's arrest by the railway police hadn't rocked Mrs Smith, and Harriet's loss of her baby had brought no sympathy.

Harriet finished her tea feeling clearer and more at ease with herself. She was determined not to let things go downhill. She had come too far to let that happen and she knew others who had not had the opportunity to rise from the depth of poverty as she and Arthur had. People were saying that this new century was going to see the huge gap close between rich and poor, but words were cheap and dreams transient.

As far as she was concerned everyone had to look out for their own welfare until they were in a position to look out for others, and she and Arthur were going to have to be strong to rise above this present crisis. She would pay a visit to Lillian Redmond this evening, and first thing tomorrow she would go to see Larry.

'Oh,' her mother smiled as Harriet joined them in

the kitchen, her new resolve showing in her face, 'this looks more like the Harriet we know.'

'Does it? And which Harriet might that be, Mum? You've seen me – what, half a dozen times since I was left at the children's home? And that was *years* ago.' Remembering what Flora had said on bouts of anger after giving birth, she tried her best to stay calm but her words had been to the point.

'You could have made more of an effort yourself,' sniffed her mother, wiping crumbs from her sandwich from the corner of her mouth. 'And you stopped in the home a day.'

'Oh, I don't know why I bother to even try and talk to you. I'm going out, Alice, to see Lillian Redmond and Polly.'

'Lillian Redmond?' Mrs Smith narrowed her eyes and sported a deliberate look of suspicious. 'Not a money-lender, is she? The name rings a bell.'

'No. A very good friend,' said Harriet. 'Lillian was Mary Dean's employer and her door's been open to me since I was a kid on the streets. And Polly's been in her care since she was born. Her mum was left high and dry and holding the baby. A sailor, I think it was, whose ship sailed quickly out of port once she was pregnant.'

'Tut-tut,' said her mother. 'Things around this way don't change much, do they?'

'No, they don't. Any changes for the good 'ave to be brought about by yerself. I s'pose it's different in South London, then?'

'In Camberwell it is. I can't say for the other parts.

You might want to think about that, Harriet, getting out of this awful area and coming over the river.'

'To mix with people like Aunt and Uncle, you mean? No, I don't fink so. You've bin around them too long, Mum. You even talk posher now. So does Alice. Not that I'm knockin' it. That'd be insultin', knockin' a place where people love to live . . . or the way they speak.'

'So you love East London, do you?' Mrs Smith's smile was patronising. 'I can't say I ever took to it. Your father should have come over to my side when we were first married, instead of dragging me over to his. But there we are. We all make sacrifices. At least I'm back where I belong with people I can talk to.'

'That's right. Each to their own, eh? Now, then, where's my cheese sandwich? I'll eat that first and be on my way.'

Alice put a covered plate in front of her. 'Shall I come with you to see your friends? Or do you want me to wait in case they let Arthur come home?'

'Wait in, just in case. He might turn up, he might not. I'll be all right out there by myself. I had a baby, not an operation.'

'Stop talking like that, Harriet. You had a miscarriage,' said Mrs Smith, sipping her tea. 'But you will have babies, all in good time, if your husband stays out of trouble. Yes, you'll have babies that'll live to make you sorry you wanted them. You see if I'm wrong.'

Harriet exchanged a wry smile with Alice. 'Oh, I don't doubt I'll 'ave a family, Mum, but not for a while. We've got a business to get off the ground.'

'Making dolls,' Mrs Smith said.

'That's right. And if we're to pay the rent on both these 'ouses, I'm gonna 'ave to get crackin' and get back to work till we've got our little enterprise up and runnin'.' She turned to Alice. 'You couldn't pop into the factory for me tomorrow morning on the way to work, could yer? Tell 'em to deliver plenty of piecework.'

'Course I could. Mind you, it's not on my way to work, is it? I'll go in my break. I can be there and back in half an hour so I won't get into trouble.' Alice turned to her mother. 'Unless you fancy a stroll up to Aldgate in the morning?'

'Oh, no, thank you. Aldgate? No. Too many old memories. All those murders. All that poverty. No, I'll stop here and give this place and the one next door a good spring-clean. It could do with it.'

The girls looked shyly at each other and grinned. They had confirmation that their mother would not fit into this household if she stayed too long. And she would certainly put Arthur's back up if she was here when he came home.

'You must 'ave 'ated livin' in Black's Buildings, Mum,' said Harriet, biting into her sandwich.

'I should say so. Love for your father brought me into the slums and left me trapped there. Still, thank goodness for your aunt and uncle, eh? I should think it'll be much nicer living in Islington, mind. A better class of people, I should think. You might want to think about where you'll settle, Harriet, once you're ready to start a family again.'

'Why would I? I love East London. People are a lot friendlier than in South London. Don't know about North, never bin there, but it sounds cold, don't it? *North* London. No, that don't appeal to me.'

With that, Harriet went out into the summer evening with a mixture of worry and hope over Arthur. Deep inside she felt that things were not as black as they appeared but she was not one to trust feelings. Maybe she would pay a visit to the Shoreditch police station after she had seen Lillian and ignore the voice inside telling her to leave things be until the next day.

She knew that Arthur would never step over that line again. Larry was on the same wavelength as herself. At least now Arthur couldn't turn down the offer Larry had made to fix him up with a better-paid job. Harder work, maybe, but financially rewarding. As far as Harriet was concerned, the Jewish people were not only warm and friendly, but clever and she not only respected but loved them for it. No, she would never leave East London. Like her mentor/Lillian, if she rose above the poverty level she would remain and enjoy living a colourful life in a colourful part of London. With enough money to make life comfortable, she could think of no better place to be.

'Why the bleedin' 'ell would I want to go to South or North?' she asked herself, as she wandered into Beaumont Square.

'Hello,' a voice said, and Harriet snapped out of her thoughts. Grace Wellington was standing in front of her, and glanced now from her flat stomach to her face. 'I didn't think your baby was due for two months.

Is the grandmother looking after it for you? Did you
have a boy or a girl?'

'Neither,' she said, offering a sad smile as explana-
tion.

'Oh, I am sorry.' Blushing, Grace was lost for
words.

'It's all right. I'm over it . . . nearly. It wasn't meant
to be. I've got plenty of time to have more.' She pulled
back her shoulders. 'So, where's your little Sarah,
then? Tucked up in bed?'

'I doubt it. I'm going out, and her nanny will let her
and her brother stay up a little later as a treat. Look . . .
I am most dreadfully sorry, really. If there's anything
I can do . . .'

'Save your baby clothes and pram for when I have
another. I'm going to get rid of everything. Give it
away and start again in a year or so.'

'That's very brave. Would that we might all be more
like you. I do admire you.'

'And I admire you. So we're evens.' She was thinking about how Grace's husband had betrayed her.

'Really? Whatever for?'

'Never mind. I just do. It's a pity we're from such
different worlds because I fink we'd get on very well.'

'Oh, well, then, why not join me for tea one afternoon? You'd be very welcome.'

Harriet was momentarily lost for words. 'Do you
really mean that?'

'Of course. Why on earth shouldn't I?' Grace
Wellington opened her silk purse and withdrew a
white calling card. 'Why not drop me a note saying

when you've a free afternoon? A weekday would suit me.'

'All right.' Harriet took the card. 'Then I can tell you all about our ladies' enterprise. Me and a few other girls are gonna start up in business soon makin' dolls.'

'Really?' said Grace. 'How marvellous. Well, I wish you luck. How far along the road are you?'

'Not sure, really,' said Harriet. 'There's a few hurdles to get over but I reckon by this time next year we'll be under way. Fingers crossed.'

'Well, I should be keen to know more. You never know, I may have something to offer.'

Peering into the young lady's lovely face, Harriet laughed quietly. 'You can't mean that?'

'Well, yes, actually. And, as a matter of fact, I've been speaking to my financial adviser of late about investment. Promise you'll come and talk to me about it?'

Harriet could hardly believe her ears or her eyes. Grace Wellington was positively glowing. This was no casual remark: she was seriously interested. 'You bet I'll come and talk to you about it. I can't wait to tell the others.' Smiling radiantly, Harriet was beside herself. 'Where are you off to this evening?' she asked.

'Oh, just another of those women's meetings, at the mission hall. One of the Pankhurst girls is giving a talk,' Grace told her.

'They're doing all right for us ladies,' Harriet responded. 'Have a nice time,' she added, and walked towards Lillian's house.

'Yes, I shall! And do keep in touch!'

Those words were like church bells chiming on a crisp snowy morning. This stroke of fortune was exactly what Harriet and her friends needed. She glanced at Grace Wellington's smart calling card and felt new hope rising.

'Oh, excuse me for breathing,' said Polly, as she opened the door to her best friend. 'Deemed fit to see us now, 'ave yer?'

Pushing past her, hiding a grin, Harriet sniffed. 'Arthur's in prison. Where's Lillian?'

'Well may you ask,' said Polly, as smug as you like. 'If you don't mind comin' down into the common kitchen, I might tell yer where she is and I might not. And don't tell lies.'

'I'm not. He was caught nickin' a bit of fish by the railway police. Kitchen'll do. If I don't slum it with the rest of yer, I won't be able to appreciate my upper-class lifestyle, will I?'

'Railway police?' grinned Polly. 'They don't put people in prison.'

'Well, that's how much you know! He won't be home for a while, and serve 'im right. Now he'll know what it's like to spend time in a cell. Shouldn't bleedin' well pinch stuff, should he?'

'Oooh, very 'oity-toity all of a sudden. "Woman of property" is what they're sayin' on the streets,' goaded Polly, following Harriet down the stairs, 'and, of course, a woman of property can't have a friend poppin' in whenever that friend feels like it – she must wait for an invitation, whether her best friend has lost her baby or not!'

'Oh, shut up,' said Harriet, flopping down on the lovely old Windsor chair by the kitchen fire. 'Pour me a drop of Lillian's best. I need a drink.'

'Well, you look a bit flushed to me and, apart from your tired eyes, I'd say there wasn't much wrong wiv you.'

'Apart from the fact that I had a miscarriage,' Harriet said, taking hold of a little bit of what her mother had said. It sounded less sad than losing a baby. 'I'm exhausted from the walk. And I've just 'ad tragic news so spare a bit of feeling. Arthur *'as* been arrested. Where's Lillian? I need 'er to cheer me up.'

'She's upstairs with a client.'

Harriet raised her face slowly to Polly's. 'I 'ope that's meant to be a jest.'

'Blimey! If looks could kill I'd be stone dead on the floor. She's in 'er snug with a client, *talkin'* business. One of the knobbers wants to buy this place.'

'What? The business too?'

'No, just the 'ouse. Use 'alf of it for business – office work an' that – an' 'ave somewhere to tuck away 'is bit on the side, no doubt. They all seem to be settlin' for that, these days. One at 'ome and one on the side.' She looked anxious. 'Business ain't too good.'

'So, will she sell?'

'Course not. She's gonna try and talk 'im into sendin' 'er more clients. Peein' in the wind again.'

'Well, she's not gonna cough up any money to 'elp set up our business, then, is she?'

'You can never tell wiv that one. She could be a

bleedin' millionaire, for all we know, or as poor as a church mouse.'

Harriet felt her heart sink again. 'Arfer's in prison, Polly. I can 'ardly believe it. The police arrested 'im today. That's why I've 'ad to get out of my sick bed.' She sighed. 'I don't know 'ow to feel about it. Angry, frightened, worried. I s'pose I must be in shock. Don't feel as if I am, mind.'

'So he got caught nickin' a bit of fish and they'll teach 'im a lesson by puttin' 'im on remand for a week or so. But he won't get 'is job back, Harriet. One of the girls who works below stairs on the square 'ad the selfsame fing 'appen to 'er dad . . .'

'It always sounds different when it's 'appened to someone else. I know it's just as bad for the ones concerned but it just don't affect you in the same way. Arfer's been arrested. Gawd know what Mary'll say if she gets wind of it. The newspapers would love it, wouldn't they, 'er husband bein' a well-to-do? They love to 'ave a dig and a poke at the rich.'

'Mary'll survive a bit of old family gossip. And there's work about for men if they're prepared to graft. Arthur'll be all right. Might even be a blessing in disguise. They pay crap to their workers, the railway.'

Harriet sat up and looked on the bright side. Polly was preening herself in a small mirror on the wall. She had lost weight and looked almost feminine. 'You're puttin' more fat on, Polly,' she said, teasing.

'That's all you know.' Polly rested her hands on her hips. 'As a matter of fact I've lost it. Twelve pounds four ounces. And once I've lost thirteen pounds, Lillian's got to gimme five guineas to go out and buy a new dress and coat wiv bonnet to match.' She glided around the kitchen, nose in the air. 'I might pop on an omnibus – an electric-driven omnibus that goes along tramlines . . .'

'They're not in operation yet, Polly.'

'Well, ain't that all you know! I 'eard different. But, then, I'm talkin' about the West End, of course, Oxford Street, where I shall go to buy *my outfit*.'

'You'd best get yer 'air done first. They wouldn't let you in a West End shop the way you look.' The sound of the street door closing stopped her banter.

'Oh, hark the herald angels sing, she's seeing out another king.' Polly took three clean glasses out of the cupboard and poured some brandy into each. Lillian would require a drink.

'Harriet!' cried Lillian, on seeing her sitting in the kitchen. 'How are you, dear?'

'Bit tired, but I've got to pull myself together now.'

'Well, I shouldn't rush it, dear. Now, then . . .' She turned to find Polly standing there with her drink held out. 'Oh, good girl.'

'No,' said Harriet, continuing, 'I can't afford to lose another day's pay now.'

'Why ever not, dear? I thought you were rising, not falling. Two properties?'

'We don't pay more'n twelve shillings for the two, Lillian. And, anyway, I only rent one. My sister and little Bo 'as got the other. I don't know what Polly's bin tellin' you but she needs to get 'er facts right.'

'Well, never mind all of that,' said Lillian, giving
Harriet a sympathetic look. 'I'm sorry for what you've
been through, truly sorry. How's Arthur taking it?'

'I don't know. 'E's in prison.'

'Oh, not another?'

'Wot d'yer mean, another? I'm talkin' about my
Arfer!'

'I know, dear – but haven't you read the newspaper
or heard it on the grapevine? The railway police
are suddenly active. Hundreds of workers have been
arrested in two days for pilfering goods. It'll pass, no
doubt. A flash in the authoritarian pan.'

'But they're gonna lock 'im up for two weeks! And
he'll lose his job!'

'No, no, no, dear. They're not going to do that
because there've been too many arrests to lock them
all up. No, Arthur will be sent home and probably not
even sacked. They'd have to sack too many, dear.'
Lillian held up her glass. 'Here's to Harriet, and you,
Polly – to your new business venture.'

'Cheers,' said Harriet pleased at least to hear that
Lillian had not forgotten the doll-making. Life, it
seemed, went on in the same old way, no matter what.
But if Lillian was right in her assumptions that Arthur
might be there when she returned home she would
have to admit the woman had insight. 'So you've had
an offer for this place, then, Lillian?' Polly gave her
a black look and she realised she wasn't supposed to
know this.

'As happens every so often, Harriet. One gets tired
of listening to intelligent men who act naïve when they

want to purchase. I go along with it, naturally, just in case their final offer is good. Once they've discovered I'm up to date on market prices, where houses such as mine are concerned they scurry away, realising that women have as much to offer between their ears as between their legs.' She emptied her glass in one gulp, then looked from Harriet to Polly. 'I wouldn't have sold to that little pervert in any case.'

'You never upset 'im, did you?' said Polly, accusingly. 'We can 'ardly afford to lose a gentleman.'

'Oh, he'll be back. Pricks are like water-diviners, my dear. They lead and the men follow.'

'It's a bloomin' big 'ouse, this one. Must be worth a couple of thousand guineas,' Harriet murmured.

'Indeed.' Lillian topped up her glass. 'But my bank account is not in the red yet so we needn't panic.' She lifted her glass and sipped. 'When I'm broke I shall sell and not before.'

'Unless someone makes an offer you can't refuse?'

'Precisely.' Lillian fixed her eyes on Harriet's face. 'Now, do you want me to be a partner in this doll-making business you intend to start up?'

Unable to hide her smile, Harriet looked from her to Polly and back again. 'With your brain for business, Lillian, we'd love you to come in on it.'

'Not your Arfer, though,' said Polly, earnestly.

'No, as it 'appens – but why you sayin' that? You'd best not be puttin' 'im down, Polly.'

'Tch, tch, tch, girls, girls, do stop bickering. What Polly meant, Harriet, and if you weren't so quick to jump you would have realised this, is that, so far, this is an all-female venture and why not keep it that way?'

'No reason not to, but why?'

'Because, my dear, the publicity will attract the thousands of women who have jumped on the suffragette bandwagon. And who buys dolls? In the main? Mmm?'

'You crafty cow,' laughed Harriet. 'Well, there's no denyin' it, between you two there's a bit of brain.'

'Less of the patronage, dear,' said Lillian, reprovingly. 'Now, I suggest that we all sit down together and have a business meeting to which we shall invite a lady of the press. We shall hold it here, of course, and be certain to have no bookings during that morning. Afternoons I cannot give you. Love in the afternoons is far more in demand than love in the mornings.

'The most important thing to get across to the reporter is that we are all part of the Women's Movement and it must never be said who comes and goes. We shall say that I am a woman of means from a titled family who live in a mansion, in the country, and I am shunned because I prefer to be in East London where there is so much good yet to be done.'

'Sounds like you've worked it all out, Lillian.' Harriet tipped her head towards the bottle of brandy and grinned. 'Wouldn't mind a little drop more of the medicinal before I go down to the station to give Arthur a grillin'. I told 'im enough times not—'

'Oh, I shouldn't do that,' said Lillian, topping up their glasses. 'Best left until tomorrow, I'd say.'

'Why?'

'Because, my dear, I can almost guarantee that your husband will be sleeping in his own bed to night. Now, let's hear no more about it and promise me that you will not go meddling in things you don't understand.' She leaned forward until her face almost touched Harriet's. 'Put it off until tomorrow and enjoy this time of day.'

From the look in Lillian's eyes, Harriet knew that she was being sent a message. But what? How could Lillian be so sure or trust what the newspapers wrote? But she was lingering on the look she was giving. 'All right, Lillian. I'll take your word for it and wait. If you're sure . . .' In answer Lillian raised her eyebrows, then returned to her theatrical, flamboyant mood.

'So, girls, we have the three of us, plus your sister, Harriet, and the new addition to your family, Bo.'

'And Flora,' said Polly, a touch icily. She had always been a little envious of Harriet's other best friend about whom Harriet had talked so much but to whom she had not yet introduced her.

'Actually, Polly, she 'asn't got anyfing to offer and neither 'as she been sniffin' round to be part of it. She's not like that. She's independent and very clever.'

'Not that clever,' muttered Polly, avoiding Harriet's eyes.

'*Girls!* So, there will be five in the team and all with something to offer.'

Harriet and Polly watched Lillian and waited. There was only one thing she had to offer: finance to set it all up. 'I'll run the business,' said Polly. 'Harriet's gonna make the dolls' clothes, Bo is to carve the model faces out of wood, and Alice will make the wigs.'

'Which leaves me to deal with the banking side of things,' said Lillian, a little smugly, money being at the root of all business ventures.

'Sounds about right,' said Harriet, holding her breath. She really wanted this to get off the ground and her gut feeling was that Lillian did too.

'Very well.' Lillian stood up and checked the time on her pretty fob watch. 'This meeting is over. We have a client due in half an hour and the girls will be arriving soon. Polly, if you could draft some kind of analysis of what is to be purchased and at what cost, I shall be pleased to study it at my leisure.' Another thought crossed Lillian's mind. 'I take it we have use of a kiln somewhere?'

'Better than that,' said Harriet, and stretched the truth a little. 'We've made arrangements to have use from time to time of a local doll factory at the back of Cambridgeheath Road, down by the arches.'

'Excellent. Now, I think we've used up enough time so . . .'

'Message received,' said Harriet, collecting her handbag. 'Mum's visitin' so I should be gettin' back anyway. Especially since Arfer'll be home – if you're sure.'

'I am,' said Lillian, 'trust me.' Had she not turned away her face, Harriet might have seen the rosy flush in her cheeks. Some of what Lillian had said about the newspaper article had been true, but exaggerated. One of her courtesans had been at the Liverpool

Street station when Arthur had been arrested and had practically run all the way to Beaumont Square to pass on the news. Having heard already that Harriet had lost her baby the courtesan felt sure that Polly would want to know straight away so that she could call on her best friend and comfort her, but she had come across Lillian first.

After she had heard the full story, Lillian had wasted no time. She had gone directly to the post office and sent a telegram to one of her clients, an old friend of her beloved Robert, and worded it thus: 'Arthur Dean falsely arrested for stealing from the railway at Liverpool Street. Please do something. Yours, L. Redmond.'

As she walked away from the square, feeling better for the visit, Harriet looked across to the house opposite and caught a glimpse of Grace Wellington at the window. Grace smiled down at her and waved, and Harriet waved back. The only problem with Grace Wellington showing an interest in the new venture was Flora. If the two women came together it would be disastrous for both of them. But the funds would help. Lillian was a wonderful person but apt to change her mind from one week to the next and might wave away the idea as a risky investment. Harriet weighed up the pros and cons, and decided in the end to let things take their natural course. If Grace Wellington became involved in the project, it was more than likely that she would prefer to be a sleeping partner and it wouldn't be too difficult to keep Flora away from her.

Flora wouldn't be involved in the enterprise so it was unlikely that they would meet. Besides, it was a little too early to worry about something that might never happen.

'Who knows,' murmured Harriet to herself, 'who knows what the future holds? Better to daydream than have no hope.'

As she walked slowly along the Mile End Road on her way home, she knew what she had to do: she had to go back to Whitehead Street and finally put to rest all of her deepest fears. She had to pass the house in which she had once lived with Mary and Arthur and continue to where the midwife had dwelled and where she herself had been imprisoned – the house from which she had taken the diary, which was still hidden in a small bundle of old clothes, kept since she was ten years old.

When Harriet arrived at Cleveland Way, she stood still, remembering how she had run for her life. Rooted to the spot, she had a choice: to turn away or go forward. She decided on the latter, and walked slowly but determinedly past the green door in the brick wall that led into the lovely Bellevue Place, where she and Arthur, as children, had sneaked in once or twice to pick flowers for Mary.

Standing at the entrance into Whitehead Street, next to the new department store, she was not trembling, as she had imagined she would be, but calm, with a warm glow in her chest. Instead of remembering the worst of things she was picturing her and Arthur sitting on the doorstep watching daft Thomas Cutbush stride by with his Bible under his arm. The one thing she did find surprising was how narrow the turning seemed and how small the houses were – and the front doors so close together. This was just a turning like hundreds of others in the area.

She strolled to the end, passing children playing hopscotch, and caught her reflection in a window. Instead of the scruffy ginger-headed urchin who had once sat on this window-ledge watching the boys in the street play kickball she saw a mature, attractive young lady. At last she was standing outside the midwife's old house where she felt nothing. This wasn't a familiar place, it was where other people lived. Other people who had no idea of what had taken place in that house and what was buried in the tiny back garden, according to what she had read in the diary.

Then, she walked back along the turning, amused that the children took no notice of her. Like herself and Arthur at their age, they were too absorbed in their game to notice a strange lady passing through. Once in Cleveland Way she decided on impulse to cross the road and push down the latch on the green door leading into the magical secret courtyard and peep once again at the lovely cottages and gardens. She was not disappointed. As she had remembered, the paved pathway leading to the far end was sprinkled with tiny clutches of forget-me-nots growing out from the gaps. The creeper-covered wall at the end was thick with ivy and clematis, and each front garden was full of lilac, roses, hydrangeas, wallflowers, lupins and delphiniums.

She retraced her steps, and closed the green door, hoping that the little tucked-away place would remain unspoiled by the outside world. In Cleveland Way, the row of terraced houses was a little less elegant than she remembered, although the steps leading up to the front doors were as clean and white as ever. She wondered if the fruit-and-vegetable seller still lived at number twenty-five or Lizzie Lisbon the pickle-bottler at number twenty-four. She would never forget either of them: Mrs Martin had given her an orange or an apple now and then, and Lizzie Lisbon smelt of pickled onions, which had always made Harriet feel hungry for cheese and bread.

As she passed the tiny dimly lit Italian café, the aroma of coffee filled her nostrils, and if she hadn't had to get back in case Arthur was home she would have gone in to see if the owners were of the same family and if they recognised her. But it was time for her to return to her own little house. Now that she had laid her fears to rest, though, she would frequent the little café again.

On her way home Harriet passed the second-hand shop where she had bought her china dinner service. It was incomplete and slightly chipped but lovely with its tiny border of blue forget-me-nots. She was unable to resist the urge to rummage in the shop so she went inside and immediately a cranberry-coloured glass vase caught her eyes. Having been in Bellevue Place with those lovely cottage gardens she had been thinking of her little back garden, and filling the house with cut flowers from it. To do this, she needed vases, proper ones, not the green glass milk bottles she had used in the past.

Twenty minutes later she came out glowing. Not only had she bought the vase for threepence but another three and all different. She also had a bundle of faded pink and green floral curtains, which would go across the window in her and Arthur's bedroom.

When she arrived home and went into the kitchen, four worried faces were looking up at her. Her mother, Alice, Bo and Larry were sitting at the table. Bo broke the silence. 'Where've you bin, Harriet? We thought you was dead.'

Larry flapped a hand. 'I don't know where you found this one, Harriet, but I swear she must be related. You're like peas in a pod.'

'I don't look nuffing like 'er, Larry, but once that 'air grows and she's a few years older, she might be lucky enough to mirror me.'

Dropping on to Arthur's Windsor chair, Harriet had to admit she was exhausted, and the string binding on the curtains had almost cut into the flesh of her fingers. She rubbed her hands together, and said, 'I'm bleedin' starvin'. Where's me dinner?'

'I've got it on steam,' said Alice.

'You shouldn't go scaring everyone, Harriet,' scolded her mother. 'It's not clever. Only just out of your sick bed and stopping out for hours on end.'

'Ne'mind, I'm back now and I've got some lovely fings from the junk shop.' She placed a foot on Bo's lap and asked her to unlace her boot. 'So I s'pose you 'eard, then, Larry? About Arthur?'

'What d'yer think? Of course I 'eard. It's all round Whitechapel. Bloody fool. And all for a bit of fish!'

'You never said that when I fried you a piece once. You said it was the best you'd tasted and you wouldn't mind some more if it 'appened to fall off the cart.'

'I said that?'

His mock-doleful eyes made her laugh. 'You know you did.' She let out a sigh of pleasure as Bo pulled off a boot, then leaned back in the chair and offered her other foot. 'God, my feet was killing me.'

'I suppose you went to the police station to give them a piece of your mind?' said Larry, knowing her better than he knew anyone.

'No, I bleedin' well never. Serves 'im right. He'll get six months, is what I 'eard. Six months' 'ard labour. Good job an' all.'

'Harriet!' The look on Alice's face was a treasure. 'That's a wicked thing to say.'

'Take no notice. I know her better than any of you. She knows more than she's letting on.' Larry glanced across at Mrs Smith, waiting for an admonishment. How could a stranger know a woman's daughter better than her mother? But she didn't seem to have heard it. She looked as if her mind was anywhere but in this kitchen.

With her second boot off, Harriet closed her eyes and rubbed her feet together. 'Ah . . . that's better. Make me a nice cup of tea, Bo, there's a good girl.'

The room went very quiet as they looked from one to the other, wondering why she wasn't she crying for Arthur. Larry was undisturbed, if not to say amused by it. She knew something they didn't – pure and simple. 'I think she's been to see him,' he said, breaking the silence to annoy Harriet. This was her scene, after all.

'What're you doin' 'ere anyway?' was Harriet's response. 'Gonna fix 'im up with work once he gets out? Well, I won't be around to see it. I'm off to live in the countryside amid wild flowers and cornfields. I've 'ad enough of London Town. I've got myself a little job in a beautiful mansion as laundry-maid.'

'Bloody liar,' said Larry, grinning. 'So, what did you find out down at the station?'

'I never went to the station, Larry. I just went out for a nice walk to see my friends Polly and Lillian over at Beaumont Square. Why the bleedin' 'ell should I lower myself by visitin' someone in a cell? Leave off.'

'You've turned hard, Harriet,' murmured her mother, knowing nothing of her daughter's sense of humour. 'I suppose it's to be expected. Not that I don't condone Arthur for being irresponsible.'

'I don't think you're in a position to condone any-one, Mum. I'm lucky to be alive and in one piece. But, there, we don't wanna drag up my miserable child-hood, do we? I got through it, one way or another.'

'Harriet,' whispered Alice, too soft for such an out-pouring of the truth, 'don't spoil things, eh? We've both come through all right, haven't we?'

'And what's that supposed to mean, Alice? Come through? You were the lucky one, don't forget. Lifted out from the depths to live in a decent place with your aunt and uncle. You never had to go without food the way your sister did.'

'No, that's true, Mum, I never did.' Alice went quiet.

'Why don't you tell Mum how you really felt, Alice, having to be a replacement wife?' Harriet asked.

'If you're referring to her being the housemaid all those years, she loved it. Took pride in everything she did.'

'Well, not everything,' said Alice, glancing at her sister and giggling. 'I enjoyed cooking, though.'

'Of course you did. You're like chalk and cheese, the pair of you. I can't imagine Harriet turning out a proper meal. Alice's laundry and ironing couldn't be faulted. She had your uncle's white handkerchiefs gleaming white and beautifully pressed.'

'Well, I did take longer on the handkerchiefs,' giggled Alice, blushing. 'Handkerchiefs are so important, aren't they?' With that she and Harriet burst into fits of giggles.

'Well,' said Larry, sensing it was time for him to go, 'I s'pose someone's got to go and speak up for your old man. I'll trot down the station and—'

'Sit yerself down and stop playin' the bleedin' saint. I told yer, he needs to be taught a lesson. Leave 'im where he is.' Lillian's face when she had told Harriet to leave things be came back to her. She knew now that she was up to something. Pulling strings.

'Whatever you say, Harriet. Anyway, I have a home to go to.'

'Course you 'ave, Larry – but I want to tell you

some good news. All of you.' She looked into his face and didn't offer a flicker of a smile. 'Well, you still in a rush?'

'All right.' He shrugged. 'I'll stop a bit longer. Go on. Spit it out.'

'Lillian's gonna put up the money to get our little business off the ground.' She smiled at their straight faces. 'Good, innit?'

'What business?'

'Doll-makin', Larry! You know that, so stop teasin' me. If you wasn't a man I'd let you put some money into it, but this is gonna be an all-women enterprise – Lillian's idea, and a bleedin' good one. Wouldn't you say so, Mum?'

'Well, no, not really. You need men to run the . . . industry. It's expected. I think Larry should go in with you.'

'I don't wanna bloody well go in, thank you! I'm quite happy with what I'm doing. Regular work, regular pay . . . with prospects.'

'Larry sells insurance for one of the big companies. I wouldn't mind bein' 'is missus when he pops his cork.'

Scratching his neck, puzzled at Harriet's strange mood, he put it down to the after effects of losing the baby. But still he couldn't quite accept that she wasn't putting on an act. He knew her well and she should be in a state over Arthur having been locked up. The old Harriet would have smashed a few plates by now before storming off to the authorities to get her man released. She had to know more than she was letting on.

'Well, if I don't get a move on I might pop my cork sooner than you imagine.' He glanced at Mrs Smith and shrugged. 'My Jewish mama goes mad if I'm not there on the dot for supper.'

'And there's another lady, a wealthy lady, who might invest in our little project.'

'Hoo-bloody-rah,' said Larry, pulling himself to his feet. 'I like your company, ladies, but—'

'Larry, before you go, I want you to do me a favour.'

'Go on.'

'Just in case this news over Arthur suddenly hits me – and just when I'm gettin' over losing my baby – I need a drop of ale in a jug.'

'And you want me to drop into the alehouse?'

'Yeah. For an old mate?'

'All right,' sniffed Larry, pulling himself up from the chair, knowing that the ale was most likely for Arthur's welcome home that evening. 'I'll go.' He stood before her and held out his hand, wiggling his fingers. He had to go through this charade of hers and if he didn't ask for money for the drink, she would guess he had caught on. This was a silly game of cat and mouse they used to play as teenagers.

'Sod off, Larry. You're entitled to treat me after all I've been through. I'll return the gesture once my business is up and runnin',' she added.

'Our business,' corrected Alice, bravely.

'That's right,' said Mrs Smith. 'You shouldn't get above yourself about it, Harriet.'

At this Harriet saw red. Her mother hadn't even

slept in this house overnight yet already she was acting as if she owned the place. 'Above meself? Is that 'ow you see me?'

Replying with a look of reciprocation, her mother simply sniffed. Silence spoke louder than words. Mrs Smith glanced sideways at Alice and raised an eyebrow, a ploy to get her younger daughter on her side.

But Alice was not as dim as she liked to appear, and her mother had angered her more than she had upset Harriet. 'I don't think you appreciate how hard Harriet's worked, Mum, or how kind she's been taking me and Bo in. It was a bit of a risk renting next door as well. What if neither of us was able to get a job? What then?'

'That's exactly what I mean. Playing God is easy but paying debts isn't. She's got to learn the real ways of the world, Alice. I think I know Harriet better than anyone. I should do – I'm her mother, let's not forget.'

'Oh,' said Harriet, hands on hips and glaring at Mrs Smith, 'suddenly you're my mother. Well, it's bin a bleedin' long time comin'! And you fink you know me better than anyone, do yer?'

'I had you under my wing from a baby in arms until you was ten, Harriet. I know the real you, not the one you're trying to grow into. I always said to your dad that, strong-willed as you were, you wouldn't make much of yourself, because of your high and mighty ways. A little lesson goes a long way.' A silence followed as everyone in the room wondered exactly what she had meant by 'a little lesson'.

'From what I can gather,' continued her mother, 'you rushed about like a blue-arsed fly, even though you were seven months' pregnant. What were you trying to prove? That you're some kind of a marvel?'

Quietly inching his way out of the room, Larry didn't want any part in this. He might just lose his temper and say too much. He had known Harriet since they were both fourteen and trying to find work, going from one store or factory to another, asking to be employed, until they each ended up on the same bench in Whitechapel sipping a cup of tea given out by the Salvation Army. This is when they first talked to each other. Found each other. And they had been good friends ever since.

From the corner of her eye Harriet could see Larry making a discreet exit. 'Wait for me outside the front door, Larry. I'll come wiv you to the tavern. And you needn't creep out, just go the way you normally would if my mother wasn't 'ere causin' an atmosphere!'

Larry didn't need telling twice – he was gone in a flash.

'So, Mum, you fink you know me better than anyone, do yer?'

'You grew inside me, didn't you? Of course a mother knows her own child best.'

'Even when she's kicked her out on to the streets at ten years old?'

'I never kicked you out! I saw you placed in the National Children's Home. But how long did you stop there? Overnight and no more. Then you go and live on the streets as if you were a vagrant. More fun, was it, than having to obey rules?'

'Well, it wasn't *much* fun – but it was better than riskin' 'avin' 'appen to me what I could see wiv my own two eyes was 'appenin' to all the other kids. But, then, 'ow could I expect you to know that when you never even went down Bethnal Green to 'ave a look a the place where you'd got me into? Just signed a bleedin' bit of paper down the Mission and that was it! Kiss your arse and off you go!'

'Don't be so crude. Alice doesn't talk the way you do and she's not had it that easy, having to abide by other people's house rules. Not that it's done her any harm. She's turned out a lovely young lady.'

Harriet looked from her mother to her sister, who was close to tears, and wanted to scream out what Alice had been through and that her lovely nature had survived despite their disgusting uncle's demands on her.

Her eyes lowered and focusing on a small garden beetle scampering across the floor, Alice spoke in a monotone: 'I think I would rather have been put with Harriet in the home. In fact, so long as we were always together in the home or running away from it, I know that's what I would have preferred.'

'Well, we can all sit and wish things had been better,

Alice. I thought *you* of all people would see how bitter Harriet's grown. Don't you think I suffered? God only knows I suffered. But I don't complain. What good would it do? Who would listen? Who would care? My husband left me stranded. Walked out just like that. I did my best, though.'

'You couldn't wait to get rid of Dad,' said Harriet. 'You was always tellin' 'im to clear off.' She tapped the side of her head. 'It ain't sawdust in 'ere, Mum, and it wasn't then. You nagged 'im silly and you moaned all the time about yerself and 'ow you was suffering before we left the old 'ouse! And you're still full of self! After all these years you're still not wonderin' what it was like to be left in a miserable children's 'ome with no family around you and listenin' to cries of kids who were being abused.'

'It was better than being on the street, I'm sure.'

'No, it wasn't! The men in charge were doing whatever they wanted with the girls – draggin' 'em into their beds! And they burned the boys with the end of their cigars! They despised us! We smelt because all you got to wash wiv was drop of grubby cold water and no clean clothes.'

'How would you know? You were only there for a day.'

'Two days, Mum – but only one night. One look at what was goin' on and I was away from there. I was one of the lucky ones. I wouldn't like to bump into them poor devils now. Them kids 'ad a lousy life. A stinking rotten life.'

'Well, then, it's your own fault for not coming and

telling me. You could have got in the bed with your sister. My family would never have turned you away. We would have managed somehow.'

'Now she tells me,' sighed Harriet. 'It's a bit late for all this, innit?' She smiled sadly. 'Mum. Mum. Mum. Do you know how much I longed to be able to say that word? I was ten years old and 'ad no one to call Mum any more. You was gone over the bleedin' river! Just like that.'

'You wouldn't have liked it in my bed, Harriet,' said Alice. 'I never really liked being there.'

'No,' Harriet said. 'Not now, Alice, eh? I've 'ad enough. If you want to say your piece, leave it till tomorrow. I'm gonna 'ave a drink wiv Larry.'

With that, Harriet left them all to it and took a slow walk to the tavern, her feelings jumbled. She didn't feel angry with her mother or resentful. She felt nothing. And that was worse than wanting a hug. Shrugging off the melancholy mood, she reasoned that thousands of children felt the same but were not so lucky to have people around them who did show love and affection: friends.

On seeing Larry standing at the counter talking to the barman she softened. His tall lanky body leaning over and his face almost touching the barman's as they talked together brought her back to reality. She did have nice friends who had stuck by her and would always be there. 'You're like a couple of gossiping women,' she said, heaving herself up on to a bar stall. 'Pour me half a pint of yer strongest ale, landlord. I need it.'

'I reckon you must do,' he said, pulling her a pint, 'but you're not the only one. There's bin a right old to-do, let me tell you. Railway police? They're not even proper coppers.'

'Oh,' said Harriet, 'so it's true what I 'eard – my Arfer wasn't the only one, then?'

'I should say not. They've 'ad a clamp-down. S'pect it'll be in the evenin' editions. Wicked bastards. You work all the hours for a lousy reward and that's 'ow they treat yer. It'll never be any different, though, no matter wot government gets in. There's a rule for the top class and another for the rest. Bastards.'

'Well,' said Harriet, reaching for her ale, 'a friend of mine who I went to see today reckoned that they've bin a bit too keen and arrested so many that they're gonna 'ave to let 'em out. The cells in every station are jam-packed.' She downed a quarter of a pint in one swallow, then wiped the froth from her mouth. 'Lovely. I needed that. My bleedin' muvver's drove me to drink. She drove me out of 'er life, comes back and drives me to drink.' She poured some more down her throat and smiled. 'Best fing she could 'ave done. This ale's beau'iful. I've not bin drunk since the Christmas before last.'

'I don't fink you've got your facts exactly right, miss,' said the barman. 'They arrested plenty but they won't be lettin' 'em out just like that.' He looked at Larry and shook his head grimly. 'Sounds like a tall story to me.'

'I never said that that's what's gonna 'appen. I said a friend said so. Lillian. She might be right. She might be wrong. But where's my Arfer? Eh? If they was gonna kick 'em out, why ain't he 'ome yet? And you, landlord, you'd 'ave heard it before now, wouldn't you? Be honest.' She finished the pint. 'Fill it up.' She pushed the glass into his hand.

'I would have 'eard, ducks, yes. I shouldn't expect 'im 'ome for a fortnight. That's usually the length of time they keep 'em. He'll lose 'is job, mind.'

'I don't care any more,' said Harriet, leaning across the bar. 'Just fill up my glass.'

Laughing, the man told Larry that he would have to carry her home if she went on like this.

Half an hour later all three of them had downed two pints of ale and were ready for another. Luckily it was quiet in the tavern that evening: apart from a few couples scattered about the small place, it was just the three of them.

'Tell you what, landlord,' said Harriet, her speech slurred by the beer, 'we're gonna 'ave a little bit of conga down my 'ouse later on. Our Alice is bloody good on the piano and Larry can sing. Oh, yes, Larry can sing!'

'And you can dance,' he said, laughing at her silly drunk expression.

'Oh, yes, I can dance.' She clamped her lips together, pushed her face close to the barman's and said, 'I can dance a lot bleedin' better than them silly cows you see on stage in the music halls. Oh, yes. They're like bleedin' elephants. I can float through the air.' She waved a hand to demonstrate. 'Can't I, Larry?'

But Larry was no longer looking at her. His eyes were on someone else. 'We've got company,' he said. 'Look what the wind's blown in.'

Turning, Harriet narrowed her eyes to focus then grinned broadly. 'Stone me blind it's my Arfer!'

'See what 'appens when I turn me back for five minutes? She's out on the booze with another man and chattin' up the barman too.' Arthur peered at her and smiled. 'You're drunk, Mrs Dean, or my name's not Arthur.'

Harriet slid down from her stool and stood, swaying, contemplating the man she loved. Then, with arms outstretched, she walked slowly towards him and fell into his arms. 'I thought you wasn't comin' back to me,' she cried. 'I thought they was gonna lock you up for ages.'

He squeezed her so tightly she could hardly breathe. 'Don't fib. I popped in to see Lillian Redmond on the way back to show my gratitude. It cost me to find out who pulled a string but it was worth it.'

'Lillian? Ah . . . so they're not lettin' the men go. She's got a friend in high places and got you off. She never said a word about that to me.'

'And *you* mustn't mention it either,' said Larry. 'The silly bugger shouldn't 'ave let on he found out. You've got a lot to learn, Arthur. If you get a mysterious windfall, you don't ask questions.'

'I would 'ave broke out of that cell in any case. Wild 'orses wasn't gonna keep me away from my wife after what she's been through. I would 'ave bent them bars and escaped if they never said I could go. I didn't 'ave a clue why I was picked out to go. I asked questions in the yard and showed a florin. They just shrugged and said whoever arrested me must 'ave made a mistake. Then I got it out of one of the beat boys. A message from higher stations said they were to let me go 'cos it'd been a case of wrongful arrest. My guardian angel was on duty today, love. No question.'

'So how d'yer know it was Lillian who pulled a string?'

'Because Harriet, my sweetheart, showin' them a florin worked.' Guiding her back to the bar and help-ing her on to the stool, he ordered drinks all round. Turning to Larry he shrugged. 'I got caught red-'anded with three pounds worth of fresh 'addock and they let me go.'

'You *must* have friends in high places,' smiled the barman.

'Crafty cow.' Harriet grinned. 'Lillian Redmond is such a dark old horse.'

'How long's your muvver stoppin'? Bit of a shock when she opened the door to me. Good Lord, the mother-in-law at a time like this. Of all people.'

'She can stop overnight then sod off back to South London. Me dad's back in 'er life, Arfer. Can you believe that? In fact, he never really left it, be the sounds of fings.'

'How comes?' he said, scratching his ear. 'Not after all this time? If I never knew you better I'd say you was kiddin' me.'

'Well, you don't know much anyhow,' said Harriet.

'I know more'n you.'

'So . . . who's this friend in 'igh places, then?' sniffed Larry.

'I told you!' said Harriet, her voice much louder than she realised. 'Lillian Redmond. She runs a very high-class brothel! A whorehouse filled with beautiful women.'

'Where is it, cock?' called a red-faced man from across the room. 'I might pop round there!'

'What – the high-class brothel? It's in Beaumont Square!' A roar of disbelieving laughter rang through the tavern.

Much later, after more beers and a song or two from Larry before he left, Harriet and Arthur made their way home. Whether Arthur continued to work for the railway or take up Larry's suggestion of working for a friend of his was neither here nor there. Both Harriet and Arthur were good, hard-working people and together they were going to make a decent life for themselves – and their children. This they promised each other that night in bed.

As for the new business venture, the manufacturing of dolls, only time could tell. But now that Lillian Redmond had dipped her toe into these waters, it was unlikely that anything or anyone would stop it happening. And what of Grace Wellington from across Beaumont Square? Would this enterprise interest her enough to make that small investment?

'Do you know what, Arfer Dean?' said Harriet, before she drifted off to sleep. 'I never knew 'ow much I loved you till they locked you up.'

'Well, that proves one thing, sweet'eart. You don't know as much as I do.'

'Huh,' murmured Harriet, half asleep. 'Well, you don't know much, then, do yer?'

SALLY WORBOYES

Down Stepney Way

In the turbulent East End of London in the thirties, Jessie Warner is growing up . . .

Emotions are running high in Stepney, with Blackshirts marching through the streets and the Jewish community under threat of violence. In the midst of this, Jessie discovers a family secret and turns to her mother for answers, but Rose is reluctant to reveal the past – for there is something that Jessie must never know.

In Bethnal Green, Hannah Blake is being forced by her cold-hearted mother to join the Blackshirts, despite deep misgivings. Next-door neighbour Emmie knows of the darkness surrounding Hannah's wretched past, but is bound by a vow of silence not to reveal it. And meanwhile, Emmie's son Tom, chipper and handsome, has just fallen for a blonde girl he wants to bring home to meet Emmie and Hannah. Her name is Jessie Warner . . .

The first of a new trilogy, DOWN STEPNEY WAY is a vigorous, lively and honest novel, full of atmosphere, depicting London in the thirties: the families, the traders, the docks and factories, and the Blackshirts.

HODDER

SALLY WORBOYES

Wild Hops

It is 1959 and emotions are running high in the Kent hop fields, where the harvest is traditionally picked by East Enders on their summer break. Picking by hand is becoming a thing of the past as mechanisation takes over. The Armstrong family – Jack, Laura and their daughter, Kay – are devastated by the news. Far from the bustle of Stepney, the hop fields offer hard work but fresh clean air and lively social gatherings around the campfires.

While Jack leads the protest against the machines, Laura Armstrong is otherwise preoccupied: will this mean the end of her seasonal love affair with the farm owner, Richard Wright? And what of Kay who, on the brink of womanhood, craves adventure and creates turmoil when she and the handsome gypsy lad, Zacchi, meet in secret?

As tensions grow between the East Enders and the local Romanies, it becomes clear that this summer will change lives for ever . . .

WILD HOPS is a vibrant tale of illicit love, firm friendships and the indomitable character of the East Enders.

'Sizzles with passion' *Guardian*

HODDER

SALLY WORBOYES

Whitechapel Mary

Suddenly and tragically orphaned, Mary Dean must find an extra source of income if she and her young brother are to escape the workhouse. The matchbox factory where she works pays poorly and she is desperate. Tempted by the lure of the House of Assignation, Mary accepts an invitation and becomes a courtesan in the exclusive establishment. Her very first client, Sir Walter, is entranced by her beauty and innocence; he insists that she be his and his alone.

But another threat lurks in the shadows. Mary's neighbour, a midwife, righteous in her hatred of prostitution, holds the key to a menacing secret – the identity of the terrifying Whitechapel murderer . . . the infamous Jack the Ripper.

Mary has no idea of the peril she has placed herself in or the intentions of those who surround her. Who can she trust . . . if anyone?

HODDER